AMONG MEN OF IRON

A NOVEL OF THE 24TH MICHIGAN INFANTRY REGIMENT

BY

BRENT RICHARD FORCE

PublishAmerica
Baltimore

First printing

This is a work of fiction. Names, characters, places, and incidents either are the product of the author's imagination or are used fictitiously. Any resemblance to actual persons, living or dead, events, or locales is entirely coincidental.

PublishAmerica has allowed this work to remain exactly as the author intended, verbatim, without editorial input.

ISBN: 1-60610-107-2 (softcover)
ISBN: 978-1-4489-0070-1 (hardcover)
PUBLISHED BY PUBLISHAMERICA, LLLP
www.publishamerica.com
Baltimore

Printed in the United States of America

For my dear wife, Shawn, whose patience and love surely must be made of iron.

And for my friend, Matthew, who has given me the support worthy of the Iron Brigade.

"The commander of the 'Iron Brigade' requested of McClellan that as he had several Wisconsin regiments, and being about to receive another, that it might be a Wisconsin regiment. The General replied: 'That's impossible, but I will send you a Michigan regiment, and they are as good as are in the service.' He sent the 24th Michigan"

—from JNO. Robertson's *Michigan in the War*

CALL TO ARMS

He felt it rise within him once again. No matter how much he prepared for it, battled it, tried to overcome it, he could never shake off his nervous attacks. Once struck, victimized, his hands would shake violently, and his stomach would churn and ache. It all hit him as he looked out his office window, three stories above a crowded street in Detroit, Michigan, staring wide-eyed at a large American flag, its colors bending and waving in the soft summer breeze.

Henry A. Morrow wasn't native to Detroit, not even to Michigan. His birthplace was in Warrenton, Virginia. It was his boyhood home. It was where his mother was buried. His native state, Virginia, now led the rebellion. For a year it had become a battleground, no longer the lively place of his memories. Those who came from the state were thought as traitors, Rebels. Perhaps this was the cause for his sudden nervous attack.

He shuffled several loose pages, scattered about his desk, into a neat and orderly pile. Slowly, his hands still shaking, he pulled out his pocket watch and noted the time. Almost time to go, he thought. Returning the watch, his eyes shifted back to the window, to the crowds growing in the street below. Wagons and carriages bounced down the roadway, pedestrians crossing quickly to avoid being hit. A police officer guided them, waving them forward or halting them with a booming voice. Morrow watched as a thick line of people crowded and pushed their way down the wide sidewalk.

Traitor. The word leaped back into his thoughts. No, he reassured himself. There shall be no one to call me such, not after this, not after today. He thought back to a conversation he'd had with his wife, the time when he told her his intentions to help raise a regiment from Detroit and Wayne County and lead it to war. At first she appealed and did not want to see her husband go. He pleaded with her, told her that he believed it his duty to do so, to go as thousands upon thousands of others before him had. He told her that he would leave his comfortable job and comfortable life if his nation needed him. Morrow argued that he had ignored the first call for troops and could not ignore a second. "I have seen war before," he told her. It seemed long ago, but Morrow had served for a year in the Mexican War, serving in the Battle of Monterey and the campaign against Tampico. Believing in her husband's patriotism, faith, and bravery, Mrs. Morrow relented. Such had been the case for thousands upon thousands of wives before her.

Morrow's comfortable position, which he would be giving up when he marched off to war, was judge of the Recorder's Court of Wayne County, Michigan. He had been a student of law, being admitted to the bar in 1854, eventually working his way up. He was educated having graduated Rittenhouse Academy in Washington, D.C. Politics entertained him even at a young age, eventually leading the youth to serve as a page in the United States Senate, quickly becoming a favorite of one of Michigan's most known sons of the time, Lewis Cass. When he was seventeen, however, the Mexican War called for him and he answered, volunteering in the Maryland and District of Columbia regiment. After his service, upon the advice from Lewis Cass, Morrow moved to Detroit and made it his home.

It had now been nearly ten years since he made the city his home. Now his nation was calling for him once again, this time to put down the rebellion which had been raging for nearly a year.

A knock came on his office door, shattering Morrow's thoughts like broken glass. The door swung open and revealed a young man, leaning into the room trying to avoid disturbing his employer. "Mr. Morrow," he said, "shall I call your buggy?"

Morrow shook his head. "No, Timothy. I think I'll enjoy the walk."

Timothy took his leave and exited. Morrow bowed his head and threw his hands together, hoping to ease their shaking. Once steadied, he reached for his pocket watch once again. Time was most important to him. He glanced to the narrow hands of the watch and concluded that it was time to go. Standing up, he opened one of the drawers of his desk, pulled out a worn Bible, and slid it in his coat pocket. More important to him than time was his faith, his religion.

He slid out the door, slowly closing it behind him. He noticed Timothy sitting at the desk just outside his office, papers spread over the desktop, several pages fallen to the floor. He looked at his young aide, disapproving of the disorder. Timothy quickly bent down and began to shuffle the pages into a pile. "Well," Morrow said proudly, "I'm off."

Timothy placed the newly arranged pile on his desk and nodded. He watched Morrow vanish from sight before he shoved the papers into a desk drawer. Timothy glanced up to check the time from the old clock on the wall. He too had somewhere to be. He too was headed where

Morrow, where perhaps the entire city was headed, to Campus Martius in downtown Detroit.

It is July 15, 1862.

The old priest's voice echoed across the walls and through the rafters of the white church. The congregation sat in silence, patiently listening to the words of a favorite clergyman. They had called upon him for a special sermon for a special time. "We all are seeking answers in our nation's darkest hour," he told them, his voice as loud as thunder. "We meet on this day to seek the Lord's guidance, to find comfort, clues to the answers we seek, within his words, within the Bible. We must remember that He is not an unjust God. He is not an unkind God. He is not an inhumane God. We must look to Him as a desperate child looks to a father." The priest's voice steadied. Years of sermons, practice, and reading equipped his voice with the power to carry on. His vocal chords were experienced, hardened by countless sermons and conversations, all providing the wisdom of the Bible, the words of God. "Our nation is reaching for our young men once again. The president has called for more volunteers. The course those brave patriots are to pursue is one of perils, but it is a most righteous path to the nation God helped create. I cannot, for those of you confronting the decision to go, tell you which way to turn. I cannot make up your mind for you. I will say, as a man of God, that I cannot condone war. Yet, as the same man of God, I cannot condone the system our southern countrymen have established and thrive upon. This cannot be overlooked by any man."

Sitting in the middle of the congregation is a young man and his wife. Like most of the men seeking God's answers, he is at a crossroads. The nation has called for him, not just once but twice. He could leave his beloved wife, whom he recently married just months prior, and go to war, or he could stay home and ignore yet another call for help. Thinking of the difficult decision before him, he wipes the sweat from his eyebrows. His eyes scan the crowded room. His ears perk at the sound of the priest's voice. The large room is packed with people. Men in search of answers, women in search of hope, and children too young to comprehend the situation their parents and their nation face. His nerves begin to get the best of him. A deep feeling of discomfort rises within him, the fate of uncertainty teasing.

His young wife notices her husband's anxiety. She carefully takes control by reaching for his hands. "Worry not, Morgan," she soothingly tells him. "The decision before you is great. Just know that either way, whatever you decide, I will be there and I trust the Lord will look upon it as right."

Morgan takes his wife's hands and wraps his around them. He feels the weight of the decision steady on his shoulders. A new sense of strength, however, begins to grow. He had not told his wife, but he had made up his mind several days ago. If there was going to be a regiment from Detroit, then he would go. He would not turn away from his country's call a second time.

"With this," continues the old priest, the congregation captivated, caught in his words and his deep voice. "We have been asked to once again furnish sons of this city, this state. We have been asked once again to send our loved ones out to the blood-stained fields where so many have already fallen. The nation has already lost many sons in this war. Michigan has paid a dear price for her services and so too have many other brave states of the Union. My friends," he said before taking a deep breath, "there is more work to be done. God has willed that the traitors and enemies of the Union shall not cease unless provoked by force. We have given them that, and they have answered in kind. We shall give them more then." He waited as the echo faded. "As a man of God, I cannot tell you that you should go or that you should stay. It is not my place to make such decisions for you. But," he added quickly, "if you bravely go, sacrificing the comforts of home, I will, as a man of God, say that you will go with God."

The sermon ended. The last echo faded. The words just spoken sunk into memory. For some in attendance, they provided reason and answers. For others, they left the church still unsure as to what to do. As for Morgan, he just sat in the pew with his wife, his hands still wrapped around hers. When the last patron finally exited the white building, Morgan turned to his wife. There was a light in his eyes, indicating to her that his mind had been made up. "I'm going," he said softly. He bowed his head and bit his bottom lip in anticipation of her response. "I need to go, Emmy," he added.

"I know," she said, not breaking her eyes from his. He lifted his head and clutched her hands even tighter. She finally dropped her head away from his. "I cannot help but think of all the times you looked upon your grandfather's military uniform. You look to him as a hero. I see the way you stare at the uniform. I know you wonder what it must have been like. And now you have your chance to find out," she told him plainly. "Well," she began, "I will be here waiting for you." Her strength was evident in her voice but so was her fear. "I can only pray for your safe return but," she stopped suddenly, fighting whether she should say it or not. "But I fear that you will not," the words finally slipped from her mouth. She pulled him close to her, rested her head on his chest and listened for his heartbeat. "I will be here for you, Morgan."

Campus Martius was full of excitement. A large stage had been erected complimented with an assortment of patriotic flags and buntings.

The crowd gathered quickly. People lined the sidewalks and paced the streets in an effort to join the gathering at the outdoor park. Police officers were scattered in every direction, deputies charged with keeping the swelling crowd in order. As people entered the park, they walked upon the massive shadow of the large man responsible for keeping the peace and ensuring the order of the event. He stood before them, towering at well over six feet in height.

Sheriff Mark Flanigan was well known throughout the city. For two years he held the office and Detroit remained in good order. Now, at the second call of his country, Flanigan was prepared to leave his lucrative position in response. He had agreed to help raise a regiment with Morrow, whom he was cordial friends with.

Flanigan, much like Morrow, could call Detroit his home but he was not a native. He had been born in Ireland, the accent still slipping into his voice when he spoke. But he had come to America for a reason. He believed it to be a land of great opportunity, and he had proved it right. Through hard work and faith, Flanigan rose to the power he was about to leave, but it would be for a worthy cause. The very nation that provided him the opportunities was in peril. The least he could do was fight for it.

As soon as word got out about President Lincoln's second call for volunteers, Flanigan's wife readied herself for what was to come. There had been few arguments between them. She had seen her husband rise to great things and knew that he was capable of even more. When it came time for them to discuss his decision, she offered no argument. She made no case for him to stay. She knew that his mind was made up and that he was going to go. Still, Flanigan had doubts about leaving her. He loved her and it broke his heart to think that he would be without her.

As the people filled in around him, he dared not to think of her, not to think of the sadness that would come on the day he left. There was great joy to be had in the event of the day. It would prove a most exciting and most patriotic day for Detroit and Michigan.

Flanigan turned his attention to the crowd at hand. He studied them for weapons or studied them in hopes of finding a bad seed before it spread. There had already been rumors circulating that the event was calling for a draft, which was not the case, and Flanigan personally assigned two officers to investigate the cause. The event had taken a great deal of planning and organization. Local businesses shut down for the day. Students from nearby and some not so nearby colleges gathered with friends and families. Politicians, city officials, and important dignitaries were scheduled to arrive for the event. Among the most important to arrive was to be the honorable Lewis Cass.

Flanigan nodded to several men as they jolted by. He waved to several others from afar. One of the officers returned to him and reported that they had come up short. Flanigan read from the short note and handed it back. "Keep searching," he ordered. "This isn't about a draft and the people should know that. I don't want it being spread anymore than what it has." He urged the young officer forward, "Do all that you can." Another officer came to him several minutes later and complained of a group of men carrying metal pipes and wooden clubs. The officer continued by describing how he wouldn't let the group enter and insisted that if they dropped their tools that they would then be allowed in. Flanigan listened as the officer told him how the group grew frustrated and began to threaten the young officer by swinging the objects at him. "Go back calmly," Flanigan barked. He pointed down to the officer's waist to the holstered revolver. "Show them the gun and see what they do. Don't draw it, but give them enough to see it." As the same with the previous officer, Flanigan urged him forward. Thinking deeper on the situation, Flanigan called the officer back. "If they still want to make a go at it, tell them you'll come and get me, and we'll give them a shot," he said with a slight smile, the Irish accent seeping through.

He rejoined his work in scanning the crowd, greeting visitors, and making his large presence known to all. Detroit rose all around him, the buildings reaching from the earth to the sky. There had been so much change, so much growth since he arrived in 1845. Detroit had become more than a city or just home to him. He met and married his wife, Sarah, there. As he looked above the crowed, out in toward the city, he thought of the first time he met her. She wore the most beautiful spring dress he had ever seen. She was calm and collective. She had a restless spirit that Flanigan had never before found in another woman, and he loved her dearly for it.

But those days seemed so long ago. Yet, even as the years whittled that lovely spring dress down to threads, his wife still held onto the spirit that had caught this young Irishman's eyes from the start. No, he thought. No matter how many years pass, she would always remain as feisty as the day he first met her.

Flanigan was politically active. Not only was he one of the founding members of the Republican Party, but he rode the Republican ticket for Sheriff of Wayne County. Prior to earning that title, Flanigan had opened up his own butcher shop in 1847, the same year he married his wife.

The noise and clamor of the crowd brought him back to reality, and he quickly realized there was still plenty of work to do.

Morrow leaped across the broad roadway, stepping beyond the reach of the officer directing traffic, and made a quick dash for the other side of the street. Checking his advance was the outstretched arm of the officer, whose duty it was to ensure that both pedestrian and carriage shared the roadway on this busy day. "Hold here, please," indicated the officer. "Nice day for such an event, Mr. Morrow," he added as he waved an arm for several horses and carriages to pass through freely.

"It is that," responded a disconnected Morrow. It seemed only a short time ago when Governor Austin Blair, in response to President Lincoln's call, asked his state for an additional six regiments to furnish the growing war effort. In turn, Morrow and Flanigan responded by attempting to recruit a Wayne County regiment.

Morrow stood patiently and waited as the carriages bounced by. His physique was not imposing, and he wasn't a very large man by nature. In his early thirties when the second call came, Morrow eagerly set to work on the development of the regiment he and Flanigan envisioned. He had a broad face with bright eyes, capable of catching anything out of the ordinary, out of place. His forehead was large, pushing his hairline back toward the center of his head. From there he combed his hair over, an attempt to stave off the balding that had caught up with him earlier than expected. At his ears, his hair seemed to roll out from his head like uncontrollable waves. Stretching down from his ears were two large sideburns, whiskers, which ended abruptly with the contours of his mouth and chin. His look was orderly and neat, that of a professional.

Dust rose from the roadway, forcing the young officer to cough. Morrow slowly dusted off his coat and turned away from the rising brown cloud. As the dirt receded, a large black carriage, very familiar to Morrow, stopped in the roadway before him. The narrow door opened suddenly, and a voice called from within the vehicle. "This is no place for a man of your stature, Henry. You shall come aboard and finish the travel in my company and care," added Detroit Mayor Duncan as he showed his face through the doorway for the first time. He extended an arm and waited impatiently for Morrow's timid response. "I insist," the politician declared.

Morrow reluctantly nodded and climbed inside. The seats were lined with red velvet, comfortable and lavish. The windows were open, so that Duncan could greet the voters as the carriage strolled on. The noise of the crowd drifted as Morrow sat down, sinking into the soft cushion that seemed fit for a king. Duncan sat across from him with another man, unrecognizable to Morrow, but probably one of the mayor's many aides. "Well," opened Duncan, "that is much better I assume." His voice was happy and clear. The raising of a Wayne County regiment would do well for support of his next election. "A lovely day is it not, Henry? One would almost think of it as perfect."

"It is," replied Morrow.

"Yes," continued Duncan, "a very fine day. I suspect that all of the county will come out for the rally. It shall be a fine and wonderful affair." The lavish carriage bounced gently as it drew nearer to its destination. Duncan pointed to the other gentleman, who in turn handed the mayor an empty glass and fumbled with a bottle of wine. The politician took a sip, licked his lips, and then nodded. "Forgive me," he said with embarrassment. "Would you care for a taste, Henry?" Morrow shook his head. "Ah," Duncan responded, "always the careful one."

The carriage turned onto another busy road, inching closer and closer to the park. "You will be pleased to know that the honorable Lewis Cass arrived for the event. The investment of one of Michigan's great heroes shall do wonders for our cause, for our regiment, Henry."

Morrow turned away, a smile coming over his face. He thought of years long passed, countless hours working with Cass in Washington. "You two have known each other for some time now," continued Duncan without missing a beat. "You, albeit in your youth, have come to know more about the political motives of the man."

"As much as a page could learn," Morrow replied carefully.

Duncan smiled before taking another sip of wine. "He is a unique fellow. I do not believe Michigan can claim another like him. He has held political offices that make the best of us jealous. It takes a strong man, a wise politician, to nearly reach the presidency." He looked down as the glass fell empty. The aide reached for the bottle, but Duncan waved him off. "And you were once a student of his, perhaps learning from Cass when he was in his prime. Are there not any political ambitions of your own?"

Morrow held his smile. Those days, that desire, had long since been over. "No, sir," he said slowly, sternly. "I'll go to war and do the fighting. I'll let others do the politicking." He gently laughed, easing the uncontrollable nervousness. "You will not find my name on a ballot opposing yours, Mr. Mayor, I assure you of that."

"Very well," concluded Duncan.

"Besides," added Morrow, sensing Duncan's anxiety, "your worries should not consist of my political ambitions, Mr. Mayor. They should consist, entirely, of Mr. Cass'."

Duncan turned away quickly and pushed the empty wine glass toward the aide, indicating that more was needed. Again the aide fumbled with the elegant wine bottle, carefully trying to steady the bottle as the carriage bounced down the street.

They pushed their way through the growing crowd developing outside Campus Martius, the flow of which remained under the watchful eye of Sheriff Flanigan, his officers, and several other officials. Morrow gazed out the windows as the carriage drove past lines of anxious people. He reached for his watch and again noted the time. The ride, generously offered by the mayor, had delivered him well ahead of schedule. This was impressive, but he despised being too early just about as much as he did being late. Arriving too early allowed for more things to go wrong, more complications to tend to, and more time for his nervousness to build and gain control. His hand shook as it delivered the watch back into his vest pocket.

In line, watching the mayor's carriage shuttle by was a sturdy looking man with a thick black beard. Abel Peck had been following the development of the war since it began. He had desires to enlist well before Lincoln's second call, but couldn't bear to leave his wife and young daughter behind. His patriotism got the best of him this time around, however, and he decided that if a regiment was going to be formed from Wayne County, then he would do his service and enlist.

As he walked toward the rally, he remembered when he told his daughter of his decision to leave her. "I must go," he softly told her. "I must go as other fathers have gone before me." She cried and begged for him to stay, pulling at his coat and clutching him toward her with little arms. He tried his best not to cry before her, did all he could to remain strong. "When you get older," he preached, "you will come to understand there is such a thing as duty. You will come to understand there is such a thing as country. And when your country calls upon you for help, often as you have called upon me, you must accept your duty and go. You must leave all that you have behind and go. And you must look to your country for guidance as you have looked to me."

When he finally turned away from her, his wife comforted their daughter, wiping away her little tears. "It has been God's will," the mother told the daughter. Peck tore himself away from the room and slid down the hall. An emotional wreck, he didn't want his little girl to see him in such a state. Men were supposed to be strong and brave. Men weren't supposed to cry. He remembered hearing the door close, finally, and the feeling of his wife's warm and loving arms wrap around him.

She turned him around and straightened his coat and buttoned his vest. "You go and do what you have to do, Abel." His eyes met hers, and he saw there were no tears, no sorrow, just pride and strength. "You go and bravely fight the war, but," she pulled him close to her, "do not think you fight it alone."

Reality came crashing back when he realized he wasn't in the safety of his home or the loving arms of his wife. His mind had been made up. There would be no turning back now. If another Michigan regiment was formed, he would go. He refused to turn his back on another of his nation's calls. Yet as he paced himself with the line, inching closer and closer to the fate that waited, he couldn't help but think of his little daughter and her little tears. And no matter how hard it was to remember her sadness, to hear her sobbing voice, Abel Peck knew that she was the reason he would go to war.

Campus Martius was at one time the centerpiece for Detroit as planned by a man named Judge Woodward. Woodward had seen the beauty and delicate architectural planning that went into the nation's capital, Washington. It was Woodward's dream for Detroit to be lined with not the classic, narrow roadways, but of wider, broader roadways and open spaces that invited nature into the industrial world of the city. Campus Martius was to be the grandest of many of such parks dotting the city.

On this day, however, it was the center for something else. It was a meeting place, and the entire county had been invited to attend. The grounds were beautiful, the sky was clear and calm, but the centerpiece of it all was the grandstand from which the presenters would address the crowd. The massive wooden platform had been built of the finest lumber and had been decorated with the finest fabrics, patriotic flags and buntings. Women devoted countless hours to the creation of the flags and buntings, donating their time for a patriotic cause. The grandstand had been a special project of Mayor Duncan, as he visited the site nearly every day during its construction to ensure it met his approval.

It was the first thing Henry A. Morrow saw as he exited the carriage. It consisted of beauty and power. It rose from the earth as if ordered by the heavens, demanding attention from all who gazed upon it. Turning toward the swelling crowd, Morrow tried to estimate just how many people had already arrived. To his left, tucked just beside the grandstand, was a band that struck up patriotic tunes as they saw Mayor Duncan arrive. Behind him, arriving one after another came the other dignitaries, invited by the mayor to either give rousing speeches or attend the event in support. Morrow reached for his watch, again wanting to check the time, again indicating its importance.

"You never could leave that watch in your pocket, Henry," a voice called from behind.

Undaunted, Morrow closed the lid on the watch and pushed it away. The voice was recognizable, unforgettable. No matter how many years whittled him away, his voice stayed the same. Swinging around, Morrow extended a hand and smiled. "You should know by now, Mr. Cass, that time is most important. Everything must be in order, sir."

Cass smiled as a father would smile upon a son. "You should run for president," he responded swiftly as he took Morrow's hand in a strong grasp. Morrow noted how much older his friend and once mentor looked. Older he was, growing older with each passing day, the youth and zeal of his life a fading memory. At one time, however, Cass had been near the height of political power, a Democratic presidential nominee. His career, developed many years before, had been born in Michigan. Cass served in the War of 1812 under William Hull, feuded with him over the surrender of Detroit to the British, and then later went on to become the governor of the Michigan Territory. An old man no doubt stood before Morrow on this day, but this old man was one of Michigan's most prominent and celebrated figures.

Mayor Duncan fell in behind Morrow and waved to the crowd. He turned back with a politician's smile for Cass, who offered a more disciplined politician's smile in return. "Mr. Cass," said Duncan, still waving toward the crowd. "I am very delighted that you have committed to such a noble and glorious cause. Detroit has always thought of you as a son. And in this time of great need, you have found your home like a noble son."

Cass nodded. "I am honored to be here for such an occasion, Mr. Mayor."

Duncan smiled again. "I trust you have prepared a few appropriate remarks…"

"I was not aware," interrupted a concerned Cass.

"Surely this rally could benefit from the remarks of a man such as the honorable Lewis Cass," Duncan stated, weaving in his political tone. "I could think of nothing more flattering to your distinguished career and reputation than to speak to a crowd of your own on such an occasion as this."

Cass shook his head. "I must decline," he reiterated. "Hurried words have never suited me, Mr. Mayor. I tend to my speeches as I tended to my battle plans, slow and steady in the planning, quick in the execution." He turned to Morrow, patting his old friend on the back. "Anything rushed will be foolish. And I will not subject my career or reputation to such."

"Very well," said Duncan in approval.

The others followed him and took their seats on the grandstand. Once seated, their eyes fell upon the sea of people that had gathered before them. Men, women, and children of all ages stood under the sun and waited for the rally to begin. Miniature flags had been passed out to persuade the patriotic feeling and were waving in the air. The band still belted out patriotic music, some of which the crowd responded pleasantly to. By this time, however, they had gone through their set twice and were about to begin a third when Mayor Duncan rose from his seat and stepped toward the edge of the stage.

The crowd quieted as he lifted his arms over them. The band fell silent. Mayor Duncan waited for another moment, for the right moment, when only the soft whirl of the summer breeze could be heard. Steadying his thoughts and urging his politician's voice forward, he addressed the crowd. "Men of Detroit, we are gathered as brave citizens of a proud and honorable country, but one that is in great need of our aid..."

Political speeches in 1862 were far less complicated and technical than what we know of today. Politicians stood before their crowd without the use of microphones, relying solely on their booming voices to carry their words. In most cases, large crowds failed to hear the words of a speaker and relied on the newspapers, issued the following day, to reveal to them what they had seen but not heard.

Crowd interaction was more present. Just as a speaker's words could carry out over a crowd, a crowd member's words could carry back up to the speaker. While most interaction proved beneficial to an event, the case of July 15, 1862 at Campus Martius proved otherwise.

Mayor Duncan briefly addressed the crowd before introducing the honorable William Howard, a dignitary, who made a wonderful address in support of the cause. A second dignitary, Theodore Romeyn followed up Howard with more patriotic words, urging the men to their duty. By the time the third speaking dignitary, T. M. McEntee, rose to make his rousing address, the crowd proved too restless and noisy to continue with the event. The fear that Sheriff Flanigan had hoped to avoid had taken hold on much of the crowd, inducing confusion and anger that prevented the ceremony from continuing.

Flanigan reported to Duncan that the crowd feared a draft. Duncan rose to silence the growing confusion but to no avail. Turning back toward the seated dignitaries, Duncan looked upon the man that vowed to help recruit a Wayne County regiment.

Henry A. Morrow walked to the edge of the stage quickly. His nervousness had devoured him while he was seated, gazing upon a crowd growing out of hand, but he managed to push it aside now. He relied on the respect the city had for him to quell the confusion and once again silence the crowd. Waving his arms over them, he made three passes before the crowd took notice of him. On the fifth pass, they fell silent enough for him to address them with a few words.

"Fellow citizens," he called them. "We are met here now in the second crisis of our country." The confusion in the crowd rose again. "There is a mistaken feeling that this meeting is preliminary to a draft. Enough can be procured without such measures. Every man who can, should go, and the men who stay at home must support the families of those who go. This meeting is for inducing men to volunteer, and I for one, am ready to go." He stopped as cheers lifted from the crowd, cracking the confusion. "Those of us who have no families should go. I do not propose that men of families shall perform duties that we young men should perform." There was another wave of cheers. Perhaps the intentions were becoming clear. "Let each man ask himself: 'Will I go?'"

A voice beckoned from the crowd. "Will you go?"

Without hesitation, the words flowed from his mouth like a river. "I have already said I would. The government has done as much for me as for you, and I am ready to assist in upholding it." Morrow fell back from the stage, the crowd's mixed cheering and confusion stunning him. Had it not been made clear enough? Had not enough been done?

The crowd began to split before their very eyes. Mayor Duncan leaped to the stage and demanded the crowd to fall silent. He even ordered the band to start playing to break the confusion and return the crowd to its normal state. A whirlpool of anger developed near the back of the crowd, pushing those not falling prey to it away, and driving toward the massive grandstand. Duncan called for the crowd to remain calm but that failed as well. Sheriff Flanigan leaped up the stairs and called for Morrow to attend to Duncan. "Get him out of here," the Irishman barked.

Flanigan busied himself by withdrawing the dignitaries, having officers securing their carriages and horses. Morrow slid toward the edge of the stage and called for Duncan to step down. "Certainly not," argued the mayor. "I will not leave this stage." He stepped ever closer to the edge of the stage and lifted a fist toward the crowd, the swirling whirlpool that spun toward him. "We are here to raise a regiment, not a draft! What has come over all of you? What has become of my city? What has become of our patriotic citizens?"

"We must leave, Mr. Mayor," pleaded Morrow.

"I will not," replied Duncan.

"We've got no time for this!" cried Flanigan, who escorted Lewis Cass off of the stage and into his carriage.

The crowd roared toward the grandstand like an unstoppable tidal wave. The officers, posted at the front of the stage, braced themselves for the coming pressure. Flanigan rushed back up to the stage and assisted Morrow in pulling Duncan away from the crowd. He had lost control of the crowd, swelling to greater proportions than his meager police force could handle. His primary concern now rested with the safety of the dignitaries. Once that was completed, he would set out to restore order as quickly as possible. "Henry!" he cried to Morrow. "We've got to get him out of here!"

It happened in a fraction of a second. As Morrow and Flanigan pulled Duncan from the scene, five men stormed the grandstand and took to tearing down the flags and buntings. It happened so fast that anybody else would have missed it. Morrow, however, had not missed it. His wide eyes caught on to them as soon as they rose toward the stage. Something had been out of place, and his eyes shifted. He instinctively pushed Duncan toward Flanigan and turned to meet the men charging toward them. The growing tide of men forced Morrow to the ground, overwhelmed by the numbers and mass confusion. The mob tore down the flags, the beautiful colors shredded as if they were torn apart by a pack of wolves. Other flags were simply stomped on, kicked, thrown about, and spat on. Morrow lifted himself and wrestled a flag away from one of them. The man clutched the flag with one hand and swung wildly at Morrow with the other. Morrow proved the better aim, landing one punch that freed the flag and sent the man sprawling backward. Morrow took his leave and jumped from the stage, joining Flanigan and several officers in securing the dignitaries.

The grandstand, now behind him, creaked under the weight, under the constant thrashing. Men worked together to pull down and break large chunks of wood. They threw the chairs into the crowd. "Burn it! Burn it all!" they shouted.

Flanigan stepped forward and handed Morrow a revolver. "I believe you used one of these in Mexico," said the Irishman, the devilish grin appearing on his face once again. He turned to several of his officers and ordered them back. "To the Russell House Hotel," he told them. "Wait for us there." The last of the carriages, protected by the armed escort, pulled away from the mob.

Morrow drove forward with the officers in hopes of reclaiming the stage. Flanigan took the lead, brandishing a rifle as well as his trusted revolver. They quickly fought their way to the stage, the sight of armed men driving the mob toward and over the edges of the stage. The anger swelled again, and the mob reformed for their push toward the stage. Flanigan met them by firing his rifle over their heads. Following the discharge, he carefully loaded the rifle before the mob, showing his desire to stand and fight.

"Burn it!" the mob cried, pointing to the grandstand.

"Hold it!" Flanigan responded, ordering the men to hold the line.

The mob surged forward, sending a small group of men toward the grandstand. Flanigan finished loading the rifle and leveled it toward the front of the approaching group. "The next one won't be a warning, lads," he cautioned them.

Morrow followed suit by lowering his revolver.

"We don't have to meet like this," called a voice from the mob. "We just want Mr. Ward and Mr. Stewart. Unionists intent on a draft should hang from an oak tree."

"You won't be getting that far," responded Flanigan, his rifle still leveled.

The mob behind the scene began to break up, spilling into the streets. Flanigan and Morrow kept their eyes on the first group, the most advanced party from the mob. When they realized there would be useless bloodshed, they turned and ordered those left with them to follow them to the Russell House Hotel.

Flanigan turned from them and waved for his deputy to join him. They would race to the hotel and further ensure the safety of the dignitaries seeking refuge there. As the Irishman vanished from sight, leaving Morrow with two other men alone on the stage, another wave of the mob inched forward, threatening the three men. Morrow met them with the revolver. "You are a respectable man, Judge Morrow," said one of them. "You will think twice before drawing blood."

"Will I?" responded Morrow, cocking the revolver.

The mob took the threat and backed away, melting into several small groups. Some of the men went home while others continued the warpath in search of the desired Unionists suspected of wanting a draft.

Morrow ordered the officers to follow him to the hotel, where they would meet up with Flanigan and assist in regaining control of the city. As he turned away from the grandstand, he saw what remained of it was a bare skeleton of its former self. The flags and buntings had been torn down, ripped to shreds, colorful strings and swatches of fabric decorating the green grass. Chairs had been tossed about, broken and battered. The massive grandstand had bucked under the weight, a crack developing at the center of the stage. He pushed the officers away from the sight and led them toward the hotel, his wide eyes shifting to the sights as he rode. Everything was out of place. Nothing was in order anymore.

"No draft!" had been the cry of the day. As the mob surged from Campus Martius, they spilled into the streets and went after anything related to the national government. Two empty mail wagons, awaiting their loads, were thrashed and damaged needing much repair. A government wagon, carrying war goods, was flipped over. The driver escaped the carnage by slipping away quickly. The wagon was looted before it was set ablaze. The chants continued as the mob inched toward the front of the Russell House Hotel.

There they were met by Sheriff Flanigan and his deputy. Again the mob demanded the Unionists responsible for the proposed draft, Ward and Stewart. Again, Flanigan met them, his revolver drawn and loaded, leveled at the closest man. "That'll be enough of this," the Irishman told them. The mob inched closer, pressing the point. Flanigan responded by drawing back the hammer and cocking the gun. The clicking noise rattled through the mob. "See how far you get," Flanigan warned.

"We will take their lives with rope!" shouted one of them, his face hidden, reminding the lawmen of the threat of hanging the Unionists.

Flanigan smiled at them. "I'll take yours without," he reminded them in turn.

As the sun began to fade, the mob grew weary of its standstill. They had all been aware of Flanigan's lucrative position and how much of his salary came from bounties collected. There wasn't a single soul in the mob that wanted to become another of Flanigan's numbers. These people, spurred on by empty rumors, didn't seek bloodshed. And if they had continued, perhaps if they had taken one step closer to the hotel, there would have been some. Flanigan had promised them as much.

By the time night set in, the streets were clear of the mob.

A fire crew arrived to extinguish to flames from the government wagon.

Flanigan and his loyal officers patrolled the streets. While the crowd had gotten beyond his control, he was able to protect the dignitaries, and then he was able to restore order to the city he was charged with protecting.

The dignitaries had been threatened. The grandstand had been virtually destroyed. Disloyalty stained the city. By this time of the evening, several companies of the proposed regiment would have been in the process of filling their ranks. There was nothing, however. All the careful planning and time spent on the rally had amounted to nothing. There was no Wayne County regiment.

Flanigan thought of this as he made his rounds through the wide streets that evening. He wondered just where everything went wrong. He cursed Confederate sympathizers, most likely crossing from Windsor and most likely responsible for the calamity. He could take pride in his quick thinking, however. The dignitaries were safe and the mob was off the street. Things could have ballooned into a full blown riot, but that had been avoided.

He rode past Campus Martius and noticed two shadows conversing on the stage. Riding in to investigate, he was relieved to see who it was and quickly spurred away to continue his rounds. He departed the scene feeling a little better. Hope was not yet lost. Perhaps Wayne County would come through yet.

"This is where it all happened," Lewis Cass said, his voice sad and weary. "It seems like so long ago," he told Morrow. The two men had stood in the darkness for some time. An hour earlier Morrow found his aging friend alone in the park. "I never thought I would see it fall into their hands," Cass continued.

"There was nothing you could do," reminded Morrow.

"There is always something you can do," responded Cass. "General Hull surrendered the city near here, near this very spot. Oh, how I can see it so clearly. I thought we could have fought on. I thought we could have held them off. I knew I was right. He thought I was wrong. Oh, how angry I was!" Cass pointed out into the darkness. "It was there, where he informed me we would be giving up the city. I remember arguing and then breaking my sword over my knee in frustration." He bowed his head, the memory so alive that it seemed as if it were playing out all over again. "And what now?" he asked Morrow. "What will come of Detroit now?"

"We shall try again."

"Good," responded Cass. "It is a fine city, Henry. It is a fine state. There is no other place like Michigan. I thought it too lovely of a place to be surrendered to the damned British. It should still be too lovely of a place to be surrendered to the damned Confederates." Cass finally pulled himself away from the memory. "This city has always found a way to

31

redeem itself, Henry. You've been here long enough to see that." He patted Morrow on the shoulder. "If you get that regiment," he paused and looked back toward the memory once again. "Do not surrender it for anything."

Morrow smiled. The aging Cass was still a fighter, still a soldier at heart. "I will do my best, Mr. Cass."

"Sadly, my young friend," responded Cass, "we must do better than that."

Morgan lifted himself from his bed and exited the room. He thought it was the heat that kept him awake, but it was the thought of all that had transpired in the day. Something that should have been great was made into something horrible. He had never seen his city or its citizens in such a manner.

He stood outside on the old porch and looked off into the darkness. He wondered just what would happen to the farm once he left for war, if he left for war. The proposed regiment would be delayed because of the violence. It was very likely that another Michigan regiment would be raised in its place. No matter, he thought. He would go with whomever to serve his country. Still, the fate of his home cautioned every decision regarding his departure. How would the farm survive? Would Emmy be able to keep up with the demands of living without a husband?

What a world it was. He had fallen for a girl whose father had money, had struck it big in the lumber industry, taking advantage of Michigan's vast forests. Morgan swept the young woman off her feet and carried her to his farm, the very farm his father worked and died upon. It was a lifestyle she was not accustomed to, but she managed and thrived. Her father would call, offer money so that the young couple could escape the dirty farm. Morgan had refused to accept the offer, no matter how many times it came up. Farming was his life. He saw how happy it made Emmy to be out in the field with him, to do work that her father never dreamed her to do.

Such work worried him. His Emmy was a strong woman, capable of many things, things that he had thought beyond her. She had proven herself time and time again. Yet she had done so with him by her side, the two of them working together. He knew she would need help. It would not be right to leave her alone to all the tasks the farm demanded.

He sat down at a small desk in the room. By moonlight, he penned a letter to her father, describing the situation and asking him for the support Morgan so often refused. He asked that Emmy not be taken away from the beloved farm, but that workers are brought in to help her with the chores. He wrote that he would send whatever income he made by soldiering home to her, in hopes that the earnings would go to things she wanted and needed. Morgan still wanted to provide her a happy life, even when he was gone. He concluded the letter swiftly, reminding her father of his decision to go to war if needed, for cause and country.

Morgan folded up the letter with intentions to send it out in the morning. With any luck, by the time her father responds, the regiment would be formed and Morgan would be off to war.

The decision to reach out to him for assistance was not liked, but needed.

Looking back out the window, into the darkness, Morgan realized it was just one of many things he would have to set in place before leaving Emmy. There was always that chance of him never returning home, no matter how much he feared it, no matter how much he fought it.

The near riot didn't hinder Abel Peck. The decision to go to war had been made, his family had been told, and preparations were being made for his departure. He would go for the sake of not just his family or country, but for the entire county. The unpatriotic actions of so few had hurt so many. Worse than that, his beloved city, his home, had been stained with disloyalty. So forward he would go into the storm of bullets, just to prove that Detroit and Wayne County still believed in the cause, and that his home was still home to brave and loyal patriots.

He had managed to squeeze into the park and inch close enough to hear the words of the speakers. Like most of the crowd, he too listened to the rumors about the nation instituting a draft. He shrugged it off as nonsense. While a draft wasn't out of the question, he knew that it had not yet come time for that. There were still plenty of men, like him, who were willing to fight for their country. It had been too bad that the actions of so few hindered the development of a Wayne County regiment. From what he had seen of the crowd, there was an ample supply of brave and willing men ready to go. As things turned for the worst, even some of the strongest of such men allowed themselves to fall in with those bent on destruction and chaos. Peck knew better. As the crowd shifted out of control, he exited the park, the words of Judge Morrow filling the air behind him.

A cool summer breeze danced across the street as he turned toward home. He paid careful attention to the shadows in the alleyways and the strange voices from afar. His tension faded as he saw Sheriff Flanigan trot by him on horseback. Soon after Flanigan passed by, another officer came toward him. Flanigan had the men make extra rounds this evening, showing the good people they were in control and reminding the bad that there would be no more trouble.

Peck walked up the steps to the house and slowly opened the door. He turned back and looked out into the street before entering. The vision of the burning wagon etched in his mind, but that now seemed so far away. Everything was peaceful now. The violence had not spread this far away from the city. He took one last breath, bade one last farewell to all that could have been on that day, and finally entered the house.

"Father's home," his wife lovingly announced to their daughter.

Upon further investigation of the violence, it was determined that a group of Confederate sympathizers had indeed crossed the Detroit River, making their way from Windsor, and infected the patriotic crowd with their rumors and lies.

The city officials worked for another war rally, another meeting that would resurrect their city's tarnished reputation, redeeming its good name from the shame cast upon it by the unnecessary violence. Other cities around Michigan were holding successful war meetings and rallies, making good on their promises to do all they could for their state and country. Knowing that with each passing day the Wayne County regiment faded into obscurity as other regiments developed, the city officials sent two electives to the state capital in Lansing, in hopes that their projected regiment would become a reality.

Michigan had already furnished sixteen regiments to the war effort and a seventeenth was meeting with recruiting difficulties. Lincoln called upon the state for an additional six regiments, bringing the expected number to twenty-three. As Detroit's appointed officials arrived and pleaded their case, Governor Blair requested that he be allowed to make his decision the following morning. He expressed slight interest in the idea but confessed that since the other regiments were suffering from recruitment shortages, that a twenty-fourth would seem too much to contend with. Raising an additional regiment, he argued, would only hinder the enlistment of another. The Detroit officials argued for redemption of their tarnished city, a restoration of its patriotic stature, and informed the governor that there would be more than enough men from the county alone willing to join.

Governor Blair took all the information into consideration, but when the morning came, he declined the raising of a twenty-fourth Michigan regiment. As the two Detroit officials prepped themselves for their sad return to their city, bearing the bad news, Mrs. Blair, the governor's wife, had overheard the conversation and stepped in on behalf of the two men and the city of Detroit. She informed her husband of the war's bleak outlook. Many men had already suffered and many more would. The nation, during such a time of crisis, needed every man it could get. Michigan, while having done all that had been asked of her, had a chance to do more. She quoted evidence from the latest papers and printed battlefield reports. Reluctantly, Governor Blair, upon the suggestion of his dear wife, granted Detroit's wish to furnish another regiment. Blair signed the needed paperwork and ordered that twenty-four Michigan regiments would be furnished, the last of which fell upon Wayne County and Detroit.

It is quarter past three on July 22, 1862.

Campus Martius is again full this afternoon. Men from all over the county had come in support of the glorious cause before them. They had been told of the meeting's purpose, to rally support for the raising of a regiment and not that to announce a draft. For hours before the event was scheduled to start, men from all walks of life formed mock companies and arrived at the park. They came from schools, mills, factories, and farms. Some were doctors, lawyers, and police officers. There were old men, too old and feeble for service but brave in their own right and young boys too young to carry a rifle but large enough to rattle war drums. From the numerous machine shops that dotted the city to the vast shipyards the spread upon the shoreline of the river, men came to Campus Martius with a new birth of patriotic zeal and courage.

The grandstand was lifted from the ashes, the flags and buntings replaced with bright and bold colors. The grounds were cleaned and cared for. There were to be no signs from the previous war rally, no reminder of the terrible acts that took place the last time so many men came together for such a cause.

Mayor Duncan addressed the crowd and again informed them of the war meeting's purpose. "This is a rally to raise a brave and true regiment," he told the vast crowd before him. "There will be no draft. Our men are far too patriotic and noble for such a measure. We told Lansing that our men would *volunteer.*" Thunderous cheers and applause rose from the crowd. There was no longer the confusion, no signs of spreading rumors. Chants thwarted Duncan from speaking much more. It seemed the crowd wanted to hear from the man that would lead the regiment to the front. They wanted to hear from Judge Morrow. Wisely granting the crowd its wish, Duncan introduced Morrow and extended an arm back to greet the man as he came up.

Morrow rose from his chair, tucking his watch away for the last time in his pocket. He had been nervous all morning. In fact, he had gotten very little sleep because of it. He accepted it, however, and used it to his advantage. He considered it good to be nervous during such a time, for he was on the brink of something great, something unknown. He was about to lead a thousand men far from their homes toward hard marches, diseases, and raging battles.

"Fellow citizens," he called to them. "We are here to rekindle our devotion to our beloved country which is in peril. This is the time of its destiny. This is the crisis of its fate. From this terrible struggle it will come forth purified and respected, or it will sink into obscurity and disgrace, known on the historian's page as the weakest of human inventions." He let his opening lines settle into place, gauging the crowd's reaction. "Our fathers thought they were erecting a temple of liberty which should last for ages, where oppression should be unknown and freedom finds an asylum. Unless this causeless rebellion is crushed, the hopes of mankind in republican liberty are blasted. This generation of loyal citizens has assigned to it the noblest work ever entrusted to a nation—that of maintaining in its integrity, the government of the United States." He took a breath before reading the conclusion to his opening paragraph. "A generous and intelligent people will not decline the labor." The crowd erupted in cheer.

He continued on at length, describing the war and the reasons for such. Morrow told his fellow citizens that the South was responsible for the war, its start and its reasons. He reiterated his point by telling them that the North had done all that could be to persuade the South from war. "The war was forced upon us," he told them. He told the story of the firing upon Fort Sumter and how Confederate President Jefferson Davis made speeches that very night. Morrow spoke of patriotism and how it "is natural to the human heart. Love of country is one of the noblest feelings in the breast of man." He told how it belonged to the Greeks, the Romans, and General Washington at Valley Forge.

His words were well crafted and pleasing, igniting rushes of patriotism. He continued on by appealing to brave young men, urging them to step forward and show their patriotism, their love of country. If the nation failed in its current task, it would sink to a fifth-rate power, comparable to Mexico. Failure could only be avoided by brave and patriotic men, he told them, again urging them to step forward.

Morrow concluded his speech in a stern voice, propelling it beyond the crowd, intending for every able-bodied man to hear. "One word for myself," he added. "I am going to the field. I invite you to go with me. I will look after you in health and in sickness. My influence will be exerted to procure for you the comforts of life, and lead you where you will see the enemy. Your fare shall be my fare, your quarters my quarters. We shall together share the triumph, or together mingle our dust upon the common field. We are needed on the James River," he said plainly. "Our friends and brothers are there. Let us not linger behind. In this time of national peril, the government turns to you. Let it not appeal in vain."

His voice silenced, accompanied by a thunderous applause and cheers. Turning away from the crowd, he listened as the patriotic chants continued. He was proud of his words, the speech carefully crafted following the first rally's failure. Quickly taking his seat, he waited nervously for the next speaker to rise and address the crowd. Pulling on the chain of his watch, he smiled when he checked the time. Everything was ordered. Everything was coming together beautifully.

Morrow's words ignited the passion in Morgan. He had arrived early, with several other farmers from the area, and gathered near the front of the grandstand. If he had mixed feelings about the decision to go or stay, he had lost them during Morrow's riveting speech. The patriotism and honor in the man's voice convinced Morgan that he was making the right choice. If he were going to war, then Morrow would be the man to follow.

His eyes lifted toward the grandstand as the honorable Lewis Cass, perhaps the most known figure on the stage, rose and paced slowly toward the crowd. Morgan stood, nearly bracing himself on his toes, to listen to the words of Michigan's most known son. "Fellow citizens," Cass began. "Standing here and witnessing the patriotic enthusiasm of the people, my heart is too full for utterance. There is no man who feels more anxious that the Constitution shall be preserved as it was given to us by our fathers. We of this generation have a noble duty to perform for mankind. We are to preserve this fair land as a heritage to our children and to freedom forever." His voice was crisp and clear. His words were swift and powerful. "Our fathers endured much in their struggle for independence, and shall we prove degenerate sons of those noble sires? It cannot be. The people of the North will rescue the government." Morgan threw his arms into the air and cheered wildly. He appreciated Cass' comments, valued them as those of a great man who had suffered many trials.

Morgan watched as Cass slid away from him. At one time in the speech, Morgan could have nearly reached out to him, shaken hands with the great man. His short and abrupt words captured Morgan's attention, however, and such a meeting was not to be. Yet like a young child on Christmas, Morgan drew nearer to the stage, the excitement etching a smile on his face.

Mark Flanigan was never known as a man of speeches. His work and lifestyle didn't dictate that he be of such. Besides, there was always a quiet and mysterious aura about the Irishman. Yet in times of great need, and when he felt he had to address the situation with his voice, he relented and rose to speak. Such was a time.

"Fellow citizens, at a time like this it behooves every man to put forth his utmost energy in defense of the government." The words rolled swift, his accent slipping through at several intervals. "Every man who is loyal to his once happy land and abhors rebellion should rise to a full sense of his duty in this hour of its adversity." He pointed back toward Morrow. "Judge Morrow and I are going to raise a regiment. I hope every man will respond to his country's call."

It was not a glorious speech. It only provided the obvious. The nation was in need of brave soldiers, another regiment had been granted, and Morrow and Flanigan needed men to fill that regiment. His words couldn't have been any simpler, but he understood that while the educated may turn away from it, those of a lesser class could relate. He had always spoken their language despite his involvement in politics and his nomination to the county's lawman. Like Morrow, as he took his seat following his short address, Flanigan was happy with his choice of words.

He once again proved that this man, never desiring to speak, could rise when called upon, delivering perhaps not the most stirring of speeches, but the most simple and the most understood one of them all.

The day was full of such speeches. Some were short and to the point. Others were drawn out and delivered as patiently as a poem. The honorable Duncan Stewart, one of the Unionists the sympathizers demanded to be hanged, made a rousing speech, pledging monetary support for men who enlisted. For fathers enlisting in the regiment,

Stewart promised support for the first twenty-five of them. He would give four dollars a month, for the duration of their service, to families where there were four children or more and he would give two dollars a month for families where there were three children. He even turned upon his fellow alderman, too old and useless for the war effort, to join him in supporting the regiment by the means they had available. He concluded his speech by declaring: "I have more respect for a drunken patriot than an unpatriotic alderman," which drew great cheers from the crowd.

Others followed Stewart, attempting to add fuel to the growing fire. One of them rose and when asked if he would join the regiment, he insisted that he was too old and that the army wouldn't let him. In his place, however, he would send twenty substitutes, vowing that if it took every last dollar he had, he would offer it to the government.

The war meeting had been a stellar success. Following the July 22 war meeting, several other meetings were scheduled around Detroit through the early part of August. Raising a regiment was difficult work. Ranks couldn't be expected to fill at the conclusion of one large meeting. Several dignitaries, including Morrow and Flanigan, traced paths around the city and county, holding smaller meetings and gatherings to promote the regiment and recruit enlistments.

Other men scampered out to hold war meetings of their own, hoping to raise enough for a company of men. Such tasks, while delegated by Morrow and Flanigan, proved competitive, as often times the reward for completing such was officer status, appointed to lead the raised company.

Upon approval, the newly designated Colonel Morrow began raising the regiment on July 19, prior to the war rally at Campus Martius. Shortly after the beginning of August, there were enough men in the loose ranks for the regiment's organization. Soon after that, perhaps a week, the regiment had reached its maximum limit and men were even turned away to other regiments.

And so, by the middle of August, the regiment descended upon Detroit Riding Park, renamed it "Camp Barns," and prepared for formal training and its official mustering into federal service for a term of three years, which would conclude on August 15.

The Twenty-Fourth Michigan Infantry Regiment was formed.

The Soldier's Studies

The air was thick and humid. Trees sat motionless, their leaves still and calm. The men moved in neat and tidy lines. Off to the right. Off to the left. Double-quick. They learned the commands, the calls that sent soldiers in motion. They were expected to master the art of the march, in formation and out. They were pushed beyond expectations. Marches were an integral part of the army. No victory was accomplished without a march of many miles. No war was won without the blistering feet of soldiers, continuously marching from one field of battle to another.

"You must keep pace with the fellow at your side," instructed a line officer. "He must keep pace with the fellow at his side, and so on. That is how an army marches. That is how this regiment will march."

Morrow sat beneath a large tree and watched as a single company drilled. He listened to the orders the line officers were giving, knowing that the regiment was learning the art of war with each passing day, perhaps each step of the march. From his vantage point, he saw the unit stumble about, learning the orders and the corresponding steps. When one soldier stumbled too much, the entire company was halted. The line officer would step toward the soldier and calmly confront him, plainly remind the man that such training was necessary to survive the war. If, once the march resumed, the same man stumbled yet again, the line officer would pull him from his comrades and belittle him in front of them.

Riding toward him, Morrow saw the impressive figure of Lieutenant Colonel Flanigan sitting erect in the saddle. Turning away, momentarily ignoring his visitor, Morrow returned his attention to the company. Flanigan slid down from the saddle and sent the animal off with an orderly. "I've seen a better trot from a mule," said the Irishman as he sat down beside Morrow. "There have been many grateful citizens of this city, Henry, all of them wanting to present me with a horse." Flanigan followed Morrow's eyes and gazed upon the company, working tirelessly in the heat. "The problem is that I haven't found a horse they've provided me worth taking into battle."

"Perhaps a man of your *build* should find a more suitable horse, possibly a pony," Morrow responded with a smile. Flanigan grunted. He was too warm to deal with the joke. "You are a large man, Mark," added Morrow. "A large horse would only make you that much more of a target, that much bigger of a man."

Flanigan relented to the joke by shaking his head. "That'd be the point," he told his friend and commander. "I figure if I look big enough, I just might frighten the Rebels."

Morrow turned toward him and raised an eyebrow. Flanigan sighed, closing the conversation once and for all. "Well," the Irishman said reaching for the papers shoved in his pocket, "we've got a preliminary roll call for companies." He slid a dirty finger down the folded pages, scanning for known names, looking at the ages of the men enlisted. "Seventy years old," commented Flanigan. "The oldest man in the entire regiment is seventy years old. The youngest volunteer is thirteen. I've figured our average age is around twenty-five." Flanigan folded up the papers and handed them to Morrow. "We've got good strong young men, Henry."

He took the papers from Flanigan and shuffled them away with several others. "I have sent for the paymaster but fear it will be some time before he can come up. I've taken the situation to Mayor Duncan. He assures me that the city will do all that it can to help the families of those now in uniform, those good strong young men." Morrow lifted himself from the ground and brushed at his pant legs with sweaty hands. He looked back toward the company, training hard. "That is Captain Edwards' company. He enlisted all of those men in two days." Morrow turned back toward Flanigan, looking down to shade his eyes from the setting sun. "We only have a few days before departure, Mark. Make sure that all company commanders generously grant passes for those who have worked so hard. I want the men to see their families before we carry them off to war. I want them to remember what it is they fight for."

"Without hesitation, sir," Flanigan replied.

Morrow inched away. "I'll see what I can do about the paymaster." He stepped away from Flanigan, forgetting to salute. The procedures were still new to him, seemed so foreign, that he often forgot about the expected formalities. He didn't mind, just as long as the men didn't see. If they were expected to remember all of the complicated orders and formalities of army life, then so was he. It all, as he knew very well from past experience, would come in time. Soon everything, the salutes, the orders, and the countless other formalities, would be a part of his life.

Until then, he hoped to keep it personal. "Goodnight, Mark," he called as he stepped away into the fading sunlight.

"Goodnight, Henry," replied the weary Irishman.

Captain Albert M. Edwards was a twenty-six year old journalist when the war first called for him. He had been in his second year of college when recruitment for the First Michigan Infantry began. Being a proud and patriotic young man, Edwards enlisted, seeing action at First Bull Run where he was captured. Exchanged after the battle, Edwards made his way back to Michigan where he waited out another chance to go to war. When he heard that Morrow and Flanigan were going to raise a regiment, he set himself to the task of doing all that he could to help.

His efforts earned him the captaincy of Company F, the last company formally organized for the regiment. Raising it, however, only took the ambitious Edwards a mere two days. When drilling commenced, Edwards again proved his worth to the regiment. His experience at First Bull Run was not only beneficial to his company but to the entire regiment as well. The young journalist turned soldier quickly caught the attention of his superiors and men alike.

Edwards wore a thick beard, extending several inches from his chin. He spoke carefully and calmly, his voice soothing and friendly. He rarely shared his feelings, keeping personal treasures locked behind his warm eyes. Edwards was an approachable fellow with the look of a well-rounded man.

It was this look that often baffled his closest friends and colleagues. For they knew that Edwards had not just been captured at First Bull Run, but that there was much more to his story. From the outset of the war, Confederate privateers scoured the waters in search of vulnerable Union vessels. Such privateers risked possible death and capture, the latter of which the Confederate government sought to free. Edwards was among the Union prisoners of war selected as hostages, a bargaining tool to obtain the freedom of the captured Confederate privateers. He served time in Castle Pinkney before being carted away to Charleston Jail. Again death haunted him, as his life was threatened by hanging, to be completed once the first privateer in Union hands was executed. Luck was eventually granted by the heavens and Edwards was freed from Confederate capture after ten months.

He realized, during his captivity, that he was a long way from Michigan University. He doubted he would ever see his state again, preparing himself for the death that had so often been threatened.

Edwards listened as the drill officer complimented his company, the voice chasing away the painful memories. They had marched well and had learned a great deal in just a few short days. Abandoning the company, the officer approached Edwards, raising a stiff salute as he stopped. Edwards responded in kind. "That will be all for the evening," he instructed the officer. He turned his head, prying it over his shoulder to watch the setting sun. As the drill officer departed, he turned back toward Company F with a smile. "You are dismissed," he ordered, sending his weary troops away for the night.

Morgan felt his legs failing beneath him. Painfully hobbling along in the darkness, he sought refuge around a growing fire, the scent of fresh coffee and food guiding him. He approached the dancing flames quickly, nearly leaping for a seat on one of the folding chairs staggered around the fire. He winced in pain when he lifted his right leg up to his left knee. His fingers clumsily began to untie the shoe, his exhaustion making it hard to grip the laces. Completing the surprisingly difficult task, he winced again as he slid the shoe off and let it drop to the ground. Immediately he tended to his sore foot.

He had worn a hole in the wool sock, soaked in sweat from the day's nonstop training. Morgan pulled on the sock gently, not wanting to provoke additional pain. A few of his comrades gathered around the fire, saw him, and watched him struggle. When he realized their eyes were upon him, he stopped suddenly. Looking at them, he felt the rush of embarrassment. He didn't want to appear weak. Just as his eyes met theirs, they must have felt foolish as well, for they reached for their shoes and began tending to sores of their own. The embarrassment gone, Morgan pulled the sock off with a sudden yank.

His foot was covered with blisters and bleeding sores. As the warm summer air hit the open wounds, the pain came back, more fierce. He winced again, gritting his teeth together to stave off the torture. His eyes lifted again to his comrades. He saw their wounds. The training had been strenuous. Morgan settled down in the chair, steadied his breathing, trying to forget about the throbbing pain. Every man in the regiment must suffer the same, he thought. He brought his other leg up and began the entire procedure again. What had once been a simple task, removing shoes and socks, was now complicated surgery, the slightest move resulting in more unbearable pain. Morgan had learned from the previous foot and tended to the work quickly. When both feet were free of the tight shoes and the sweat-soaked socks, he propped them up on a log and leaned back in the chair. Suffering from the same, his comrades followed suit.

There were no words between them. These were working men. They had walked their share of miles. As for Morgan, he often worked out in the fields of the farm from dawn to dusk. His feet carried him from one place to another, rarely stopping for anything except food and an occasional moment's rest. There were many days where he returned to the house with sore feet, blisters hampering his movement. None amounted to anything like the pain he was in then, however. He figured he'd never marched more in his life, his feet never carrying him farther.

He nestled into the chair, closing his eyes. Just as they had done before, his comrades followed suit. It had been a long and trying day. It would just be one, however, in a long and difficult line of them. But these men knew the value of a good day's work. They knew how to look ahead and see the work before them, knowing the success their efforts could bring. As they began to drift to sleep, they knew there would be plenty of work in the days, months, and years that followed. Despite such thoughts, they dreamed of victory, epic battles, and the glory to be sought when they finally reached the front lines, when their blistered feet finally carried them to the war.

"I cannot recall a finer group of men," said Lewis Cass, touring the camp with Colonel Morrow. "You should be most pleased with their conduct. There has been much forced upon them. They have met it, with what I see, with great enthusiasm. They have risen above all expectations."

"Indeed they have," replied Morrow.

The two men shuffled about the quiet camp. Life had steadied for the evening. The men retired and the fires faded. A few conversations could be heard in the distance, as night-owls discussed what kept them awake. Morrow led Cass to the training ground, showing him where the men had marched countless hours in training. He showed him the guards, learning their duty, posted at each corner of the camp. "They do so," Morrow said of the guards, "with borrowed weapons. We are to return them in the shape they came once we get our own. We anxiously expect the shipment tomorrow morning. If not, then we expect it the following morning. The men are ready to get their hands on the rifles, I assure you. For the marching, they use sticks, branches, and chunks of wood nearly the size of a rifle. They are ready to go to war, Mr. Cass."

Cass nodded. "It is a regiment's purpose."

"Yes."

"And what of Mrs. Morrow?" asked a concerned Cass.

Morrow shook his head. "It pains her to see me go. There are times, late at night, where I ask myself if I have made the right decision. It is only momentary." He sighed. "And I always reply in the affirmative. I always come to the conclusion that this is something that I must do, no matter how much it pains her, no matter how much it pains me to abandon her."

"If I could go, I would," added Cass. "If the president called upon me and was willing to give me a command, an army of my own perhaps, I believe I could make a short go of this war." Morrow looked to the aging warrior and nodded. Cass had always been confident, on the verge of arrogant. His friend, his one-time favorite page in the Senate, had come to accept it. "I would give it until Christmas," declared Cass.

Such predictions had been made before. All had failed. The war had continued longer than anyone expected, anyone had believed.

Morrow continued on with the tour. Cass continued on with how he would end the war and how he would run the war if he were in charge. Eventually the conversation came upon the subject of slavery and its relation to the war. When Cass asked of Morrow's opinion of the sensitive subject, Morrow froze. The cheerful expression on his face retreated like a sunset. "It is an economic system with great flaws," he told Cass. "The idea that one people does the work of another while being held in bondage is improper and uncivilized. I do not know if one black man is capable of the same exertions as one white man. I do not know if one is of the more intellect. I have seen many freedmen here. I know what they have done and what they are capable of."

"And what if the war turned against slavery?" asked Cass. Morrow slightly tilted his head to gauge the question. "There is much clamor in Washington to make this war not only about the preservation of the Union, but to abolish slavery as well."

"Slavery is an economic system with great flaws," reiterated Morrow. "Eventually those flaws will collapse the system." He took a breath. The subject had appeared in newspapers all across the state. Abolitionists held rallies and meetings in attempt to build their voice. "I have enlisted for a term of three years," he added. "I will serve my country and government for that term no matter what course of action they pursue at the conclusion of this war. If slavery must be abolished with our victory, then let it be so. If we fail in our righteous mission and a compromise must be met, regarding the issue of slavery, then let it live." He pulled his hand away from the tree, ushering Cass forward for the remainder of the tour. "Slavery will die eventually, Mr. Cass, one way or the other."

Cass stopped. "And what, my dear friend, if it must end at the tip of your sword?"

Morrow moved on without hesitation. "Then I shall unsheathe it bravely."

Lieutenant Colonel Mark Flanigan scribbled his signature on the piece of paper and handed it back to the government official. He watched as the first wagonload of rifles appeared before him, bearing over five hundred arms. It would be the first of two such shipments. "What are the makes?" he asked the official in regards to the weapons.

"Springfields, Enfields, and some Austrians," replied the young man. "You'll be getting an assortment for now."

"Very well," responded the Irishman. "A rifle is a rifle."

"They are all suited for .58 caliber, some a .57 caliber. Don't worry about ammunition. You'll have plenty of it when you get to the field. For now, I've delivered what you'll need for training and what you'll carry with you when you depart for the front. Once you arrive at your destination, your brigade commander will distribute further ammunition to you."

Men began to swarm about the wagon as Flanigan and the young official discussed the arriving weapons. The regiment had waited for several days for their arms, hoping to at least have a few days to practice their marksmanship and rifle care. Cheers rose from the men as the first rifle cases were pried opened, their contents revealed. "Expect the second wagon sometime this afternoon," continued the official, raising his voice above the cheers. "By this time tomorrow, you should have your arms and uniforms. I'll remain in camp until the last of the wagons arrive to see that everything is properly coordinated and dispersed." He turned away from Flanigan, hiding a yawn. "You must excuse me, sir," he said quickly. "I've been on the road for several days and have had little rest."

Flanigan nodded. "Never mind," he said warmly. "If you seek rest, please take a room at the hotel for the evening. All costs will be covered."

"I believe I will do so, sir," replied the young man. "Cost is no worry as the government covers such."

"The government has paid enough. Your room, as well as the rooms of those accompanying you, shall be covered by the good citizens of Detroit."

The young man nodded gratefully. "Cities across the country shall know of Detroit's honor and patriotism."

Flanigan bowed at the waist. He called for a few men to escort the official and his attendants toward the hotel. Seeing the guests satisfied, Flanigan turned his attention to the newly arrived rifles. The men continued to gather and cheer around the wagon. He climbed aboard and waved for three officers to join him. They began prying open the wooden crates, checking the makes of the rifles. "We must get all serial numbers," Flanigan told them. "We will assign a rifle to a man and list his name, make of the rifle, and the rifle's serial number." He grunted as he pulled the lid off one crate. "We will not disperse the rifles until all have arrived. When we do so, see to it that the different makes are scattered about the regiment. I don't want one company to have just one make. These are new and fine rifles, but they still may not operate properly, lads." A grin came over his face when he lifted a new Springfield rifle from the box. It was oily, slippery to hold. It was wrapped in paper, greased onto the stock. "The last thing we need out there is a company with failing rifles."

Abel Peck lowered his rifle and took careful aim at the target. The long rifle swayed as he tried to settle it into place. He squinted, looking down the lane to a board propped against a tree. Once he found the target, he closed his right eye to take better aim. Quickly he propped the sight up, lining the cross-hairs with the board. He took a breath and then pulled the trigger. Crack! The board spun around on impact, dancing to the ground. Peck lowered the rifle, pleased at his accomplishment, and waited for further instructions.

"Very well done," said the young official. With the rifles dispersed, he stayed the extra days needed to properly train the regiment. "You see," he told the company before him, "Mr. Peck was capable of firing three shots in one minute. He hit the board twice. The primary concern should not be how fast a man can fire, but how accurately his fire is. It should be remembered that upon the field of battle there will be another line opposing you. There will be another line firing back. I assure you that it will become much more difficult to fire under such pressure, but you will learn."

He moved out in front of them and ordered the company commander, Captain Crosby, to arrange Company C in lines of fire. As the maneuver completed, the young official paced out before the readied company. "The front row will kneel," he said, pointing to them to do so. "The second row will step forward and take place directly behind the first row. This will present a precise line of fire, a massed volley from the first and second lines." He strolled into the line, stopping at the backs of the kneeling first row. "Now, if there is no time for the front row to kneel, things have to be rearranged slightly. It is not complicated, but it must be done swiftly." He signaled for the front row to rise and aim their rifles forward. "As the front row readies to fire, the second row will immediately move to the right. Each man in the second row will move a length of eight inches to the right of the man in his front. If done accurately, the volley of the second row should safely hurl over the shoulders of the men in the first row."

The officer slid away from the company, scampering to a safe distance. "Now, we shall commence firing by row. First row will kneel." He turned to Captain Crosby and waved for the officer to give his order. Crosby barked the orders, his voice thundering above the men. The first line knelt to the ground and leveled their rifles. The second line inched behind them, their rifles steadied. Crosby ordered the company to fire by line. The first line opened a quick volley. The second line waited only a few seconds before Crosby ordered them to commence, their rifles cracking.

Black-powder guns produced a lot of smoke. As the thick blanket of smoke warmly covered the men of Company C, the young official moved out before them. When he first spoke, his audience couldn't see him. "Where am I?" he asked them. Hidden from their view, he moved around frantically. "Where am I now?" He moved around again, sliding up and down the line. He moved forward and backward. "How about now?" he asked. The men in line searched the smoke but could not locate his position. Finally, he drove toward them, his sword pointed at them. He screamed when he leaped out from the smoke, crashing toward the startled men like a wild beast.

He stopped only inches from one man, the would-be victim's eyes wide with fear. The young official took a deep breath, collecting his thoughts. "You will not always see your enemy," he told them. "They will not always see you. The field of battle is a dark and confusing place. You will see little. Your eyes will fail you." He took another breath. As the men of Company C settled back into place, the official continued. "Your training will not. Look into the smoke for flashes. Use your ears to listen for them." As the smoke lifted from the field, the men understood the lesson. Their eyes shifted toward bright red swatches of fabric, placed about the ground before them when the official was running around in the smoke. "Each patch represents a man, perhaps a group of men." The patches, ten of them in all, dotted the land before Company C. Some were in line, others were back several feet. A few were placed just two or three feet away from the front row.

"Aim low," continued the young official, his energy regained. "Very well," he said turning to Captain Crosby. "Commence the drill again, this time firing while standing. When the smoke falls again, rely on your senses, rely on each other to locate my position. If you think you've found me, shout out the position and have the man standing there raise his arm." He smiled at them, approving of their work thus far. "We shall see if you are learning anything or not."

Splotch. Splotch. The rain fell heavier by the minute, generously providing a thick curtain for the men to march through. Feet were pulled in attempted rhythm from the thickening mud. It had rained for two days straight, but the drilling never ceased. The regiment only had a short time to learn the art of the soldier, the soldier's studies. Clap! Clap! A solid crash of thunder shook the world around them. Still they marched. Still the formation was held, their eyes forward, their aching feet moving. "Keep your feet moving, boys!" shouted Colonel Morrow, moving alongside them on foot. "Keep your eyes ahead, boys. You're marching like soldiers now!"

The line splotched through the mud into another torrent of rain. This regiment, consisting of men from all walks of life, had grown into a cohesive and disciplined force. They were still rough around the edges, but such was expected of a new regiment. They received vast amounts of training in a short time. Morrow pushed them forward constantly, demanding great things from them. They pushed themselves to unbelievable levels for him. They vowed to go above and beyond his expectations. They respected Morrow, not just for his civilian work and his approachable attitude, but because he often would march with them, would learn with them, in the rain or in the heat. And at times, when needed, he would become the rash disciplinarian, a trait expected of a commander.

The army had prided itself on such distinctions between the men of the rank and file and their officers. Weather, however, especially the Michigan weather, made no such distinctions. The men, marching and dirty, were soaked. The company commanders, keeping their men in line, were soaked. Colonel Morrow and Lieutenant Colonel Flanigan, ordering the line forward, praising their effort, were soaked.

"Three cheers for the Twenty-Fourth!" shouted Flanigan.

The men responded by hoisting their kepis, those short government supplied hats of the common soldiers, and cheering away.

Onward they marched, the rain unrelenting, unforgiving. "Three cheers for this Michigan weather!" shouted Captain Edwards.

Again the kepis rose, and the men cheered three cheers once more.

The march continued. The rain continued.

A fine regiment was being constructed.

"No, they didn't," said Morgan quickly. He lifted his eyebrows in interest. Several men had gathered under an oak tree to swap stories and discuss the war. Because of the regiment's hard work, Morrow had given them an afternoon off. The men accepted. "You mean to tell me," he quipped again, "that the government, our national government, made this fellow a general because he raised a regiment and supplied them himself? And then you tell me this particular *general* doesn't know how to ride a horse?"

"The truth," his comrade responded. "It's said that old Abe signed this fellow to a generalship and even provided him with a special wagon for transportation."

"What? Lincoln gave this fellow a wagon?"

"Yep," the soldier said with a smile, "a covered one at that."

Morgan laughed in disbelief. He had heard of ridiculous things since the war started, but this was one of the worst. "I don't believe it," he confessed.

"True as day," replied the soldier.

"That's just the thing of it," said another. "I grow weary of the papers and all their talk about the *great* men fighting this war. The way I see it, not everybody in uniform, in an army, fights the war." He slid forward, drawing closer to his comrades. "You've got your generals, like that fellow there, and they don't fight the war, they command it. They make the decisions for us grunts to follow. You know what I'm saying? Yet they get their names in every paper while those who fight, good men like us, get nothing."

"Our names go on a casualty list," chimed in another.

The conversation died. The men sat around in a rough circle and looked at each other. Morgan turned away, still not believing the story of the wagon-general, still not sure if there were no generals in the thick of the fight. He had read papers and heard stories of brave commanders, men who risked their lives for the men under them. He could recall countless stories of commanders riding out before their men, in the middle of the fight, urging them forward, praising them, and fighting alongside them. Unconvinced of the story about the general, Morgan turned back. "You really read about that general?"

"Ah, hell, Morgan," the soldier replied. "Don't worry on it anymore. We'll probably see him when we reach the front. Hell, he'll probably be in charge of our brigade. Wouldn't that be something?"

The men shared a laugh, easing the tension brought on by the casualty list statement. The sun splintered through the branches and leaves, warming the men sitting below. The rain and storms had long passed. The countless marches and drills through such horrid weather faded to memory. Resting comfortably under the large tree, the men sprawled out on the green grass and bathed in the sun's warmth.

Morgan fell back with them, propping his head up with his arms. He looked to the sky and wondered just how long they would stay home, just how long they could be kept from the bloody war. He thought of Emmy and wondered if she was troubled with the work he left behind for her. He hoped his letter had reached his father-in-law. Emmy would need help. If Morgan couldn't be there for her, then he would at least guarantee that she did not go through it alone.

Scrambling toward them, searching for a comfortable spot, a curious soldier could no longer hold back. Approaching them, a smile on his face, he beckoned the group. "What did you say about a general who rides in a wagon?"

Colonel Henry A. Morrow completed his paperwork and signed the last of the remaining documents for the evening. He rested his hands on the small desk and thought about his decision. He had wrestled over it for several days. A color bearer, the single most important soldier in a regiment, was needed. Throughout the regiment's training, Morrow inspected the men to see who met the precise qualifications. The color bearer was more than just a soldier. It was considered a great honor to carry the nation's flag, the pride of the regiment, into battle.

After much consideration and conversation with Flanigan, Morrow had come to a decision. There had been many good men considered for the position, but one man stood out above them. His busy work completed, Morrow lifted himself from the chair. He had made his decision, and he would confront the soldier about it, testing whether or not the man appointed wanted the position. The color bearer was often the first victim of a fight. Not only did the colors help direct its regiment, but it also presented a vital target to the enemy. The colors would often move with the command. Considered a centralized location, there was no more important of a position to be.

Perhaps it was the most dangerous position in a regiment.

Morrow shook away the thoughts. There is no time for that. Such thoughts should not be introduced to the man appointed. The color bearer must be a man of respect, responsibility, and courage. Above all, he must be loyal not just to his regiment but to the country as well. Morrow firmly believed he had selected a man that met all of those qualifications.

Skimming across camp, Morrow eventually stopped at a blazing campfire, a single soldier tending to the flames. Abel Peck slowly prodded the fire with a steel rod. He moved the burning chunks of wood in different directions, hoping to keep the fire alive as long as possible. For the first several minutes, he seemed not to notice his colonel standing before him. It mattered little, as Morrow was in no haste. His eyes, just as Peck's, had become transfixed on the dancing flames and orange glow. After prodding the wood once again, Peck finally looked up and acknowledged Morrow's presence. "Are you having trouble sleeping too, Colonel Morrow?"

The question broke him away from the flames. He shook his head quickly. "No, Abel," he said. "No trouble at all. I'm not much for sleeping nowadays."

Peck nodded. "My daughter would be up right now." He looked to Morrow with sad eyes. "She would have woken us only moments ago.

Whether from a terrible dream or just difficulty sleeping, she would crawl into our bed and nestle in between us." He dropped his head and gently laughed. "I wonder how her mother is putting up with it without me. I wonder if my little girl will get back to sleep."

Morrow fell silent. "Are you a father?" asked Peck.

"Not yet," replied Morrow.

Peck fiddled with the fire some more, hoping to ward off the depressing feelings. He hadn't even left home yet, and he was homesick. "It'll be another few hours before my wife settles the girl down."

Morrow unbuttoned his vest and sat down on a log across from Peck. "I have come to speak with you about regimental business, Abel." He spoke carefully, not wanting to offend the soldier. "We have made an important decision that concerns you."

Peck smiled. "And what'll that be, sir?"

"You have been selected to carry the national colors."

He took the moment in and offered no response to Morrow. His eyes fixed back upon the flames. When he finally spoke to Morrow, he didn't look at him. "I will carry the flag," he said softly. "I consider it a great honor that you have chosen me above all others."

Morrow nodded. He was pleased with his selection. He had watched Peck since the training began. Not only was he eager to learn the ways of a soldier, but he was eager to help those who needed it. Peck was the first to volunteer for drills and never questioned the authority of those in charge. "You will have many duties and great responsibilities," he told Peck. "Explanations of such will come in time. For now," he said while bracing a hand on Peck's shoulder, "you have other important things to take care of." Morrow lifted himself from the log. "You are aware that the officers of the regiment have been granting passes for those who have earned them. It is our wish that the men see their families before we depart for the front. Seeing that there is no record of you receiving such, I am officially granting you leave for two days." He read Peck's reaction, the surprise and happiness. "Your two days will begin tomorrow morning," Morrow continued. "What you do between now and then shall not be counted against your time. You are free to go home now, if you wish."

Peck stood up. "You mean…"

Morrow interrupted him. "Go home, Abel, and put your daughter to bed." He turned away from Peck. "I will see you in two days, Mr. Peck. Do not be late in your return. There is much for you to learn." He took out a piece of paper and jotted down the pass.

Peck moved around nervously, swiftly. The generous offer by Morrow would not be denied. He began shoving his personal items in his issued haversack. Morrow handed him the paper that granted his leave. Peck smiled when he received it. "Such generosity will not be forgotten, Colonel Morrow. I assure you I will return on time and shall be ready to assume my responsibilities."

Morrow nodded and shuffled off into the darkness.

Peck stuffed the haversack full and made his way toward the nearest guard station. His legs carried him quickly, his hands bearing the pass from Morrow. He could not wait to arrive home and see his wife and daughter, to help put the little one to bed. Two days away from the regiment. Two days to spend with his family.

Jaunting through the darkness, the depressing thoughts were left in the wake.

Abel Peck was on his way home.

Captain Albert M. Edwards rubbed his sore hand. He had written a great deal of passes, allowing the men to vacate camp and head home for a few days. As he slowly walked across the grounds, he saw his company melting away. As the sun rose above the trees, above the buildings of Detroit, he watched them gather what little they had and leave for home. Some men would just simply walk away without anything. Others would cram whatever could fit into their haversacks.

The scene reminded him of his time in Confederate captivity. Brave and patriotic Union men, dismantled and broken behind bars, contemplated on escaping. They would hold meetings in the middle of the night. Crude plans would be drawn over paper. As he watched the men of his company pack their things for their two days leave, he could not help but compare the sights of present and past. Oh, how the brave men thought they could escape, he thought.

His memory carried him back to a dark night. The wind blew cold circles around their prison, sneaking in and blowing out their candles. The men had just finished their meal of stale bread and sour coffee, settling in for the night. One man, who had long since been planning an escape, whispered to them that the time was right. "I am going," he proudly told them. "You can go with me, but if you fear it, I understand." He shoved several small personal items into a makeshift haversack, gently sliding the Bible in last. Not a man around him moved or made motions of joining him. When he concluded packing his gear, he looked back to them. "I shall go it alone, comrades. I have spent too much time in this rotten place." The others, including Edwards, simply looked at him. Then the man chewed on his last small piece of bread. Surely he would need energy if he was going to be successful in his attempt. Standing up, he looked at the steel bars; the cage kept them locked away like animals. He then turned to his comrades with a soft smile. Edwards raised a hand in the darkness, offering his bread from dinner. The other men followed, offering what little they had left. The man accepted them warmly, thanked them for their support.

A Confederate guard, a polite gentleman by the name of Howell, arrived at his usual time to check up on the prisoners. This time he came with the ring of keys in hand, inserting the key to the cell quickly, his eyes shuffling from side to side. The steel gate swung open. Edwards propped himself up to look outside. He momentarily thought about joining his comrade in the daring escape. The escapee slid through the large opening and received further directions from Howell. "You are a good man," he told the Confederate. Before departing one final time, he again turned to his comrades. "I will not forget you friends and all that you have bravely suffered through. If I get out, I shall make your sacrifices known." He nodded to them. They nodded to him. Howell, very anxious to move on, indicated that they were running out of time. The plan had been in formulation for nearly a month. The escapee had sought out Howell and attempted to bribe him. The Confederate gentleman would have none of such. He told the prisoners that he had no heart in the war and did not like to see his northern brothers treated so harshly. He would aid them because he believed it God's will to do so.

When asked again if something could be done in return for his help, Howell rubbed his dirty chin and smiled. "I met a fair woman in New York when I went to school there," he told the prisoners. "I would like to see her again." The escapee assured Howell that if the two of them got out he would take him to New York to find his girl.

Howell closed the steel door and said goodbye to those left inside. Edwards gave him and the escapee an encouraging nod. As another gust of wind broke into the dark chamber, the two men made their escape toward freedom.

"I shall see you in two days, Captain Edwards," said a voice, beckoning him from the past to the present.

"Excuse me?" replied Edwards, lost in the daze.

"I shall see you in two days, Captain Edwards," Morgan said again. He showed Edwards the signed pass. "I have never been more excited to head home in my life."

"Very well," Edwards responded. He shook his head, forcing the memories to retreat, forcing his mind to accept reality once again. "You have earned it, Morgan. Return to your wife and your peaceful farm. For in a few days we will be marching to a war that will not be as comfortable."

FAREWELLS

Newly promoted Color Sergeant Abel Peck awoke that morning feeling rejuvenated. He had arrived in time to help put his daughter to sleep, in her own room, but she managed to slide in between her parents sometime in the night. They were delighted to see him when he arrived, although his wife initially feared that her husband had deserted. Peck assured her that he hadn't by showing her the pass signed by Morrow. He explained how the pass didn't come into affect until the following morning, but that Morrow had let him go early.

He spent his first morning attempting to help his wife with breakfast. She would have none of it. Her husband had worked very hard with the regiment. It would do him well to sit and rest while she prepared the morning's meal. When his daughter woke, she jumped into her father's arms. Peck smiled and laughed. Never before had he felt more comfortable. Never before had he felt so confident. For the first time in a long time, the three of them ate a meal, together, at the table.

Peck spent that afternoon finishing some of the chores that had escaped him before he left. The roof needed some minor repair, a task that Peck completed in good time. There was a window at the side of the house that needed to be replaced, so that too was completed. Other chores came at him, but he accepted the challenge. By the time the sun began to set in the sky, his chores had been completed.

After putting the little girl to bed, Peck and his wife sat out on their front porch and listened as the night settled in. It was a peaceful moment, one that Peck enjoyed very much. Hand in hand they sat on the front steps. There were no words between them. He looked at her with loving eyes. He felt he needed to say something, but the words never came. When her eyes met his, he moved in for a kiss. It was reminiscent of their first kiss, so long ago.

His life was a good one. He knew that as he sat with his wife that evening. While he tried not to entertain the thoughts of leaving his family behind, they snuck up on him anyhow. When he felt them rise within him, the sadness taking control, he wrapped his arms around his wife and brought her in close to him.

She sighed as she looked up to the stars. "I do not want to let you go," she confessed. "I cannot bear to let you go."

Peck kissed her on the cheek. "Oh, my dear wife," he said soothingly. "I have thought much about it, and it pains me so to leave. But as much as I cannot bear to see you hurt, I cannot bear further ignorance to our nation's trial."

She nodded. A tear rolled down her face. She understood what her husband had to do. She understood that he, as a proud man, as an American, couldn't stand by after another call and watch thousands more answer in his place. She wrapped her arms around his, holding tightly.

Peck kissed her on the cheek once again. "One more night, dear wife," he said. "We have one more night together before I must go."

The farm had been tended well in his absence. As he walked the road leading to his house, the farmer in him was pleased to see the progress made. When Morgan climbed up the front steps, the creaking wood signaling his arrival, he heard his wife shout from inside the house. Excited and surprised, she ran out to him, nearly leaping into his arms.

"How long?" she asked regarding his stay.

"A full two days, Emmy," he responded proudly.

She hugged him and kissed him. Leading him by the hand, she took him into the house. It was clean and beautiful. The house had been recently swept. He could smell bread baking in the kitchen. Morgan wondered how his little wife had found so much time for everything. He wondered how she managed the farm and the house at the same time. Her skills impressed him.

Emmy forced his haversack away from him, hanging the leather bag near the front door. The drifting scent of fresh bread nearly pulled him toward the kitchen. She wrestled him away, leading him up the stairs toward their room. At the top of the stairs, she kissed him again. He followed her down the hall and into their bedroom.

She closed the door behind them.

He awoke a few hours later to the sound of a carriage rolling down his drive. Morgan rolled over and saw his wife's side of the bed was empty. From the cracks in the wooden floor rose the scent of not only fresh bread but a full meal. He slid on a clean shirt and looked out the window. A black carriage, adorned with red curtains, slowed at the front of the house.

Morgan paced down the stairs to confront Emmy about the visitor. He found her in the kitchen, finishing the preparations on the meal. He leaned on the doorway, turning toward the front door to watch for the visitor. "Your father has arrived," he said to her. Morgan walked in and sat in a chair at the table. "I wrote to him for assistance," he said ashamed to admit it.

"I know," she replied, not pulling her eyes from the meal. "He arrived here two days ago and told me the contents of your letter."

"And?"

Emmy turned toward him, finally pulling herself from the meal. She walked over to him and put her arms around him. "You are a strong and proud man, Morgan. Reaching my father for help must have been painful." She smiled at him. "You did it out of love for me, concerned for my well-being." She leaned in for a kiss. "I have never loved more than what I do now."

Morrow stayed in camp. His wife had come to visit him, bringing lunch and dinner. She didn't mind visiting him because she was all too aware of his duties and his devotion to them. He didn't mind her joining him either, as it brought him great joy. "I will come and see you as often as I can when you are there," she told him lovingly.

"I know," he responded.

As the evening blanketed the sky, dismissing the bright sun for another night, Morrow and his wife sat outside under a large oak tree and gazed upon the shimmering stars. She imagined how things would have been different had the war not called her husband away, not beckoned for thousands of young men to pull from their loved ones' arms. He wondered just what was developing under those watchful stars on the front. He wondered who was dying, praying, and looking to those same stars for answers, for salvation. He pondered at the plans generals were making under the stars and wondered if those plans would lead the brave armies to victory or tragic defeat.

"What will come of it if we don't win the war?" she asked, pulling Morrow away from the intriguing thoughts that entertained him.

He rolled over and looked at her. "We will be successful," he replied.

She shook her head. "What if we are not?"

Morrow sat up and collected his scattered thoughts. "Oh," he confessed, "I imagine things will be no different here than before. Life will go on in the northern states, I believe. I cannot see a nation, one such as the Confederacy has proposed, surviving more than a few years, their mark on the world little more than a gentle ripple in a vast ocean." He turned to her. "I do not see us losing the war. When it is over, whether it be tomorrow or well beyond, I see their argument will settle upon the idea that a much stronger more industrious people, with better arms and more soldiers, brought about their final defeat."

"And?" she asked innocently. "Are we not the more populated and the better armed nation for such conflict?"

He chuckled. "Foolish talk," he said. "History has shown that even an outnumbered and out-supplied force, if trained well and led well, is capable of winning a war against a much larger force. This is not a war of nations," he added carefully. "This is a war for the restoration of a nation. This is a war to put down a rebellion."

She nodded. Her husband's patriotism was strong, his feelings evident in his voice. She fell to her back once again, down to the cool summer grass. Her eyes fixed upon the stars hanging above them again. "This reminds me of a night long ago, when a young man came to call upon me in Niles."

Morrow smiled. The memory played.

Flanigan gently closed the door and came into the room. His wife had not expected him and had fallen peacefully asleep. Entering the room, he took careful steps in attempt to silence his large frame. He did not want to disturb her.

She was nestled warmly in the bed, a hand resting upon his pillows. He bent down to her and thought of kissing her on the cheek but decided against it. His beard would only tickle her and wake her from her slumber. Flanigan quietly slid across the room and sat in the rocking chair, the same she had used to rock the children to sleep. From there he watched her dream, perhaps of him, perhaps of the war's end. Her lips curled as if she intended on saying something, and her eyes would gently shutter as if they were about to open and fall upon him.

He watched her sleep, burning the image into memory. There he was in his uniform, an officer. There she was sleeping. To her, at that moment, the war was a distant thought. There was no need for him to go to war, not in her dreams. Flanigan thought of this as he leaned back in the chair and closed his eyes. Such horrible things as war do not belong in dreams. Dreams should be of happiness. He prayed that she wasn't dreaming of his departure or fearing of his fate.

Fate should not be questioned. God has a plan, he thought. I am to go to war. I am to leave my family and go to war. His eyes opened and closed, struggling to stay awake. He was tired and worn out. Never before had he worked so hard. Slowly the chair began to rock back and forth. The motion began to carry him to sleep. Pulling himself up with his arms, steadying the chair, he opened his eyes once more to gaze upon his wife. He loved her so. She had never looked more beautiful. Remember, he told himself. Remember this moment and carry it into the whirlwind of war, the din of battle. Let her be your will to continue and let God be your strength to see the great task through.

Leaning back, giving into his weariness, the chair began to rock again. The fight to stay awake had faded. No longer could he hold it back. He needed rest.

The old chair creaked as Flanigan fell asleep.

Across from him, his wife, her eyes open, lovingly looked upon him. She had been awake the entire time.

The old man extended a warm hand as he stood on the front porch of the farmhouse. He looked beyond his grievance, his only daughter marrying a poor farmer, and awaited Morgan's response. Morgan took the hand and welcomed it, a smile on his face.

"You do a great deed," said the old man. "There were many times I questioned your values," he said as he ran his fingers across the brim of his hat. "I did not see what I should have, and for that I apologize sincerely." Morgan nodded, silently accepting. "When I received your letter, much was to be assumed of its contents. Upon reading it, I have never read a more understanding and kind letter. You have a love for my daughter which I thought you couldn't offer. I see now the errors of this thinking."

The sun began to rise behind them. Emmy came out to them, Morgan's haversack in her hands. She had filled it with fresh vegetables and warm bread. After handing it to her husband, she turned to her father and hugged him. "This war has called a great many young men," said the old man. "I have seen many of them leave me for it. It has taken from me a great workforce, but I cannot complain. I saw those men depart, and I wished them farewell and warm wishes, hoping for victory and their safe return. They were brave young men," he concluded with a nod. "But I have not seen a braver man than you."

Morgan smiled. There were no words to express his emotions. The old man extended another hand which Morgan accepted happily before walking back into the house. Emmy watched her father disappear and then turned to Morgan with sad eyes. "How the days have passed," she confided. "I did not want them to end."

"They will not," Morgan replied. "I will carry them in my heart and I pray that you will do the same."

She nodded and clamored down the steps into his arms, wrapping hers around his shoulders. Emmy looked at him, read his eyes, and then kissed him. "You have your Bible," she stated. "And you have my heart."

"I will return, my Emmy."

"I pray that you will."

They kissed again as he pulled himself away. The regiment called. He was due back at camp within the hour. He had promised not to be late.

As he marched down the long path, Emmy fell to her knees and watched him go. "I will pray that you will return to me," she whispered, "for I cannot live without you."

Abel Peck had to pry his little girl from him. He had called her out to the front room and told her that he was leaving. He reminded her to be a good and pleasant little girl, minding her mother and paying attention to her studies. Peck also told her that he would no longer be there to help her to sleep, no longer there in the large bed when the girl came bouncing in. She was not to expect him home for a great while. "That nation is calling me," he told her. "I must go to her assistance."

The girl cried. Her father pleaded that she wipe her tears and be strong. She ignored his desire and let the tears fall. Clutching her, he lifted her into his arms. "You do not worry for your father," he told her. "I will be fine."

His wife came and removed the girl, cradling the sobbing child in her arms. Peck turned away and wiped a tear of his own. He had thought a great deal about leaving them, but he had not expected it to be this trying. He was not prepared. "I will write you often, little one," he said, offering some hope. "I will tell you of the great accomplishments of your father and his comrades. I shall make an effort to render you every thought of my return to you in my words. I will tell you of our adventures. I will tell you of our battles, always writing after them to indicate my safety." Peck reached for her, brushing back her brown hair to see her face. "I will depend upon you and your mother to tell me of the goings of home. I will be far away from the life I love, and I will need to be reminded that all is well."

Finally the little girl nodded.

His wife put the girl down and reached out for her husband. "You are brave," she whispered to him. "We will be here when you return. Come back to us and live a happy and long life. I pray that your departure will not be for too long. I pray that you will once again walk though that doorway and fall into my arms."

"I will."

She let him go and he watched his daughter run upstairs to her bedroom. "Abel," his wife called to him. "You should be going. The regiment awaits the return of its color bearer."

He leaned in and softly kissed her. Before exiting the house, he turned to her and gave her one last smile. "The Twenty-Fourth shall be the pride of the state," he exclaimed. "You will read of us in the papers. You will hear of our journeys in the streets. Read and tell the stories to our daughter," he insisted, "so that you both can be proud."

She brought him toward her, kissing him again. "I am proud." Her lips recoiled, her eyes were closed, but she felt him pull away. When the door closed and he was gone, she went to the window and watched him depart, vanishing into the busy street.

From her room on the second-story, the little girl followed her father until he melted away in the distance. In her hands she clutched the stuffed bear given to her as a birthday present from her father. It had always been her favorite.

Hundreds of other brave men suffered the same. When the sun rose on that final day with their families, the men found it hard to depart, found it hard to leave them behind. They had a duty, however. Some of the men played one last time with their children. Some helped their wives with unfinished chores. Others paid visits to the sweethearts they had been planning to marry. Some said their final goodbyes to their mothers, fathers, and siblings. All of them suffered the lonely walk back to the regiment.

They marched into camp and presented themselves to their company officers, notifying their commanders that they had not lost their patriotism. They were indeed brave men, willing to separate themselves from their families, and go to war.

And as their loved ones sadly watched them depart, they wondered if they would ever see their brave men again. Some of the women sought out the Bible. Others entertained their children or tended to the work at hand.

Mrs. Morrow replayed countless memories, hoping to stay strong.

Mrs. Flanigan tended to the sad children, shaken by their father's departure.

Morgan's wife sat alone on the front steps, praying.

Peck's wife kept herself busy in the kitchen. His daughter fell asleep on her bed with dried tears on her soft face, the bear still nestled in her little arms.

All of them just as strong and brave as the men they watched depart.

Alas, the War Is Calling

It is August 25, 1862, one day before the Twenty-Fourth Michigan's flag arrives. Colonel Morrow had kept the regiment in fine fashion. He ordered the uniforms to be cleaned and inspected by all company officers. Rifles were to be cleaned as well. The regiment was to look as splendid as possible for the flag presentation.

His work was cut short, however, when several of his close friends came to him and beckoned him back to headquarters. He took the bait and when he arrived, he saw a large number of people, Mayor Duncan included. It seemed that nearly a hundred citizens received invitations to the private event. Morrow, startled, stopped and had to be urged forward by his friend William Jennison. With his friend's guidance, Morrow came upon the group. Arriving, they immediately ushered forward the most beautiful and powerful horse Morrow had ever seen.

"Colonel," Jennison addressed, "it seemed but yesterday when you pledged the people to organize a regiment. That pledge stands redeemed, and one thousand brave men await your command to march to the front." He took a breath and saw Morrow marveling at the horse. "With grateful pride at your success, your neighbors ask you to accept this living token—

in peace the emblem of labor. Amid the storm of battle, may it bear you triumphantly against your country's foes."

Morrow carefully slid up to the animal. He patted the sturdy neck and looked into the eyes of the beast. Perhaps the animal knew the perils in store. Applause erupted from the audience. He swung around, bowing at them. Lifting a hand above them, he quieted them. "The worth of this present is a thousand times enhanced by the fact that it is a gift from the citizens of Detroit, among whom I have passed all the days of my manhood." The words flowed steadily. "This camp, the roll of yonder drums, and these brave men, all seem like a dream. But yesterday, I was in the quiet pursuit of my profession. I am here because my country needs my services. I came to Detroit ten years ago, an unknown boy." He looked to them as he spoke. "Its people adopted me, and I have had honors beyond what I see fit to deserve. If, by leading this regiment to the field, I can repay the debt of gratitude I owe them, I welcome the opportunity." He took a slow breath. The audience was captivated by his words. He was captivated by the generous gift. "I shall take good care that the high character of my state sustains no injury, and my battle cry shall be *Detroit and victory!*"

The audience exploded with cheers. Morrow's friends congratulated him, shaking hands with their city's colonel. Mrs. Morrow came forward, a warm smile on her face, and lovingly embraced him. With the cheers around them, and his friends patting him on the back, she looked up to him. "Your friends are very kind, Henry," she said softly.

"Too much," Morrow sighed.

She smiled. "They thought it too little."

Colonel Morrow checked the time once again. His watch read slightly after five o'clock. The time had come. The regiment would receive its flag. For nearly an hour the men stood still as stone. This is what they had been waiting for. As several important delegates arrived and took their places on the grandstand at Campus Martius, a large crowd gathered to witness the event, for they too had been waiting for this.

Morrow stood with Flanigan on the stage, anxiously waiting for the show to begin. There was still much to be done. The regiment was leaving for the front in three days.

Three days wasn't that far away, Morrow thought. He looked over the orderly ranks of the regiment with judging eyes. Are they ready? Have you done enough for them? Are you ready? The nagging questions filled his mind, so much so that he began to suffer from a severe headache. Ever so carefully he regained his composure, wiped the sweat from his forehead, and straightened his posture.

Finally, the greatly anticipated moment arrived. All eyes turned toward two men, the massive regimental flag rising between them. The crowd gasped. The soldiers lifted their chins to gaze upon the bright colors. Morrow turned to Flanigan with a smile. What a flag it was. It flapped freely in the wind, its bold colors dancing. He saw the careful craftsmanship, the attention to detail. In bold gold letters, standing out from the patriotic colors, was "Twenty-Fourth Michigan Infantry." Never before had Morrow seen such a beautiful flag.

Pacing before the silenced crowd, the two men stopped and one of them stepped forward toward Morrow. "Colonel Morrow," he said loudly, his voice proud and strong. "Your regiment has been raised sooner than any other that has left the state. Messrs. F. Buhl and Company request me to present, through you, to the regiment this beautiful banner. It is the gift of generous, loyal men to patriotic soldiers. It symbolizes our Union, its power, grandeur and glory." He slowly handed the flag to Morrow. "In the smoke and din of battle, may its beautiful folds ever be seen till victory shall bring peace to our distracted country."

Morrow extended his hands and took the flag. He looked out over the crowd and then to his regiment. For a moment the words seemed to escape him, slip away from his tongue. For a moment he felt as if he were all alone, embracing the mighty flag. "This is the flag of the United States," he uttered, "and it shall never be any other. I have a check from a citizen of Detroit for the color bearer, Abel G. Peck, of Nankin, and a further assurance of one hundred dollars in the event of the flag not being lost in battle—as it never will be." Thunderous cheers arose from the crowd. Peck, standing with the elected color guard, those charged with protecting the great flag, marched to the grandstand and received the flag from Morrow. "It is a great honor," reminded the colonel to his color guard. Peck nodded, saluted both Morrow and Flanigan, and then quickly rejoined the regiment.

As Morrow watched the flag melt into position, forever becoming one with the regiment, an old colleague of his, Judge Campbell, approached and presented Morrow with a magnificent sword. His words returned Morrow's attention to the moment at hand. "Colonel Morrow, the people of this old country feel a deep interest in those under your command, who belong to their own households. It is my pleasant duty to offer you this sword from those who will renew their proof of confidence when you lead them in battle," he lifted the sword with his hands, showing the crowd before turning it back to Morrow. "Let it gleam at the head of your columns until there is no longer an enemy to meet them."

Morrow accepted the kind gift. "I thank you for this handsome gift," he told Campbell. "It shall never be used except in defense of my country. If I die it will be with my face to the foe. Once more, and it may be the last time, I bid you adieu."

He turned toward Flanigan and issued the orders to have the regiment move out. Sending Flanigan off, Morrow turned and said his goodbyes to the dignitaries and close friends on the stage. They responded with warm smiles and affectionate handshakes. Many of them were businessmen, their workers departing the factories and foundries for the regiment. Morrow was the man that would lead them into battle, was charged with their wellbeing and responsible for their hopeful return from the front. Others were politicians, Democrats and Republicans, there not in light of their position on the war, which was proving to be much longer than expected, but because they were willing to support the men in arms.

Morrow thought of all their various positions as he accepted their hands and embraced them warmly. Behind him, the regiment melted away. Company after company pulled toward the road that led them back to camp. Amid cheers and waves, the regiment spilled into the street like a river, bending and winding its way.

His hand sore and aching, Morrow was relieved when his horse arrived. Having said farewell to all on stage, he slid down the steps and mounted the horse. Flanigan met him there and informed him that the regiment moved in good order. "They are good men," replied Morrow. "They are good men, Mark." Turning back to the companies that remained, preparing themselves for the march, Morrow raised his voice, "move out!"

The rest of the regiment complied, marching in perfect line, cutting a neat path through the crowd. Cheers still sent them off and the men responded in perfect fashion: eyes forward, feet moving, rifles on shoulders, and chins held high. A magnificent sight it was.

Settling in his saddle, Morrow waved one last farewell to the dignitaries and the crowd. He followed the rearguard of the regiment, proudly following the bold flag at the helm, still visible in the fading sun. There were many a "God bless you" from the faithful citizens sending off their brave soldiers, their husbands, sweethearts, brothers, and sons.

Morgan sat alone under the shade of a large tree. It is August 29, 1862, and the Twenty-Fourth Michigan is preparing for its departure. He had been dwelling on the notion of writing Emmy a letter all day, but the words eluded him. He knew what he had to say. He just didn't know how to tell it. He shuffled through his belongings and found some paper and a pencil at the bottom of his haversack.

My dear Emmy, he began slowly, etching the paper carefully. *I hope this letter finds you well and in good spirits. Do not let the sadness of our separation upset you, as I believe it the will of God that keeps me from your arms. I will go and fight, as He deems fit, but I do so with a heavy heart.* His eyes remained focused and fixed on the paper, his hand commanding the gentle strokes. *Your father assures me that all will remain well. I have written mother, and she will send James out to the farm twice a week. My brother is a good young man and capable of doing things of a grown man, under watchful eyes of course. He thinks he is old enough to join the regiment. He is not. His age will not allow him to fight, but it will allow him to help with the progress of the farm when needed.*

He began to feel the great pressure upon his shoulders. The weight of his decision began to eat away at him. He was leaving her. There was nothing more to it than that. *I miss you already,* he wrote quickly. He pulled the pencil away until he fended off the sadness, and the depression that was building within. *We are a fine and splendid regiment*, he wrote, burying the pain. *We have been drilled considerably since enlisting. I believe we excel in nearly every aspect of the soldier. Colonel Morrow is a good man. I know of no man who will not do his duty and follow Colonel M. into battle. We are excited and anticipate our chance at the Rebels.*

I am not of the belief that this war will be short. And there are those among our ranks that believe we will not be needed at the front. I do not share this belief either. There have been many more before us, and I fear there will be many more after. The pencil stopped as he attempted to imagine the perils he faced. How many more will it take? How many more brave men must fall? *Please pray for me*, he continued. *I will pray for you and all I care for. Please let your thoughts be of happier times and not this dreadful moment we now find ourselves in. We will have peace.* He took a deep breath and thought carefully before scribbling the last of his letter. *I will return.* Satisfied with its contents, he concluded the letter slowly. *Love, Morgan.*

He gently folded the paper into thirds and slid it into his haversack. As he replaced the paper and pencil, the expected drum roll called his attention. Morgan had finished the letter just in time. The regiment was preparing to leave.

As he stood up, he saw men in blue dash in all directions. Company officers were directing their men into place. Colonel Morrow rode through the camp on a wonderful horse, ordering the men to form ranks, marching columns. Men gathered their belongings, slinging the excess gear over their shoulders. Some quickly finished packing their haversacks or rolling up their blankets, officers barking in their ears.

Morgan stepped away from the tree and headed for his company. His gear was packed and he was ready for the challenges that awaited him. He took his place in line, rifle at his shoulder, gleaming in the sunlight, the letter to Emmy in his haversack within quick reach. If he saw her, and an opportunity arose, he would give it to her.

Woodward Avenue chocked with people. As had been customary since the regiment's formation, the city was lined with flags and patriotic buntings. From nearly every window down the avenue, the bright colors waved in the summer breeze. As the Twenty-Fourth Michigan marched through the thundering crowd of at least a couple of thousand, the two large parties could not help but think it might be the last they ever saw of each other. There seemed no end in sight for the war. Michigan had already sent many men to the bloody front. Now it was parting with yet another regiment.

The Twenty-Fourth had been organized faster than any other Michigan regiment. Much was due to competent officers such as Morrow and Flanigan, and the diligent work of men like Captains Edwards and Wight. As important, however, were the women of Wayne County. As their men rallied behind the national cause, they rallied right behind them. Enormous efforts were made in the raising of funds, caring of poor soldier families, as well as taking over the duties left as the men departed. The women could not go to war, no matter how strong, no matter how patriotic. War, they had been told, was no place for women. Despite being constricted to home duties, the women contributed to the formation and solidification of the regiment just as much as any man. They could not carry a rifle or march to war, but they still found a way to become the stable foundation the regiment needed while in training and beyond.

As the regiment slithered down the road, they passed the women that had supported them so. They were waving flags, crying, and shouting out to their men, hoping their words could be heard. As one company slid past a group of sobbing young women, one of the soldiers summed it all up. "We do the nation's bidding," he proudly told his comrades, "but *they* do the chores, the raising, and the praying. Hell," he confessed to his comrades, "I do believe we have the easy part."

Colonel Morrow led the regiment through the wide Detroit streets. He responded kindly to the shouts and cheers of the citizens, but remained steady and stiff in the saddle. He was no longer their neighbor. He was an officer now. Calm, crisp, and cool was his demeanor. It delighted the crowd. They had a brave officer leading their brave regiment.

He bounced up and down in the saddle. Slowly he turned around to check on the condition of the regiment. He was immediately pleased. The men showed good form. His eyes skipped around as he saw their faces. No longer did he think of a regiment as a singular object of military value, but of a group of loved individual men, a father, son, husband, or brother. Would he bring them all back? Was it within his power to do so? He very much wanted to vow to each and every family that he would bring their soldier back. He was much too wise to make such a promise. He had seen war before. The words of such a promise, however, would settle the nervous families. It would be an empty promise, though. The words hollow. He would be foolish if he vowed such.

War is a constant struggle. Men die.

Morrow swung back around, forcing himself away from their faces. It was as if he could already hear the drums, the clamor of battle, off in the distance. It was almost as if a great battle awaited them just beyond the city, out into the rolling countryside of Michigan. His eyes squinted as he looked ahead. He could almost make out rising pillars of black smoke. He could almost smell the distinctive stench of rotting bodies. He had seen it all before, a long time ago. And yet he knew that more was in store for him.

Alas, the war was calling.

Color Sergeant Abel Peck's arms were already sore. The large flag was blowing wildly in the wind, and Peck used his frame to steady it as best he could. To make matters worse, it seemed they had been marching forever, but had yet left the city. He swore he saw the same street corner a dozen times.

The war will be much harder, he told himself. You will march greater distances. You will pass through greater trials. It will improve. The flag will become lighter as you get used to it. Keep at it, he ordered himself. Keep your feet moving and your eyes forward. Let the flag settle in its place and wrap your hands around it. Steady now, keep the pace. You will get there soon enough.

Just then he saw his wife and daughter. The woman lifted the child. The little girl waved and smiled at her father. Peck released one hand, the flag no longer heavy, and waved back.

For that moment, it seemed as if time stood still. His arms no longer ached. His legs continued the pace, but he remained transfixed, staring happily at them. The little girl continued to wave at him, calling out to him. He saw the tears roll down her face. Then he saw his wife, saw that she was crying, and he cried out that he loved her, that he loved them both. They continued to wave, tears streaming down their faces.

Peck watched them as long as he possibly could. He cranked his neck as far as it would go, looking behind him, in hopes of catching one final glimpse. He had hoped and prayed that he would see them. The night before, as he said his usual prayers, he had asked for nothing more than the chance to see them in the crowd. He wanted it more than anything else.

His prayers had been answered.

Thank God, he thought.

The march continued and his family faded into memory.

Captain Edwards guided his company through the deafening crowd. When he turned to look at them, he could not help but think of what would come. How many more would be sacrificed until the cruel war was over? Despite his best efforts to shake the darkening feelings, submerging him into a deep and depressing mood, he could not. As he led his company of men down the wide streets and avenues, listening to the thundering cheers, he was reminded of the first time he left for such and how tragic that ending turned out to be. Would it happen again? Would fate be so cruel?

He listened as soft patriotic melodies belted through the cheers. He had seen it all before. He had already marched with brave men toward war. Their cities and homes gave them generous sendoffs, proper memories to take into combat. Even when that regiment emerged from the crowd, marching away until the old scenes of home faded, the men held their chins high and bravely looked ahead to the war that called them. They firmly believed they would have a hand in the Union victories that were to come once they reached the field. Edwards himself had believed it.

Fate had other plans in store for that regiment, for the war, and for the innocent and raw Edwards. The great Union victory never came. The great regiment ended their enlistment after three months. Edwards played out his captivity, in the hands of the traitors he had hoped to defeat.

The innocence had died.

He was no longer raw.

Edwards had seen battle. He had witnessed men fighting and dying. He had seen the flood of confusion on the battlefield. The cannons boomed and thundered. The rifles cracked and whipped. Shot and shell burned into the sky, the projectiles screeching to the earth toward brave rows of soldiers.

No longer would such seem foreign, not anymore.

Edwards broke through the memories when he ordered his company to keep pace. "Steady, boys," he calmly told them. "Ease into the pace like good soldiers. Make your friends and families proud."

But as his words faded, the tragic memories triumphantly returned.

Would fate be so cruel again?

Morgan vigorously searched the crowd for Emmy. The march had nearly concluded, the buildings growing smaller and sparser as the regiment pushed away from the city. His body carefully maintained his position, rifle in hand and on shoulder, in sync with everyone else like a well oiled machine. How perfect it must have looked from the outside. They were vastly different men, of different ages and different occupations, moving together in unison, harmony. It mattered little where they came from, what work they did, or how much of an income they had earned. They were soldiers now. All of them equal. And equal soldiers march in equal steps. Oh, how the drilling officer would be pleased! The Twenty-Fourth was marching beautifully.

While his body remained stiff and in position, his eyes anxiously scanned the crowd. When they locked onto Emmy, he felt relieved. At last he had seen her. Getting her the letter, however, would prove a much more trying task. Orders had been made very clear: there must be no breaks in the line.

He had anticipated this by switching positions with the man on his right, which left Morgan on the outside of the marching column. From there, if needed, he could risk the consequences of breaking the line and quickly step out to meet her, handing her the letter. It was his only chance.

Having approached her, he reacted quickly, extending his free arm as long as he could, the letter outstretched in his fingers. The undeniable momentum of the pace pushed him forward, where he again stretched out to reach her. She in turn reached out, her arms as far as they too would go, but to no avail. It was simply too far. The women around her reacted and pushed her forward, extending her reach by several inches. They clung to her dress to prevent her from falling into the street. The teamwork, while beneficial had fallen short; her fingers could still not reach his. Morgan's comrades stepped into the mix, having witnessed the attempt. His entire row shuffled their feet, keeping the desired pace with the regiment, moving their bodies to the right. This pushed Morgan out toward the sidewalk, out from the line. Not only was Morgan tossed to the side, in disobedience of orders, but his entire row was as well.

The tactic prevailed. The women worked together from the sidewalk, the men from the rank and file. Emmy's hand met Morgan's, and she grasped the letter before feeling her fingertips slip away from his. Morgan, the current carrying him further away, turned back with a smile, and melted back into the line.

No officer cursed him.

There were no consequences.

Perhaps every man who witnessed the touching scene believed that it would be the last time the two young lovers saw each other. Yes, they told themselves, it may very well be. Everyone thought it.

Everyone, that is, except Morgan.

Pushing through the city in timely fashion, the regiment met the party of General Orlando Wilcox. Wilcox had been wounded and taken prisoner in early fighting but had healed and was ready to return to the front. "Colonel Morrow," he beamed, "looks like you have a fine and mighty regiment, sir. Michigan will earn its share of laurels when your Twenty-Fourth takes the field."

"We are confident of such, General," Morrow replied. He spun his horse, turning to face the regiment. "Your reputation," he said to Wilcox, "of a brave and daring officer is well known within the regiment. The men are honored to make this trip with you. I trust your command has long awaited your return."

"Well," said Wilcox, shrugging his shoulders. "We shall see, Colonel. All in good time," he added. "All will come in good time." He turned to his personal entourage, aides and personal guards, waving them to move on. "To the front, Colonel Morrow," he said proudly. "Your services are most needed."

The regiment inched toward the Detroit River, then to the Michigan Central Wharf, where two vessels were waiting patiently to send them off. Morrow watched from his saddle as his regiment lined up, stacked in place like cattle, and began to board the vessels. He watched them move slowly, the line inching forward every few minutes.

He thought of their training. Had he done enough? The regiment had been instructed in such haste. Had he prepared them enough for what was to come? Would he live up to the great task before him? The horse, the beautiful mount he proudly rode, had been a gift, but also a reminder of his responsibilities as regimental commander. When he leaned down to pat the animal on the neck, to perhaps settle its fears as well as his, he thought of such.

He was personally responsible for a thousand men.

A distant bugle call shattered the cheers. The crowd had not faded. It seemed as if the entire county had turned out to wish their regiment off. The men, in response to the cheers, lifted their kepis and waved. Another bugle call arose announcing that the regiment was nearly onboard, being split between the two vessels. Their journey was about to begin.

Morrow took a deep breath, one last gasp of Michigan, before directing his horse on board. His hands trembled. The crippling nervousness had returned. As he watched the gates being lifted and heard the vessels rumble, he knew there was no turning back now. It would be three long years of service, perhaps more if needed, before he could return to Detroit's shoreline, his home. And there was a chance he wouldn't survive the war.

But as the vessels pulled away from his home, he wasn't thinking of his fate. He was thinking of his men. If he had to sacrifice his life to ensure the safety of theirs, he would do it.

He shook his head, reminding himself again that he was responsible for a thousand men.

It's too late now to dwell on it, he thought.

The Twenty-Fourth Michigan was off to war.

Morrow pulled his thoughts back to the men. Some of them would return. Some of them would not. Some would be wounded. There would be heroes as well as cowards.

Such was the fate of a soldier.

The Twenty-Fourth Michigan had a rough night passage of Lake Erie, but arrived in Cleveland, Ohio, the next morning. From there, they were shuffled into rail cars and driven through the Ohio countryside and into Pennsylvania, making a stop in Pittsburgh. The soldiers were received kindly, and Colonel Morrow made a patriotic address in which he expressed his appreciation for the city's kindness and said such would be returned when the war was over and Pennsylvania regiments marched through Detroit to take and capture Canada. As for the rank and file, the young women of Pittsburgh seemed to immediately fall in love with them as soon as the regiment arrived. Personal items were exchanged, including ambrotypes and rings, before the regiment was again loaded onto trains and carried away.

From there, the regiment went to Harrisburg, Pennsylvania, and then switched cars for Baltimore, Maryland. Following that ride, the regiment marched to the Washington depot, and was forced to wait as other regiments had arrived before them. The wait ended early the following morning with the regiment boarding the cars in complete darkness.

Washington, the nation's war torn capital, was a forty mile ride.

With each passing hour, the regiment drew nearer to the great conflict that awaited them.

WE SHOULD
GROW ACCUSTOMED

As the Twenty-Fourth Michigan traveled to Washington, the newly created Union army, the Army of Virginia, under General John Pope, fought the Battle of Second Bull Run. Confederate General Robert E. Lee, in command of his Army of Northern Virginia, decided to move north and engage Pope before Union General George McClellan and his massive Army of the Potomac, could link up with the new Union army under Pope. If this happened, Lee's Army of Northern Virginia would be outnumbered two to one.

The desperate fight raged over already sacred land, the exact location of the war's first battle. Two days after the two enemies eyed each other, Pope fell back toward Washington, leaving the victorious Confederates the field. His army disintegrated toward the city, meeting the first elements of McClellan's army sent to reinforce them. The campaign had been a complete failure, another sour spot on the Union's war record, happening again on the fields near Bull Run, sight of the first meeting between the two contending forces. Pope's new army was disbanded, never again to be fitted or designated. General McClellan was then charged with the protection of Washington City, as well as the reorganization of his Army of the Potomac.

Washington, to say the least, was in one of its darkest hours. Many citizens feared the city could be immediately sacked by the ruthless Confederates. Wounded soldiers came in by the thousands, bouncing in innumerable wagons or hobbling into the city. Soldiers scattered into the darkness. Officers trailed them, hoping to regain control of their commands. Confusion reigned supreme.

This is what the Twenty-Fourth came upon when they first saw Washington.

Colonel Morrow leaped down from the crowded car and looked over the busy train station. His journey had been a long and painful one, his regiment enduring great lengths of time confined to cattle cars, packed together tightly to maximize space. As Morrow walked down the train, ordering the officers to open the doors and organize their companies, he realized just how close to the front they were. He could smell it, feel it building and boiling around him. The atmosphere was tense, thick, and heavy.

The air reeked of thousands and thousands of sweaty men, gunpowder, smoke, and horse manure. Hundreds of soldiers gathered around the regiment and Morrow ordered them pushed aside. His eyes fixed on their empty faces, their thinning bodies. The soldiers present were not the victorious soldiers imagined, not the powerful sons of Liberty, the boys of Lincoln. What had come of them?

These soldiers, dirty and bloody, angry and violent, scattered about the landing area. They begged for food and money. They told tales of tragic defeat. They pleaded with the new soldiers to turn back home. Morrow identified several officers and sought information, but they proved helpless. No matter how much he called to them, they kept ignoring him. There was no order and to a neat and orderly man, as Morrow was, it was a nightmare. He swung around in search of an exit, some order in the confusion. A man stumbled to him, a bandage over his left eye. He grabbed at Morrow's coat, saw that the uniform was new, the gold buttons and trim shiny and bright. "Kindly spare something to eat," he begged. Morrow brushed the soldier away, the burning stench from the man too strong to take. Reaching back to his saddle, Morrow dove into his haversack and brought out a single chunk of bread. He pushed it into the man. "God bless," replied the wounded soldier. "God bless your kindness, sir."

In the background an unknown voice called for the regiment. "Twenty-Fourth Michigan!" the voice cried over the confusion. Morrow saw the man slide out of the crowd, his head turning to the left and right, calling out the regiment again.

Morrow raised an arm, calling the young officer over. "I seek the Twenty-Fourth Michigan," said the officer. "I have yet to find them in this God forsaken mess."

"You have found them."

The officer quickly looked up. "You are with the Twenty-Fourth Michigan?"

"I am the commanding officer," stated Morrow.

"Splendid," he said. The man slightly buckled at the waist, catching his breath. "This is what it has been like all day," he said of the crowd. "General Pope retreated from Bull Run and came here. They are all over the city. All day, I tell you. What a mess."

"General Pope's army?" asked Morrow.

"Well," said the officer, "this is what is left of it. General McClellan has been called back to take control of the situation. Rumor has it that Lincoln is going to name him commander of all Union forces."

Somebody had to take control. Morrow had never seen a more panicked city. "You will hear more on this, Colonel," the officer pointed out. "For now, I will direct your regiment. You hungry? I'm sure you are. Follow me, Colonel, and I will take you to food. You will find out all you need when we arrive, sir."

Morrow mounted his horse and Flanigan joined him. The marching orders were issued, with specific instructions not to stop and not to give anything away. There would be a great many needy soldiers along the way, their needs far outstretching the abilities of the regiment.

Flanigan handed Morrow a newspaper. "Pope was defeated," the Irishman declared. "He blames McClellan for the disaster. There has been much politicking between the two of them." Flanigan rubbed his beard as he gently spurred his animal into motion. "Some of the papers blame Pope. Some of them blame McClellan. I know nothing of either of them, but I believe such assumptions are based on politics. All the papers," he identified, "are calling for revenge."

Morrow flipped through the thin pages. "They always call for revenge."

"And if it is achieved, Henry?"

"Then they call for the conclusion."

Their escort, the young officer, had listened to the short conversation and could no longer keep from it. "Pope got whipped," he said, "but McClellan is still in the field. Lee had attacked Pope because he could not afford to attack McClellan. That's the way I see it, Colonel."

Morrow looked to Flanigan and returned the paper. "Well," he said turning his attention back to the officer, "there is only *one* army left in the eastern field. It looks as though Lee can now *afford* to move against McClellan."

Captain Edwards had seen Washington more than once in his life. He had marched here with the First Michigan Infantry Regiment. He had passed through here when he was released from his captivity. Washington had been a permanent fixture in his mind. For when he first marched upon it, he realized what he was fighting for. The buildings, the entire city, had a distinct greatness that he had never felt anywhere. This was the centerpiece of a new and experimental nation, the likes of which had never before been seen on the known earth.

Calm and professional, Edwards went stride for stride with his company. When he saw his men get nervous, he soothed them by telling them that it would all go away in a few days. "There will again be a great rush to Richmond," he told them. But he knew that it would be much more difficult than that. He knew that reorganizing a scattered army takes time. His experience in battle had proven that much.

And when his men gasped at the horrendous wounds of weary comrades, Edwards ordered them to look away. "We shall see plenty when we reach the field," he lectured them. "Let us not contend with such matters, boys. These men have had a rough go of it and in time we will get ours. We must resurrect from our plights. We must rise again and rally around the old flag. These men will."

The men of Company F listened and hung onto every one of Edwards' words. He had led them through the grueling training process, worked with them, and cared for them. Above all, he was a man of experience. He vowed to make them the best company in the entire regiment. They responded by doing all that he asked of them.

No matter how difficult it was not to look upon the poor souls of the once proud Army of Virginia, the men of Company F did just that. They cocked their heads forward, straightened their rifles, and drove onward.

"Very good," said Edwards, praising his men.

The praise from their captain pleased him. Morgan worked tirelessly to keep pace with the regiment, while the horrible scenes played out around him. He had never been to Washington, had never dreamed he would see it. He had seen pictures and illustrations of the magnificent city, but the one featured in those works was not the city that met his eyes on that day.

This Washington was black. It was cold and ugly. There was no evidence of its humble beginnings, no evidence of its political clout, and nothing to indicate that it represented such noble figures as George Washington and Thomas Jefferson. Everywhere he looked he found soldiers, wounded, hungry, confused, and angry. He watched them scatter about the streets. Some were in gangs, rifles still in their possession. Their uniforms were tattered and torn, muddy and bloody. Officers frolicked about them, clinging to the hope of corralling their loose commands.

As the regiment moved on, inching its way toward their destination, Morgan shuttered at the sights around every corner. He came across a church, rising high into the darkening sky, where a funeral procession was taking place. Women in black lined the steps of the church. A wooden casket trickled down slowly from the large wooden doorways leading into the church. One woman reached out to touch the wood, to say her final goodbyes, but she collapsed upon her knees in tears, in anguish. Her sobbing was heard by all as the regiment slowly slithered by. The casket stopped as the bearers stood paralyzed by the heartbreaking scene. Finally, a man from the funeral crowd urged them to continue. Morgan forced his eyes away, upward toward the church's steeple.

He noticed a lonely angel, guarding the holy cross of the church, high above him.

The regiment slid across the road, tilting the march so the funeral procession could continue undisturbed. An open wagon carried the sobbing woman, three young children, and the casket. The crowd, dressed in black, urged the woman not to ride in the same cart as the casket. She would have none of it, planting herself next to the rectangular wooden box. The crowd followed closely behind, their heads low, their shoulders buckled from sadness.

Morgan carefully watched the rest of the world, the commotion around the funeral procession. Its pace continued, seemingly ignorant of the depressing scene before it. Not a man stopped or seemed to pay their respects to the fallen. Women and children continued on quickly, not wanting to be out in the streets longer than needed. The world continued to move swiftly. The funeral procession progressed slowly, painstakingly.

He had come from a different world, a distant land perhaps, where the people in the streets would pay their respects to the departed. The men out and about would remove their hats. The women would drop their heads in sorrow, some of them clutching even tighter to their children. This was different. Washington had hosted far too many funerals since the war began. There had been too much heartache, too much pain, for the city to bear. So the world continued around such depressing scenes.

The people went on, not ignoring, not forgetting, but simply trying to survive. The war had taken its toll on the city and its people.

He finally lifted his eyes from the trying scene. Turning away, he forced himself to believe that it wasn't real. Perhaps if he believed enough, this world, the Washington City around him, would cease to exist. He sighed. He knew it was there, knew it was real.

He also knew that he was a long way from home.

And how distant a land it did seem.

Colonel Morrow wasn't hungry. He broke away from the regiment and ordered Flanigan to keep the men in line. He instructed his officers to allow the men ample time to eat their first government meal. "I must go for a walk," he told the Irishman before he departed. It would do him good to tour the city once so familiar to him. He wanted to see about the organizational efforts, perhaps lend a hand if he could. There were other items he sought, rumors that circulated and needed verification. So he pulled away from the regiment and slid out into the confused and busy streets.

He moved along quickly, stepping around the disorganized force that was once a proud army. He stepped over newspapers, discarded orders, supplies, and armaments. There were canteens, rifles, and haversacks thrown about. It looked as if the battle had raged about Washington, tearing through the streets and alleyways. Morrow pushed on, hoping to find some relief, some sanctuary.

Shuffling about the crowd wildly, resembling a lost child, Morrow expressed relief when he found a small bench just outside the War Department. To further pull himself away from the confusion of the streets, he broke open his trusty Bible. Slowly, carefully, he read the words in the small book. Slowly, carefully, his nervousness settled, the confusion faded away, and Morrow found the peace, the sanctuary, he had desperately sought. In this calm state of mind he wondered what his wife was up to. He wondered how things in Detroit were going without them. Did things change? The thoughts were not depressing, were not of sadness. He simply wondered if life continued the same without him. He imagined it would and rightfully should.

His dirty fingers skimmed across the narrow black text. The world continued to swirl around him, but he buried himself in the divine book. He had fallen into the soothing words so much so that he did not notice when a new shadow came about the bench, requesting to sit a spell, in which Morrow nodded but never lifted his eyes.

There was a soft grunt when the man's frame settled into place next to Morrow. "I must walk this path a thousand times a day," said the man. "Sometimes I'm there so late," he said of the War Department office, "that I sleep on a couch there. Oh, it must be a sight to see my long legs hanging off of the end. The little wife," the stranger continued, "does not like it when I sleep there. She worries that I care too much about the work of our generals and tells me I should leave the commanding to those more suited."

Morrow closed the book and turned toward the man. He was delighted to stumble across such a friendly soul. His eyes fell upon a weary man, lanky in size. He wore a beard that slid from his hair across his chin, clean-shaven around the mouth and the upper part of his cheeks. Immediately, Morrow recognized the stranger. "Forgive me, Mr. President," he pleaded, making a quick attempt to salute.

"I beg you," Abraham Lincoln confessed, "save that for your generals.

Where I come from," he said warmly to Morrow, "we shake hands." Morrow accepted Lincoln's large hand. Lincoln then directed toward the Bible. "You find comforts in those sacred words. Have you come from the field?"

"No, sir," Morrow admitted. "We've just arrived."

"And your home?" asked Lincoln, seemingly pleased with the brief break from his hectic schedule. "Where do you come from," he stopped and noticed Morrow's rank, "Colonel?"

"Michigan, sir," he replied.

"Ah, I was there once, in Kalamazoo, I believe. It was long ago, I fear," said Lincoln. "It was long before these most unpleasant times." Lincoln patted his knees. His lips moved as if he were speaking to himself. "How is your Michigan regiment, Colonel? Where do you believe your men will go in this war?"

"As far as we must, sir," stated Morrow.

Lincoln smiled. He stood up and towered over Morrow. The president ran a hand across his forehead, pushing his hair into place. He looked weary and worn. Morrow had only seen pictures of course, but the president before him looked much older, much more fatigued. "You say you are from Michigan," said Lincoln. "Michigan has given many sons. The nation owes her more thanks than most of her loyal siblings."

Morrow stood up to see the president off. "With kindness, Mr. President, I must assume that you say the same when you greet a man from any other loyal state."

Lincoln smiled again and broke into laughter. He leaned toward Morrow, bending down to whisper into his ear. "I must confess that you caught me, son." Lincoln pulled away. "Now," he said, the smile still on his face, "which Michigan man am I speaking with?"

"Colonel Morrow, Twenty-Fourth Michigan Infantry, Mr. President," was the quick reply.

"Well," replied Lincoln, "we shall see how the Twenty-Fourth performs in the field, but I hope to hear much more from it and its Colonel Morrow." Lincoln gently waved to a young aide and then nodded to his armed escort. "We will see how far the war must take you, Colonel Morrow. I look forward to hearing." The president then said farewell and turned toward the War Department.

It had been a chance meeting and Morrow relished it. Not only had he found comfort in reading the Bible, but he found hope and kindness in the short conversation with President Lincoln. Not wanting to forget the occasion, he reached into his haversack and pulled out a notebook. He noted the date and the time before scribbling the three words that would reignite the moment later on: met the president.

He stood up and melted back into the confusion a rejuvenated man.

Abel Peck sat down at the large table and looked down to his plate. What was placed before him, he did not know. What it was made of, he cared not to know. No matter what, however, he was expected to eat it. It would probably be the last cooked meal he would get for some time. Even the new soldiers understood that food had little time to cook and little time to settle while in the field. There just wasn't enough time for either.

His first instincts were to push the plate away from him, but he held his manners. This wasn't his idea of a meal. And it sure wasn't his idea of a meal prepared by an army cook, someone paid to cook instead of fight. One would think that if the paid soldiers were expected to fight well, then the paid cooks would be expected to cook well. But this was war time

Washington. There were more things to worry about than the condition of the food served to the soldiers.

Peck eventually gave up and lifted the spoon to his mouth, much to the amazement of his bewildered comrades. Closing his eyes and holding his breath, he took a quick bite, swallowing the slop as fast as he could. The men around him shuttered and waited for their comrade's response. Peck opened his eyes and winked at them, a smile built on his face. "Not bad," he told them. They offered nothing in response, only silence. They glanced down to their plates, unsure of what to do. Peck took another bite. "Not bad at all," he reiterated.

The hungry soldiers loosened up. "Well," said one of them, "it can't be half bad if Abel enjoys it so." He took his turn, slowly lifted his spoon to his mouth. He watched a glob of the unknown substance slam back onto his plate with a plop. He turned to Peck, watched him take another hearty spoonful and eat it.

"It's not bad once you let yourself taste it," added Peck.

The soldiers listened to their stomachs growl, announcing their hunger. Peck lifted his eyes from his food and saw them dive into theirs, lifting spoons full of the slop. In unison, the men slid the food into their mouths and chewed slowly, trying to find the taste that Peck had found so enjoyable. In the meantime, Peck had dropped his spoon, using the hand to cover his mouth, keeping his laughter from his comrades.

Nearly every spoon fell to the table. The men looked around, eyes wide, stomachs violently churning. They turned to Peck, whose laughter became uncontrollable. He rose from the bench and headed for his escape. "You son-of-a-bitch!" shouted one of his comrades. "This is horrible!"

The soldiers leaped from their seats and chased after Peck.

Peck slammed through a doorway, hoping for a quick escape, only to be corralled by three armed guards posted outside the building. When he saw them, there was little choice but to surrender to his comrades.

He quickly grabbed a hold of his white handkerchief and waved it frantically before the charging soldiers. "Treasure this day, fellows," he told them. "This will be the last time you see me wave a flag of surrender. For you have won today's battle."

Lieutenant Colonel Mark Flanigan had always considered himself a passionate man. He was passionate about his political beliefs, his occupation, and his family. So passionate in his occupation, however, that he had more than once been accused of taking the law into his own hands. Despite such claims, he was never fond of violence. That is not to say that he didn't understand it, however. He was a man who believed that there were special cases where only violence could quell violence, but such actions should only be used if all other respectable measures had been considered and attempted.

Such was the case for the war. Politics had attempted, for better or worse, to block the rising tide of hostilities. As the raging storm built before the nation, Flanigan knew that it would result in violence. There was no turning away from the bloodshed anymore. Where politicians had failed, soldiers would prevail, one way or the other.

As he toured Washington, there was no violence. There was plenty of chaos and confusion, but there was no violence. There were, however, countless painful results of such. These were the horrible reminders of how cruel the war was.

Ambulances bounced up and down the streets. Surgeons and doctors rushed bleeding patients from one cart to another, sometimes throwing the recently deceased or mortally wounded off to the side. One wounded soldier limped by him, a short stump all that was left of his right leg. Wooden crutches carried the poor soldier from one place to another. How can I live like that? Flanigan shook his head at the thought. He prayed for the soldier. Death upon the field of battle would be better than to live a life wounded, permanently disfigured, disabled. He prayed that it not happen to him. He didn't know how he would live in such a state.

He shuffled across a broad street and entered a hospital. The congestion and confusion of the street had gotten to him, made him weary. A hospital would not have been a proper retreat from such for many, but Flanigan wanted to see, needed to be reminded of the great sacrifice and dangers of war.

There were plenty of examples inside.

Flanigan stepped around tired surgeons, nurses, and hospital attendants. The entrance to the building was once a large open room, but had been cluttered with suffering bodies and bore scents of blood and alcohol. Tables were a precious commodity, badly needed and in short supply. There was a bar in the room, one of the most impressive countertops he had ever seen, used as a makeshift operating table. He stepped around puddles of blood that filled the gaps and cracks in the wooden floor. The sounds were both unique and horrific. Saws cut bone. Men screamed in agony or moaned in constant pain. Many of them could be heard praying out loud, asking God to forgive their sins and let them live, let them return home. Surgeons pleaded with attendants to provide more alcohol or to bring more cloth. The curtains, perhaps the last of the unused cloth in the building, were pulled down before his eyes. Every bit of the precious fabric was needed, used to bandage a bleeding wound.

While standing in an entryway of one room, looking to be the operating room, he was pushed in by a group of surgeons returning from a short break. One of them nudged him, pulled at his elbows. "You look like a sturdy man," said the surgeon. "I need you over here with me."

"I'm no doctor," replied Flanigan.

"I don't need one to hold him down," the surgeon said while pointing to a waiting patient. "I'll need you to keep him in place while I amputate the arm."

Flanigan studied the bloody soldier. He had been laid upon a door, acting as an operating table, and had a couple of bloody shirts tucked under his head for comfort. The soldier's left arm had been shattered at the elbow, loose skin and bone fragments as jagged as rocks popped out of the ghastly wound. The soldier gritted his teeth, fighting the pain with the same intensity as he had fought the enemy. "I can't," Flanigan confessed. "I can't help you with this."

The surgeon looked up. His eyes were dark, black rings circling them. He was tired, weary. He had tended to the same bloody work for days. Such trying work took a severe toll on the man. He looked much older than he was. His hands were stained red with blood. His body ached. His legs were sore and numb. His senses burned from all the use of alcohol. "You'll want to remove your coat, Colonel," he insisted. "Blood will splatter. Just pin him down and let me do the work." The surgeon turned his back on him and began cleaning his tools. Flanigan watched as bloody rags were dipped into bloody water. Quick attempts were made to clean the tools before the operation began.

"Colonel," a whisper called to Flanigan from the makeshift table.

Flanigan looked down to the wounded soldier.

"I had a good colonel once, you remind me of him," the soldier said in pain. "He was a fine man indeed." His raspy voice cut in and out. "He led us to them, right up to them. You should have seen us. Not a finer body of men in the army. A good colonel he was." His teeth gritted and his body shook as the pain set in again.

The surgeon, hearing the soldier speak, turned to him and ordered him to be still. "You need to rest. I'll need you to keep steady. I will go as quickly as I can." As fast as he had turned around, the surgeon went back to his tools. Time was a concern. There were more wounded waiting.

"I never thought I would end up here, Colonel. I never thought I would be meeting the bloody saw." The brave soldier smiled at the irony. "I thought I would die in battle. Never did I think I would end up here. How foolish of me," he reasoned. "How foolish it is to think that I would be lucky enough to fall on the field."

"You must be still," said Flanigan. "Do what the surgeon tells you and you will soon be home with your friends and family. The war will be a memory."

The soldier smiled again. "Kind of hard to forget," he said as he looked over to the bloody wound. He dropped his head back down to the bloody shirts, allowing himself to get as comfortable as possible. "I was with him, you know. I was there when our colonel fell. They all looked to me. They all looked to me for orders. I had none to give, Colonel. I had nothing to offer them." He struggled as the pain came rushing back, overwhelming his body in spasms. "I just hollered to go forward. I went forward, believing that I would die. Meet the Lord in Heaven. Go forward and die like a brave soldier, die like our good colonel."

Flanigan clutched the soldier's good hand. "You live," he told him.

"And what life is this?" asked the soldier.

"It has been by the grace of God that you live."

The cleaning and inspection completed, the surgeon rejoined the table. He lifted a bottle of alcohol and poured a conservative glass. He pushed it forward and forced the soldier to drink. "The best *southern* whiskey around," said the surgeon. "We have nothing left to offer." He turned back to Flanigan. "Now, I'll need you to hold him steady." He brought the saw into view. "This has to be clean, quick, and careful."

Flanigan took off his coat before sliding around the table. He braced his large hands on the patient's shoulders, determined not to give an inch. The surgeon stood at the other side, preparing for the operation. He took several deep breaths, gathering his will to perform another agonizing task. "Keep him steady," he ordered Flanigan. He gently placed the saw to the skin, about an inch above the horrible wound. At first he started sawing slowly, carefully, waiting for the saw to catch the bone.

The soldier flinched in pain. The saw sliced through the skin and muscle, reached the bone and dug in. As the surgeon increased the speed of the passes, the soldier nearly shot up from the table, nearly knocking the large framed Flanigan off his feet. The pain, the sight, and the sounds of the sawing proved too much for him to bear. His body twisted as every ounce of strength fought to free himself from the table, to end the operation. Flanigan held him down firmly, his face turned away, his ears flickering at the grinding sound. "Please," the soldier pleaded, whispering in pain. "Please."

Flanigan pushed down even harder, not wanting the surgeon to slip because the terrified soldier moved too much.

Grind.

Crack.

The saw tore into the bone with steady passes, the dreadful work nearly complete.

Grind.

The soldier struggled again, his body shaking from the paralyzing pain. Grind. He gritted his teeth and looked up to Flanigan. Grind. His eyes were wide, his senses ablaze. He struggled to blink, keeping focused on Flanigan. Tears streamed down his dirty face. Grind. The soldier's body shook with more intensity. He tried in vain to fight off the pain. Flanigan saw in amazement as the helpless soldier gently smiled at him. The soldier must have thought once more of the irony of it all. Flanigan forced himself to turn away. Grind. Grind. Crack.

"I'm through," announced the surgeon. Without breaking stride, he called for attendants. "Clean it and dress it," he ordered them. "Place him out on the back porch. Then pull me another one."

The soldier was lifted from the table and carried away. Flanigan sighed in relief that it was over. He watched the surgeon turn back to clean the saw, again with the bloody cloth. Flanigan reached for his coat, but the surgeon stopped him. "You'll want to wipe the blood from your face, Colonel."

Flanigan took the damp cloth, pink with stained blood. "Lieutenant Colonel," he said, correcting the surgeon's mistake in rank.

The surgeon shrugged it off. "You'll stay and help more, I assume?"

Flanigan wiped his face quickly. The cloth stunk of sweat and blood, a foul and nauseating stench it was. "No," he said as he returned it to the surgeon. "I can help no longer. I must be getting back."

This place, wrote a disgusted Morgan, *is not the place I envisioned it to be. When we arrived here, I thought it nothing of the city named for our first national president. I have yet to see a hint of its renowned greatness, my dear wife. Yet,* he added, *I will fight for it. I believe it to be a sacred place, an honorable place. If it takes many more battles, many more deaths, I believe it a just cause for such a place, such a nation.* He dropped the pencil and scratched at his head. Fleas and lice had invaded the camp. Army life had already proven miserable and dirty. An endless stream of men clogged the arteries of the city. Disease ran rampant.

My dear Emmy, he wrote. *You would not believe me to be your husband if you saw me. There is little time to groom. We are drilling and shuffling about constantly. We move regularly, trading one camp for another. The miles have broken me into a thin man.* She will worry, he thought, stopping the pencil, holding the thought. *I am well. We are eager to meet the enemy. We have heard many stories. I cannot say of their truthfulness. Some of the men were really whipped. They tell us to prepare for our own licking. I care not to listen. I suspect that all defeated men say as much.*

I must bid you farewell, my Emmy. Pray for me and our glorious cause. I will write you again as soon as time permits. Love, Morgan.

He folded up the letter and slid it into a pocket. He enjoyed writing to her and reading her letters. He missed home very much. Yet he knew he was doing the right thing, leaving her, leaving all that he knew. The nation had called for him.

But the nation had called for others before him. He had seen a great many of them, confused and helpless, roaming the streets of Washington. Morgan had overheard the stories of their hardships and defeat. He listened as officers scurried about, shouting for their commands to return. He saw several men placed under arrest for desertion. The men he saw were defeated, their bodies exhausted. They had been beaten by a better army. Some blamed their commanders. Others blamed the nation. It was disheartening to see his comrades in such a state. He couldn't help but wonder if he too would end up the same. Would he too curse the national cause which had brought him so far from home?

He shook away the thoughts.

It was in God's hands. Everything would be determined in time.

He peered toward the soft glow of the fire, gently cracking and popping, soothing the men around it to sleep. Morgan watched them, wondered how many would return home after the war. He stopped, cursed himself for thinking on it. Only time will tell, he thought. One day the war would be over and then those left would go home. Just how many of them there would be, Morgan had no way of knowing.

His eyes shifted above the fire. Bright stars hung in the night sky. How strange it was to him, realizing the peacefulness in the sky above and the carnage on the earth below. It was as if the two worlds collided into a bloody struggle for dominance, each wanting just one more inch. The sky wanted to fall. The earth wanted to climb. Neither of them understanding that what they had was all that they would get, no matter how much they struggled, no matter how much they bled.

Morgan smiled at the irony.

The north fights for preservation. The south fights for recognition.

Perhaps both have come as far as they could, achieved all they could. Perhaps this bloody storm of war was needed to clean the slate. Morgan pondered at it.

He wrestled with the thought before finally surrendering to the enchanting rhythm of the fire. Drifting to sleep, his river of dreams would take him to where he wanted to be most, home.

And while this lonely soldier slept for the night, the chaotic battle between the sky and the earth raged on silently in the background.

One wanted to fall. The other wanted to climb.

Captain Edwards shot up from the earth as a soldier nudged him from his slumber. After rubbing his eyes and coming to his senses, Edwards quickly turned to the soldier. "What is it?" Groggy and confused, he waited impatiently for the answer.

"You must come, Captain," said the shadow. "Your attention is needed." The soldier helped Edwards to his feet. "I apologize for waking you, sir," grumbled the soldier. "We have a man. He is sick. He is calling for an officer."

Edwards rubbed his eyes again, forcing himself to wake. "What company?"

"He's not ours," replied the soldier.

"And you called for me?"

The soldier stopped. "You are the nearest. Colonel Morrow is still in the city. Lieutenant Colonel Flanigan is out there as well. You are the nearest, Captain." The soldier rolled back into his strides, pulling Edwards behind him. "He came up on our pickets, sir. He stumbled in looking for his horse. He never rode in on a horse. We got him to settle down and gave him coffee, but then he started to get sick. We called the surgeon, but all are busy in the city."

Edwards stumbled across the camp. He watched the passing fires fade, the soldiers tending to them falling to sleep. He was envious. Edwards hadn't slept in several days. His brief rest of the evening had been the first in a long while. Good things never last, he told himself as he shuffled through the camp.

After several minutes, the soldier led Edwards to the sick stranger. There were half a dozen men standing over him. Edwards immediately ordered them to retire. He bent down to one knee, sinking into the soft earth. He studied the shadowy face and quickly searched for obvious wounds. The stranger, now used to being studied, coughed a few times before looking up to Edwards. "I need an officer," he said.

Edwards nodded. "I am."

The soldier, his face sweaty and white, looked to him with dark eyes. His mouth opened as if to speak again, and with a severe cough he vomited blood. Edwards pushed the soldier down to his back and began to search through the dirty uniform for any wounds not obvious to the eyes. The soldier struggled, coughed up more blood, before asking for water. Edwards relented, still unsure of the man's condition. "Bring him a canteen," he ordered.

The soldier's uniform was soaked, the reason for such Edwards couldn't tell in the darkness. A canteen, full of cold water, was brought and the man drank freely from it. The canteen was pulled away and the soldier thanked them for the water. Edwards tore into the uniform, his hands scouring the man's chest for wounds. The soldier moaned and then asked for more water. Edwards relented again, his hands still searching. As his fingers slid toward the stomach, they fell into a soft, warm pool. The wound had been found. A large hole had been blown into the man, the uniform keeping the entrails tucked inside.

The canteen was pulled away. The soldier distributing the water asked Edwards if he should fill the canteen again. Edwards nodded. Pulling his hands up, the other soldiers noticed the red liquid, dripping from his fingertips. "Should we call a surgeon again, sir?" asked one of them.

Edwards shook his head. "No," he told them. "Give him more water. Stay with him. He is dying." He wiped his hands on the cool grass.

The men took a step back. Edwards rose to his feet and looked around. He knew he needed to say something, but he struggled with the words. A man, a brave man, was dying at his feet. Edwards could say nothing. His head turned as he saw the faces of the Michigan men look to him, questions burning. Edwards had no answers.

The canteen came back.

"One man stay with him," Edwards ordered. "The rest of you return to your posts or camps. There is nothing more we can do for him now." He turned away and heard the dying soldier beckon for his horse once more. Before leaving the scene, the weary Edwards stopped and asked one of the soldiers to grab a horse.

"It won't be his," replied the soldier.

"It doesn't matter now," said Edwards. "Let him see the animal. Let him believe it his. We owe him that. Give this man all that he wants if possible." He turned back toward the soldier's pleas, his desperate calls for his horse. "That may be me out there, someday. I only hope that you would do the same for me."

Edwards finally pulled himself from the scene. He found out later that the soldier had died less than an hour after he left. A horse was brought in, which the dying soldier believed was his, and he died as happily as he could. Edwards was told that the soldier expressed his final words, which were written down to be mailed in the morning. The letter would go to his mother, whom he had named his beloved horse after.

It was the first death witnessed by that small band of Michigan men that night, and Edwards doubted if any of them would forget it.

He knew too well from experience that there would be plenty more.

Colonel Morrow danced through the confusion as politely as he could. Wounded and disgruntled soldiers paced by him. Dirty and bloody hands reached out to him, begging for food and drink. He had nothing left to offer them. His haversack was empty, as well as his canteen. The sights were overwhelming, sickening. To think that this had been a once proud and mighty army, ready to take the field before the enemy. There was nothing left of it now. It had been shattered, the remains scattered about the countryside.

There was a brewing hatred seeping from their words, their eyes. There was distrust in a once trustworthy man's voice, his promises. Officers didn't trust their soldiers. Soldiers didn't trust their officers. Few had faith in Washington and the national government. There were even less with favorable opinions of General McClellan. McClellan seemed to be the target for the survivors of Pope's army.

Rumors of impending disaster paced the streets alongside him. Perhaps more crippling to an army than even disease, rumors had the power to shake a soldier's morale, his will to carry on the fight. This is what Morrow saw as he scampered through the thick crowd that evening.

As the street lamps glowed, Morrow came upon a busy hospital. Officers were standing outside comparing roll calls. Women and children gathered, hoping their loved ones weren't among the unfortunate souls inside. Surgeons, their clothes bloody and soaked with sweat, wearily walked from the building seeking a short rest, a moment to gather their emotions. Politicians and generals toured the building, shaking hands and commending many of those inside, at the very least offering words of encouragement.

He found Flanigan near there, standing in the middle of the sidewalk. His coat was unbuttoned and his shirt and face had dried blood spatter on them. Morrow approached his friend slowly, calmly. When he got up to Flanigan, Morrow put out a hand. "Let us retire, Mark," he said.

Flanigan remained silent and still. He brought his hands to his face in attempt to clear the last of the blood. He scrubbed until the fluid smeared into his skin. Morrow called for him again, trying to imagine what Flanigan had seen. There were no words. He looked to Morrow, his expression confessing all, but never opened his mouth. Morrow nodded. He looked back to the hospital behind them, knowing that Flanigan had come from there. No words needed to be spoken. Morrow understood.

He gently put a hand on Flanigan's shoulder. He looked into the eyes of the weary Irishman. "I know," he said in a low voice, reaching out to Flanigan. "I know." Morrow turned him down the road toward the regiment, finally rejoining their men. "Oh, it is a shame that we should grow so accustomed," Morrow added.

They departed quickly, leaving the haunting images behind.

THE LAND OF SECESSIA

Washington proved to be a short stopover for the Twenty-Fourth Michigan Infantry Regiment. Soon after their first meal as federal soldiers, ranks were formed and the regiment marched up Pennsylvania Avenue, turning south to cross the mighty Potomac. Despite recent events, General McClellan, with his Army of the Potomac, danced around Lee's Army of Northern Virginia in a game of chess. The war still raged. One Union army had been completely routed, but another was still in play.

The Twenty-Fourth quickly presented itself as an available pawn in the deadly game. As the regiment left Washington, the men believed they were headed directly for the front. Fate proved otherwise, however, and the regiment skirted Washington, while the military bureaucrats contemplated their next move, hoping for a checkmate. Crossing the Potomac impatiently, the regiment imagined the glory that awaited them once they set foot on southern soil.

The sights they beheld in the land of Secessia gave them a glimpse of reality, what really awaited their arrival.

And glory was not evident.

Morgan shuffled his feet. His ears twitched, and he hummed along with the delightful tune of *Dixie*. The regiment had just crossed the Potomac, veering off into the land away from Washington, away from the eerie darkness. He was glad of it. The city hadn't impressed him, nor had the relics of General Pope's great army.

Beads of sweat rolled from his hair, trickled down his forehead, and seeped into his eyes. They burned and squinted. His hand shot up and feverishly rubbed at them. The march had been long and tiring, the heat grabbing hold of him. To make matters worse, there had been many delays. First the roads had to be cleared, the remnants of brave soldiers pushed from the streets. Once the regiment began to roll, there was another delay, as a small wagon train broke down and blocked their path. The men had been ordered to stand in line for nearly half an hour.

Morgan's patience had run out.

Pleased that the regiment had finally crossed the river, Morgan began to relax. He believed the march would improve once the confusion and congestion of Washington faded away behind them. Comfortably steadying his pace, however, his patience was again tested when the command came down the line for the regiment to stop and slide off the road.

Clear of the road, he collapsed in the cool grass with his company. He saw Captain Edwards pass them, to which Morgan questioned the officer about the delay. Edwards gave no response, passing without giving much notice. Soldiers stood up and pointed, calling their comrades to attention. Leaping up from the horizon was a massive cloud of smoke. Soon the familiar sounds of wheels squeaking and creaking, bouncing over the loose dirt of the road, could be heard.

Morgan stood up too, giving into curiosity. The first wagons passed slowly, their cargo visible to the Michigan men. Limp and bloated bodies bounced uncontrollably in the carts. Morgan saw open mouths and wide black eyes. Many of the men were naked or nearly so, their clothes having been stripped for bandages or by the Confederate vultures after the battle. Arms and legs hung over the sides, freely swaying with the motion of the ambulances. The drivers, those poor devils, wrapped cloth around their noses and mouths. The stench was terrible.

Morgan felt a hand clutch his shoulder, as the soldier next to him buckled and got sick. The ambulances moved on, but the horrible scent lingered for several minutes. The soldier braced himself once more against Morgan's shoulder as he vomited again. Once the hand lifted, Morgan pulled away. He bravely inched toward the road, watching the ambulances pass. He prayed that the line would end soon, that the stench would be lifted from them. Turning his head down the road, away from Washington, he saw an endless stream of suffering.

He gathered himself, breathed in the tainted air, and sat back down. Morgan knew that they would be there for awhile. With the sights and stench of death all around him, he buried himself in the picture of Emmy.

Colonel Morrow rode up from the rear of the line. He had ridden the path many times since the regiment had been stopped. He issued orders for the men to stay with their companies and not mingle with those passing. Morrow made it very clear that as soon as the road was cleared, the regiment would move.

The ambulances bounced past him, their deceased or suffering occupants jolted from side to side. He tried to pay little attention to them, but it could not be helped. The sights were both fascinating and frightening. He could not help but wonder if he would soon find his regiment transported in such a manner.

Flanigan, completing duties of his own, rode by him. He saluted Morrow as he passed.

Morrow said, "You appear much better, Mark."

Flanigan stopped and turned his horse to meet Morrow. "I am."

"That is well. We should not let the men see us…"

"I know, sir," interrupted the Irishman.

Morrow nodded. He remembered meeting Flanigan in the middle of the street, just outside the hospital. Blood was visible on his shirt and face. The Irishman's eyes seemed drained of hope, of confidence. Morrow had never seen Flanigan as he did then. He never wanted to again.

Losing the reprimanding tone in his voice, Morrow spoke again. "You must forgive me, Mark," he said. "I did not mean to imply, well, I did not mean to offend you."

He saw Flanigan shake off the brief conversation. Flanigan then said, "Do not worry, Henry." His horse pushed away from Morrow. "There will be many more offenses in our trials that I will consider far more unjust." Flanigan nodded, accepting the apology, and then spurred his horse off down the line.

Morrow too had other business to tend to. He guided his horse, the three hundred dollar gift from his friends in Detroit, toward the helm of the regiment. He would need to hurry and finish his marching orders. The road would be cleared soon and the regiment was needed elsewhere. The delays around Washington had been costly. Too much time had been lost.

He pulled out his watch and noted the time. The ambulance train had been passing for nearly an hour, and he saw no end in sight to the long line, the thickening dust cloud still blanketing the land. He watched the brown particles float across the sky, sliding under darkening clouds building in the sky. Looks like rain, he thought. We are out in the open with no shelter, no tents for the men. They will suffer dearly if we don't move along soon.

As he slid the watch back into its pocket, his eyes caught glimpse of a familiar face. He squinted, catching view of the man's features with more clarity. Yes, he realized, I do know that man. He watched as the lifeless body, an officer, well known in Detroit, bounced with the melancholy rhythm of the ambulance.

He turned in his saddle and watched as the eyes of the regiment fell upon the familiar face, one of Detroit's first great heroes of the war. Morrow quickly removed his kepi and pressed it firmly against his chest. He bowed his head and began to silently pray.

Every head in the regiment followed suit.

"That's Colonel Roberts," said Captain Edwards to several of his men. "I served in the First Michigan with him. He was a veteran of the Mexican War. I believe he even knew Colonel Morrow from that excursion." The soldiers replaced their kepis as the ambulance carrying the deceased officer creaked by. "If there was one soldier I served with in that regiment that I believed would survive this war, it was him."

One of them commented, "Seems to me there aren't many of you left from the old First, Captain."

Edwards shook his head. "I do not know. Perhaps it is better that way." He turned away from them and watched the cart bounce out of view. "We will all come to understand that sometimes it is better to not have all the answers. When this war is over, however long it takes, I would sooner hope I could forget our trials and our sufferings than remember what little glory we gained." Once he realized what he had said, he quickly uttered an apology, asking the men to forgive him.

He changed the subject by pointing up to the road, clearing as the final ambulances drove toward them. "Ready up," he ordered them. "Colonel Morrow will want us on the road as fast as we can, boys. I will not have Company F be the last in line." Edwards broke away from them. "Finish your coffee and then fall in."

The ambulance bearing Roberts' body had long since vanished from his sight, but he could not help but wonder how the good officer fell. Edwards struggled to imagine the battle that took his life, the Confederate who aimed the shot, and the ball that tore through his body. He wondered if Roberts had suffered or if he had even known he had been hit. Death upon a battlefield could be a cruel thing. A life could be taken quickly, the victim never feeling pain or a life could be drained by a horrendous wound, the victim feeling and sensing the coming death.

He had seen both cases before. At Bull Run, Edwards was posted near a man who took two shots to the head, dying instantly. The sight was horrible and blood was everywhere, but the soldier never suffered. He never reacted to the impact. There was another scene, just as Edwards was being carted off in captivity, where he saw a young soldier crawl, a trail of blood staining the grass in his wake, toward the Confederate line. A Confederate officer ran out to aide the dying soldier, offering his canteen to his enemy. Within seconds, the poor soldier stiffened with death. The blood trail stretched for several yards behind him.

Edwards carefully stepped into the road as the last two ambulances rumbled by. These were perhaps the worst of them all, bearing those still alive with horrible wounds. There were men sitting on the edge of the cart with one leg or no legs at all. Several of them had bandages around their heads, shoulders, arms, and legs. One soldier was standing, as the cart was too full to sit down, and he just stared at Edwards as he passed. Edwards noticed the man was missing both of his arms, bandaged stumps hanging down from his shoulders. Embarrassed, he turned away.

He heard Morrow's booming voice in the distance, calling the regiment to attention. The road had been cleared. The regiment was ready to move.

Pushing aside the haunting images, Edwards barked to his beloved Company F. "On your feet, boys. It's time to move."

Lieutenant Colonel Mark Flanigan received word of the regiment's destination and was disappointed. Since they had left Detroit, the men wanted nothing more than their chance to fight. They were eager, their anticipation and frustration simmering with each passing day. Morrow had just told him that Fort Lyon, perched above Alexandria, Virginia, was their destination. "The men want to fight," Flanigan replied, tugging on his gloves.

He turned in his saddle and stretched out his back. It had been sore, having been in the saddle the entire day. Thirsty, he pulled out his canteen. The water was refreshing. He poured a little over his face, washing away the dirt and the sweat.

His thoughts turned to earlier in the day, when he vainly attempted to wash the blood from his face following the visit to the hospital. He remembered the wounded soldier staring at him, his eyes wide as the surgeon cut through skin and bone. He could distinctly hear the surgeon telling him to keep the soldier pinned down. Grind. Grind. Each pass of the saw continued in memory.

Flanigan wiped his eyes, brushing loose beads of water from his face. He looked around and realized he was with his regiment and not at the hospital. The canteen fell to his side, bouncing against his haversack. He was relieved to be with the regiment, away from the bloody hospital and the wounded soldier.

Dark clouds built over him. The last remaining sunlight, streaming down from the breaks between the clouds, rolled up and disappeared in the growing shade. The weather very much reflected Flanigan's mood. He felt alone, despite being surrounded by a thousand men. He felt depressed, despite beginning the greatest adventure of his life. The Flanigan on this day was not the same Flanigan that left Detroit. He was not in search of glory or ambitious to undergo the rigorous journey before him. Flanigan missed his wife and missed Michigan. He had seen very little of the war, but on this day he had grown tired of it. He looked as if he had been among those already defeated, circulating Washington in anger and confusion.

He spurred his horse forward, trotting toward the helm of the regiment. Things would change. The day would pass. By morning, he knew that he would return to his normal self. The depressing thoughts would escape his mind. The war, the regiment, would become his biggest concern. He would once again be hopeful of victory. He would once again anticipate meeting the enemy in battle.

Flanigan drove his horse up the hill that led to Fort Lyon, the city of Alexandria nestled comfortably below. He looked up and saw the massive guns of the fort, extending from the walls, pointed down to the rebellious city below. He wondered if the gunners would actually fire into the old town. The church steeple was visible from his vantage point. Flanigan began to silently count the buildings below. It was a beautiful old town but a hotbed for secession. He frowned at the thought that Virginia would be full of such towns, their people loyal to an unjust cause.

The clouds above him began to rumble. As the regiment reached the peak of the hill, rain began to fall. As the rain fell heavier, Flanigan called for the regiment to settle as best it could. They hadn't been issued tents yet and there was little cover from the severe storm.

His body shivered as he looked through the sheets of rain for Morrow. He had taken care of several companies, assigning them positions. The men had scattered themselves about the hill, blankets covering their cold bodies. Flanigan turned and looked back down upon the town below him. His day just continued to worsen, adding to his grim mood. With a sigh of relief, he found Morrow, who was waving for Flanigan to join him. Through the pounding rain, he heard that shelter had been found for several of the officers and a few of the men.

Knowing that a warm and dry room would do him some good, Flanigan pulled away from the shivering regiment and broke through several curtains of rain. He needed time to gather himself. He needed time to clear his head. He simply needed time away from the regiment, away from the tragic thought of awaiting conflicts. Flanigan met Morrow warmly, greeting his friend with a smile.

It was his first smile of the day.

"You men look like good men. I saw your regiment today, marching from Washington. They are men of good order. I believe they shall make excellent soldiers, the highest caliber," said General Joseph Hooker. He had just returned from the field. Having run into Morrow and the Twenty-Fourth Michigan in a blistering rain storm, one of the worst he had seen, he offered the house he accommodated to several of his new comrades.

Morrow, enjoying the warm fire, listened carefully to his words. "Our government was foolish to believe this war would be over in three short months," Hooker continued. "We have good men, worthy men. Our ranks will swell with brave men, like your Twenty-Fourth, sir, and we will again strike at them." Morrow studied Hooker as he spoke. There was clarity and strength in his voice. Hooker was an opinionated man, one of the worst of such in federal uniform. He was outspoken against General McClellan and several other Union commanders, for which he blamed the poor results in recent battles. He cited that he had seen the First Battle of Bull Run as a civilian. Seeing the confusion and aftermath of that battle, he wrote to Lincoln offering his services and calling for a commission. Despite his dislike for General Scott, the overall commander of Union forces, Hooker was accepted.

His first commands included stints with the Army of the Potomac, before being welded into Pope's Union Army of Virginia, where Hooker led a corps into battle at Second Bull Run. Following Pope's defeat, Hooker was called back to the Army of the Potomac where his services and known fighting qualities could be used.

"You see, Colonel Morrow," Hooker instructed, "fighting war can be as simple as entrapping your enemy without firing a shot. A good commander must not only make attempts to spare the lives of his good soldiers, as McClellan is known, but must use those soldiers as soldiers are intended. Battles must be fought, sir. But, if a march can be stolen on the enemy, placing his army in a vulnerable position, and your soldiers are used as soldiers should, then the chances for defeat are far less than if you meet the enemy face to face on open ground."

Morrow nodded.

"Your regiment there," Hooker said, pointing out into the rain, "they are eager to fight, yes? And you have a thousand patriotic souls in your ranks, Colonel?"

"Yes."

Hooker said, "Then your regiment, shall it ever fall under my care, will be considered one of the finest. While I should use it to quell many dangers, I would do so with only the best consideration of your troops in mind."

Morrow nodded again.

Hooker smiled. Morrow felt relaxed, accepted. Immediately the two befriended each other. Morrow came in with a new regiment, fresh and green to war. He praised their conduct on the journey from Michigan, but didn't over do it. Hooker spoke loudly, accepted Morrow and his regiment as it came. There were great expectations between the two of them for the untested Twenty-Fourth.

Hooker mesmerized Morrow and his company with tales of his success in recent battles. He often spoke of his impatience with military blunders and those in command. More than once, he mentioned how he would conduct the war if he were given an army. He spoke of how the south should be choked off and how Richmond should be sacked with one army while another deals with the Army of Northern Virginia. Such a dream, he relented, would never develop because those in power had little knowledge of war. Furthermore, he cursed rumors and political distinctions within the armies. Hooker claimed that politics had no rightful place in war. Let the lawmakers make the laws and rebuild the country. Let the soldiers and generals, who know war, fight.

By the time the two officers retired for the evening, a friendship had been cemented between them. They respected each other. Before retiring to his room, Hooker turned to Morrow and company and bade them goodnight. "Whatever different paths this war will take us," he said to them, "I hope that I may someday come across the Twenty-Fourth Michigan again."

It had been another chance meeting for Morrow. Within the span of twenty-four hours, he had met the most influential politician of the war, Lincoln, and one of the most distinctive generals of the war, Hooker. Morrow went to bed that evening hopeful of a distinguished military career.

Color Sergeant Abel Peck was selected as one of the few to venture a few miles away to Mount Vernon. George Washington's estate was then considered the country's most hallowed ground. Peck was honored to be among the few to see the place, to walk the path of the greatest American.

Prior to entering the mansion, the men separated themselves from their rifles. No arms were to be taken onto the grounds. He followed the line of soldiers stumbling about the property, transfixed on the large dwelling, and taking leisurely walks down the paths. It was a peaceful moment, the war far from their thoughts. Peck nearly seemed to forget about the war in its entirety, until he looked to one of his comrades in uniform. Then everything came back to him. He very much enjoyed his time outside, relaxing under the shade of the tree Washington himself had planted so long ago.

Their tour included the slave quarters, which sparked much debate between the men. While they questioned the institution of slavery, they did not question Washington's stance on the subject. Slavery was not a political and moral issue in his time, they reasoned. Peck was among those who agreed.

He slowly paced about the old mansion, wondering if his steps matched those of the great American. Peck toured the rooms. He imagined what life was like in Washington's time, if it were anything similar to his. He imagined Washington pacing the halls or climbing the stairs. Life seemed to continue without the master of the house. Peck silently shuffled into the room where Washington died, standing shoulder to shoulder with his comrades. He quickly removed his kepi, as did the others, in respect. There was a soft haze streaming through the window, as the sun reclaimed the sky from the dark clouds. The warmth bathed the men standing before Washington's deathbed. There was a profound sense of patriotism and strength building within them. Everything seemed divine, soft and angelic. The spirit of Washington was very much among them, Peck believed.

As the men exited the property, they seemed to fully comprehend the great task before them. They were called upon to save the country that Washington helped create. The visit had only solidified their determination to save it, to preserve the Union. Peck understood what was asked of him. He accepted the challenge with a full heart. Having seen Washington's tomb and the place he called home, Peck felt a renewed rush of confidence. It was the same confidence that had been shaken by the sights of a depleted army, battered soldiers, and a frightened Washington City.

This renewed confidence pushed the soldiers even harder on their trek back to the regiment. Once there, they found their comrades in motion, with orders to march as soon as possible. Peck hurriedly returned to his post, reclaimed the flag, and waited for the orders. His trip to Mount Vernon had been delightful and peaceful, reminding him of the proud nation he defended. He contemplated on what Washington had envisioned for the country, smiling at the thought of what could have been.

As the gears of the regiment drove the massive body of men forward, word came down the line that their destination was the front. Peck learned from Morrow that Confederate General Robert E. Lee had invaded Maryland, and that the Twenty-Fourth Michigan was called to give pursuit with the Army of the Potomac.

He was glad that his confidence was restored, that his visit to Mount Vernon returned the faith he had in the nation. It was a good thing because the war was calling them. It seemed their first taste of action was only days away.

And Abel Peck knew he was ready.

The Twenty-Fourth had received orders to march for Leesburg, hitting the road at nine in the evening. They marched by moonlight, knowing that Lee had stolen a march on them and was pressing on national soil. Morrow instructed the men to carry only the necessities, to move quick and light. All other objects, no matter how valuable, were to be left behind. Nothing was to hinder the regiment's motion to the front.

By the time they reached Alexandria, the familiar cannon of Fort Lyon staring at them from above, the regiment stopped for rest. The men replenished their canteens and hurriedly made coffee or ate from their haversacks. Following the short break, the regiment was again on the move, nearing the bridge that led them back into Washington.

The regiment learned that because of an error by the War Department, the Seventh Michigan Infantry Regiment was sent to Leesburg instead of the Twenty-Fourth. There would be no great chase of Lee and his Army of Northern Virginia. And there would certainly be no great battles for the regiment to partake in.

Fort Baker was the eventual destination for the Twenty-Fourth, while Antietam was the bloody destination for the Seventh. Morrow and his men had missed out on the bloodiest single day of the war.

It was another setback in a line of disappointments since they had parted with their families and homes. Their stay at Fort Baker wouldn't be long, however. By the end of September the regiment was marching toward the Army of the Potomac, having recently fought at Antietam. October 9, 1862, was the regiment's formal date of admission into the army.

They were assigned to the Fourth Brigade of the First Division of the First Corps, known as the "Iron Brigade."

POTOMAC'S PRIDE

General John Gibbon, commanding the Iron Brigade, had requested of the War Department another western regiment to fill his ranks. He wanted one from Wisconsin or Indiana, being that the Second, Sixth, and Seventh Wisconsin Infantry Regiments and the Nineteenth Indiana Infantry Regiment comprised his brigade. The War Department denied his request, stating that regiments from those states were not readily available. They sent him a Michigan regiment, the Twenty-Fourth, and he reluctantly accepted.

The Iron Brigade was an entirely western brigade caught in an eastern army. The brigade had become famous for its hard fighting style, aggressiveness, and determination. It was an honorable brigade, widely known as such by its comrades and enemies alike.

General John Gibbon stood before the Twenty-Fourth as calm and still as a statue. He stared at them, studied them, with his sharp eyes. His lips remained frozen as his eyes traveled up and down the ranks. Known for building one of the most effective fighting brigades in the Army of the Potomac, Gibbon judged his new regiment with passionate and critical eyes. The regiments under his command had forged their growing reputation through blood and sacrifice, glory and honor. He demanded supreme authority. His brigade was destined to become the pride of the Potomac.

The veteran regiments standing behind Gibbon had seen hard service. These were the men who rode the first wave of patriotism, enlisting when Lincoln first called for volunteers. The regiment joining, the Twenty-Fourth, had needed a second prodding from the government, a second call for assistance. For a year the war raged on without them. For a year thousands of men suffered.

The Iron Brigade was unique not just because of their western states, but because of their distinctive dress. Instead of the traditional kepi, worn by most of the army, the brigade wore the official hat known as the Hardee. It was tall, towering above the kepi, and was black instead of federal blue. The wide brims of the hats were pinned up on one side, a feather extending from that point. This distinctive look made the brigade easily identifiable to its comrades and enemies. The hats were a prized commodity for the soldiers who earned them. Receiving one meant the regiment had earned it through bravery and fierce trial. Gibbon expected nothing less.

The veterans stood across from the Twenty-Fourth in tattered rags when compared to the dress of the new regiment. Their uniforms showed signs of campaigning, the wear and tear of battle and drill. There were a number of different styles of coats, many shades of federal blue. Some were fairly long. Others were short. All appeared stained with dirt, sweat, and blood. The black hats were dirty. The feathers were old and bent. Their appearance mattered little to them. They knew there was more to war than shiny brass buttons.

The Twenty-Fourth's uniforms were dirty from marching and garrison duty, but were still relatively new. The blue was still sharp, the buttons still glaring in the sun. There were no tears or holes, no signs of combat. The worst wear and tear, in fact, came from the bottoms of their pants. The pressures of drill and marching had begun to take their toll on the ends of the pant legs, slowly shredding the dirty fabric.

There were two different colors clashing on the field that day. One was the old, stern federal blue. The other was the bold, untested federal blue.

The brigade also knew that war was a game of numbers. The new regiment before them nearly outnumbered them two to one. The price of war had been costly for the Iron Brigade. At one time, each of its regiments boasted nearly a thousand brave men. The trials of war, campaigning, and disease took their toll on them. They were a battered, ragtag brigade, having just come out of the slugfest at Antietam. There was still plenty of fight left in them, perhaps more than most brigades in any Union army.

Numbers were indeed important as they gauged the Twenty-Fourth, but what mattered most was if their new regiment had the same intensity, the same fight in them.

Captain Edwards had never seen a finer body of men. Despite their tattered uniforms and depletion of ranks, Edwards knew that the brigade was more than capable of holding its own. He had followed their stories in the papers when he could get them. He heard rumors of their ferocity and fearlessness, all the while wondering if such a body of men ever existed in reality.

If he had to imagine the men of that storied brigade, these would be them. They were burly men, seemingly built for combat. They had come from the western states, where work was done mainly by hand and outdoors. These men appeared rough around the edges but obedient in military manner. They had seen more combat and had been thrown in more perilous situations than nearly any other brigade in the Army of the Potomac. Their faces, their eyes, silently told their tales.

He saw them stand there, tucked behind Gibbon, reluctantly accepting their new comrades. Edwards turned and listened as Colonel Morrow proudly listed the qualities of the regiment, its determination, and the bravery of the men. In turn, Edwards turned back to the rank and file of the brigade, searching for reactions. There were none. Even after Morrow finished addressing Gibbon and the brigade, there were no cheers, not even a polite response from Gibbon.

Edwards felt cold and alone. He was pleased to be at the front, with the army at last, but the reception was cool. He felt uncomfortable, unwanted. These feelings triggered the painful memories of his captivity, where he had felt the same things.

He quickly pushed aside the thoughts.

Gibbon paced the line before him, still not uttering a word, still looking as cold as the brigade behind him. Edwards watched the officer stop and study how one of the Michigan soldiers held their rifle. Keeping his silence, he shifted the rifle over, pulled the man's bottom hand forward a few inches, and then shuffled away. Gibbon stopped, when several men in Company F frantically scratched at their heads, hoping the officer hadn't seen them. Lice had invaded the regiment. The dirty lifestyle of the soldier was becoming well known to the Twenty-Fourth. He watched as Gibbon drove toward the men and raised a hand, demanding that they be still. Edwards was sure that Gibbon would address the men for their misbehavior, their shameful conduct.

Again, no words were uttered.

As Gibbon turned toward Edwards, recognizing an officer, Edwards took a deep breath and lifted his chest. He adjusted his head to look forward. His eyes shifted steadily into place. He had been through the routine before. Gibbon stepped up to him, looked up and down. He bent his head to the side, studying Edwards' stance, his presentation. Approvingly, Gibbon nodded. As the officer pulled away, Edwards exhaled. He lowered his chest and fought off a smile. His discomfort was improving. He had impressed the general.

Color Sergeant Abel Peck stood erect and tightly gripped the flag. He was nervous, excited, and frightened at the same time. To make matters worse, his head itched as the lice continued their assault on him. He dared not react to it, to scratch at his dirty hair. He did not want General Gibbon to come down on him as he had done with several others.

He too watched Gibbon stroll down the regiment's line. He also felt the eyes of the veterans, standing across the open ground, fall upon him. He noted how proud the small band, no bigger than his regiment, stood before him. They were lean and rugged. Their skin was tanned from the sun, blistering down on them during numerous engagements and endless marches.

Peck closed his eyes. He wanted to pull away from the judging eyes. He shook away the fear, the discomfort. It is better than garrison duty, he thought. At least with the brigade he was part of something. His thoughts trickled back to the dull rhythm of garrison life. The regiment had worked on fortifications and drilled constantly. Often times there would be a call for the regiment to gather arms and prepare to meet an enemy that never advanced, the threats never materializing.

He smiled at the comfort of being with an army. At least here we are bound to meet the enemy, he assured himself.

As he waited, he thought back to the previous nights, when the regiment first arrived. Their assigned position was in between a barn containing Confederate wounded and a pile of amputated limbs. The stench was terrible, forcing him to wake suddenly in the night to get sick. Several members of the regiment complained to Morrow about the location, but nothing was done. There was little room on the field to accommodate such a large mass of men, so the regiment was told it would have to make due.

Several men from the regiment ventured off into the barn containing the Confederate wounded. They held pleasant conversations with the enemy, sharing stories of home and adventures. Peck chose not to join them, hoping instead to find rest. Of course he couldn't sleep with the stench and the sight of the limbs piled high, so he listened to the stories as the men trampled back from the barn. He heard that many of the Confederates were planning on rejoining their army as soon as they were healed. A few of them were contemplating on making an escape, in hopes of joining their old comrades. While they entertained their Yankee captives and cordially accepted them, they reminded their enemies that if they met again in battle then all cordial ties would be broken. They were soldiers from two fighting countries and should fight as such.

The dedication of the Confederate wounded impressed Peck. He had envisioned the same for his Union comrades as they came upon Washington. This was not the case. Instead of dedicated and loyal soldiers, Peck found confusion, anger, and depression. Most of all there was fear, thick and heavy fear. His comrades in Washington, those left of Pope's army, had been defeated and were uncertain of what the future held in store for them. Not only did they question their country's chance of survival, of Union preservation, but they questioned their will to continue in the face of that pressing uncertainty. The world had seemingly crashed around them. All that they knew and loved had crumbled. This was not the case with the wounded Confederates. Even after the terrible battle of Antietam, even after horrible wounds, these southern men wanted nothing more than to heal and live to fight again amongst their comrades.

Peck had not seen the same qualities in Union men since he arrived in Washington and his journey began. But as he stood across from the Iron Brigade, Peck felt relieved that he had finally come across such men. These men had indeed seen hard service. They watched as their friends and relatives fell around them, but they bravely banded together to survive, to carry on the fight.

Peck knew these men weren't just fighting for cause and country.

They were fighting for each other.

"You are the Twenty-Fourth Michigan Infantry Regiment," Morrow heard Gibbon say. "You have been sent to me for service. It will be hard service, I assure you. You have been selected, I believe, because you are a western regiment and we a western brigade." The voice was stern and cold. "Your arrival bears little on your acceptance, which will come only after you have proven your worth as soldiers." Morrow watched as Gibbon's posture stiffened before the regiment, demanding attention. "This brigade is trained and disciplined in the conducts of war," he said. "I expect the same of you."

Gibbon added, "When cowardly men pillage enemy towns and villages, we shoot the cowards. When a single brigade is called upon to stop an enemy army, we volunteer. We succeed where others fail." His eyes prowled the new regiment. "We stand where few dare to stand."

Morrow froze in place. He silently battled the nervousness, hoping to contain it without his new commander noticing. It would be a shame to be presented as a coward, to be afraid. "This is a unique brigade," continued Gibbon. "You will have your chances to join it, to march with its hardened veterans, to don the black hat. I pray that you will make every effort to do so, to give as these veterans have given. Only then will you be considered a member of this brigade." As his voice settled, Gibbon's feet shuffled and he paced the line once more. "You men," he said sternly, "will fall in line next to men from Wisconsin and Indiana. I look forward to seeing the qualities your commander has expressed. I look forward to seeing what sons Michigan has provided us."

The speech concluded with Gibbon turning his back to the regiment and conversing with several aides. The men of the Twenty-Fourth relaxed. Several pockets of men began to gently pull away from the ranks, their focus lost. Gibbon swung around quickly and reprimanded them, reminded these soldiers that they had not been dismissed. As the small pockets quickly meshed back into the regiment, Gibbon's voice grew loud and stern again. "You are an eager and proud regiment," he said. "You desperately seek the opportunity to meet our enemies in a good fight, this I can tell. Well," he confessed, "you have been assigned to the right brigade."

With the wave of a hand, Gibbon dismissed the regiment. Morrow, regaining his composure, winning the bout with his nervousness, turned to Flanigan. "I want as detailed of numbers as we can get," he ordered. "We will let General Gibbon know what we have to offer." Flanigan soaked in the order, saluted, and then rode off.

The regiment broke apart as the individual companies shifted away from the line. Morrow could see their frustration and disappointment. They had come a long way from the rolling landscape of Michigan. This was certainly not the welcome they had anticipated.

Morrow watched as Gibbon still conversed with several aides. It took him several seconds to realize that one of the general's aides had approached with a note. When it was handed to him, he pulled open the note to read that Gibbon wished a private conference with him. As Morrow's eyes scanned the paper, he read aloud Gibbon's compliments to the regiment and its officers. Sliding the note away, he noticed Abel Peck watching him, listening to the words. "He sends us his compliments," Morrow pronounced with a cynical smile.

Peck smiled. "Very well," Morrow said with a sigh. "We shall see what comes tomorrow, Mr. Peck. I have great faith in the men."

"And we in you, Colonel," replied Peck.

Morrow nodded. "Unfurl the colors," he ordered. "Let the boys retire under the bold banner." Just as Morrow spoke, Captain Edwards came up with his company's numbers in hand. He had finished the work early in the morning, knowing that Morrow would eventually ask for it to present to General Gibbon. Edwards thought the short remark was beautiful and the gesture would do much to inspire the men, to brighten their spirits after the gloomy reception.

Morgan nervously shuffled about the encampment. His regiment had settled and perched alongside their new comrades in arms. Brave men, curious to explore their new life, ventured out beyond the regiment. They hoped to hear stories of glorious battles and brave soldiers. Most of all, they longed for something that reminded them of home. To some, the chance of stretching their legs provoked them to explore. Others simply wanted to use the short window of freedom to break away from the everyday rigors of marching and drilling. They had just arrived among men of iron, the famed Iron Brigade, and they were eager to learn about the soldiers.

The land Morgan strolled through had lost all its beauty. War had been hard on it. The army had been even harder. Trees were stripped of bark, either by rifle or artillery fire. Dead horses were scattered about, being clumped into piles for burning or quick burial. Bloated bodies, some with horrifying and disfiguring wounds, rendered identification of the individual soldiers impossible. The stench was terrible, a strong odor that made the senses burn. Escaping the sights by an open pathway, Morgan sprinted past a pile of rotting limbs. He saw the emptiness of the world around him. What once had been a farmer's field, golden and profitable, was torn apart and blackened by the gods and generals of war.

If the land around him seemed cold and distant, then his new comrades seemed a world away. They huddled closely together, in packs like wild dogs. Their eyes watched Morgan as he passed them, their hands stretched out over warm fires. They happily cooked meals, told stories, exchanged goods, and played games. Morgan could see all of this and wanted to join them. As they recognized that he wasn't one of them, one of the great veterans, they shunned him. Their stories would fall silent, the goods would get shuffled away, and the games would stop. Their eyes, those judging white eyes, would break from whatever had previously commanded their attention and focus on Morgan. Every set of eyes gazed upon him as if he were a lonely deer in wolf country.

He stopped when he came upon a group of soldiers, huddled around a fire, whose stories didn't fade when they saw him, whose happy games continued despite his presence. He stood there, foolishly, for a moment. Surely they had realized he was there. Surely they would say something, react to him, for they were the only ones who weren't staring at him. They were the only ones who continued despite the newcomer, a green recruit, a lonely deer, stumbling into their country.

Morgan watched with enthusiasm as dirty and bent playing cards were shuffled around, tossed into dirty hands. He listened carefully to their stories of home. With each murmur of the lips, each flicker of the cards, he moved closer, hoping for the chance to join them.

And they continued to ignore him.

Yet he came closer, nearly standing over them. He came close enough to feel the warmth of their fire, to bask in the glow. One man, holding a hand of tattered cards, finally lifted his wide white eyes and looked to the intruder. No words were spoken. A silent caution had been issued, sent from the lead wolf of the pack: stay clear.

Morgan ignored the warning, tempted forward by curiosity. Slowly, carefully, he inched closer. Once he got close enough, the lead wolf called out to him. "Is there something you want, boy? Is there anything we can help you with, hmm?"

Morgan shook his head. "No, sir," he pleaded. "I just thought I could join you. It has been a long while since I played a game of cards."

The others around the fire lifted their heads in response. The man with the cards, the lead wolf, fiddled with them, shuffled them over and over again. The others brought their eyes from Morgan to him, seeking direction. "What makes you think you can join us?" he asked of Morgan. "The last I heard, Michigan was setting up just beyond those trees yonder." His eyes dropped from Morgan and went back to the cards. The game continued despite the interruption. "You best be on your way, boy. You stick with your regiment and you'll be fine, no harm done."

"My company was dismissed," Morgan informed him. "I figured I would pass through camp and get to know those I'll be fighting with." He heard the cards still again, as the lead wolf grew increasingly annoyed. "It sure would be a pleasure if you showed me how to play that game. I haven't seen the likes of it before."

"No," said the man. "Go back to your company and stay put."

"We were dismissed."

To which the man replied, "We weren't. My company hasn't been dismissed yet. We have important business to attend to." He turned back and collected the cards from his comrades, commencing the start of another game. "I don't recognize you, *Michigan*, as part of our company. Does anyone else?" The others grunted, their heads shaking.

Morgan steadied his nerves. "The name is *Morgan*, not *Michigan*."

"We'll call you by name when you earn it."

"And what of your company?" asked Morgan. "I see but a handful of men."

The man stood up in frustration. He tossed the deck of cards to the ground and pointed to his comrades. "This is my company. This is all that is left, boy." He sat back down as the anger cooled, his arms reaching to gather the scattered cards. "God damned fool," he muttered. "Go back to your regiment, *Michigan*. This is a place for soldiers."

Morgan backed away. He had ignored several warnings and continued on, hoping to join them. They didn't want him. There would be no stories, no card games for him. He pulled away from the group and retreated back to the regiment, the eyes of the hardened soldiers of the veteran brigade upon him. They didn't want him there, but they didn't want him to retreat.

It would be a lesson for him to learn in the coming months. This brigade despised newcomers, foolish and ignorant soldiers, because so often they had to bury them. They were testing the mettle of the new Michigan soldier, to see just how far the young soldier would go alone. They approved his efforts but were critical of his quick retreat. Morgan had come so close.

The lesson would come in time, but for now the lonely deer limped away from the weathered pack of wolves with only a slight wound.

Colonel Morrow moved slowly through the darkness. He inched his way toward Gibbon's headquarters, cutting a path through the veteran ranks. They smelled the green soldier, the raw commander. They stared at him. They questioned him. With each step came new dirty faces, judging eyes. There were no words. There was no need. Their eyes said enough. Morrow was not welcomed. He could sense it. His nervousness began to grow, violently build inside.

He scurried past fading fires, those gathered around the warmth slowly falling to fatigue, giving in to sleep. He heard the soft crackle as numerous fires retained their lives as new logs were tossed toward the dancing flames. Still he moved on.

A strong wind came through camp, forcing shivers down unsuspecting spines. Morrow felt the gust hit him, the chill passing through his wool coat, his shirt, and his bones. His teeth clattered lightly. He pulled the heavy coat even closer to his body. Onward he went, weaving around makeshift camps, stepping over the bodies of exhausted soldiers. The darkness was thick. The crackle of the fires filled the air.

He spun himself around to avoid disrupting a few poker games. He struggled, much to the amusement of the witnesses, to keep his balance.

Morrow fell to one knee but quickly brought himself back to his feet. He heard their laughter, felt their judgment. His hands began to shake uncontrollably. The nervousness exploded. He anxiously rotated his head to the left and right, hoping to come to his senses and remember the path to Gibbon's headquarters. The strange laughter continued, mocking him. He shoved his trembling hands into his pockets, but this only proved to shelter them from the chill. Morrow struggled to regain control, desperately fought to steady his hands. No use, he thought. No matter how much he tried, his nervousness could never be brought under control. It had been that way for too long now.

Morrow felt lightheaded. The laughter continued in the background. He stepped over a log here and there, moving in a circle, hoping to pull out of his nervous tailspin. He pulled his hands from his pockets and brought them to his face. What have I done? He felt the anxiety come back to him. Why am I here? He spun around again, trying to claw his way out of the darkness. His hands trembled. His thoughts raced through his head.

He tried to push the paralyzing thoughts from his head. He was a soldier, a patriot. He had been called by his country. That was why he was there. He had raised a regiment of brave and patriotic men and led them to the front. That is what he had done. Steady, he told himself. This is not the conduct of an officer, a commander. The men need you, he thought.

As the world around him rocked back to stillness, he regained his composure and stepped forward, probing the darkness. It had been a long and tiring day. He had had little sleep in over four days. He had eaten very little.

Suddenly the laughter stopped. Only the crackle of the fires was evident.

"Never mind them, Colonel," said a reassuring voice. "They don't mean to offend. They're just boys who fight like devils. Like all boys they like to play games."

Out of the darkness stepped General Gibbon. "I apologize if I startled you, Colonel Morrow. Mr. Haskell saw you approaching when you fell. Finding your way through a brigade in the darkness can be tricky business."

"Indeed, General."

Gibbon stood erect, his arms folded across his chest. He lifted his right arm and pointed off into the darkness. "My tent is just beyond that small hill, if you wouldn't mind the walk, Colonel."

Morrow nodded. His sense of direction returned. Gibbon continued to talk as the two of them melted into the thick black curtain of the night. "You have a fine regiment. With training they will become an even better regiment, perhaps one of the best in the entire army. It is a fine regiment, indeed. They are worthy men for a worthy cause."

"You must forgive me, General, but we are under a different impression."

Gibbon chuckled. "Ah," he sighed. "There are two sides to first impressions, Colonel Morrow. On one hand, you have the first impression with new comrades. It matters little, really, to the commander or those comrades on how you impressed them the date of arrival, for they are waiting to be impressed by what they see in the field, in battle, Colonel." Gibbon smiled, leading Morrow toward his tent. They could see the massive canvas dwelling rising from the earth, a large fire out front. "On the other hand," Gibbon continued, "you have the first impression with the enemy. This matters greatly, for it is how you impress them on the first meeting which will stay with them throughout all subsequent meetings."

Gibbon added, "If you have a regiment that breaks and runs immediately upon meeting the enemy, then that is how that regiment will be remembered by the enemy, no matter how much improvement has been made in later battles. But," Gibbon nodded as an aide lifted one of the flaps and let the two men enter the tent, "if you have a regiment that stands against every shot, every shell, every attack, then that is how your enemy will remember you, whether your army claimed victory or defeat."

Gibbon sat down in a wooden chair next to a small writing desk. Atop his desk were scattered orders and loose pieces of paper, information regarding the strength of his brigade and the losses from the recent battle. He pointed to another chair and invited Morrow to sit across from him. "What of the brigade?" he asked of Morrow.

"I have never seen such," Morrow confessed. "It is vastly different from what we saw on our journey here, General."

"And how is it in Washington?"

"It is not the place I remember it once was, sir."

Gibbon stretched out his legs. He looked weary. "I am told that along your journey you met General Hooker."

"Yes," replied Morrow.

"He is very impressed with you and your regiment, Colonel Morrow. He was wounded in the fight. We are now led by General Reynolds. He is a fighting man like Hooker. I think he will do well while Hooker recovers."

"I did not know."

Gibbon pulled his eyes away. "Battles will do that," he added. "There have been many vacancies and many appointments. Since the battle of late, the army has already undergone several command changes." He shifted his eyes toward the desk, the loose papers. "There will not be a brigade untouched by such in the coming months. Battles will do that."

The conversation momentarily fell flat. Morrow could sense that there were more pressing things on Gibbon's mind. He could see his new commander was tired and worn out, and nearly sick. He stood up to take his leave, but Gibbon lifted a hand, motioning Morrow to sit back down.

"I understand you are Virginian by birth, Colonel Morrow," Gibbon said, reigniting the conversation.

"Yes," Morrow reluctantly replied. Too many times his loyalty had come into question since the rebellion began. Virginia had seceded from the Union. Morrow had not. He sat still, patiently waiting for Gibbon's response.

Gibbon said, "You have nothing to fear in my company. I too am a southern man by birth, Colonel. There are those in this army that remind me of that every day. I get looked upon as a traitor, as no better than those we fight. Yet I stay. I chose to fight for the country, my country. To me it is more important than state, more important than a way of life. We have the chance to build something better, I believe. Preservation of the Union is the first step." He took a breath and gently leaned back in the chair. "Despite our efforts, these are dangerous times for men like you and I. We must be careful where we step, who our friends are, who we talk to, what we order, and how we conduct ourselves against our southern brethren." The words flowed perfectly, results of thoughts long since deliberated in silence. "Therefore, we must rise above the highest expectations."

"It is my hope," replied Morrow, "that all men in federal blue be looked upon as Union men."

"We shall see, Colonel Morrow. Only combat will tell."

Morrow watched as Gibbon ruffled through the paperwork on the desk. "I received your numbers an hour ago." He found the paper and lifted it from the scattered mess. "Your numbers bring great strength. The brigade is low on men. You must understand that the Twenty-Fourth's arrival is appreciated."

Morrow nodded.

"Mr. Haskell has done much to inform me of your regiment in such a short time. You have done very well with the resources at hand." He tossed the paper back to the desk. "I will keep the Twenty-Fourth very busy, Colonel Morrow. Army life is tiring. There is a constant stream of dress parades and drills. I expect your regiment to arrive as ordered for the daily dress parades."

"We will."

"I expect your regiment to keep pace with the veteran regiments, drilling four hours a day prior to the commencement of dress parades."

"I will drill them for six."

Gibbon smiled. "Your confidence in your regiment inspires me, Colonel Morrow. I look forward to see what men you have in your ranks."

Morrow nodded. "Good men, sir."

Gibbon went back to the paperwork and Morrow knew it was time to leave. He stood up, saluted stiffly, and stepped toward the exit. Before leaving, he turned around. "General, sir?" he asked. Gibbon pulled himself from his work and looked up. "Those men out there, the men of this brigade, what makes them stand like men of iron?"

Gibbon rubbed his chin, deep in thought. "Faith, Colonel Morrow." He nodded and then smiled at Morrow. "They believe in something greater, I suppose. But it is faith that makes them men of iron."

Fall of Discontent

As the Twenty-Fourth Michigan settled into their new position within the Iron Brigade, they received a delightful treat from home. Several important dignitaries from Detroit, including the wives of a few officers, ventured down to see their homesick men in camp with the army.

Colonel Morrow was granted permission to take five hundred men from the regiment and tour the Antietam battlefield. Marching loosely over the sacred soil, the men witnessed the devastation left in the wake of the great battle. Trees were toppled. Bullet holes riddled fences and buildings. The earth was scorched and trampled by the feet of thousands of men and the wheels of hundreds of artillery pieces. Among the most disturbing sights, however, were the numerous humps of dirt where soldiers had been buried. Often time buried where they had fallen, the task of covering the bodies was done with such haste that it was common for the tourists to see a hand, a foot, or even a skull protruding from the soft soil.

As the month of October neared its end, the regiment marched away from Sharpsburg, as the Army of the Potomac finally shifted away from the haunting grounds. Across the Blue Ridge Mountains they would march, battling blistering winds and bitter cold. Stopping for rest, the regiment's government issued knapsacks, stuffed with fresh clothing, arrived from the massive storage depots of Washington. A government official then expressed that the men of the Twenty-Fourth had the opportunity to enlist in the regular army, vacating their status as volunteers. Colonel Morrow argued against such an act, stating that the designation of a volunteer was honorable and glorious. The government official was forced to retreat with not a single enlistment from the proud volunteer regiment.

The crowded and dirty life of a soldier rapidly caught up with the regiment. Disease, aided by the coming winter, struck violently at the rank and file. As the men waited to cross the mighty Potomac at Berlin, Maryland, many a cough and moan could be heard.

Captain Edwards ordered his men off of the road once again. It had been customary for such actions while on the march. The regiment would make several miles and then would be ordered off the roads. Artillery trains, cavalry, and ambulances would then clamor down the road. He could hear them rolling in the distance.

Several men of his company were ordered out of line and back onto the road. They had been sick for several days. Officers jolted down the line picking up these men in wagons, quickly pulling them away from their healthy comrades. The sick would be taken by train to Washington, where they would receive the care they needed. As this task was completed, Edwards pulled a sheet of paper from his coat, the latest roll call, and crossed out the names of the departed.

The rolling wheels of the carts cluttering the background, he looked to his remaining command. There were still plenty of them, but he could tell they had suffered, and they were yet to see combat. Edwards couldn't help but wonder what would happen when battle finally came to Company F. How many more names would be crossed off? How many more would be loaded and pulled away from their friends, their comrades? There will be plenty, he thought. His experience told him that much. He had not seen the last of the long ambulance trains or officers removing the weak and sick from his ranks.

Edwards then turned his attention to the craftsmanship and skill of the pontoon bridge floating atop the Potomac. The hostile fields of Virginia rested on the other shoreline, impatiently awaiting the coming intruders once more. He watched as the massive train streamed over the bridge, gently bouncing in the water, and climbed the banks of Virginia's soil. His eyes scanned the earth before him, squinted off into the distance. He wondered what awaited him on the other side.

Several of his men huddled together closely with dear friends and families. A cold wind sliced through the ranks. Edwards pulled away from their gaze and checked his watch. Chaplain Way had asked permission to offer a prayer before the regiment crossed onto enemy soil. It was due to start within twenty minutes. "Alright boys," he told his men. "Chaplain Way would like to offer some words. Get back on your feet. We don't need to take the road."

Without hesitation, the men stood up and formed in line. They slung their knapsacks over their shoulders and listened as Edwards gave them the order to march.

It would do them good to hear the soothing words of Way. The regiment had battled everything except the enemy. The men were tired, cold, and hungry. They missed home more than ever. Morale had yet to become an issue, but Morrow was determined to prevent it by any means necessary. He hoped that Way's suggestion of offering prayer to the regiment before they crossed into Virginia would ease the cold and dampened minds of his faithful soldiers.

Edwards hoped that it would do the same for him as well.

Lieutenant Colonel Mark Flanigan sat atop his horse, proudly watching the regiment step onto the pontoon bridge. He had always been inspired by the men, but on this day he had never been more so. They marched with a new determination, jaunting forward like an unstoppable machine. It seemed that the perils that awaited them in Virginia did not frighten them, did not slow their steps.

His mood was pleasant, having just seen his wife depart for home.

He loved having her in camp with him. The soldiers loved it as well. She busied herself greeting the soldiers, preparing meals, and mending tattered uniforms. As her husband tended to his work and the soldiers tended to their drill, she worked tirelessly in the background. For her husband, she brought with her stories of home and of the children. For the soldiers, she brought letters from loved ones and assurances that all was well back in Michigan.

Having traveled with several wives, Mrs. Flanigan enjoyed spending a portion of the day gathering with them and discussing all they witnessed and the events that led their husbands to war. Mark Flanigan enjoyed the conversations thoroughly, thinking it marvelous that the women, despite their lesser knowledge of war and politics, dared to converse on such matters. Following the long discussions, Mrs. Flanigan would return to him and relay all that the women had discussed. He would kindly listen, but be quick to remind his dear wife that war and politics were for men and that women should not be concerned with such dirty and dark affairs.

She always responded that one day things would shift, that one day women would enter a world once forbidden. Her response never contained a harsh word and her voice was never raised. She loved her husband. Mrs. Flanigan knew that he was, just as she was, a product of their time. So, she relented and tended to "women's" work, repairing clothing and preparing meals.

Flanigan smiled when he thought of her deep passion.

She was gone, however, heading back home to the children.

He gently urged his horse forward, matching the pace of the regiment. The animal's hooves stomped on the wooden pontoons, a distinct drumbeat to the dull rhythm of the march. The men met him there with warm smiles. He responded by gently bowing his head and touching the brim of his officer's kepi. Chaplain Way's words had done much to empower the men, to warm their souls. For this, Flanigan was grateful. Knowing that God was looking over them and that their friends and families would be waiting for their triumphant return, aided the men in taking the needed steps to complete their journey.

Across the Potomac the regiment surged, guided by the long blue line ahead of them and the tune of *Yankee Doodle* blasting from the Virginia shoreline. Flanigan quietly hummed the tune as he trotted forward. His spirit had been warmed. His confidence had been renewed. He felt new and fresh. The urgency of the situation was not on his mind, not for the time being. For now, he and the Twenty-Fourth Michigan strolled forward as if on dress parade, as if there wasn't a war raging. It was a peaceful and wonderful crossing for him.

As he guided his horse up the jagged Virginia shoreline, Flanigan thought of nothing other than returning home to his beloved wife and family when the war was over. And for what it was worth, he believed at that moment that he would do so in victory.

Morgan knelt down behind the fence and paid close attention to the house before him. He had been watching the position for several minutes. An old man lived there, rumored to have sons serving in the Confederate armies abroad. Morgan had heard several soldiers speak of how this old man boastfully told the Union men of this fact.

His pocket was full of his soldier's pay, separated into two divisions: a small amount for himself and the rest to be sent home to Emmy. Yet this wasn't on his mind as he scoped out the house and watched as the man settled comfortably inside. Morgan had not seen the man exit the house and assumed that he had bedded down for the evening. All was quiet and dark.

Kneeling next to him were men from the other regiments of the brigade, tossing their distrust for the green Michigan soldiers aside. They waved for Morgan and his comrades to follow them into the yard behind the house. There were several neat humps of haystacks, ideal for soft bedding. Chickens could be heard somewhere in the yard. The thought of more comfortable bedding and a good meal provoked these men onto the old man's land.

"Should we be doing this?" Morgan heard a soldier ask.

The response was sharp. "It's no worse than how they'd treat our homes."

Onward they went, sneaking into the yard, their bodies hunched over, low to the ground. A few men scampered ahead, making sure the area was clear. Bypassing the stacks of hay, these men headed straight for the chickens, opening the gate and pulling birds out of the darkness. The others, Morgan included, quickly followed. They did not want to be left empty-handed.

Morgan quietly instructed a friend to go ahead and grab a chicken while he collected hay for the both of them. He closed his arms around the pile and swallowed up more than enough hay. Pressing his bounty against his chest, he looked back and saw his friend racing toward him with a chicken. The bird cried once before its neck was snapped, silencing the alarm that surely would have gotten them caught. Sprinting past Morgan, the soldier looked back with a smile and boyish giggle.

Reaching the fence, Morgan quickly handed half the pile to his friend and stuffed the other half into his coat. They had been successful at this point, but it would be hard to bring a large amount of hay and a chicken into camp without getting noticed. So the chicken was stuffed into a knapsack before the two of them hurriedly left the scene. As they departed, a guard detail thrashed through the darkness to put an end to the pillage.

Escaping, Morgan could hear the cries of the old man as he realized what was taking place. His property was being stripped from him. By the time the guards got there, there was little left. Immediately several of them dispersed into the crowd in search of the stolen goods. Orders came through the ranks that officers were to check their companies and have all stolen goods returned.

Morgan reached his tent and unloaded the hidden hay. He clumsily pushed around in the darkness, stuffing loose hay under his blanket. Quickly, nervously, he shoved equal amounts in every direction, flattening out the blanket as he went. His friend, merely a tent away, collapsed to the ground and began digging a hole. Morgan could hear fabric being torn. His work finished, he inched closer to the exit and listened to see what came of his friend and the chicken. His stomach growled in hunger. "Finished," said his friend, just a tent over. The man climbed from his tent and crawled toward Morgan. "It's wrapped up nice and tight and buried. They won't find it. We'll roast it tonight."

A frightening commotion was all about them as Captain Edwards quickly strolled through camp. Morgan tensed up, perhaps believing to be caught. He quickly looked behind him, into his tent, and saw his bedding was flat as could be. Good, he thought. Edwards approached them and asked if the two of them had anything to do with the mischief, to which both of them denied having a hand in it. They sat in agony as Edwards probed the area around them, looking into Morgan's tent, and looking to both of them with judging eyes.

Morgan's stomach churned, not in hunger but in nervousness. Edwards leaned down toward them and Morgan knew the gig was up. "You have made great efforts to hide your prizes," he told them. "I suggest that it would be wise to share them with your company officer. He will return your generosity, I assure you."

Both men nodded, not wanting to risk punishment for their actions. Edwards departed and left them to their prizes. Morgan climbed inside the tent and rested on one of the softest beds he had since leaving Detroit. His friend went to work digging up the chicken and cleaning it off. It had not been a part of their plan, but their newly found supplies would have to stretch to the use of three instead of two.

Morgan rolled around comfortably. It didn't bother him that he would have to share a portion of the hay with Edwards. He was very much impressed with his company officer and thought highly of him. Morgan was fortunate to have a solid veteran leading him into battle and through the work of a soldier. A small portion of hay and a hearty piece of chicken was a small price to pay for Edwards' leadership.

The thought of his little adventure excited his mind. Reaching for his knapsack, he pulled out the pad of paper to pen a letter to Emmy. She would enjoy reading of his minor exploit. He could imagine her smiling as she read the words, as she read about how her husband almost got caught in the act by his officer.

He happily picked up the pencil and began to scribble away.

Color Sergeant Abel Peck enjoyed the regiment's new camp. It was wooded, offering protection from the gathering winter elements. He also enjoyed a moment without the great responsibility of carrying the flag. Colonel Morrow had called his company forward for a demonstration on how they should conduct themselves in battle. Peck had requested a break from the flag, and Morrow granted that he switch position with one of the color guards, so that Peck could partake in the demonstration.

He watched as Morrow stepped out in front of the company and politely told the men to relax. This was not a drill. There was no need for formalities. He explained to the men that what he was offering was information, advice, on how they should act in battle. Peck listened to the words carefully, knowing that Morrow had experience in Mexico. "Do not leave the regiment," Morrow explained, "unless wounded or dismissed by an officer. It is unmanly to vacate your position in the face of the enemy, to leave your comrades behind." The words seemed to echo through the woods. Morrow's distinct tone slashed through the pine needles and flimsy branches. "You will wait to fire until ordered," he continued. "An entire line of fire will do more than a single man. Do not think your single services useless, instead as a member of something greater, something more powerful. On the field of battle, we will act as one."

Peck watched with anticipation as a relaxed Morrow discussed with the company several possibilities. "We should be ready for them all," he told them. Peck smiled at the thought of the regiment in battle. He wondered how the men would conduct themselves, if they would live up to Morrow's high expectations. He wondered if Morrow would live up to theirs.

Morrow went on about how it would become necessary for the men to collect arms and ammunition from the dead and wounded. "Worry not for the fallen patriot," he said, "for he would give you all that he had if he could. He would not think it intrusive." Morrow then instructed the soldiers to keep an eye on the flag. During a battle, it would be hard for orders to be heard. Once loud bugle calls would fall silent to the thunder of armed conflict.

Peck thought about the men taking ammunition from their fallen friends and family. He wondered if any of them would do it. Would their own desire to stay alive and defeat the enemy drive them to commit such a desperate act? Only time would tell. He believed that despite its initial cruelty, stealing from the dead and wounded, it would become a necessity. He had never seen battle before. He had never witnessed the fury of man. If ammunition or arms was needed to hold precious ground, then who among them could honestly say that taking such from the fallen was beyond the conduct of a brave soldier.

He studied as Morrow displayed the proper firing stance, both standing and kneeling, while reiterating the importance to aim low. Then

Morrow moved on to discuss the proper way to fill the gaps left by fallen comrades. "We will do so without breaking stride, without slowing the movement of the regiment," he said.

After several more minutes of pleasant instruction, Surgeon Beech stepped forward to take over the demonstration. Peck moved closer to listen, to find out what the good surgeon had to offer. The voice he heard was raspy, weary, but calming. "Colonel Morrow has just offered advice on how we should conduct ourselves in battle," he reminded them. "A good soldier would put those words to use. And I have been called here to further instruct the conduct that is expected of you, mainly if you are wounded. It is far more likely you will be so, rather than killed in battle. I should remind you that it is possible to die from wounds received on the field. I will help you. I will advise you on the best measures to keep yourself alive if wounded."

Peck stared as Beech was handed a rifle, complete with a fixed bayonet. "The bayonet will prove instrumental in close combat. I must confess that one of these sharpened tools can be run through a man, in any number of places, without killing him." The brief lecture went on describing the expected areas of bayonet wounds and what to do in case it happened to any of the men. "The immediate response, as with all other wounds, is to put pressure on the wound. Blood lost is life lost and we cannot refill you as we do our water canteens." Beech continued with great clarity. "Prepare a bandage from your clothing and wrap it tightly around the wound."

Peck took in the information. He watched as Beech demonstrated the proper way to dress a wound and how to care for it without the presence of surgeons. As the surgeon's words concluded, ending the demonstration, Peck believed he had a solid understanding of how to conduct himself in battle. Much of this, while beneficial to the infantryman, would prove only as knowledge to Peck, as he was responsible for the flag. There were plenty of duties of his own he had to worry about, but he was pleased to witness the demonstration and primarily how to care for and dress a wound.

Before their dismissal, Morrow called them back to attention. He said, "If you are captured by the enemy and are asked where you come from, I insist that you tell them the truth." He smiled. "Tell them you come from the *United States of America* and proudly serve with the Twenty-Fourth Michigan."

The nervous men shared a hurried laugh while being dismissed.

As Peck slid away from his company to reclaim the flag, he heard the distant rumbling of artillery. His eyes followed the thundering, looking off over the trees toward a series of rising heights, a faded blue in the distance. He pondered the battle that was being fought and wondered if it would turn into the fight his regiment had long awaited. The rumbling continued, however, without creating much of a disturbance in camp. The only motion was that of Captain Edwards' Company F, being sent forward for picket duty.

A chilly gust of wind pushed him toward his tent, forcing him to move faster. It had been a wonderful day, the sky a clear blue with a few clouds dangling peacefully, but the strong wind picked up and reminded the soldiers that winter was vastly approaching. And when he pushed his way back into camp, he saw several men being carried out of their tents on wooden boards. Off to the hospital they would go, having fallen ill with the deteriorating weather and poor sanitary conditions of life in the army. He found no end to the spectacle as nearly every other tent seemed vacated by a poor sick soul. The wind came back again, slamming into the forest and cutting through the protective shell of the trees. Peck wrapped up in the warmth of his coat as he reached his tent, the color guard eager to exchange the heavy flag for his rifle.

He sat down inside his tent to escape the growing cold. The distant rumbling of cannon and the doctors' cries for the sick entertained him as he struggled to keep warm. His fingers too cold to flip through his Bible, he sat huddled on his blanket with his knees pressed against his chest, reciting the lessons learned from the demonstration. His shivering under control, he lost himself momentarily in glorious memories of home.

Suddenly he coughed. He brought his hand to his mouth to silence it. Then he coughed again, this time more violently, uncontrollably. His eyes grew wide and white at the thought of him suffering from disease, of being pulled from his comrades. Peck quickly fell to the blanket and covered himself with as many layers as he could.

What had started as a beautiful day was ending terribly. He prayed that by the time he woke in the morning, he would be free of the cough, free of the disease that ran rampant through the regiment.

Fighting off the cold and the pain, he finally reached out for his Bible.

Maybe the holy words would offer him some comfort.

The Twenty-Fourth Michigan continued its trek through Virginia. By early November, because he was senior officer of the brigade behind General Gibbon, Colonel Morrow took temporary command of the Iron Brigade following Gibbon's promotion to division command. This act further alienated the green Twenty-Fourth from the hardened veterans of the brigade. Not only having to deal with new recruits, the hardened soldiers of the brigade had to see their beloved commander replaced by a new and untested officer. Gibbon, perhaps sensing the growing animosity between his regiments, sought out Morrow and requested that Morrow refuse the command of the brigade. Remembering Gibbon's talk about rising above expectations, Morrow could not bring himself to relent to Gibbon and accepted temporary command of the brigade.

As Morrow led the brigade forward, the army commanders busied themselves searching for a replacement to lead the already storied Iron Brigade.

Colonel Morrow pulled ahead of the lead elements of the brigade. From the moment the column turned down the old road, Morrow knew it was familiar. When he saw the picturesque buildings rising from the rolling hills, he knew he had returned to his boyhood home, Warrenton, Virginia.

Lieutenant Whiting, selected to be Morrow's aide, moved out to meet his commander. Upon reaching Morrow, he found the officer stopped in the center of the road, watching the last line of Confederates pull away from the quiet town. "You mustn't ride too far ahead, sir," Whiting lectured. "It will do us no good if something were to happen to you."

Morrow smiled. "I am fine, Mr. Whiting."

"I see that, sir."

"Well, then."

Whiting sighed. "You should let the brigade enter first. The enemy has just departed and, if I may say so, sir, it would be foolish for you to enter before it."

"I know this place," replied Morrow.

"It is a disloyal town, sir."

Morrow nodded. "I was born here, grew up into boyhood. I learned to ride a horse here. I can remember it very clearly."

Whiting paused. "I mean no offense, Colonel."

"Oh," cried Morrow with a smile, "none taken, Mr. Whiting. This place was only home at birth and a few years beyond. My home is much farther north now."

"Indeed, sir. Shall I send a company forward?"

He nodded again. "Very well, send them in. I will ride in with them, though, Mr. Whiting. I would very much like to see my old house, the yard I played in."

Whiting departed and ordered a company forward. Morrow heard their footsteps approach, the shouts of the officers urging them on. He turned in the saddle and watched them come up behind him, eventually passing him and marching into the center of town. As the last row of men made the turn, Morrow spurred his horse forward. Whiting ordered another company in before bringing up the rest of the brigade.

Again venturing from the safety of the brigade, Morrow turned down another road and headed for the familiar house. Along the way he retraced the steps he took there in his childhood, remembering it as a happy and loving one. The building, like the rest in the town, was closed and dark. A few old secession flags hung from dark windows. As he looked toward the house he had known in earlier life, it saddened him to see the large traitorous flag hanging from a window.

He inched closer to the house, remembering it as being vastly different in his youth. The streets were vacant and empty; while in his memories they were bustling and alive. He could remember friendly neighbors and citizens. None greeted him then, not as he slowly rode through the town in federal blue. Turning his horse around, he drove the animal toward the cemetery. Behind him he could hear the clamor of Whiting and an armed escort approaching. He had not gotten used to it all, commanding a brigade. Things operated differently from what he had known with the regiment. He sometimes struggled with tasks, but always worked to complete them. Morrow knew he was learning valuable lessons that would one day, if he were fortunate enough, help advance his career in the army.

Ignoring Whiting's pleas to wait up, Morrow dismounted and calmly made his way into the cemetery toward his mother's grave. The young aide, not wanting to let his commander escape from his watch once again, steadied himself when he saw the name on the stone from the cemetery's entrance. He no longer called for Morrow's attention. Whiting simply turned and ordered the escort to wait and bellowed that he would receive all incoming messages to Morrow for the time being.

Morrow slowly approached the stone. Fresh flowers had been placed at the site, perhaps just days ago. He wondered if a longtime friend, still mourning the loss of the women he called mother, had carefully placed them there. The memories of her filled his head. They were happy, joyous. He remembered watching her work in the kitchen. He remembered the fresh scent of warm bread. Morrow remembered her as a devoted mother and southerner. She was a true example of a southern woman. There was class, charm, beauty, and strength. All of those things he remembered of her. All of those things she wanted to instill in her little boy.

And what had come of him? What had come of her beloved son?

He had returned home to her, albeit momentarily. Not as the youthful boy she remembered, but as a man, a loyal Union man at that. Morrow wondered how she would react to her son fighting against her home, the people she called friends and family. He asked if she would have been proud of him, no matter the blue uniform. Perhaps their ideals would have been different. Perhaps their views would have collided, a compromise unreachable, a dream. Yet she would still look to him as her son. He would still look to her as his mother. It was a bond that remained strong, no matter feelings or opinions. It was this bond, Morrow believed, that would have her open the door to greet him as he rode into town, blue uniform and all. But she was gone. There were no open doors. The building he once called home was dark and lifeless. The town he had once roamed was empty and damp.

Wiping a tear from his face, he turned around to meet Whiting. "You must excuse me, Mr. Whiting. I have not returned here for many years. It is a shame that I should do so at a time like this."

Whiting tapped on the black iron fence enclosing the cemetery. "There is no shame in returning home, Colonel Morrow."

Morrow mounted his horse and looked back toward his mother's grave. "No," he said quietly, "it is a shame that I can no longer call this place home." He pulled the animal away from the cemetery. An aide approached with news that Confederate guerillas had attacked several wagons in the rear. "And how holds the good Twenty-Fourth?" asked Morrow. The aide replied that the wagons assaulted were not guarded by the Twenty-Fourth, and that all was well with Morrow's regiment. "Well," Morrow said turning to Whiting, "Mark has the boys holding their own back there. We should call them up in a hurry and give them some rest. I believe it best to leave this place and distance ourselves from it."

Whiting saluted, accompanying the gesture with a warm smile. "Indeed, Colonel, sir. I shall move the brigade out immediately."

To the aide, Morrow said, "Call up Lieutenant Colonel Flanigan and the Twenty-Fourth, for I am homesick and seeing the boys again would do me some good."

The aides departed, veering off into opposite directions. Morrow felt the armed escort gather around him, politely telling him that it was time to move. Turning back once more in the saddle, he silently said farewell to his dear mother.

He cared not to see his old boyhood home with the secession flag draped from the window. Morrow preferred to remember the house as it was in his memories.

Perhaps that was how God meant it to be.

Morgan marched into Warrenton with sore feet. The regiment had hurried its pace to catch up with the rest of the brigade, having successfully defended a portion of the wagon train. He was tired, cold, and hungry. It was extremely dark by the time he trampled into the town. Fires scattered across the landscape, as the men finally settled. It was well after midnight.

Ordered to meet up with the brigade, Morgan pushed even harder to maneuver the last few hundred yards. Finally reaching his destination, he collapsed to the earth in exhaustion. Sweat rolled down his face. His clothes were drenched. He thought of removing his outer layers to cool down, but thought otherwise to avoid disease. Morgan had been fortunate enough to avoid the crippling sickness that took its toll on the regiment. He wasn't about to push his luck.

Falling upon the solid ground, Morgan struggled to pull out the gear needed to bed down for the night. He was too weary and frustrated to fiddle with his tent, so he compromised by wrapping himself first in his blanket and then with the canvas. Anything to help his body fight off the cold that was growing in the night, hunting for those less fortunate and those less prepared.

His stomach bellowed in hunger, but he was too tired to eat. He had become comfortably warm in his improvised shell and was quite impressed with his ability to fight off the hampering elements. Several men from his company gathered around him, simulating the method that seemed to work for Morgan. A few of them, not yet ready to settle for the night, agreed that they would build and tend to a fire, in hopes that its radiant heat would do much to warm the cold men through the night.

Morgan didn't mind the usual noise of men settling down. He barely heard their quiet conversations and didn't even hear the rustling of the logs as the fire was pieced together. It was too late and he was too tired to be concerned with such. And, like Morgan, as soon as the others wrapped themselves in their makeshift cocoons, they quickly drifted off to sleep.

The throbbing pain of his feet finally faded away as Morgan closed his eyes.

A fresh gust of wind swept through the trees around them, sweeping over the rolling hills protecting their campsite. Only those left up to handle the fires guessed at what the midwinter-like weather would bring. And even they too, having prodded the fires to life long enough, settled down and quickly fell asleep.

It looked to him as if hundreds of small snow mounds had been built overnight. Captain Edwards had gotten little rest, but when he awoke he found himself dusting off a few inches of snow. Standing up, he wrapped his arms around his chest and shivered in the chilly wind. The elements had struck again, covering the regiment with a blanket of snow in a few short hours.

He struggled as he pushed himself through the snow toward headquarters. He had been out of food for two days. There had been no sign of supplies coming toward camp and he was growing restless. His men came to him and pleaded that he give them food, but he could only tell them to conserve what they had, that food was coming. For a while he believed that the trains would arrive, but now he thought otherwise. Perhaps they had been bogged down by the terrible weather. Perhaps the trains had been captured or burned by Confederates. Either way, Edwards hoped that Colonel Morrow could give him better answers. It was the first time the Twenty-Fourth had to suffer without sufficient supplies. The hungry men sought out any officer available and voiced their concerns.

The sun was climbing into the sky behind him. He could feel the warmth of its rays catch him. Again he shivered. His clothes were wet and damp. He hoped the sun would shine long enough to help him dry his uniform. The dark clouds gathering above him told him otherwise, however.

Slowly the men around him broke free from their snow coffins and brushed the white flakes from their bodies. A few fires dotted the hazy landscape, as soldiers began to rise. Some of them called to him as he went by. They begged for food. They repeatedly told Edwards of their hunger. They asked when the supply train would be up. He could give them no answers. He had none. Edwards simply paced by them without muttering a word, his arms wrapped around his body, still trying to warm himself.

Closer and closer he slid toward Morrow's headquarters. There he would find the answers he sought. As he trekked through the snow, he saw Lieutenant Colonel Flanigan approach from the right. The Irishman stooped his body against the icy wind, his head low as his feet plugged away. In his hands was a cup of coffee. Edwards could see the steam dance into the air above the tin cup. He had run out of coffee and desired the drink more than ever. Battling the wind, he turned to meet Flanigan.

"Captain Edwards, lad," greeted the burly Irishman. Flanigan leaned in and looked Edwards over as a surgeon would look to a patient. "You look worse for wear," he commented. "This ought to do you some good." He quickly handed the steaming cup of coffee over to Edwards.

He quickly accepted Flanigan's offer. The steaming hot liquid burned his cold lips when they met. Edwards guzzled slowly, sipping the liquid, hoping to savor the flavor, the warmth. Embarrassed, he shoved the cup back to Flanigan. "I mustn't take it all," he said. "I insist that you drink it with me."

Flanigan raised an arm in protest. "I've had too much."

"Please, it does not seem right."

"I must decline, Captain Edwards. You drink it."

Edwards took another sip. The liquid slithered down through his body, warming his cold soul. When the cup was empty, he handed it back to Flanigan. "You are most kind," Edwards stated. "When the time comes for you to drink from my cup, I shall surrender it politely."

The wind rose up between them, blowing snow in their faces. Flanigan tucked the cup away in his knapsack and turned toward Morrow's headquarters. "I assume," he said to Edwards, "that you and I are here for the same objective, Captain."

He nodded. "The men need food."

Flanigan replied, "Then we shall see what is keeping it from them."

His health slightly restored, Edwards marched through the snow toward Colonel Morrow's tent with stronger strides. The coffee had indeed done him some good.

Colonel Morrow wasn't at his headquarters. Like most of the officers of the regiment, he had slept little in the night. He spent much of it looking over paperwork, organizing reports, and trying to locate the brigade's supplies. Morrow worked tirelessly through the night, but by the time the sun rose from the treetops, he felt as if he hadn't achieved anything at all. The paperwork, it seemed, never had an end. There was always some commander with this concern or that concern. There was always the need to write reports, to keep his superiors knowledgeable as to the condition and placement of the Iron Brigade. The work streamed like a massive river, its current carrying Morrow further downstream.

To seclude himself from the workload, he tried to sleep. When this tactic failed, he turned to the Bible and slowly read from the crisp pages. It was important for him to try and read from the book every night before he retired. The words soothed his soul, and during the previous night, had warmed his shivering body. An hour before the sun rose, he was outside and mounted on his horse. He had grown weary of the paperwork, he could not sleep, and he had read the desired passage from the Bible several times. The supplies had not yet arrived and Morrow wanted to personally check on the condition of the regiment. After informing Whiting of his plans, Morrow trotted off through the last of the snowstorm which had buried much of his command.

Despite the weather, the ride was a pleasant one. The men were buried under the snow, sleeping, gaining strength, as Morrow rode between them. He came across several officers from the brigade taking a morning stroll to warm their bodies, and he had polite conversations with them. They briefly discussed the terrible weather and pondered if the army would advance for one more campaign before the full weight of winter fell on them. Rumors had circulated that General McClellan, in command of the army, had soured his ties to Washington and was in danger of being relieved from command. The officers dared not debate on if such should happen, but concluded that if the army were indeed preparing for a campaign, then a change of commanders would be risky.

Morrow departed the gentlemen and toured the camp of the Twenty-Fourth. By the time he reached it, the men were rising from their slumber and working feverishly to build fires. When they saw him, they waved to him and called out their needs. Before long, Morrow rode to a chorus of "Hardtack!" The men shouted impatiently, for they had waited long enough for supplies. With each trot of his horse, Morrow listened to their cries. He attempted to respond to the complaints, telling them that he was seeing to the matter and that the supplies were expected later in the day. The men again shouted, "Hardtack!"

He pulled away from them feeling the full burden of his command. The weather was impeding further movement. The supply train had failed to arrive on time. Just as the men were, Morrow too found himself growing impatient. He grew increasingly frustrated with the brass of command, primarily McClellan. The army was motionless and suffering. Surely the enemy was trapped just the same, bogged down by the building winter and the tangled web of military bureaucracies. Morrow wanted quick, decisive action. The supply trains should have arrived by now. His men should have been fed.

As he rode back to headquarters, he could not help but think of a recent conversation he had with General Hooker. "McClellan is a capable bureaucrat," Hooker told him. "He is good at entertaining social events and completing all expected paperwork. Mac is very meticulous in this regard. He has built and organized a worthy army. He just fails to use it. And for this his command of this army should be sacked." The words rattled through Morrow's thoughts as he returned to his tent. Hooker was clearly anti-McClellan, his stand on such ruffling the feathers of high command and Washington alike. Yet Hooker had made an impact on Morrow. Both men were immediately impressed by the other. Perhaps this was the reason that Morrow sided with the fiery Joseph Hooker. But Morrow had been with the army long enough to realize its defects, resulting from its commander, and to realize its untapped potential. He knew the army was more than capable of meeting their Confederate opponent in battle and winning, sweeping the field in victory. Antietam should have been an indicator to McClellan of just what kind of power he held at his command. The Army of the Potomac was a powerful tool. It just needed to be used properly.

His horse plowed through a bank of snow and stopped short of the tent. Whiting came out to take the animal away. He informed Morrow of the most recent news and that the supply train was well on its way to the brigade. "Marvelous, Mr. Whiting," Morrow replied. "Tell the drivers to cut straight through the camp. The men will enjoy the sight."

"Right away, sir," replied Whiting. Then the young aide fumbled about his coat, finally revealing a small envelope. "This arrived from your wife, Colonel. I thought you'd want it as soon as possible."

Morrow took the envelope. "Thank you, Mr. Whiting." His lips curled into a smile. It had been a couple of weeks since he had seen a letter from her. Having sent Whiting away on errands, Morrow happily retired to his tent to read the letter, alone, in peace.

Outside, the distant rumble of a wagon train serenaded the hungry men of the brigade. Eagerly they stood from their huddled groups, hoping that supplies had finally arrived. And when the first two wagons appeared on the snowy horizon, the moaning cries were replaced by thunderous cheers and applause.

My dear Emmy, wrote Morgan. *Our hardships and trials have yet to pass. I fear there will be many more days like the ones we have suffered of late. We have come near a place where Colonel Morrow knew as a boy. It is a very dark and disloyal place. Not a soul greeted us. I find it hard to believe that such a noble patriot could have risen from such a traitorous village. He toured the streets before we got here, but I am told that he did not stay but awhile.*

He gently tapped his chin with the pencil, trying to pull words from his thoughts as they floated by. *We were close enough to see the fires of the enemy's pickets. We have seen no action as the Rebels vacated the village once the brigade arrived. There are those among us that fear they are whipped. Of this, I am not sure. I have seen little of them other than of prisoners and wounded. For the most part, they are sociable and well educated. I find it hard to believe that they would fight for such an unjust cause. But I imagine that they think the same of me. The weather has been very intolerable here. It is cold and we have been brought to a halt. There are rumors that the army will move one more time before winter sets in. For this also, I do not know. I think it better to leave such decisions to more educated soldiers in the ranks above.*

I hope that all is well at home and getting along without me. I ask that you send another picture of you with your next letter. I am afraid mine has been broken through service. Please remember to pray for me and all our brave patriots. Love, Morgan.

He folded up the paper and slid it into an envelope, the last one he had, which reminded him that he needed to purchase more in the morning.

Crunching through the snow, he heard footsteps approaching his tent. He crawled out the flaps and met a comrade standing against a tree. Reaching back into his tent, Morgan pulled out his rifle and slung it over his shoulder. "I am ready," he told the comrade.

Morgan's company had once again been assigned picket duty.

The work of a soldier never ended.

WINDS OF CHANGE

General George McClellan was relieved from command of the Army of the Potomac and took his farewell leave on November 10, 1862. The rumors that had persisted, entertaining anti-McClellan men and terrifying pro-McClellan men, had proved to be true. General McClellan and Washington could never come to the same conclusions. The man that had built the Army of the Potomac was tossed aside for the final time, being replaced by General Ambrose Burnside.

It was clear that the government wanted action. Burnside took to the maps in construction of a grand scheme that would give them just that, and hopefully bring the war to a close in the east.

Change came once again for the Iron Brigade as well. Colonel Morrow, having successfully led the brigade as temporary commander, was returned to the Twenty-Fourth Michigan, and General Solomon Meredith was called to duty. Meredith was a proven veteran, having served in the Nineteenth Indiana. A disagreement between him and then brigade commander Gibbon forced Meredith's departure. Since he left the army, he spent his time lobbying for an all Indiana brigade, hoping to extract the Nineteenth from the Iron Brigade. His dream, however, was unattainable. Meredith, upon Gibbon's promotion, leaped upon the chance to command the brigade.

Despite the sour mood resulting from McClellan's dismissal, the rank and file of the Army of the Potomac was ready for another go at Lee's Army of Northern Virginia. If they could get the chance, many a soldier believed they would be in Richmond by Christmas.

Having served just a month under McClellan, it mattered little to Abel Peck as to who commanded the army. He had little to say about the dismissed commander, and dared not criticize him in the face of the veterans. The hardened soldiers had a bond with McClellan that seemed near unbreakable. There were those among the veteran ranks that threatened to leave the army if McClellan wasn't reinstated.

Peck had signed for three years. He would serve just that, no matter who was in command. He hoped that the veterans would feel the same as well. Those soldiers spent a better part of their day grumbling about bad politics and cheerfully remembering days long passed when McClellan loved them, looked over them, like a father.

For his part, Peck thought of only the future. There was no use dwelling on the past. McClellan was gone. Sooner or later the army would get used to life without him. Burnside was, after all, a good friend of McClellan's. The angered soldiers should have taken that into consideration.

There were more important things on his mind anyway. The regiment had suffered its second death since leaving Michigan, and Peck knew the deceased. The man hailed from Nankin, the same town as Peck. The two had enlisted together and were good acquaintances. Peck had learned a great deal about the man during the regiment's travels. He enjoyed the time they spent together. It was sad to see such a friend leave without touching upon the possibility of glory, without meeting the enemy on the field of battle. The deceased soldier had been pulled from the ranks and trained to Washington for better care. Peck heard that the doctors and nurses did all they could for him, but he died ten days after arriving. The last time Peck had seen the soldier was when he was being helped into a cart when the regiment stopped in Berlin, Maryland.

Peck questioned whether he should send a letter off to the soldier's family, detailing his bravery, commitment, and courage. It would be a sad thing to write such a letter, to describe how the soldier died. His death was not the glorious death sought after by soldiers. Yet, somehow, his abrupt end of life, taken by disease, was the most prevalent threat. Peck was beginning to learn that few died in actual battle. His chances, he believed, of dying in an engagement were pretty slim. If anything happened to him at all, he would be wounded. With any luck, the wound would be minor and he would be back on his feet with the regiment in a few weeks. If his luck was worse and the wound was more terrible, then at least he could be sent home with his wife and family.

There would be no going home for his fallen friend and comrade. Peck assured himself that he would send a letter, through his wife, to the family. He was certain of that. What he wasn't certain was of how he was going to tell them, how he would break the news. The letter would have to be immediately penned and sent with the body or else the wooden casket would arrive before it. He did not want the soldier's family suffering the pain of seeing the pine box. Not before they were told how he perished and how he had conducted himself as a soldier. He knew the words would offer very little comfort, but they needed to be sent anyway. The soldier had earned that. His family had too.

The situation forced Peck to think about his own death, should it come during the war. It pained him to think of his wife and daughter struggling without him. He didn't like to think of it, but he could not shake the thoughts. He could only accept them and hope they would not come true. And, should he be among the fallen, he only hoped that one of his comrades would send a caring letter to his family, just as Peck would do for the deceased soldier.

Peck was tired and weak. He had been battling a cough for several days. He did his best to continue with his training and marching, but made sure he didn't push himself too far. Disease was always on the doorstep, as too many of his comrades had fallen ill over the last few days. The short rations, the cold, the drilling, and being penned together like cattle created a proper breeding ground for all sorts of illnesses. Peck himself had grown tired of the poor sanitary conditions within the army. There never seemed to be enough latrines for all of the men. There never seemed to be enough hospitals. And there never seemed to be enough room between the healthy and the sick.

And then he thought of the irony of it all and a smile came over his face.

He had three solid years of this left.

Colonel Morrow slid into the hospital tent and gasped at what he saw. He had heard stories about the place and its condition, but he never expected to verify them all. Pneumonia had spread across the scattered camps of the army, withering able regiments down to skeletons of their former numbers. Yellow skin and shallow black eyes of disease had been the decoration of the army, and the hospital tent was its horrifying centerpiece.

Upon entering the tent, he wanted to leave but stayed. Better judgment got the best of him, and he was determined to do all that he could for the poor souls inside. So he moved among them, sometimes fighting off the urge to turn his head away from the sights, the smells. The tent was filled to near capacity and the space that was available for each man wasn't fit enough for a young boy. Men were scattered about the tent, some on tables and cots, and other rested on boards placed on the cold ground. Nurses fluttered about like angels, tending to those calling for them. Chaplains came and went, offering prayers to those who sought the assistance of God.

As he slid between the staggered rows, men reached out to him. Some were familiar and from the regiment. He bent down and greeted everyone he could, offering encouraging and hopeful words. At several times his voice broke and shuttered, as he struggled to hold back his emotions.

Retreating back to the entrance of the tent, he found a nurse carefully tending to one of the patients. "Excuse me," Morrow called to her. She turned around as if she expected to see a sick, thin body. Her eyes looked to Morrow's and he could see her exhaustion, her frustration. Morrow said, "Who's in command here?" The woman shrugged her shoulders and then softly told Morrow that she had just arrived that morning. She had only seen nurses tend to the sick. Not a doctor or surgeon had stepped inside the tent that she knew of. Morrow shook his head in disappointment. "Would you mind," he asked her, "if I send my surgeons?" The women shook her head. They could use the help, she told him. "We need to get the sick out of here," Morrow replied. "What good can we do for them here, like this?"

He left the hospital tent and called for his surgeons. Beech was the first to arrive and Morrow told him of the predicament, the conditions of the tent. Beech agreed that the sick would have to be moved and that it would be better if they were contained in a building, away from the hampering elements. "I'll go and see what I can do for them," Beech said. "You find a more suitable place."

Morrow dashed off to find a capable dwelling. Along the way he came into contact with Flanigan, who rushed to him with news from the regiment. "They don't want to bury him here, Colonel," pleaded the Irishman.

"What?" replied Morrow.

Flanigan barked, "Curtiss, of Company C, sir." He caught up and matched Morrow's frantic pace. "The men feel it would be better to send the body home."

"We can't." Morrow moved faster.

"Something must be done for them, sir. The lads don't want to leave him behind here. This is not a place he knew." Flanigan's long legs struggled to keep up with Morrow. Finally, he extended an arm that brought Morrow to a standstill. Stepping in front of him, Flanigan bent down slightly to look Morrow in the eyes. "Colonel, sir, Henry, the men do not want to see him buried here. He'll be too far from home."

Morrow nodded, finally paying full attention to the matter. "As trying as it is for us to see a Michigan man buried in this soil, we must come to the conclusion that although he will be far from home, he will not be alone. There are hundreds of others being buried from other states, further away than Michigan. It is a lesson that the men will have to learn, that we are forced to accept."

"Understood, Henry, but the men are stubborn."

He nodded again. "There is nothing we can do, Mark. We both know that. We will bury him with full honors."

Flanigan agreed. "What do I tell them?"

"Tell them they have done all they could for him. Curtiss will be buried here, where he fell. And tell them that he will share equal ground with other fallen soldiers from other states because they were all Union men and they died in service of it."

Flanigan took his leave and left. Morrow continued his search for a suitable building but came up empty-handed. There were several houses, but none of them were available. Officers scampered toward the dwellings and quickly made them into their headquarters. Morrow pleaded his case but to no avail. When he brought his case before a fellow officer in the streets, Morrow was directed to General George Meade. It was a coincidence that just might pay off, as Meade had served in Detroit while preparing a survey of Michigan's coastlines. The two had met on several occasions in the city and had formed a warm acquaintanceship.

General Meade proved a worthy audience. After hearing Morrow's complaints about the hospital tent, he toured the sight himself with several of his aides. Meade immediately issued a court martial and placed the building in the hands of reliable surgeons.

Morrow had accomplished his task of removing the sick. A house was selected, its army occupants sent packing, and the sick were carefully carried inside. Morrow and Beech themselves oversaw the movement, making sure that every sick soldier received the most thorough care available. As for the hardworking nurses, Morrow ordered them to retire for the evening so that they could get some rest. He even detailed several volunteers from the Twenty-Fourth to serve as aides and care for the sick.

And when he finally retired that evening, he could not help but think of Curtiss, the poor deceased soldier. He understood the concerns of burying the man so far from home, but there was nothing Morrow could do. It was just another situation that Morrow had no control over. He was getting used to seeing them. But getting used to them and growing adjusted to them were two different things. While Morrow accepted the fact that there was nothing he could do, he still made an attempt. So when he returned to his cold tent, he made a formal request to General Meredith to send Curtiss' body back home to Michigan. He knew that it would be denied, as the army was preparing for another campaign and Meredith would have more pressing things on his mind.

But he still handed the request to Whiting and asked that it be delivered immediately. It was the least he could do for the deceased soldier. It was the least he could do for his men.

The air choked with the sounds of shovels, axes, and saws. Morgan added to the deafening clamor by driving his shovel into the cold earth. His arms were sore and weary. He had a headache. His frustration level had peaked. Normally mild-mannered, Morgan exploded from his shell by complaining of the workload to his comrades. He strayed away from profanity, struggling to keep at least a little dignity. "We march. We train. We drill on parade. We dig. We eat a little and then sleep a little," he howled. "Then we rise and do it all again."

His comrades remained silent. They didn't like the work anymore than Morgan, but they kept their opinions to themselves. Instead of voicing their frustrations, they used the emotion to fuel each drive into the soil. The steadier the pace, the quicker they could retire for the evening. As their tools slammed into the earth, Morgan entertained them with his surprising rant. After wiping the sweat from his forehead, Morgan continued. "Some campaign this is, boys. We move a little. We dig a lot.

Then we move a little more. It's a snail's pace, it seems." He dropped his shovel. Stepping up from the growing trench, he pointed across toward the woods in the hazy distance. "We know they're there. Why don't we just go greet them? Why do we stop and dig trenches every few feet?"

His argument was one of the many complexities of war that Morgan and the common soldier, for the most part, did not understand. To them, the war was as simple as grabbing their rifles and sprinting off toward the sound of action. Especially to Morgan, who was trained in the art of the soldier but had yet to see combat, the idea of strategically placing the army against the enemy was useless and ineffective. Fueling his beliefs were the countless Confederate picket fires burning in the night, seemingly only a short march away. So his philosophy was simple: they are there, so go get them. The commanders, however, viewed it differently. War had developed into so much more than men simply shooting at each other. War could be won by maneuvers, quick marches, and even a dramatic show of force.

Not wanting to abandon his comrades, Morgan reluctantly went back to digging. Despite the continuous growth of his frustration, he held himself in check. He had rattled off and spewed more than enough fire for one day. Like his comrades, he realized it was better to see to the task at hand than to complain about it, for that too proved useless and ineffective. And his comrades, despite their initial amusement of Morgan's spectacle, had grown tired of his complaints, so they were careful not to trigger any more outbursts that would surely draw the attention of their officers.

The trigger, however, would come from somewhere else. The clamor of the tools meeting the cold earth silenced the arrival of the wolves, those soldiers from Wisconsin whom Morgan had met when he first toured the camp. They stood above the trench and watched the Michigan men work with excitement, smiles on their dirty faces. They took great interest in Morgan, instantly recognizable as the deer who had stumbled into their camp not long ago. "Hey, *Michigan!*" was their call. Morgan quickly glanced up, his bottled emotions boiling. The wolves continued their taunt, "Keep at it, boy. Take your time. We'll do the fighting while you do the digging!" A comrade quickly reacted by calming Morgan. Soft words of forgiveness were spoken, but Morgan's only thoughts were of revenge. His dignity still intact, Morgan continued to work, continued to ignore the calls from above. "That a way, *Michigan,*" they mocked, "you're digging like a soldier now. I bet your pretty girl back home is mighty proud of you."

His frustration exploded and he tossed the shovel aside and threw his kepi down to the ground, amid the laugher of the wolves above. He immediately looked up to them. The sun blocked his view and hid the faces of his aggressors. They responded with more laughter, knowing they had rattled another raw soldier. "By the way, boy," they called to him again. "You missed a spot!"

Morgan's response was immediate. "Come down here and show me where, you son-of-a-bitch!" The shovel was kicked aside, tumbling against the cold earth one final time, and Morgan took to pulling himself out of the trench. As he quickly got to his feet on the ground several inches above, the wolves had scattered. Captain Edwards had heard the commotion and set out to bring it to an end. He met Morgan at the base of the trench, the officer's arms folded across his chest. Morgan shuffled his feet backward, struggling to get away from Edwards' grasp. He felt foolish for his rant and even more foolish for his behavior. Never before had he been so rattled. Never before had he wanted to kill a man.

Fortunately for him, Edwards had heard the banter of the wolves, had known they had lit the fire under Morgan.

"Back to the line," Edwards muttered. "I don't want to see that happen again."

"It won't, sir," reasoned Morgan.

"See to it," he said.

Morgan leaped back down into the trench and grabbed his shovel. He was angry and embarrassed, a volatile mix if not cared for. So Edwards made sure that he straddled that portion of the line, to watch over the aggravated Morgan and to protect the deer of Company F from the Wisconsin wolves.

And Morgan thought of nothing other than revenge.

Lieutenant Colonel Mark Flanigan removed his kepi before offering a few solemn words to the small congregation, gathered around a pine box and a dark hole. The burial was the second for the regiment in couple of weeks. It was the third official death since they had left Michigan. The oldest of those enlisted, James Nowlin, had died just hours before. While at the time of his enlistment he listed his age at forty-three, he was actually seventy. Morrow and Flanigan were onto it, but could not help but admire the aging soldier's patriotism.

Flanigan admired Nowlin's bravery and his peaceful words reflected such. As he spoke, the few soldiers around the box huddled together and offered their final goodbyes. Another Michigan soul had departed before it could shine, before it was given the chance to prove itself as an honorable soldier. This too, was added into Flanigan's thoughtful words. The words themselves were of pure beauty and elegance, perhaps fit more for royalty than and old soldier. Never one to offer any public words or address such situations, Flanigan found himself breaking from his shell, if only momentarily, to honor the old fallen soldier. Once his words were completed, Flanigan stumbled back to his old self and stood awkwardly gazing at the small, depressed group before him. He quickly slid away into the darkness before he had to say anything else.

The pine box, fresh from the Quartermaster, was lowered into the earth behind him, forever entombing the oldest member to have served with the Twenty-Fourth. Flanigan shook his head at the tragic thought that it was another homesick soul resting too far from home. It was just another Michigan man laid to rest in Virginia soil. How many more would there be? How many more pine boxes?

He did not know.

All around him, seemingly oblivious to the small funeral service, the army was bustling with excitement. The veterans were relaxed, calm, cool, and collected. They prepared their arms with ease, careful attention. The green soldiers, those new to war, fumbled over their equipment, listening to stories of what to expect when they met their enemies. The excitement had swallowed up Flanigan too. As soon as he left the service, he swelled with pride, anticipation for what was to come. No sooner had Nowlin's body been covered with black soil and Flanigan asked himself how many more would suffer the same, did he look forward to an open engagement with the traitors, a deadly exchange that would surely send men to their graves. It was just another irony among countless in the war, but Flanigan was too excited to dwell on it.

Just when the engagement would come, he could not guess. There was still much to be done before the army could move. No marching orders had been established, and Flanigan believed that the army would stay in camp a few more days. He had even been told that a few days before a battle, the commanders would stop all drills and training, giving the rank and file much needed rest. Of this, he was not sure either. It was all new to him. The excitement and thought of battle were foreign.

He made his way toward regimental headquarters. It was only then, when he thought of issuing the latest report to Morrow, he thought again of poor old Nowlin. The old soldier, so hopeful in his efforts, did not live long enough to meet the Rebels. There was no chance of glory. It saddened him to think of it. The idea that the old faithful soldier wouldn't partake in the regiment's battles seemed too much to bear. The journey for the men of the Twenty-Fourth had just begun, while Nowlin's had come to an abrupt end.

The thoughts circled and danced about. Tragic they were, but he could not push them away, could not shake them. He stopped outside headquarters to collect his thoughts before entering. His emotions changed in little time. From excitement to depression he sank, his soul battling the tragic thoughts. It proved to be a weight that was hard for his massive frame to bear, falling upon his broad shoulders. He took deep breaths, hoping to regain composure, to steady against the raging tides of thoughts and questions, all of which concerned a path he did not know, a fate he could not control.

Color Sergeant Abel Peck stood at the center of the line as the sun rose from the trees before him. The flag in his hands was unfurled and flapping in the chilly wind. His hands gripped the wooden staff to balance the heavy cloth. As had been the same with the days before, he was tired, hungry, and cold. He, with the rest of the regiment, had been awoken earlier than usual. The soldiers stumbled about camp and quickly gathered their breakfast, forcing themselves to wake up, to prepare for another hard day of digging trenches. Like rusty machines they practiced the routine, finishing breakfast and then separating into their individual companies for the morning roll.

Unlike machines, however, the men quickly grew tired of their assigned busy work and the harassment from the veterans, who seemed to keep their hands clean of dirt and hard labor for the time being. Peck struggled as he watched his comrades work hard and endure the torture of the brigade. The work, he knew, was needed. The army needed trenches. Someone had to dig them. Why shouldn't it be the new regiment? But Peck was one of the few fortunate souls who did not have to bear the demanding workload. He simply followed Colonel Morrow around with the flag, setting up where the officer set up. Being responsible for the flag was just as tiring of service as manual labor, but there were those in the regiment's rank and file that did not see it as so. Knowing this, Peck received permission on a few occasions to join his company at work. He got in with the men and got his hands dirty. His comrades loved it.

He stood with admirable patience as he waited for Morrow to dictate the day's work. As the officer rode before them, inspecting the lines, a few of the men grunted and commented on what the army would ask of them next. There were a few childish giggles from a small group of soldiers, which immediately fell silent when Morrow rode out before them, his eyes meeting theirs. To this, Peck smiled.

Quickly adjusting his posture and checking the proper position of the flag, Peck shifted his eyes forward and brought his feet together. The regiment had been called to attention. They listened for the expected workload. Again the question of what the army demanded of them was passed between the neat rows behind Peck. Again it was met with short and quiet laughter.

Colonel Morrow toured his regiment exactly on time, just like he had every other day. He would come upon the rows of men, shuffling off behind them to stay out of sight. From there, he would check his watch for the time, commencing the inspection and concluding with the announcements at nearly the same time everyday. Having already verified the time, Morrow pulled his horse next to Flanigan's and met his subordinate with the usual polite greeting. "Beautiful morning, is it not, Mark?"

Flanigan looked up toward the blue sky. There wasn't a cloud visible yet. "It is that, Henry," he happily replied. He took a breath, feeling the cool crisp air scratch at his throat. "The Twenty-Fourth is ready for inspection, sir."

Morrow said, "No need." Spurring his horse forward, he felt the eyes of the regiment fall upon him. He could sense their frustration and weariness. They had done all that was asked of them and he heard little complaint. "You men, of the Twenty-Fourth Michigan," he said in a booming voice, "are to be thanked for your tireless efforts to complete all that has been asked of you." He studied the white faces as he spoke. The ranks before him were silent, the only noise stemming from the commotion of the brigade around them. "It has come to my attention of particular difficulties which have plagued our efforts to accomplish the tasks demanded of us. I assure you that I have taken this to our commanding officer and he has assured me that it shall not happen again.

That said," Morrow quickly added, "the addition of more trenches has been requested of this brigade." The silence was broken by a string of grunts and moans. Above the din of harmonious sighs, he continued, "Seeing that we are the newest addition to the brigade, it is generally accepted that such a demanding chore be assigned to us."

"God damned fools," Morgan whispered of the army's high command. As Morrow sat atop his horse and began to issue the day's work, Morgan knew what it meant for the regiment. They, once again, would be the ones stuck digging into the frozen earth, struggling through the cold mud and muck.

He was beginning to think that digging was all that an army did. There was great talk about a coming battle, but Morgan could not see how it would come if the army didn't advance. In order to advance, they would have to stop digging holes and trenches in the earth wherever they stopped. Those more educated in the ways of soldiering replied to him that such work was needed for defense. Morgan quickly concluded that the Confederate army wasn't going to advance on such a large force. From his vantage point, among the dirty rank and file, the army clearly held several advantages over their enemy, primarily in numbers. Since joining the army, however, he had seen those advantages slip away from a seemingly careless commander.

And so he realized that more digging was ordered. The army, for the time being at least, was staying put, despite the fact that the enemy was within its reach. But Morgan's job was to carry a rifle and dig trenches, not to make tactical decisions concerning thousands of lives. He accepted that.

Preparing to hear the day's workload, Morgan was ready to lay down his rifle once more and pick up the shovel, but he didn't like it, not one bit. "God damned fools," he whispered again. "They should try digging if it sounds entertaining enough to keep at it."

Morrow saw the regiment stiffen their sore muscles, bracing themselves for more work. He looked back to Flanigan and offered a simple smile before swinging his head around to address his command. "But it will not be, not today." He heard the collective sigh and read the blank expressions. Morrow said to them, "We will not be digging trenches today, men. We have received a day of rest, in thanks of your hard work." He watched with pride as his soldiers relaxed, their frustrations withering away.

"There will be no picket duty," he continued, "no drills, and certainly no digging. We have been ordered to the rear of the brigade. We are to set up camp there for the day." He turned once again to Flanigan and spoke to him directly. "Mark, see to the location of the camp." Sending the Irishman off, Morrow turned back and faced the regiment. "Company officers," his voice thundered again, "you have been issued your orders. I trust your companies will arrive in good order and behave themselves." After the brief but exciting announcement, Morrow spurred his horse and slowly began the trot down the lines toward brigade headquarters. "Twenty-Fourth," he ordered, "you are hereby dismissed."

No sooner had Morrow concluded and began his departure, had a voice from the shivering ranks called to him. "Colonel Morrow?" Upon hearing his name, he slowed his horse and gently guided the animal back around. He heard his name called again from the ranks. Steadily riding toward the voice, Morrow came upon a thin soldier waving his arms about in the air. The comrades around him quietly demanded that he keep his mouth shut and not spoil the news. Unfortunately for them, the soldier had to address something of his own. "Colonel Morrow," the young man said as his officer approached, "you say that a trench is needed and that a regiment is needed to dig it."

"That is correct," Morrow replied.

"Then who's digging?" asked the soldier.

"The Sixth Wisconsin, General Meredith's orders."

The regiment exploded with cheers. Kepis were tossed high into the air. The Sixth Wisconsin had done most of the tormenting and some of its soldiers were the wolves that often growled at the green Michigan recruits, Morgan especially. By the time the kepis fell back to earth, the men had swarmed Morrow's horse. "Thank God for Colonel Morrow!" was a general cry. They extended long arms and dirty hands up to him and he tried to shake as many as he could. The soldiers crowded him, offering their thanks for his efforts in obtaining them a much needed break.

Morrow replied that it was not he who was responsible. "Do no thank me," he cautioned them. "For it has been the work of your company officers. They had brought it to my attention. I simply passed the report to higher authorities." He spoke while he greeted the soldiers. "They deserve your thanks and blessings, not I."

He finally managed to pull away from the regiment. He pleaded with them that it was not he they should be thanking, but they swarmed to him no matter his words, his confessions. They loved and respected Morrow. He had done them no wrong. It didn't matter if he had anything to do with obtaining the day of rest. It mattered that he was there, sharing in their trials, just as he had said at the rally back in Detroit. Perhaps that is why many of them were thanking him, reaching out to him to shake his hand.

As Morrow pulled away, the Sixth Wisconsin marched past the regiment, in which the Twenty-Fourth gave three hearty cheers in celebration of being replaced. With joy and excitement, the Michigan soldiers noticed that the rifles on the shoulders of the Wisconsin men had been replaced with shovels, axes, and tools of all assortments.

The cheering sputtered on, fading as each company was pulled from the line. Morrow heard his regiment fall silent before a chorus of patriotic songs sprung about from his ranks. He could hear them happily singing from a distance and it put a smile on his face. His men were happy.

Captain Edwards sat alone and watched the daylight quickly fade away. The cold, crisp, relaxing afternoon became a memory as the sun dropped below the vast ridgelines in the distance. The moment was peaceful and calm. He only hoped he would live to experience many more of them. His thoughts did not lead him to fear, and he certainly wasn't in the mood to question fate. The day had been enjoyable. His workload had been lifted. Edwards spent much of the day catching up with his men of Company F, joining them in card games and listening to them sing songs.

He watched as the weary line of the Sixth Wisconsin staggered by. He did not envy them, nor did he join in the revenge many of his men were taking. The Wisconsin men had done their work for the day. At the same time, however, he didn't move to quell the taunts from his men. He considered it just punishment for the way the Michigan regiment had been treated by the Sixth since joining the brigade. Let the boys have one day of redemption, he told himself.

As the darkness began to blanket them, Edwards saw three weary Wisconsin men slowly pacing the last of the regiment's line. These men seemed more tired, weaker than their comrades. When they saw him sitting alone, recognizing him as an officer of the Twenty-Fourth, they quickly pulled from their line and made their way toward Edwards. For his part, Edwards immediately recognized the men as those who had been having their way with his company when the Twenty-Fourth was assigned to dig the trenches. These weary men before him were the wolves, tormenters of Company F.

Stumbling from the darkness, the leader emerged and quickly saluted. Before he addressed Edwards, the soldier identified the officer's rank. "Captain," said the beleaguered soldier, "We have a grievance, Captain." The two other soldiers caught up with him and crashed through the darkness behind him. Edwards reacted kindly, offering the men a seat around his fire.

Edwards said, "Please, tell me. What is it you need from me?"

"We have seen you with your company, Captain. We knew who to approach."

"Concerning what?"

"Our trench," was the hasty reply. "Our trench is gone, Captain." The soldier settled and spread his hands out before the fire. "It is gone, I tell you. We spent the entire day digging it and now it is gone."

"Shove on with it," interrupted one of the other soldiers.

"Yes," replied Edwards. "Please, continue."

"We did not notice at first, Captain," said the soldier. "We finished our portion of the trench, the last to do so. We could hear our regiment gather about, preparing to leave. We were all hungry, sir. We had worked all day without the slightest break. But our work took us longer and we stayed behind. The regiment moved on and ate dinner. Oh, our bellies did growl in hunger. But our work had to be finished before we could eat. We worked quickly, finishing nearly an hour later, our hands bloody from the tools, our muscles as sore as they have ever been." The soldier took a breath. He looked around as his comrades listened, their heads low, their bodies exhausted. "So we grabbed our tools and began to make our way down the freshly dug trench. We ourselves were responsible for a hundred feet. From the end of the line, we made our way toward the regiment. It was getting dark now. We could see fires sprouting from the ground before us. We were anxious to return, Captain. It was then that we noticed something peculiar about our fresh trench," he said with wide eyes. "We lost sight of it, Captain! It was gone! I myself did not believe it, so I threw my shovel toward the trench and heard the blade slam into soft, fresh soil. The trench was gone!"

Edwards listened with great interest. The soldier continued, "We moved up and down our little line, but the trench was gone. Our hard work was gone. We moved further up the trench and found that beyond our portion, the line remained intact. No effort to fill in the greater portion of the trench was made, Captain. More than half of our hundred feet of trench was filled in. We didn't hear anything more than the work of our regiment. There were no indications of such a cruel act. We didn't see anybody."

"It was dark when we were still working," said one of the others.

"It was," replied the soldier. "But our little trench was gone, Captain."

"And you believe that some of my men were responsible," added Edwards.

The soldier replied, "Certainly. We saw them ourselves. There were at least six of them, all of them with tools slung over their shoulders." The soldier clasped his hands together, rubbing them to keep them warm. "They approached us, whistling as they marched. I saw the leader of the pack and recognized him. I called out, the anger in my voice evident, '*Michigan*,' I said to him. He looked to me as he passed and replied, '*Wisconsin*.' We all heard him say it. We all saw them march away with their tools."

Edwards nodded. He immediately knew who was responsible. He shuffled toward the weary soldier and patted him on the knee. "I will see to it that each of those men receive punishment for their actions," he assured the three men. "Colonel Morrow will hear of their misbehavior." He turned away, struggling to hide his smile from them. "But I cannot, gentlemen," he said to them, "inform Colonel Morrow until your commander has been brought aware of your conduct as well. If we are going to settle this matter once and for all and assume that no further revenge be taken against our two opposing parties, then we should do so to the fullest extent."

"That won't be necessary," cried one of them.

"No," added the soldier. "It won't be necessary, Captain. We just thought you should know what had happened. We have to go back in the morning and finish it, sir."

"Then I will order those men to assist you," replied Edwards.

"We must decline, Captain," said the soldier. "It is our trench. Perhaps," he muttered as his eyes shifted toward his comrades, "we are the ones responsible in the first place. If so, then we should be the ones to fix it up." He brought his tired eyes back to Edwards. "There is no need, Captain, to take this matter further. We just wanted you to know."

Edwards said, "Very well." He looked again to their eyes and saw how tired they were, how hungry they were. He felt confident that there would be no further aggression between the two parties. Standing to see the three Wisconsin soldiers off, Edwards offered a simple handshake instead of the customary salute. "I will consider the matter closed, gentlemen. I will inform those responsible of the same. I trust that you will consider it as well." The men nodded and wearily departed the warm fire. Edwards watched them stumble back into the darkness from which they came.

The smile grew once again, but he shook his head. His company was a good one, but even good ones are a handful. Glancing back toward the fire, he thought of finding Morgan and interrogating him about the events, reprimanding the young soldier for his foolishness. Had the news of his actions reached higher authorities, a far more severe punishment would have been in store. The three disgruntled veterans sought out the first Michigan officer they saw and Edwards just happened to be at the right place at the right time. The matter would go no further. There was no need for it. As he watched the flames dance to the rhythm of the crackling wood, he continued to smile at the thought of his boys seeking revenge. Oh, he thought, how they put one over on those sturdy veterans.

Entertaining himself by prodding at the fire with a stick, Edwards stopped when he heard distant whistling. Morgan and his band had returned to camp, finally victorious over their tormenters. Half the trench was filled in.

It seemed, for the first time, that the helpless deer of Company F had driven off the aggressive Wisconsin wolves, revealing that the green Michigan soldiers were learning how to fend for themselves in the army.

Revenge had been taken.

Colonel Morrow watched as his regiment slowly slid past him on the muddy road. He had been pleased with their conduct and anticipated more of the same in the coming battle. The regiment, falling in place with the rest of the Iron Brigade, began its march to a distant field. The pieces of the grand chessboard aligned in preparation of Burnside's great assault.

Everything was coming together. The regiment was on time and the march commenced at the hour appointed. Morrow made sure that his men went by the clock, obsessively coordinating the movement of his troops with that of his watch. Things had not soured, not yet. The brigade was off and moving in fine condition. The men envisioned the battle before them. The Twenty-Fourth marched forward with excited steps, for they were about to receive their chance to prove their worth. The patient veterans, long awaiting the campaign, moved forward with steady and unnerved strides. They were the ones who knew what to expect when the din of battle rose.

Morrow could hear the hooves of an approaching party. He turned away from his marching command and saluted as General Solomon Meredith rode up and warmly greeted Morrow. "Henry," Meredith said, "how are you holding?"

"Well, General. What about you, sir?"

"As good as can be expected," replied Meredith. "What is the condition of your men on this morning?"

"They are ready." Morrow smiled. "God knows they are ready."

Meredith followed the line quickly, "This is good, Colonel. I believe we will have a trying time against our enemies. There are those among us," he said quietly, "that believe the army should have moved sooner. They fear the traitors have had time to dig in. They believe we are moving too late."

Morrow nodded. He too had heard of such talk. Some of which was warranted, but much of it was foolishness. He would have liked to have seen the army move sooner, work its way to meet the enemy on open ground. "What do you think of it, General?"

"We will soon find out, Henry."

He shifted his eyes away from Meredith and looked to a colorless field. He wondered what the land had looked like before it met war. "It is a shame," added Meredith. "Look at what we've done to her, this land. Look at what has become of it. There is nothing left for the fox or crow. How dark it is. How empty we now find it." Meredith reflected on the sight. The land was vacant and bare, cold and damp. "We see the destruction we are capable of, yet we still cry for more. There will still be blood shed into the winding rivers and ravines. I have seen rivers run red too many times in my career, Henry. Yet I will see more of it, I know. We men of arms are creatures of war. It is a flaw that haunts the very best of moral men. Even you, yourself, command a regiment that desires conflict more than most I have seen. The Twenty-Fourth is well aware that good conduct in battle will lead to full admission into the Iron Brigade and it is itching for a go at it." Meredith leaned back in the saddle. "As creatures of war, we must all come to ask ourselves one simple question: is war a desire or an obsession? What do you think of it, Henry? Is war a desire for you? Or is it a dark obsession?"

Morrow didn't hesitate with an answer. "It is whatever it takes to bring this sad war to its conclusion, General Meredith."

"Good," Meredith chuckled. He lifted his canteen and took a slow drink. He then handed it over to Morrow. "On to Fredericksburg, Henry," he muttered. "Let us drink to the hopeful conclusion of this bloody affair." Morrow gladly took a drink. Capping the canteen,

Meredith pulled his horse away. "You have a fine regiment, Colonel. I look forward to seeing it in combat, to its earning of the black hats. For now, I must bid you farewell. See you at the front, Henry."

Morrow sent Meredith off with a formal salute. He turned back and watched his regiment cross before him. They were happy. Their feet were moving in near unison. Their chests were raised and their eyes looked forward, off into the distance. They were ready. Once they had been nothing more than farmers, lawyers, doctors, merchants, and anything else a man could be labeled, but now they were soldiers. All of the countless hours of drill and instruction had shaped them into stronger, better men. No longer did the questions of whether they would live up to expectations or if they would be successful in their trials swirl about his thoughts. He was proud of them. They were proud of him. There was an unbreakable bond between them, faith in each other. Morrow had promised them combat, and he was about to make good on his word. Where they had stumbled, he stumbled. Where they had progressed, he progressed. It led to the undeniable conclusion that while there would still be a Twenty-Fourth without him, he would be nothing without them. Morrow firmly believed that. The men of the Twenty-Fourth would know what to do, what was expected of them, if he fell. He, on the other hand, would simply be lost without them, without his brave regiment. But for now they needed him just as much as he needed them, both agreeing that there was no better regiment to serve in, than the Twenty-Fourth Michigan.

"To Fredericksburg," Morrow whispered, finally urging his horse forward.

SEEING THE ELEPHANT
—THE BATTLE OF FREDERICKSBURG—

General Ambrose Burnside's grand scheme pitted the Union Army of the Potomac against the Confederate Army of Northern Virginia at Fredericksburg, Virginia. By the time the Army of the Potomac arrived, they found their enemies entrenched on the high ground outside of town. The Federals moved quickly and spanned the river under relentless Confederate sharpshooters. With the bridges secure, the first Union elements crossed the river and pressed the defending Confederates through town.

The Twenty-Fourth Michigan arrived at the river on December 11, 1862, listening to the sound of the Union guns thundering further upriver. There, they received their two month's pay from the paymaster and many of the men entrusted Chaplain Way with the checks to send back to their families. Not yet ordered to cross, the regiment bedded down for the night near the bridges. The green Michigan soldiers, eager to "see the elephant," as a soldier's first engagement was often called, had great difficulty sleeping under the growing noise of battle.

Those who did sleep awoke the morning of December 12 to bugle calls.

Morgan glanced downriver in amazement as the Union guns continued their assault. He was tired. The night had been rough on him. His blanket did little more than cover him from some of the cold. There was no support against the frozen earth, so he awoke with a sore back. About a half hour before the first bugle call, Morgan had finished his breakfast and downed a small portion of his coffee, mostly hot water, because he wanted to ration enough for later. As the bugles cried, Morgan grabbed his rifle and gear and slid into the ranks of Company F.

His knees were weak and nervous. Thoughts raced through his head. This was foreign to him. He had never seen a place like it. Of all the times he tried to imagine what a battlefield would look like, he never imagined such a place as where he then stood. The town of Fredericksburg, from what he could see, was one of beauty. Even during the torrent of artillery fire, there was still evidence of its peacefulness. There was something wondrous about the town, but he could not guess at what it was. There was little time to ponder on it, in fact, as before long the regiment was ordered to move out.

His nervous legs carried him. As the regiment adjusted their marching columns, it gently shifted over to take position on the right of the Iron Brigade. The move was fluid and flawless. The men were quick and confident. Despite struggling to catch sleep, Morgan moved well, suddenly refreshed.

He thought of Emmy and home. He wanted to be with her and missed her very much. Keeping him moving, however, was the thought that he did not want to let her or his family down. Morgan was a proud young man. He had made a commitment and intended to see it through, no matter what its conclusion. Fueling that thought was his commitment to his comrades. He had vowed to stand with them, to fight with them. As long as there was a line braced by the mighty Twenty-Fourth, Morgan would rush to stand with it. He wanted to ensure that there would be nobody, within his ranks or at home, that could call him a coward. His image, his name, meant too much to him.

As a few of his comrades struggled to keep pace, staggering over the rough ground, Morgan drove forward. He would not be slowed.

Colonel Morrow watched as the last of his regiment filed into position. He sat nervously in his saddle, paying close attention to his men. It was the first time they had heard the roar of battle. He studied their faces and eyes, hoping to catch a glimpse of their thoughts. He wanted to tell them that it would turn out alright, but he had no right to say so. He did not know what was in store for his regiment, so he refused to imply that he did. Instead, he waited for the company officers to join him before addressing his nervous regiment.

"Today," he bellowed, "you will meet the enemy. Your skills, developed from constant training and constant drill, will lead you into the fight. You know what you are to do, as you are brave and intelligent men." Morrow steadied his horse, as the animal trembled slightly from the thundering cannon. How strange it was to see his horse startled, but he led himself to believe that the animal was less nervous than he. The animal too was anxious to get the contest on and over with. "Remember your training," he told the men. "Follow the orders given. Keep pace with the line. Step lively and bravely. Wayne County expects every man to do his duty."

He lifted himself in the saddle to continue but was interrupted by an aide from General Meredith. "The Twenty-Fourth is to move out at once, Colonel," said the aide. "You are to cross the river with the brigade. Positions will be provided once you reach the other side. Move immediately, Colonel, by order of General Meredith." There was no apology offered for this interruption. There was little time to do anything but order the regiment forward. "You will take the second bridge, Colonel," instructed the aide. "There you will follow the brigade across for further orders."

"Send General Meredith my compliments and inform him that the Twenty-Fourth is moving up as ordered," stated a nervous Morrow. The aide shuffled off to deliver the message to the rest of the brigade. Morrow turned back to his command and told the men to get ready. To his company officers he said, "See me when we get across the river. Move your companies along with haste." He sent the officers back to their commands. "Well, Mark," he coolly told Flanigan, "we must cross the river."

He would have liked to have offered the men a few more remarks, but Morrow knew that his time was up. Besides, it was clear the men didn't need patriotic words to prompt them to duty. They didn't even need to be told what was expected of them, but he could not help but remind them of all of those counting on them back home in Michigan. With these burdened men, Morrow made the turn and began the trek across the river over the pontoon bridge.

The cannons still rumbled in the distance.

The Twenty-Fourth Michigan crossed the Rappahannock River at what became known as Franklin's Crossing, reaching the opposing shoreline sometime after noon. From there, they marched downriver before halting to allow troops and artillery to move into position before them. At this point, they bore witness to the enemy's entrenched guns on the hills spanning the horizon.

The Union Sixth Corps had already crossed the river and had formed a solid line of battle when the Twenty-Fourth arrived. The separation between the Union and Confederate lines was less than half a mile. General John Gibbon's division hooked to the left of the Sixth Corps. The old veterans of the Iron Brigade cheered as Gibbon rode across the field to urge his new command forward. From there, General Meade posted his division to the left of Gibbon's. General Doubleday's division, which included the Iron Brigade, fell in as a reserve line behind Gibbon and Meade.

The Iron Brigade nestled on a slight ridge. Their guns were stacked and the ranks were broken. The men quickly nibbled on hardtack and drank from their canteens, anxiously awaiting the call for them to engage. As the brigade settled, however, the Confederate guns on the heights took notice of their position and began dropping shells their way. It was the first time the Twenty-Fourth Michigan came under fire.

Color Sergeant Abel Peck wrestled with the flag in the December wind. He stood erect, standing near Colonel Morrow, as the flag waved about above him. The thundering of the cannon downriver seemed to grow fainter, but he couldn't tell if the action was ceasing or if he had just gotten used to the distant rumble.

Suddenly the thunder became louder, much closer than it had been before. The ground trembled and the sky lit up with glowing shells, cutting through the winter haze. On the opposing ridgeline, where the enemy was known to be, he could see small white puffs of smoke sprinkle the hillside. He initially wondered what the Confederate artillery was firing at, but he soon found out.

At first it was a soft hum, followed by a loud screech that tore into the eardrums, concluding with a large explosion. The ground shook as the projectile slammed into the earth in the ranks of the Twenty-Fourth. The display of force and shock sent shivers down their spines and created much commotion. Peck looked through the thick blanket of smoke to see if anyone was wounded. He saw several officers and men leap into the darkness to offer aid. Peck held his breath and prayed that no soldier was injured. To his disbelief, the officers and soldiers vacated the hole as the smoke cleared. They shouted to the startled regiment that there was no harm. The men, still shocked, offered few cheers.

Peck saw Colonel Morrow spur his horse toward the commotion to settle the regiment down. "Relax, gentlemen," said a surprisingly calm Morrow, "there is no need for such excitement. Lightning has never struck twice in the same spot."

There was another hum, louder, more defined. An explosion raised flames, dirt, and smoke into the air near Morrow, nearly knocking the officer from his saddle. Peck took the flag and ran over, but Morrow had quickly recovered from the scare. "*To hell it don't, Colonel!*" one man replied to Morrow's statement from the ranks.

When Morrow saw Peck come to him, the officer met the color bearer kindly. "I am fine, Mr. Peck. Another few feet to the right and that would have been the end of my service, but I am fine."

Captain Edwards ordered Company F down from the rise into safer ground. "We shouldn't attract enemy fire from here," he told them as they moved along. He was glad to see the position vacated. There were too many close calls. Several shells fired toward the brigade landed within the lines of the Twenty-Fourth Michigan. The men were slightly rattled, but Morrow calmed them down. Despite the Confederate artillery pressure, the regiment had come out unscathed. As far as Edwards knew, not a casualty had been suffered under the sudden barrage.

It seemed that as soon as the men got settled, they were ordered back to their feet. There were grumbles and complaints, but Edwards was used to short stops, he had experienced enough to know that armed men will seldom stay in one place too long. So again he ordered his company forward. He saw their heads turn toward the Confederate position across the field and on the rising heights. Surely they consider the opportunity missed, he thought. They don't know any better. They have much to learn. Edwards shook his head. "We will have at them soon enough, boys," he shouted. "For now, just keep pace with the man in front of you and all will be well."

Further downriver he could see a large house. Already he noticed a great number of figures moving about the yard and through the entrances. Edwards could see many horses. He first wondered if the building was temporarily set up as army headquarters, but he realized that it was positioned too close to enemy lines for that service. The next thought, the more practical of the two, was that the building was going to be used as the frontline hospital. The latter seemed to be more likely and Edwards felt foolish that he would have guessed it to be Burnside's headquarters. His experience should have told him that such a place wasn't suitable for army command. It was on poor ground, too far left of the central locations for both armies.

Whatever the house's purpose, it was clear the brigade was headed for it. Even as the men moved out of position, the Confederate gunners worked to cause a ruckus, entertaining the brigade as they stepped. They continually tossed fiery shells toward the moving columns, which did little more than hamper the movement of the brigade. The veterans urged the new Michigan recruits forward. They promised there would be rest at the approaching house. But the Michigan men weren't looking for rest, they were looking to fight.

"Do you think we'll see the elephant today, Captain Edwards?" asked an excited soldier from Company F.

Edwards replied carefully, "I don't think so, but I don't imagine it will be too long before we see it." He moved forward, stretching out ahead of his men. He dared not think of what combat would bring, how much suffering there would be for the regiment. There was no room to think of such when entering a battle. He knew that his mind had to be clear and ready at all times. Clouded thoughts in battle often meant lesser chances for survival. Edwards wasn't just responsible for himself, but he was responsible for an entire company of men. So he forced the dangerous thoughts from his mind and kept his eyes on the approaching house.

All the while his gut told him that his veteran experience would soon come in handy.

And that made him nervous.

December 13 opened early with Union troop movements. General Meade's lines shifted to confront the enemy presence on the hill, while General Doubleday shifted his lines to cover Meade's old position. From there, Meade and Gibbon stepped off and led the charge over the open ground and up the hill toward the first line of Confederate works. The battle opened that morning but was not limited to the center of the field, where Gibbon and Meade were making their combined assault. Off to the left of the line, Confederates could be seen gathering. General Doubleday responded by shifting his division to face this danger.

Battery B, Fourth United States Artillery, rolled into place and the Iron Brigade was ordered to support it. As the excited men of the Twenty-Fourth gathered in line, their wait would not be long. Their service was called for.

Lieutenant Colonel Mark Flanigan calmly urged the men in place. He guided them with his officer's sword, pointing toward the various positions the men were required to fill. His large frame was comfortable in the saddle. His feathers had not yet been ruffled by the shot and shell of the enemy or the clamor of battle toward the center of the Union line. Nor was he thinking too much on the task at hand. He simply guided his men into position, taking one step at a time.

The Twenty-Fourth had been ordered to clear the houses and buildings in front of them. The enemy was lodged there, creating a nuisance for the Union artillery bouncing into position. It seemed like several minutes, but the regiment had shifted in little time. Flanigan could see the lines steady into place. His heart began to beat faster. His ears perked at the sound of explosions, cannon blasts, and small arms fire in the distance. His eyes turned toward their objective, the houses. He could see shadows streaming in all directions and Confederate officers on horseback ordering their men forward. He wondered if they knew what was coming, if they knew the Twenty-Fourth had plans to meet them, to push them from their improvised nest.

Then he saw the first of the wounded falling back from the center of the field. One man limped by him, a foot nearly severed. Another man was carried on a stretcher, his chest ripped open and his insides exposed. The man was breathing steadily, holding strong. Flanigan couldn't believe the soldier was still alive. The Michigan men staggered and their faces fell to a shade of white. He could see they were uneasy. "Steady, boys," he guided them. "Clear a path and let them through. These men have done their work."

The battle raged in the distance. Flanigan could hear the savage storm.

Another wounded solider was carried past them. Both of his calves had been shot away to the bone. He was in pain and agony but fought to keep it in, to hide it from his comrades. When he saw the formed ranks of the Twenty-Fourth, he leaned up, with tears in his eyes, and said, "God bless you, boys. May He keep you from this terrible slaughter."

Before Flanigan could coach his men and excuse the warning, the regiment was ordered forward. He watched as the men looked at each other, offering silent farewells. Flanigan spurred his horse forward, streaking past the regiment. He couldn't look at them, not then. He did not want to think of what would become of them, the brave soldiers. So he steadied himself in the saddle and rode as an officer should, giving no indication of the worries that suddenly plagued him.

Colonel Henry Morrow let his horse drink from the ravine. The regiment had moved slightly more than a mile forward, driving the enemy from the buildings. It was peaceful, despite the desperate conflict raging in the background. He could see the enemy before him, but they had not yet made an effort to greet him.

His regiment was ready at a moment's call. He had deployed skirmishers out to the front, and watched them disappear into the fog. Morrow had just remounted his horse when the enemy opened with artillery fire, but the shots passed too far overhead or had come up well short of the intended targets. He took a breath. He was relieved that the fog offered some protection. Riding down the line to inspect possible damage, he found nothing and again thanked the winter fog for obstructing careful aim. Not one injury once again. Luck seemed to be with the regiment, he thought. Will it stay?

Ahead of him, however, he could hear the skirmishers clash with the enemy. At first it was a slight engagement, only a few cracks of a rifle now and then. Soon the sporadic firing evolved into a steady pace. He knew what it meant. The skirmishers could go no further. The enemy line had been found.

Immediately he received word to move the regiment forward again. He gave the directions and watched as his men stepped forward in unison with the rest of the brigade. Morrow spurred his horse onward, shouting words of encouragement. "Step lively, boys. We'll meet those devils and drive them from the field!" The line inched forward until it met several skirmishers. They had identified the enemy's position. Concealed in the woods before them, they had encountered horsemen and infantry but to what number they did not know.

Again the line slowed. Morrow rode through the ranks to settle the men. To his amazement, he found them calm and collective. They were close enough to battle now that their excitement could be contained. It was nearly destined for them to meet the enemy soon. They could feel it. Quickly touring his lines, he realized that he was the only one visibly nervous. His hands shook as they held the reins, and he nervously cocked his head from side to side to see all that transpired. As he looked behind him, he saw the rolling guns from Battery B fall into position.

Once the gunners readied their cannons and found their bearings, trained on the woods, they announced their presence. The blast of the guns shook the earth and blanketed the brigade in smoke. Morrow remained in the saddle, trying to watch the shells careen toward the woods. He knew what would come after the big guns fell silent. The brigade would tighten their lines of battle and then move against the enemy. And he knew he was correct when he saw a thin line of sharpshooters spread out and melt into the land before the brigade.

Battery B boomed away. Explosions ripped through the woods.

An aide approached unnoticed, as the noise was too great to hear and Morrow was far too distracted by the woods and the spectacular explosions that ripped the trees apart. He told Morrow that the Twenty-Fourth would advance in line with the Seventh Wisconsin. "Those woods need to be cleared, Colonel," the aide shouted. "The artillery can't do it alone."

With a nod, Morrow began to envision the plan. He called for Lieutenant Whiting and informed him to designate a litter corps. It was a sad task and Morrow nearly choked up when he gave the order, but he knew that it was needed. His regiment was moving to the front soon, and there was sure to be casualties that needed evacuation from the field. It would be up to the litter corps to make sure that all wounded were accounted for. Morrow then went over and instructed Flanigan on how the regiment should advance toward the woods and reminded the

Irishman that a unit of United States Sharpshooters had already advanced and were engaging the enemy. On his ride back to the center of the regiment, the men cheered him, for he had delivered them to the enemy. He raised a hand, silently urging them to save their energy for the coming fight.

Satisfied that he had done all he could, he nervously took his place and awaited the order to advance. His hands continued to tremble uncontrollably.

When the call came for the advance, Captain Edwards politely ordered his men forward. They were anxious to meet the enemy, and Edwards reminded them of their duties and how they should conduct themselves on the field. "We are Company F," he told them, "and if we believe ourselves to be the best in the regiment, then I expect to see it today."

He had come to know these men. Maybe not so much back in Detroit, where their lives kept them separated, but from the time they had spent together since leaving the city. There were countless drills, marches, and innumerable hours spent digging trenches, latrines, and graves. Edwards came to know them as family. He could name many of their children. He even prided himself on knowing several of their favorite Bible passages.

Such knowledge was frowned upon per military standards. An officer mingling too much with his men would come to know many personal things about them. Therefore, it would be harder for him to order them into battle, harder to see them wounded or watch them die. While Edwards found some truth in the teachings, he could not help but come to know the men he commanded. If he expected the men to believe in him, then he would have to believe in them. It would be those soldiers,

216

under his care, that would attempt to do the worst of the bidding, the bloodiest of tasks. To him, his soldiers were more than numbers.

The least he could do was learn their names and a little about them.

He gently slid from the ranks and watched the men pass before him. He was proud of Company F. They had come a long way since he first met them, first organized them. But standing before them, he could not help but think it the last time he would see some of them. Some would be wounded. Few may be killed. Every man knew it was possible. Yet they continued onward, bravely driving toward their objective. There was a name to make for their regiment, glory to be shared.

As Company F marched gallantly by, Edwards silently called the names of his beloved soldiers. Lewis Chamberlain. George Ross. John French. The list went on as the company slithered by, toward the regiment's first engagement of the war.

Lieutenant Colonel Flanigan brought his horse through the smoke and much of the field became visible for the first time. He felt nervous and uncomfortable remaining in the saddle, but it had been ordered. On level ground, he spurred forward to better assess the situation the regiment confronted. Pop. Pop. Pop. The sharpshooters had reached a stalemate with the enemy in the woods. Pop. Pop.

He quickly turned his horse back to the regiment. With large arms he waved and pointed forward. "There, lads!" he shouted. "We are needed there!" Guiding his horse past the two lines of battle, he waved to Morrow before taking his place directing the right side of the regiment. When he turned back to look forward, smoke again obstructed his view as the rifle fire grew.

As the thin blanket of smoke was carried from the field by the December wind, Flanigan gasped when he saw the sharpshooters bogged down behind a small wooden fence. He watched them try to return fire, only to quickly seek shelter again as Confederate infantry and horsemen opened up. Crack. Pop. Flanigan could make out the wooden splinters explode from the rails of the fence. He saw a dead sharpshooter several feet off to the side of his comrades and two wounded ones stumbling back toward the rear. He saw the Michigan men open up small gaps and continue past the wounded.

Flanigan swung back to Morrow, hoping to point out the trapped sharpshooters. His efforts were in vain as his commander was far too occupied and too far away to take notice. Turning back to the right side of the regiment, Flanigan unsheathed his sword and hollered for the men to keep moving, the small fence and sharpshooters nearing their reach.

Colonel Morrow's confidence didn't buckle under the pressure of his nervousness. At the center of the regiment, tucked behind the lines, he urged his men forward. He could see Abel Peck standing firm, leading the regiment toward the fight and he could see the fence and trapped sharpshooters. "Forward!" he shouted as they reached the fence.

The captain of the sharpshooters, a young man with a scruffy beard stumbled toward Morrow and explained that he could not get his men moving anymore. Ignoring the growing danger of Confederate fire, the soldier demanded only one thing from Morrow. "Give my men a kick over the fence, will you, Colonel?"

Zip. Morrow heard the shot just miss him by inches. "On the colors!" he bellowed to his command. "Do not break from the colors! Over the fence, boys! Forward!" Zip. Whip. More shots sailed past him. He knew it was only a matter of time before the Confederates zeroed in their aim and the shots began to hit their marks. The best thing, the only thing to do was to keep moving forward, to drive the enemy from the woods.

The regiment drove over the fence, swallowing the sharpshooters in their path. Inching closer to their enemy, the Confederate aim improved. Zip. Thud. Bullets slammed into the earth and wooden rails around him. His horse stepped over the debris and calmly followed the regiment as it moved forward, the engagement playing out with each step.

Morrow raised his sword and shouted, "To the woods!"

"Forward, Company F, forward!" Edwards shouted as he ran. Entering the woods, he saw the surprised Confederates scatter, a few of them preparing to make a desperate stand. He raised his revolver and fired two shots toward them, striking one man in the arm. When he reached a large stump, he leaped upon it and continued to order his company forward. The Rebels were on the run.

As he climbed down, one Confederate soldier, dirty and thin, wrestled him to the ground and struggled to pull the revolver from Edward's hand. The soldier demanded that the Yankee surrender or perish, but Edwards wasn't bound to give into either. After a brief struggle, Edwards came out on top and punched the soldier to the ground. Staggering to pull away, the soldier regained momentum and grabbed at his feet. Quickly lowering his revolver, Edwards pulled the trigger once before he was cut free from the dirty clutches of his would-be captor.

He was determined not to fall into their hands again.

Clear of the struggle, Edwards stepped over the soldier's body and followed the regiment forward, rejoining his company nearly a hundred feet into the woods.

Morgan steadied his rifle and took aim at a Confederate cavalryman destined on making his escape. Not wanting to miss the opportunity to down an enemy, he pulled the trigger. Too low to hit the rider, the slug slammed into the horse, sending the animal plummeting to the ground, violently tossing the rider from the saddle.

Instantly Morgan leaped upon the fallen soldier, his rifle swinging wildly behind him. The soldier struggled to pull his revolver from its holster, but Morgan never gave him time to draw the weapon. The rage of war filled the young man as Morgan struck at the fallen horseman. Again the Rebel tried to pry himself free of Morgan's grip. Lifting the rifle over his head, holding the barrel end with both hands, Morgan swung the solid mass of the wooden stock down upon his enemy. Blood spattered all over his face. The struggle continued, one last fight still left in the wounded Confederate, but another sturdy swing settled the matter for good. Again blood spattered. It was just enough for him to taste the salty fluid.

Standing victoriously over his fallen enemy, Morgan wiped the blood from his face with a sleeve. The rage had filled his body, ignited his soul. His comrades moved about him in slow-motion, chasing, shooting, and capturing their enemies. He stood in the middle of the storm, ignoring orders to move forward, ignoring the danger of the bullets zipping past him. He carefully turned his rifle around. With the calmness of a soldier on drill, he slowly reloaded the weapon.

The rage of war had made an effective killer out of him.

Color Sergeant Peck planted the colors where Morrow directed. The brigade had done enough. The enemy had been driven from the woods, and General Doubleday wanted to set up a new line over the ground fairly won. As color bearer, it was Peck's responsibility to indicate the new position, to hold the flag so that the regiment could find its way to the new line.

Throughout the brief fight, he wanted to join his armed comrades. The soldier in him wanted to shoot and capture, but those responsibilities were out of his hands. He had his own work to worry about. Being a color bearer in battle wasn't easy work, he quickly found out. Bullets and slugs sliced the air around him. Each time the danger seemed more pressing, his faithful color guard moved in to protect him and the flag.

Colonel Morrow joined him there within minutes. The officer was pleased with the conduct of the regiment and anxiously waited for the ranks to return. "Did you see that, Mr. Peck?" Morrow beckoned. "Did you see how the boys conducted themselves?"

Peck nodded. "It was a splendid sight, Colonel. Marvelous to see the boys have at them. I think the veterans would be most impressed." Pop. Pop. He looked ahead and heard the rifle fire of the new skirmish line flirt with the enemy.

Morrow flashed a piece of paper, holding it tightly in his fingers. "General Doubleday sends his compliments, Mr. Peck."

"The men earned them, Colonel." He relaxed as he watched Morrow sit nervously in the saddle, guiding the men back into line. He had come through his first fight unscathed, uninjured. He had carried the flag across open ground under enemy fire and did not stumble in fear, did not turn his back. There had been no thoughts of retreat. There was no fear of death. There was no time to think of such when the march began. All he could do was steady the flag and proudly lead the regiment forward. He had done that. It was only then, after the charge, did he crumble from exhaustion.

He gave in to the weight of his legs, arms, and his body buckled under the pressure at the waist. Peck turned his head and noticed several Confederate prisoners and horses being carted off under guard toward the Union rear. They had done well, the green Michigan regiment. He did not think it could have been done better.

Peck closed his eyes and thanked God for protecting him.

His prayer concluded and his thoughts turned to his wife and daughter.

The Twenty-Fourth Michigan received little rest. Battery B, known as "Bloody B," rolled into its new position and began to pound the Confederate artillery in its front. As had been the case before, a regiment was called forward to support the battery, and the Twenty-Fourth Michigan was selected for the task.

As the opposing artillery battles slugged it out, the regiment moved toward a ravine and took shelter in a ditch, half filled with water. From there, the men tucked their heads low as shots from three angles battered the earth around them. Battery B continued to fight a lopsided battle and the unit took many casualties. Several men of the regiment volunteered for service in the battery and bravely stepped from the ditch into artillery fire as thick as hail.

Fearing the battery's position in jeopardy, the Twenty-Fourth was ordered to move against the enemy artillery and drive them from the field, thus securing Battery B and the ground won by the brigade. Headquarters had been pleased by the regiment's conduct thus far and wanted to see more.

Colonel Morrow ordered the regiment from the ditch. The officers took to securing their lines and ordering their companies forward. Morrow rode impatiently from one end of the line to the other, hurrying his soldiers along. They were in the open again and the Confederate artillery made them pay.

As the fiery shells rained down upon them, Morrow quickly ordered his command back toward the ditch. The regiment swayed with the force of the explosions, throwing mud and debris into the ranks. Again Morrow pleaded from horseback, frantically shouting for his command to return to cover. Crash! Boom! "Back to the ditch!" shouted Morrow. "Get back to the ditch!"

The fog that had offered so much protection earlier had failed to cover the Michigan regiment from the tremendous fire. The line staggered forward, stubbornly holding the ground in front of the ditch. Morrow spurred his horse and rode down the line to order the men to back down, to fall back to safety. As he did so, he heard the cries of several men as the screeching and humming noise of solid shot riddled the ranks. Morrow watched, helplessly, as the solid masses of iron bounced across the field and slammed into his command. "Fall back!" he shouted.

His horse raced across the regiment as the rider tried to order the men back down. He tried to guide his horse to the front of the line, but an explosion sent the animal back a few steps. Mud and leaves floated into the sky, caking to his uniform. He continued on, however, urging his frightened animal forward through the black smoke and chaos.

Morrow had to get his regiment back to the ditch, out of the line of terrible fire.

His pleas went unnoticed and the line actually took another stubborn step forward. Again he tried to reach the front, force his way to the proud flag and order his regiment to retire. Again he met with disappointment, as a solid shot careened through the ranks and nearly took the legs off of his horse, that wonderful gift from his friends in Detroit.

Lieutenant Colonel Flanigan heard the desperate cries and rode forward to investigate. He found several men hunched together over two fallen soldiers. The Irishman quickly dismounted and ordered the men back to their lines. He fell to his knees when he looked at the bodies of the young soldiers, spread out on the cold ground.

One of them was still alive, having had an arm wiped away by solid shot. The soldier was squirming in pain and coughing up blood. Flanigan reached out for him and told him that things were going to be fine. "We'll get you back, lad," he said calmly, his eyes wide with shock. Immediately turning to one of the soldiers gathered about, he ordered the litter corps forward to take care of the fallen. "Get them here, now."

Stepping over the sobbing, wounded soldier, Flanigan came across a headless body. The sight was sickening, but he could not look away. He carefully searched the body for pictures, letters, or any other form of immediate identification, but none was found. He then directed another soldier to see to it that the body's ammunition and rifle was taken back to the regimental quartermaster. There was no telling when the extra supplies would be needed, but he wasn't about to leave them on the field.

As he stood up to remount his horse, his eyes glanced to an object resting still on the ground several feet away. He looked to see and found that it was a piece of the soldier's severed head, the rest having been carried away with the shot. He instantly felt sick but quickly kicked it away. He did not want the men to see it. In shock, he climbed back into his saddle and rode back to his position, fresh blood on his boots.

The carnage continued around him.

Captain Edwards had never been under such relenting fire before. His past service had done much to solidify his confidence and bravery, but never before had he witnessed such an onslaught. His beloved Company F was bogged down under the pressure from the Confederate guns. Explosions ripped the earth around him and solid shots bounced wildly through the ranks.

"All together now," he told his company. "Keep at it, boys."

Like demons the cannonballs shrieked through the air. Word got around of the recent casualties and the names of the dead soldier. The line began to waver and the company officers scattered about to hold them together. Edwards himself had personally sent two men back into line, telling them that the safest place was with their comrades. He knew it was a lie, as the safest place was back at the ditch, but he wasn't about to let his company fall apart in the face of the enemy.

Again the entire line staggered and confusion began to break out. Edwards heroically tried to curtail the madness, but to no avail. As soon as he received word that Colonel Morrow was trying to draw the regiment back into cover, he pleaded with his command to move out. The men, however, had suddenly become frozen in the face of the artillery fire. Everywhere they moved, it seemed, they were worthy targets.

Colonel Morrow knew that no body of troops could withstand such a fire without being able to fire in response. He had seen his line bend, but he wasn't going to let it break. Finally forcing his horse toward the screeching shells and thundering, he broke through the ranks, reeling the horse around to address his faltering command.

As if instructing on dress parade, he unsheathed his sword and lifted it into the air, demanding the attention of his regiment. "*Attention battalion!*" he shouted, mustering all the voice he could to rise above the din of battle. The regiment clumsily stumbled forward, not believing the orders they heard. Again Morrow bellowed, "*Attention battalion! Right dress! Front!*" he ordered, his voice carried across the field. The regiment aligned with precision, finally ignoring the tormenting shot and shell about them. "*Support arms!*" was Morrow's next directive.

Nearly a thousand men held the position, under the tremendous artillery fire, until their officer gave the final order for them to move out. Morrow watched them with pride. His nervousness had faded. Fear wasn't an emotion. Pointing the sword back to the ditch, he ordered the regiment to retire in the face of the Confederate artillery.

The act was done with skill and confidence, with faith in their commander and faith in each other. As they sank back into the ditch to escape the danger, Morrow rode among them commending them for their bravery. They responded by cheering him and calling out his name.

The men had indeed done the duties expected by Wayne County.

As the Union assault of Meade and Gibbon was snuffed out at the center of the line, the Iron Brigade was again pulled from their position to ward off a suspecting counterattack by the victorious Confederate army. As the men moved, they could hear the southern cheers from the heights above.

The Twenty-Fourth came under severe artillery fire two more times before the night of December 13 ended. Again they were the recipients of paralyzing fire but could offer nothing in return. At one point, the regiment had even been close enough to be confronted with enemy canister fire. They could see the shrapnel spread out over the sky as they huddled, officers and men alike, in another large ditch.

During December 14 and 15, portions of the regiment were sent out for picket duty, offering no time for the weary troops to rest. Colonel Morrow received an important reconnaissance operation by order of General Franklin. With him, Morrow took two full companies and less than half of another. The adventure gathered information but came close to making prisoners of the lot, having danced nearly to the grasps of the Confederate lines. When the group returned, they received the thanks of Franklin and his staff.

Near sundown of December 15, the dead of the Twenty-Fourth were finally accounted for and buried. Later that night, amid a severe rainstorm, the regiment received word that the army was pulling out of Fredericksburg. Ordered to be silent, the men moved as quickly as possible, leaving the tragic field of battle behind them.

In all, the regiment suffered thirty-six casualties, more than any other regiment in the Iron Brigade at Fredericksburg.

Morgan slowly stumbled up the hill. Behind him and across the river, was the sad battlefield where so many gallant men had fallen before the enemy. Just a few short days ago, the hill he was on was crowded with anxious soldiers. Now there was nothing more than a seemingly empty shell of an army, retreating back up the hill that it had just recently bravely marched down.

As Company F marched past several regimental bands, they heard the soft melody that was all too familiar to them. Perhaps by order of an officer or just by decision of the veteran bands, *Amazing Grace* was the tune their instruments beautifully belted out.

He looked to them in confusion. Had the bands not witnessed the terrible struggle? Did they not know that the mighty Army of the Potomac was driven back across the river in defeat? Had they not toured the many hospitals or seen the burial parties complete their work? Did they not know all that transpired?

Morgan was not alone, as several of his tired comrades gathered with him and watched the bands play on. Death and sadness was all around them. It was raining and the men were cold and hungry. Brave men were dying in the hospitals as overworked surgeons and nurses tended to their grievous wounds.

Not a word needed to be spoken between Morgan and his weary comrades, for every one of them asked the same question: where was the grace in all of this? But onward they marched past the regimental bands playing in the rain. With hope they looked to the future, but with sadness they looked to the past.

Yes, where was this *Amazing Grace* at Fredericksburg?

WINTER INTERMISSION

The Twenty-Fourth Michigan settled into their winter camp at Belle Plain, naming the place Camp Isabella in honor of Colonel Morrow's wife. She stayed with the regiment for most of the winter, and the regiment stayed put for nearly four months.

The men set to work building log cabins and makeshift shelters complete with chimneys, roofs, and elaborate fireplaces. They soon began to take pride in the art of building cabins, offering advice to neighboring regiments on how they should construct their winter dwellings.

From this camp the men performed their drills, held dress parades, and handled all business regarding the regiment. They were happy to receive anything from home, and, once in a great while, a couple wagonloads would arrive to surprise them. They received letters from loved ones and wrote happily back to them. Deserving officers were promoted into the vacancies created by the Battle of Fredericksburg and the entire regiment was ordered out for the presentations. Disease still lingered in the darkness and shade, growing more violent as the winter months steadied. There were several deaths in the regiment due to disease, in which the regiment gathered and buried the fallen soldiers with full military honors, doing all they could to give them a proper burial.

There were several other instances, however, that kept the regiment busy. Some of the events were happy and enjoyable, while others caused more pain and heartache.

As I close this letter, my dear Emmy, I must confess that I have seen the elephant. I have heard the roar of battle and have been face to face with the enemy. I know not how to describe it. Our endeavors have earned us great recognition from the veterans. Never before have we been so welcomed. We are now considered full members of the brigade. Colonel Morrow is very pleased with our conduct and says that we are one of the finest regiments in all the army. He stopped writing when he heard commotion outside his cabin. Tossing the pencil down, he exited the small room to see what the fuss was about.

Three men met him outside the cabin, rifles in their hands. "Have we been assigned picket duty again?" asked an intrigued Morgan.

"No," said one of them. "We have a deserter, a murderer."

"Murder?" he asked. "What murder?"

"They've found Walters of Company E out in the forest. He has been killed by one of our own. Poor fool never had a chance."

Morgan stormed back into his cabin and grabbed his rifle. He glanced down to the unfinished letter and knew that it could wait. Stepping back out into the cold, he sought more information from his comrade. "What are we to do?"

"Colonel Morrow has issued a search party. Company F has been selected to find the deserter and bring him in."

"How do we know it was one of ours? I would think it is the work of a Rebel."

The soldier shook his head. "It is far too cruel for even Rebel standards. Besides, this happened a few hours ago. There would have been an attack by now if they were at fault." He slung the rifle over his shoulder. "Come on, boy. We should get moving. Captain Edwards will not tolerate us being late and I will not be the reason he gets out of the woods."

Morgan agreed and quickened his pace. There was no order as to how the men were to prepare for the search, so as he slid through the camp, he could see various men gather about their rifles and join the march toward the starting point. With each stride he felt the rage of war build within him again, this time brewing against one of his own comrades. He could not help but wonder why a Michigan man would be responsible for taking the life of one of his comrades. Good, moral men would never consider such.

He followed the growing stream of angry men into the woods.

Lieutenant Colonel Mark Flanigan had his hands full. The camp was alive and thriving, the men thrashing and combing the land in search of their prey. Morrow had ordered Flanigan to lead the chase, relying on the ex-lawman's ability to apprehend such ruthless criminals. He had done it before. He would do it again.

His law instincts had failed at that point. The victim, a young man standing guard, had lived only a short while after being confronted and stabbed by the deserter. It was apparent that the deserter's escape route was blocked by the sentry and that the two met in desperate struggle. By the time Flanigan arrived to properly question the victim, the young soldier had passed on. The only viable witness to the horrible crime was silenced.

Before announcing the establishment of a search party, Flanigan ordered that all companies hold an emergency roll call. He demanded the officers conduct the roll silently, without alarming the men. He advised them to go through every cabin and every makeshift shelter and account for all of their men.

Flanigan rode steadily through the thickening forest. It was cold and wet. Clumps of white snow fell from the trees above them. He quietly urged the men of Company F to search everything that could be a hiding place. He told them to look to the trees they reasoned sturdy enough to climb, as the deserter may have taken to one of them. The men were ordered to crawl under fallen trees, to dive into banks of snow, and to search every foxhole. Flanigan moved them forward in a wide line of battle, the ranks thinned to cover as much ground as possible. "Hold all fire," he told them. "We don't want him killed, not yet."

The line searched on. Flanigan spurred his horse forward, pointing off into the distance. He could barely make out several fires dotting the landscape. "We have to be careful, lads," he said. "We are fast approaching Confederate pickets. Continue slowly. We are not looking to start a battle."

Colonel Morrow nervously paced the floor of his winter cabin. He had a company of men thick in the woods in search of the murderer. For the past two hours, Flanigan had sent him a courier to keep him updated of the events. Morrow called the matter to the attention of General Meredith, who responded clearly: *cowardly murderers will not be tolerated and shall be put to immediate death.*

He broke his nervous stride several times as Isabella, his wife, questioned him if there was something wrong. Morrow did not want to bother her with the details, but found it hard to keep them from her. When he explained the situation and the punishment resulting once the murderer was captured, his wife quietly informed him that he was not responsible for the cruel actions of one of his men. "I understand," he told her, "but how am I to put one of my own to death?" She could give him no answer and so she busied herself in mending one of his blue jackets.

He sought comfort in his watch and carefully counted the ticks as they passed. Again he nervously paced the floor. Just as he fell into his nervous habit, a knock came on the door and a young man presented Morrow with the ordered roll calls. After the soldier confirmed that all companies had reported he took his leave. Morrow took the papers over to his desk and sat down in the creaking chair to review them. His fingers twitched and he found it hard to concentrate on the scribbles, but he took his time, not wanting to make a mistake. He read carefully, not wanting to miss a thing.

Isabella rose from her work and walked over to him, glancing down at the papers. "If all of these are complete," he said to her, "then we shall soon know who was responsible for this barbaric act." He tore his eyes from the paperwork and looked at her. "And then may God help him."

Captain Edwards covered the extreme left of the line. He moved slowly, carefully. His eyes scanned the trees and white mounds built up over the winter. He ducked under large branches of pine trees and searched the shade under. He probed snow banks gently with his sword. Anything that he thought could be a hiding place he looked over, carefully checking for signs of use, something to guide them in their search.

He heard the clamor of the men down his line search through the land. Then he heard a noise off to his left. He stopped and listened. Snap. He recognized the sound of twigs breaking, a man in motion. Desperately, he called for another man to join him, but his whispers were carried off by the howling wind. He would have to check it out alone.

Edwards moved toward the tree line, his sword at the ready. His other hand slid up to the leather holster and unsnapped the cover. One man had already been killed. He was determined not to become the next.

Snap. Snap. He moved toward the sound until he stepped on a small twig himself. Snap. The noise immediately stopped. Edwards knew that he was close, perhaps just around the other side of the tree from the murderer. Gathering his confidence, he quickly slid around the tree and pulled his revolver.

"Don't shoot!" was the cry.

Edwards opened his eyes and saw a dirty Confederate soldier standing before him. "Don't shoot!" he cried again.

He stepped back. Had he stumbled into a Confederate picket line? When an officer rose from the snow, Edwards knew he had indeed done so. "Well," said the Confederate Captain, "looks like we've found ourselves a stray. What brings you out this far from your lines," he noticed Edwards' rank, "Captain?"

With ease he sheathed his sword and holstered his revolver. He wasn't frightened. If they were going to take him in, then he wouldn't fight them. There was no use. "There has been a murder," he told them. "One of our sentries was killed this morning."

The reply was sharp. "Wasn't us, Captain, if that's what you're getting at."

"No," Edwards said. "It was one of ours."

"Good God." The officer ordered his men to lower their weapons. "How many do you have out there searching with you, Captain?"

"A company," he replied.

After a moment of deliberation, the Confederate officer turned back to Edwards. "We haven't seen much of anything this morning. If your man would have come through here, we would have seen him." The soldier shrugged his shoulders. "I'll pass the word that y'all are looking and mean no harm. We've got a line that stretches from here all the way to those woods yonder, Captain. I don't think your man came through here, but you are welcome to look. We'll cause you no harm."

Edwards saluted. "Your generosity is appreciated, sir."

The Rebel officer sighed before returning the salute. "'Till we meet again on the battlefield, Captain," he said.

With that, Edward departed, determined to push his line further to the right. He did not want his men to stumble into any surprises as he had. Perhaps they wouldn't be so lucky.

The great chase would have lasted much longer, but Flanigan had led the company well. It was an organized and intricate search. As the line shifted to the right to avoid the Confederate pickets, it didn't take long until there were shouts from the extreme right of the line. Dashing toward the shouted directions, Flanigan rode to the cries that the murderer had been cornered.

The men broke into small pockets, flanking the cornered fugitive and surrounding him to prevent further escape. They were determined to end the chase once and for all. Several of them leveled their rifles and thought about pulling the trigger. Flanigan's arrival, however, thwarted any immediate revenge. "He's surrounded, sir," they told him. "We saw him through those bushes there, and he made another run. He didn't get too far, sir. We've got rifles on all sides of him."

He climbed down from the saddle and thanked the men for their efforts. A soldier guided him to the fugitive's location, and Flanigan bent down to identify the murderer. "Move back," he barked to the soldiers. "Give me some room." He tried to look at the soldier's face, but he remained huddled. The young man was crying and praying. Flanigan reached out and touched his shoulders, hoping to see the man's face. The soldier's uniform was soaked in sweat, and there were signs of dried blood on his hands and cuffs. Flanigan lifted the soldier's dirty chin with his hand and managed to catch a quick glimpse of the soldier. "Dear Lord," the Irishman stated. "It was you, lad. It was you."

Morrow heard the wooden door creak open. Then he heard the heavy footsteps of a large man. He didn't need to turn around, for he knew it was Flanigan. The ruffled pages of the roll calls were scattered about his desk. Mrs. Morrow greeted Flanigan warmly, asking if she could take his coat and inviting him to sit a spell to warm up.

Flanigan removed his kepi and ran his fingers through his hair, which was plastered flat with sweat. "We have apprehended him, sir," he opened. He glanced over and saw the papers on the desk. "I think you should know before the regiment, sir, who was responsible…"

"It was Timothy," interrupted Morrow. The young man that in Detroit had been Morrow's faithful aide had committed murder. "His name wasn't on the rolls. He wasn't present in camp."

"He's outside under guard, Henry."

Morrow moved over to Flanigan and put a hand on his shoulder. "Was anyone else harmed, Mark?"

The Irishman replied, "No, sir."

"Good."

"I trust you've relayed the information to General Meredith." Flanigan struggled, trying to comprehend the situation. "What do you wish me to do with him, Henry? What are your orders? What did General Meredith say?"

"We must put him to death."

"When?" asked Flanigan.

Morrow replied quickly, "Tomorrow morning, before the entire regiment." He glanced over to his wife, who held her head low. She tried desperately to ignore the conversation. He did not mean for her to have to listen to it, to bear witness to such horrible atrocities. "Keep him under guard and let no soul near him. There is a universal feeling of revenge among the men, but it must wait until the morning."

"Very well, Henry."

"And get some rest, Mark. You have done more than enough."

He saw Flanigan reach for the door and open it. A cold wind rushed into the small room and sent shivers down his spine. "It has been a hard day," the Irishman sighed.

"Indeed it has."

Flanigan bade the Morrows farewell and exited out into the cold. Morrow went to the doorway and watched his subordinate depart with Timothy in his grasps. He wondered what had come over the young man, what could have provoked him to murder one of his own. Isabella Morrow rose to comfort her husband. She wrapped her arms around his shoulders and held him tight. "There are some back home that say war changes men," she said. "It is a shame that it should change a young man like Timothy."

Morrow could only nod.

At daylight the regiment was summoned and placed on two sides of a small open field. The regimental band struck up a sad melody, but the men felt no sympathy for the condemned. By that time, all knew the identity of the murderer and all sought vengeance. If the soldiers had had their choice, Timothy wouldn't have made it out of the woods. He would not have been given the satisfaction of living another day.

Twelve armed guards stood at ease near the designated spot. They had been charged with ensuring that the condemned didn't make an escape, and they too were eager to get the event over with, to see Timothy laid to rest once and for all. Then came the condemned, Timothy, escorted by Chaplain Way and two armed guards. His head was low, his character shattered. He walked the path of a guilty man. Following closely behind him were twelve more armed men. These soldiers would be responsible for executing Timothy. Morrow himself armed the rifles. It was customary to load one of the twelve rifles with powder and no ball, ensuring that one of them wouldn't fire the fatal shot. The rifles were then mixed up and distributed back to those selected. And when the smoke cleared and the execution was finished, each man could believe, if he wanted, that he had held the empty rifle. The other eleven, however, were primed and loaded.

Following the armed procession came four men bearing the pine coffin. They shuffled out ahead of Timothy and the executioners, and quickly placed the box down on the ground before the entire regiment. Timothy was then brought to it, and seated on its end, facing the twelve executioners as they lined up. There, a soldier, a friend of the slain, approached him and removed any military insignia from Timothy's uniform. He did not deserve to wear them. After that, Lieutenant Colonel Flanigan read what the condemned had been charged with before the entire regiment, concluding with the established punishment: death by firing squad. Before stepping away, Flanigan tied a black cloth around Timothy's eyes.

From there, Chaplain Way moved in for final words. The conversation was short and to the point, but as Way pulled away, Timothy grabbed at his robe. Way bent down to settle the frightened spirit and Timothy said a few more words before he let the holy man go.

Colonel Morrow then gave the order for the twelve executioners to take their aim. There was a moment of eerie silence before Morrow gave the command to fire, and every soldier in the ranks could feel the tension. Perhaps for that brief moment their thoughts of vengeance had passed. Perhaps they actually felt sorry for Timothy. But before any of the scattered thoughts could settle, Morrow ordered the executioners to their duty. There was a loud crash as the small wall of musketry ignited. Timothy's arms shot upward, his chest taking the brunt of the blows. The impacts went off with thuds, the slugs slamming into flesh and grinding into bones. The body fell back into the coffin, the weight of the shots driving it toward the ground. As the pocket of smoke rolled across the small open field, the men could see Timothy's legs sticking out of the pine box, one of them twitching as the last of the blood flowed. Two men immediately dashed toward the coffin and pushed the legs inside, adjusting the body before the lid was nailed down.

The regiment filed quickly past the pine box. They saw the blood on the lid, on the edges of the coffin, and spattered on the white ground around the box. Morrow himself did not want to see the coffin but did so anyway. If he expected his men to bear witness then he would have to as well. It would serve as a reminder. Cowards and murderers would be punished to the full extent of military law.

And without further ceremony, the box was tossed into a large hole and buried.

In late January, the Twenty-Fourth Michigan worked its way through General Burnside's infamous "Mud March." The roads had been holding well prior to the great movement, but by the time the army slithered from its camp, the weather made a turn for the worse. A plastic mud swallowed the feet of men, the hooves of horses and mules, and the wheels of the artillery and wagons.

Wagons were emptied and left vacant. Multiple teams of horses attempted to free the artillery from the muddy trap. Drivers cursed at their stalled mules and horses. Hundreds of soldiers were gathered and employed to build corduroy roads, cutting down trees and setting them over the mud and muck to create passable roads. For two days these soldiers battled the elements on the road project. Finally, General Burnside called it quits. He ordered the Army of the Potomac back into their winter quarters.

Days after returning, General Burnside was relieved of his duties and replaced with General Joseph Hooker, the cordial friend of Colonel Morrow.

Colonel Morrow found General Joe Hooker alone in his tent. At first he hesitated before entering, but once Hooker saw him arrive and rose to greet him, Morrow stepped inside. Taking Hooker's hand, Morrow said,

"I owe you congratulations on your promotion, General. I wish you great success. I can think of no man who deserves it more."

Hooker beamed at the compliment. "I can't tell you," he replied, "how proud I am to be at the head of so noble an army as the Army of the Potomac, Henry. I sincerely believe it the finest army in the world." Hooker invited Morrow to sit and join him. The two embraced each other as old friends returning from a long separation.

"With so noble an army and you in command," stated Morrow, "I believe we will really whip the Rebels when we meet them."

"Yes, yes," Hooker quickly replied. "I fear that they will slip from my grasp before I can have a chance at them. As soon as I can get back across the Rappahannock I will give them a go. I will fight such a battle that has not been seen on this continent before, Henry. I know how to fight it. I will fight it." He tapped his fingers on the desk as he thought. "Fredericksburg was a two-penny affair. Burnside sent them in detail by detail. I will not commit such an error, no, sir. I will give *all* our troops business. Politics," the word struck a cord in him, "our commanders worry too much on politics. I want none of it. There is no greater position for me than at the head of this army. That fool General Taylor tainted my name in politics. I wanted nothing of it then and I want nothing of it now."

Morrow nodded, attentive to every word.

"And how is the Twenty-Fourth, Colonel Morrow? I hope they are doing well. I have formed great expectations for them."

"We are indeed well, General, sir."

"Yes," Hooker returned. "I am very glad to see you well. I am never too engaged in business to see any of my brave officers. I wish to see all of them." Hooker turned away momentarily, his thoughts racing about.

"I reviewed General Sigel's corps today. They are a most splendid body of troops. As soon as the roads permit my travel, I wish to see the Twenty-Fourth and the old Iron Brigade and I hope they wish to see me." When he returned and confronted Morrow again, his mood changed. His face seemed more careworn and tired. His eyes lit up with frustration. "What of General Franklin? Has he received his Court of Inquiry for his dismal performance at Fredericksburg?"

Morrow could only shrug his shoulders. "What do you think of it?" beckoned Hooker.

"I think you should dispose of all officers who will only fight under *one* general. There has been too much foolishness in this army. You have a grand opportunity."

Hooker smiled. It was exactly what he wanted to hear. "That is being done very fast, I assure you." A slight smile grew upon his face. "McClellan's grip on this army is coming to an end, Henry."

Morrow stood up to take his leave. He kindly congratulated Hooker on the promotion and again stated that he looked forward to serving under him. "The Twenty-Fourth will be ready when you call upon it, General," Morrow added proudly.

"And I shall call upon it," replied Hooker. "When I get across the river, I shall give old Bobby Lee the whipping he deserves. I want the mighty Twenty-Fourth at the front when I go rushing into Richmond."

As April of 1863 rolled around, General Hooker was preparing for his campaign. Colonel Morrow, following a few leaves of absences to tour Washington and Baltimore with his wife, had quickly become a favorite officer within Hooker's Army of the Potomac. He was recruited heavily by General Abner Doubleday, who was awaiting his promotion to Major General. He also received several compliments from various commanders, including General Meredith and General John Reynolds. The most flattering, however, was when Morrow attended a cavalry review, in which President Lincoln was present. There, General Hooker called Morrow forward and gently took him by the arm and in the presence of several important officers said, "We are old friends. They tell me you are most noble soldier. I observed your regiment the other day. It was as fine as silk. You *are* a noble soldier. I will take care of you."

Morrow was then introduced to Lincoln and the two made brief mention of their first meeting while Morrow was in Washington awaiting deployment. General Hooker approached again, this time swinging an arm around Morrow's shoulders, and whispered, "*Mon ami.*"

The Twenty-Fourth Michigan was anything but idle that April. In the middle of the month, they joined the Fourteenth Brooklyn Zouaves and one gun of Battery B, for an expedition to Port Royal, Virginia. Crossing the river under a blanket of stars, the force entered Port Royal. Driving off a small detachment of Confederate horsemen, the party re-crossed the river with six prisoners, fifteen captured horses and mules, Confederate mail, and two women sympathetic to the Union cause and seeking safe refuge from the hostile town. All was completed without firing a shot, but as the force returned to the other shoreline, a large Confederate force appeared but it was too late to have done anything. Arriving back at camp, the expedition won acclaim from General John Reynolds, commander of the First Corps, in which he said the Twenty-Fourth showed themselves to be "tried and experienced soldiers and entitled to the highest admiration and praise."

With growing confidence, the Twenty-Fourth Michigan looked

forward to Hooker's coming campaign. They had proven their worth to the Iron Brigade, winning acceptance after their brave and stubborn performance at Fredericksburg. Following that battle, an order was placed for the regiment's black hats, the Hardee Hats that made the Iron Brigade so distinctive. The Twenty-Fourth had earned them, but they would not have them in time for their next bout.

But that didn't matter. They still believed they had something to prove.

CROSSING THE RIVER
—THE BATTLE OF CHANCELLORSVILLE—

Union General Joseph Hooker, known as "Fighting Joe," had developed a master plan; a grand strategy that he hoped would steal a march on the fabled Robert E. Lee. He would split his command. A smaller force would move a few miles below the old Fredericksburg battlefield to direct Lee's attention, while Hooker crossed with the main wing of his army and pressed the Confederate rear and flank, forcing Lee to withdraw from his strongly fortified position.

The Iron Brigade, with the Twenty-Fourth Michigan in tow, was selected as part of the body to make the demonstration near Fredericksburg. While it was to draw attention away from the main Union force crossing further upriver, Hooker wanted the men across the river as soon as possible, so that they may reunite with the rest of the army in time for the grand assault against Lee.

Fitzhugh Crossing would be where the Iron Brigade would cross the Rappahannock, and the Twenty-Fourth would once again attempt to earn its laurels.

There was a dense fog rising from the river. Morgan thought that he could see the enemy on the other shoreline. He knew they were there, but his eyes played tricks on him. Shadows danced about on the opposite bank, and he could hear them converse and hear their laughter as they swapped stories. He wondered what the homes and families of his enemies were like. Were they like his? Did they have sweethearts back at home impatiently waiting for their soldiers to return? He rested his chin on the barrel end of his rifle and watched with curiosity. Were they so different than he?

There was rustling off to his right. He could hear men in motion, the clamor of the anticipated engineer detachment. These soldiers struggled to pull the pontoon train down the bank of the river. Morgan could hear them curse and could hear their officers urge the weary men forward. The boats were needed for the crossing. If they failed to arrive on time, then the brigade would lose the element of time. At this point, there had been no exchanges between the two opposing shorelines, nothing to resemble even a small skirmish.

Morgan watched in amusement as several engineers fumbled with the boats. As more of their detachment arrived, the men worked quickly to unload them. There was more cursing, and the men seemed ignorant of the close proximity of the enemy. Several officers from the brigade slipped down the shoreline and demanded the engineers work quietly. Morgan heard the response and assumed the Confederates across the river had heard it as well.

As the engineers began to unload the boats for the pontoon bridge, the Confederate line on the other side opened. Morgan nearly stumbled in surprise when he heard the sudden roar of musketry. He drew his attention back to the engineers, who continued to work under the growing pressure. The dense fog had not passed, but Morgan could make out muzzle blasts from the opposite side. Flames sprouted from the barrels and pushed through the thick haze.

It was an eerie sight.

Morgan patiently loaded his rifle. Since the engagement at Fredericksburg, he had learned a great deal. He had learned how to read a growing fight and when to trust his gut feeling about a coming adventure. His regiment was near the front of the brigade, so it was very likely that if a fight was going to break out over the river, they would most certainly be involved. So, with the calmness of a hardened veteran, he slowly tended to his rifle. Those around him did the same.

And as he tore into the powder and emptied it down the barrel, he no longer wondered if the Southern soldiers across the river were anything like him. They quickly returned to being nothing more than the enemy. That's how it had to be. Those men across the river, with human hearts and human minds, couldn't be valued as equals. War was indeed that cruel, that cold.

Lieutenant Colonel Mark Flanigan strangely thought of the wounded soldier he had met in Washington. The haunting images of the man's amputation dominated his thoughts. He remembered how the soldier bravely battled the pain and agony. He remembered how the surgeon continued to work despite the man's pleas, despite his own exhaustion. It was a dedication like no other. The surgeon sawed and stitched every hour of his day. Flanigan found himself wondering how a man could endure so much and still find the will to continue. He knew that he would see much on the front lines, but he believed the most ghastly of images, the saddest sights of all, took place in the darkness of the hospital tents and buildings.

He watched the engineers work under fire. He saw their guards respond with volleys of their own, but this small body of men was simply outclassed by the larger force across the river. It would only be a matter of time before the engineers pulled back up the shoreline and a line from the brigade would be tossed forward to combat the threat. The pontoon bridge had to be built in order for the First Division to cross. The First Division had to cross in order to keep up with Hooker's master strategy. It was simple, really. The division had to cross, one way or another. Be it by bridge or boat, the First Division was needed on the other side.

Forcing the terrible memories from his head, he instructed the men around him to prepare to offer the enemy a response. "The engineers cannot hold alone forever," he told them. "I believe we will be called to assist them and get the bridge built. I think the Twenty-Fourth is up for the challenge."

The enemy fire continued to grow hotter and the engineers continued to struggle. Their efforts paid off, however, as one boat was pushed into the water. Then another one came down and Flanigan could hear the splash. It was a pleasant sound that reminded him of fishing in the streams back home. He could almost feel the cool Michigan water rush between his bare feet. The thought made him smile but was shattered when another Confederate volley sent a few of the engineers dashing up the hill to safety.

Out of the corner of his eye he caught sight of Morrow receiving orders from an aide. Flanigan couldn't hear the words but knew what they pertained to. After the young aide concluded with Morrow, Flanigan watched the soldier jaunt over to the Sixth Wisconsin to relay the order to Colonel Bragg. Before long, Morrow rode up to him and instructed Flanigan to prepare the regiment. "We are to go down to the bank and try to ward off the Confederate fire. We must buy time for the engineers to finish the bridge. They must be protected and we have been selected to provide that service," Morrow quickly said, his nervousness clearly detectable.

Flanigan turned his horse away from Morrow. The animal was calm despite the clamor of musketry and the rattle of the boats as the engineers struggled to get them into the river. "Just give the word, Henry," he told his nervous commander. "The Twenty-Fourth shall go in full force to meet them. The lads are looking for another go at them. This will be another chance."

Morrow said, "I know, Mark. Let's be sure to tell the boys to fire steadily through the fog. Have them look for the muzzle blasts and discharges. Tell them to fire at them."

Flanigan saluted. "Consider it done, Henry."

Color Sergeant Abel Peck stepped down toward the bank and leaped over a few jagged rocks. He hoisted the colors to guide the regiment down to their position, his color guard matching his steps. The fog had thinned slightly, and he could nearly see the opposite bank. As he stumbled down to the shoreline, three more engineers sprinted past him. They had been under a severe fire with little support. They had managed to get only a few boats into the water before they were driven off.

Peck gazed across the river in anticipation. He wasn't frightened. He wasn't worried. With him was his trusted regiment, and they would not abandon him. As he settled at the center of the line, he felt the companies on his sides latch on, embracing each other as a complete unit. No, he wasn't frightened. He almost actually felt pity for his enemies across the way. The Twenty-Fourth had come to greet them, to ensure that the bridge was completed and the First Division would accomplish its objectives.

He heard the orders for the soldiers to take their aim. Hundreds of rifles steadied in the soft spring wind. He heard them swing into position. Peck anxiously awaited the order to commence firing, but it did not come. Instead, there was a single volley from the opposite shore, the blasts indicating to the Twenty-Fourth Michigan and Sixth Wisconsin where to place their aim. Before the smoke settled and the flames vanished, the combined Union line delivered a response. The mass eruption made the ground shake under Peck's feet, and he felt the vibrations in the heavy wooden flagstaff. Pushing the flag even higher into the air, he screamed in support of his comrades. "Give it to them!"

Several birds flew through the fog and were brought down by the exchanging volleys. Two of them dropped within the lines of the Twenty-Fourth, and the closest soldiers shouted their intent to keep the birds and try to eat them later. Peck heard the brief, friendly squabble between comrades and thought it marvelous that men could think of such while under fire, while engaging the enemy. After several short exchanges, the soldiers apparently agreed to share the bird and went back to keeping up a hot fire.

The heat grew intense as the two lines, standing across a river, and under the cover of fog, blasted away at each other. The sweat rolled down his forehead and the flag was getting to be quite heavy. The deafening thunder of the rifles, just feet from either side of him, momentarily made him lose hearing. He could see the lines exchange, but he couldn't hear the volleys, the orders, or the cheers of the men.

His eyes had not yet been affected by the burning smoke of gunpowder, so he could begin to clearly make out the opposite shore and its entrenched soldiers as the fog lifted from the river. To his amazement, both lines stood their ground and battled it out despite the rising fog, despite the loss of the protective blanket that had settled between them. For every volley from the Confederate side, he watched the Michigan and Wisconsin line respond in kind, both lines tossing lead over the river. Both lines determined to hold it out, no matter how long it took or how great the cost.

The large flag wildly flapped in the breeze generated by the fight. His hands gripped the staff even tighter, bracing himself to keep it steady. As he turned away, he saw the first of the wounded vacate the Michigan line and head toward the rear, several hundred yards behind. There he also saw Colonel Morrow, sitting on horseback, offering the men encouraging words. He watched as the officer strode over, ignoring the bullets and slugs about him, and checked on the wounded falling back. With a quick nod and a pat on the back, he sent the soldiers to the rear.

Colonel Morrow saw the soldier's bloody arm and dismissed him. The soldier argued with him, but Morrow would have none of it. "I ordered you to the rear. You are wounded. You have done all that you can today," he barked. He watched the soldier climb the bank back toward the rear. There is a great deal of fight in these men, he thought. They wish to stand with each other to the end.

The thought made him smile. His regiment had become what he knew it would become. His thoughts, however, were short lived as another aide dashed through the smoke and ordered him to fall back. Morrow had trouble hearing the soldier and asked the young man to speak up over the roar of musketry. Again the aide repeated the order for the Twenty-Fourth Michigan and Sixth Wisconsin to withdraw to a safer distance. Morrow looked ahead across the river, plainly seeing the outlines of the enemy's trenches and making out a few cannon rolling into position. The enemy line looked well placed and well manned from what he could see. "Very well," he told the aide. "I shall order my regiment back."

Captain Edwards was cheering on Company F when he received the order to fall back. With each passing minute, their enemy shuffled more troops into position and began to bring in cannon. It was useless for the Union line to continue firing across the river. He knew there would be several more tries at building the bridge, but he believed the efforts would fail as they had before. But the regiment had done enough, buying ample time for the engineers to rest and recover. He knew the Twenty-Fourth was capable of holding steady against enemy infantry. The idea of holding, unsupported, against both infantry and cannon, however, would be much more trying.

As the regiment shifted back, Company F slipped out of position and found themselves out from the rest of the regiment. The error, Edwards identified, had happened when two men were wounded on the right side of his line and their comrades did not want to leave them behind. He hurriedly ordered the wounded recovered and again shifted his lines to meet back up with the regiment. There was safety in numbers, he knew, and he dared not stay out alone on the exposed shoreline too long without support.

Edwards was leading his company back up toward the regiment when he heard a massive volley that tore into his line. He saw the dirt and grass fragments fly about him as the slugs met the earth. Racing across his line, he ordered the men forward at the double-quick. "Get up the hill!" he shouted. Surging up the slight rise away from the enemy fire, Edwards turned to another portion of his company and saw four men stop to return fire. It was a brave and foolish effort. There was no need to reply to the Confederate volleys, as the company was nearing safety. He ran over to them and immediately ordered them back to the line. One soldier pleaded with Edwards that he had not gotten the chance to shoot a Rebel and that there seemed to be no better time than the present moment. Reluctantly, Edwards allowed the solider to take aim. Turning back to check on the rest of his command, Edwards heard a thud as the soldier collapsed to the ground behind him. Reaching back and pulling on the body, he saw the small hole in the soldier's forehead and the stream of dark blood it quickly produced. Three soldiers, having witnessed the event, ran toward them and fired across the river before pulling both Edwards and the dead soldier up the bank.

There, Edwards watched as the soldier's body was pulled from his hands. He did not want to give up the boy, but his soldiers urged him to do so. "I should have ordered him to the rear," Edwards muttered. "I should have ordered him." The pain of having witnessed the death and having allowed the soldier to take his shot gnawed at his soul. He sat alone for several minutes, deep in thought. I should have ordered him to the rear, he told himself again. His soldiers gathered around him and tried to pull him from his depression, but he ignored them. Chaplain Way was called to offer assistance, but when he arrived, Edwards instructed him to leave. "I am well enough now," he told Way.

He returned to Company F amid praises and admiration.

Commanding the Union First Corps, General John Reynolds didn't want his First Division stopped in their crossing. The engineers made several more unsuccessful attempts at unloading the boats but were thrown back by the Confederate line holding the opposite shore. The pontoon bridge was vital to the crossing and if the Confederates couldn't be frightened away, then Reynolds would drive them away by force. The only other option left was to storm across the river and take the heights from the pesky Rebels. Only after that could the bridge be built without hassle.

Storming the heights was considered a forlorn hope. There was an entire Confederate brigade stationed in the rifle-pits and trenches across the river. The river itself, at this junction, was quite wide. The attacking Union men would have to cross the wide river under a relentless fire before they could even set foot on the shore. From there, the bank rose steadily and very steeply. It was covered with thick undergrowth that would hamper the movements of an attacking force. Trees had been felled, further obstructing forward motion. The position, it seemed, was near impregnable.

Reynolds had made up his mind, however, and the Twenty-Fourth Michigan and the Sixth Wisconsin were assigned to the storming party. Three companies from the Second Wisconsin were detailed to run the pontoon wagons down to the bank and get the boats into the water. The First Division had to get across the wide Rappahannock and the two Iron Brigade regiments had to take the opposite shore.

Morgan heard the thunderous order and the Union men gave a cheer as they dashed down toward the bank at the double-quick. He ran as fast as his legs could carry him. His rifle was loaded but was held tightly in one hand. There would be no time to stop and fire. They had been ordered to get the boats and push across the river.

Pop. Pop. Pop. Boom! Crash! The Confederate line came to life. Slugs slammed against the boats carried by the Wisconsin men and tore into the soft muddy earth of the shoreline. Morgan drove forward with all his might, rushing toward the first boats being tossed amid heavy fire into the water. He slid on some mud that nearly sent him sprawling to the ground, but he regained momentum and splashed into the cold water. Tossing his rifle into the boat and leaping in, he turned to aid others in jumping into the vessel. He hollered for them to give him their rifles so they could leap in. Once in, the brave Wisconsin men gathered behind the boat and pushed it forward into the river.

Oblivious to the rain of lead, the men used whatever they could to propel the boat forward. Morgan turned his rifle over and used the butt-end of the stock as a makeshift paddle and urged the others to do the same. As they began their trek across the wide river, two of the men stood to exchange shots with the opposing shore.

Quickly nearing the bank, Morgan ducked as a Confederate volley cut across the river. His head nearly fell between his legs but his arms kept rowing. He pushed the water with every once of strength, nearly breaking his rifle stock in half. The men bravely cheered as they neared the shoreline and several of them leaped over the sides into the shallow water and began firing toward the shocked Rebels. A foothold had been made.

Colonel Morrow climbed into the boat and cheered the men on as they battled the river's current and fought their way to the other side. He continuously bobbed his head up and down to avoid the volleys, even though he realized the Confederate aim was too high. Nervously he looked to the other shore and wondered what his regiment would come up against.

To his left he could see Flanigan standing in the boat, his large figure towering over the water. The Irishman was ordering the men of his boat to row faster, telling them that the Rebels were waiting to be driven from the field. Morrow could hear the cheers and laughter of the men in response to Flanigan's ramblings. It was strange to see Flanigan and those men so cool and calm under fire, unable to return it. It made Morrow damn his nervousness in the face of combat.

But the men in his boat thought their Colonel was just excited, eager to strike. For his part, Morrow relaxed once the boat came upon shallow water and three men climbed outside to pull the boat onto the shore. Without hesitation, he stepped from the vessel, unsheathed his sword, and ordered the regiment forward.

His uncontrollable nervousness suddenly faded.

"Forward! Charge!" he shouted to his beloved Twenty-Fourth.

Color Sergeant Abel Peck threw himself from the boat as it slammed onto the shore. He unfurled the colors and drove forward against the heights. He passed several comrades who had formed short lines and fired quickly before ascending the bank. Peck drove headlong into the undergrowth, clinging onto thick weeds and struggling over felled trees.

As he stormed the heights, he heard the cries of the Sixth Wisconsin as they entered the fray. He saw two of their companies surge forward and reach the undergrowth with the lead elements of the Twenty-Fourth. He also saw the Sixth's color bearer rush from a boat and, having seen Peck nearly to the top, dash forward for a friendly race. A game was soon played between the two as they neared the end of their climb. Peck smiled and laughed, ignoring the danger of the attack.

He pulled upward with his free arm and reached the top, sprinting past a surprised Confederate soldier, who froze and lifted his arms to surrender as the Twenty-Fourth spilled over the rise. To a soft plot of soil Peck dashed, stride for stride with the color bearer of the Sixth. The two met together and drove their flagstaffs into the ground amid cheers from Michigan and Wisconsin men alike. Their friendly competition over, they embraced each other with a warm handshake.

A fight still raged as the Twenty-Fourth stormed the heights. Peck stood guard alongside the regiment's flag and eagerly watched the event unfold. Too tired to join in the chase but not wanting to sit it out, Peck raised his arms and pointed forward, yelling for his comrades to drive the enemy from the field.

Lieutenant Colonel Mark Flanigan easily stepped over the edge of the boat and watched as a dead Confederate solider slid down the bank and tumbled through the thick undergrowth. He immediately ordered the boat cleared and sent the vessel back across the river with two volunteers to help the rest of the brigade cross.

His eyes lifted to the heights where he saw a Michigan soldier buckle from a shot and slump to the ground. He waved his sword forward and directed the men to climb and join their brave comrades. Pacing down the line urging the arriving Michigan men forward, Flanigan came across Lieutenant Wheeler of Company I. Wheeler was huddled to the ground and when Flanigan first came upon him he thought the young officer had been wounded or killed. To the Irishman's amazement, Wheeler was unscathed but refused to go forward. Flanigan pleaded for the officer to do his duty and catch up with his company, but Wheeler refused.

Finally Flanigan demanded Wheeler to go forward, whether he wanted to or not. Unsnapping the holster of his revolver, Flanigan then threatened to shoot the coward if he did not do his duty. "We are all scared as hell, lad," Flanigan preached, "but we have signed up for this and it is our duty. We should all see to it, no matter the cost in the end."

Pulling the young officer to his feet and again threatening him, Flanigan drove forward with the rest of the regiment. He could hear the firing settle over the slight rise, and he could hear Morrow shouting orders to the Twenty-Fourth.

Behind him, crossing the river, were the first elements of the rest of the brigade.

Captain Edwards looked back and saw the regiment's flag planted in the soil. He pointed to three Confederate prisoners and politely ordered them toward the flag. Edwards was pleased with the conduct of the entire regiment. The heights had been stormed and taken in short time and the enemy was sent fleeing across the field. The elaborate sets of rifle-pits and trenches had offered no protection as the Michigan men surged over them.

There were several wounded comrades that sat back behind the line as Edwards ordered his company to regroup. As he toured the field in search of his soldiers, he saw a large batch of prisoners being escorted toward the river. There were several lifeless bodies of Confederate soldiers who had died making a last stand. Joining the captives were a few artillery pieces, which were proudly displayed as trophies.

His men cheered when they saw him, lifting their stained kepis into the air. "We have done well, Captain!" they called. "Tell Wayne County we have done our duty!"

Edwards nodded to them. He was relived the attack went so well. When he had stood on the opposite shore, just moments before the charge, he wondered if the intimidating heights were even possible to take. He had counted a great many soldiers confronting him and he wondered how many more were behind them. He saw their trenches and cannon. What had begun as a near impossible task was completed remarkably and in short time. The attack had gone so fast, in fact, that Edwards believed it took less than ten minutes for the two regiments to get across the river and successfully storm the heights.

How marvelous it was!

Colonel Morrow checked his pocket watch and smiled. "It took seven minutes, Mr. Peck," he told the color bearer, "just seven minutes for us to drive them away." He shook his head. "Beautiful, isn't it?" he asked. Before he received an answer, there was a shout from the river bank that General Wadsworth was crossing.

Swimming his horse across, Wadsworth appeared before the Twenty-Fourth just as the regiment gathered in line. Morrow watched as the general rode before them, his horse dripping wet. Wadsworth removed his hat and pointed to two bullet holes, in which drew a large cheer from the Michigan line. He exclaimed, "God bless the gallant Twenty-Fourth Michigan! God bless you all!"

The men responded with an explosion of cheers, followed by several cries of "God bless you, General."

Once Wadsworth departed for the Sixth Wisconsin, Morrow turned back to his regiment and ordered that a defensive line be prepared. He sent out skirmishers and ordered they keep an eye out for the enemy. "We should elect not to give this ground so nobly won," he told them. After finalizing several other orders, Morrow took a lone stroll down toward the riverbank. He needed a moment alone to gather himself, to reflect upon the quick assault. His regiment had performed splendidly and was already winning great acclaim from the division. It would all sink in eventually, he knew. Let it come. The men deserved it, all of it.

There he came across a group of thin Confederates being loaded into the boats to be carried off to captivity. To their guards, recognizing them as Michigan soldiers, they said, "You boys crossed at Port Royal the other day and are not afraid of anything." To this the guards replied that they had indeed crossed there and that there was in fact nothing that frightened them. Morrow was pleased with their response. They were his soldiers and he was their commander. Most of all, the Twenty-Fourth Michigan belonged to old Wayne County and Michigan. He was pleased that his constant drill had not broken them, but had in fact turned them into hardened soldiers. He was pleased that they did not abandon him when he made them work so hard.

Watching the prisoners being sent off, Morrow sat down on a large rock and listened to the distant thunder of artillery. At first he thought it could have been thunder, but the roar was too constant. He wondered what his friend Hooker was up to, if he had indeed stolen a march on the enemy. Morrow wondered where the Twenty-Fourth would be called to next, what duty they would have to perform.

The pontoon bridge was near completion by the time he stood up to make the climb once again. Several officers noticed him and congratulated him on a brilliant assault. One of them, a captain in the artillery, stopped and said, "Colonel, your charge across the river was the most brilliant act I've ever seen. God bless you and your men, Colonel." To which Morrow replied, "If you would be so kind as to do me a favor, and climb that hill there and tell this to the regiment. I'm afraid that I cannot take the credit for the work those brave men have done. I simply pointed my sword, Captain. They were the ones who did the work." Again the captain expressed his congratulations and told Morrow that he would congratulate the men as well. Morrow kindly thanked him for the compliment and watched the officer climb up the steep bank.

So much acclaim, he thought. Oh, how the men deserve it.

At Fitzhugh Crossing, April 29 and 30, 1863, the Twenty-Fourth Michigan suffered twenty-five casualties. The regiment secured the lines for a few days after the crossing and met heavy cannonading from the enemy and several sharp skirmishes. One day, while the distant battle could be heard raging, the Confederate line before the regiment happily cheered as the sounds of battle grew nearer. Colonel Morrow rode along his line and ordered the regiment to give a rousing cheer in response, which was carried well beyond the Michigan line.

Shortly after, the division was relocated to the Chancellorsville battlefield, finally attaching to the Army of the Potomac. The land they occupied was terrible for armed conflict. The regiment found it heavily wooded and broken. The great battle continued to swirl around them, and it appeared that General Hooker was driving Confederate General Lee from the field. As had been before, the noise of battle inched toward the Twenty-Fourth. The men prepared their rifles and wrote letters. Colonel Morrow viewed pictures of his wife and baby for the first time. Lieutenant Colonel Flanigan penned a loving letter to his wife. Morgan wrote to Emmy, and Peck wrote to his wife and daughter.

General Wadsworth soon called upon Colonel Morrow and instructed him to prepare his regiment to move. While meeting with Wadsworth, Morrow learned that General John Sedgwick had taken the heights behind Fredericksburg from the Rebels. The message was passed to the regiment where it was received with lively cheers.

A day after Morrow prepared the regiment, it was moved. The Twenty-Fourth Michigan was shuffled across the field to the extreme right of the Union line, toward the fight they had listened to for days.

"The Eleventh Corps made fools of us all," the aide told Morrow. "Those damned Dutchmen ran a foul again. They were swept from the field. We would have won the day had it not been for them." The aide pointed toward a road in the distance, "We'll take that one, Colonel."

Colonel Morrow nodded. He had not been on the field when the Eleventh Corps was attacked so he couldn't rightfully criticize their behavior. He had heard from several officers, however, who spoke very badly of their conduct. But this didn't matter anymore. The Confederates had pounded Hooker's line but it had not yet broken. The Army of the Potomac was standing strong. He could sense the bravery, the desire to whip the Rebels as he rode. It was a comforting feeling.

"You're probably asking yourself why it is you and your regiment have been called so far away from your brigade, aren't you, Colonel?"

"It has crossed my mind."

"It is so good, Colonel, that I cannot keep it from you," the young aide stated. "I called upon General Hooker to give him a report on the condition of things on our right. Just as I finished, the general asked me what troops were positioned there. I told him." The aide rubbed his chin as a smile grew. "He fell silent for a moment and was deep in thought. He finally looked up to me and said 'I wish Colonel Morrow and his regiment were there.' Then he nodded. 'Yes,' he said, 'tell General Reynolds to send the best regiment he has to guard those roads. Tell him to send Colonel Morrow and the Twenty-Fourth Michigan.' So that, Colonel," said the aide "is how you came to be called, sir."

Morrow smiled. It seemed very much like Hooker to offer such a flattering compliment in a time of conflict. He beamed at the faith Hooker had in the regiment. The regiment had in fact come a long way from being ignored by the veterans, earning respect and acclaim in nearly every aspect of military life. It was winning such attention and fame, no longer for their presentation during drills and dress parades, but because of their mettle in battles and expeditions.

"I trust you will give General Hooker and General Reynolds our compliments," said Morrow. "The Twenty-Fourth is honored to have been selected, and we will not disappoint our faithful commanders."

Morgan heard rustling in the trees off to his left. Company F had been sent forward on picket duty, and contact had been made with the enemy all through the night. It was dark and the troops could hold no fires, so their eyes struggled to see in the thick darkness. The eyes often played tricks on those out beyond the safety of the line. Shadows leaped from treetop to treetop and strange noises alerted the men on guard. Morgan had fallen victim to these tricks on more than one occasion that night, even firing at what turned out to be a deer caught between the two opposing lines. He cursed himself for giving away his position and wasting ammunition, but such mistakes happened often that night.

But the noise he had heard didn't fade. He could almost make out the sounds of each careful footstep. They could not have been of his own company, for Morgan was well aware of his comrades' positions. So he waited, perhaps not wanting to give away his concealed location or not wanting to waste the ammunition, to see what came of the noise. Before he could adjust himself he heard several men shout, calling support toward the left of the picket line. Morgan took a breath and sprinted over that way, drawing nearer to where he heard the strange noises that sounded like men shuffling through the woods.

Pop.

"To the left!" was a shout through the darkness.

Pop.

Crack.

The rifle exchange was limited as the men struggled to find their bearings. The Michigan men were careful not to open fire on their own lines or detachments, so they remained still and waited for the firing to continue before moving forward and joining in. Their wait wasn't long as soon the night was lit up with musketry. Pop. Pop. Pop. Crack. Pop. Crack. Pop. Pop.

Morgan pumped his legs even harder, determined to reach the fight before the thin picket line was overrun. Zip. Bullets buzzed his head.

Twang. Slugs tore into the trees around him. Still he ran, knowing that his comrades needed him. Pop. Pop. The musketry grew more intense as he shuffled across the line, stumbling over rocks and large branches as he went. Pop. Pop. Pop. Pop. He inched close enough to see the muzzle blasts of the enemy and gauge their distance from the Michigan line.

He heard the moans of one man wounded but couldn't tell whether it was one of his comrades or one of the Confederates. Ignoring the man's pleas, he stepped blindly through the darkness and fumbled his way onto a group of comrades who were targeting enemy movements in the darkness. Carefully listening to their directions and watching for the muzzle blasts to give away the enemies' position, Morgan steadied his rifle and joined the heated skirmish.

As soon as there was a flash several yards in front of him, he pulled the trigger.

As the sun climbed into the morning sky, the growing light splintering between the trees, Captain Edwards checked the condition of his company's picket line and was satisfied that it had not been broken. There were several times in the combat during the night before where he feared the Confederates had broken through his thin ranks. Company F, however, wouldn't be outdone or victimized by the pressing Rebel forces. They had held firm yet again, despite being harassed all through the night.

Pacing the thin and weary line, Edwards quietly complimented the men under his command. He was proud of them and wanted them to know it. He wasn't afraid of telling them what a job they had done and how the entire army would be grateful. On his little tour he saw a few of his wounded. These men stayed with the line because their wounds were not deemed enough to force them to the rear. There was still plenty of fight left in the soldiers. It would take more than cuts and bruises to move them.

The damaged trees scattering the position and the makeshift fence the men put up the day before showed the markings of a hard fight. Bark was stripped off of several trees, including two where Edwards himself had sought shelter while issuing orders. In some parts, the makeshift fence had been collapsed as the bullet holes forced the quickly compacted branches and logs to bow and break. Even his jacket bore signs of hardship, as he counted five small holes scattered about him. He never realized that he had come so close to perishing in battle. Had he shifted an inch or two either way then the slugs would have found their mark, and he would have been killed instantly or horribly wounded.

Such was not his fate, however, at least not from the previous night. God granted him another day to live and fight, but Edwards questioned how many more lucky chances he would get before his time ran out. He studied the proximity of the holes by holding up his jacket and sticking his index finger through them. Several of his soldiers witnessed the sight and cheered for him, knowing that their officer had once again escaped death or capture. He politely waved for them to be quiet and still. They were still on picket duty until relieved, and he wanted his line to be ready in case the Rebels tried to strike during sunlight instead of relying on the darkness to press their attacks.

He didn't have to keep his weary troops attentive very long, however, as Colonel Morrow furnished another company for picket duty. As the tired men of Company F saw their replacements streaming toward them, they grabbed their gear and sleepily formed into line without being ordered to do so. Edwards didn't waste the time correcting them or punishing them for their actions. He was far too tired to worry on such matters. His men were ready to go. There was nothing more to it than that. He was ready to go as well. It had been one long and dangerous night and the boys of Company F were ready to march back to the regiment for supplies and rest.

Several of the men had fallen asleep with their rifles in hand, still ready at a moment's notice. Edwards wearily found these men, woke them, and ordered them into line. "We are leaving," he told them. "It is back to the old regiment for us. We'll get a good night's sleep tonight, boys. I promise you that."

The men said their farewells and wished their comrades luck in holding the line that night. Edwards gave whatever information he could to the officer in charge and even informed him how and which way to construct the makeshift fence and other fortifications that helped solidify the thin line. "Keep the men close enough to support each other," Edwards instructed. "They will come at you from all angles in the darkness. Do not be timid in your defense. I believe your men will succeed as long as they fight for every inch of ground. If the Rebels advance forward, then so does your line. If the Rebels fall back, then you continue to advance your line until they will no longer pester you or create a nuisance."

Edwards eventually pulled away from the fresh company and joined his men on the march back to the regiment. They had done their job and withstood a constant skirmish that lasted all night long. When the sun rose the following morning, the men still held their original positions. He was thrilled with their conduct. Company F had once again outdone themselves and surprised their veteran commander.

He was growing used to it and should have expected it.

After all, he had hoped to make it the best company in the Twenty-Fourth.

General Joseph Hooker's plan never materialized the way he envisioned. Chancellorsville proved not to be the grandest victory of the war for the Army of the Potomac, but one of its most tragic and humiliating defeats. Hooker believed he had no choice but to again cross the river and silently pull his army away from the victorious Confederate Army of Northern Virginia.

As the Union army began to pull out and quietly flush troops, artillery, and trains across the river, the Twenty-Fourth Michigan, sent out by order of Hooker himself, seemed to be forgotten. Had General Paul not stumbled into the regiment's camp and informed Colonel Morrow that the Michigan regiment was the last Union regiment on that side of the river, then the Twenty-Fourth surely would have been captured. Taking action immediately, Morrow called in his pickets and ordered the regiment out as silently as possible.

A terrible rainstorm set in that drenched the men as they marched back to where the massive Union army sat just a day ago. To their amazement, the army was gone. The Michigan troops quickly realized that the army was in retreat and had vacated the field to the Confederates. Morrow drove the regiment for miles, seemingly wandering around in the dense woods and thick growth, almost becoming captured on a few occasions, until they stumbled onto the main army crossing at the United States Ford. During the night march to that location, however, five companies became separated from the regiment and were feared to be captured. The companies eventually turned up at the crossing and rejoined the regiment just as the Iron Brigade redeployed back across the river to protect the rear as the army finished crossing the pontoon bridge. Back to the woods the brigade went to fend off an attack that never materialized. Finally, the brigade again crossed the bridge and its soldiers were the last Union men to leave the Chancellorsville battlefield soil.

The entire day of the crossing the regiment marched through the rainstorm. They waded through creeks and struggled through mud nearly knee deep in some spots. The regiment marched with the retreating army for fifteen miles and eventually stopped for rest that night. The men were wet and hungry. Having marched constantly for the past two days, the men of the regiment quickly fell asleep within the first ten minutes of being settled.

The Twenty-Fourth Michigan questioned the retreat of the army. The men had been under the impression that the army was driving back the enemy, with few exceptions and errors. Colonel Morrow attributed the retreat to the rumors of cowardly conduct by the Eleventh Corps and General Sedgwick's failure to keep the heights behind Fredericksburg. He could not answer from positive knowledge, however. The reason for the retreat was a mystery that escaped the Michigan soldier and officer alike. All that Morrow knew was that it seemed that half of the Army of the Potomac had not fired a gun, but to this, he also had no reliable sources or concrete evidence.

Colonel Morrow, perhaps seeking reasons for the army's retreat, paid a visit to his friend General Hooker. He hoped to find answers there.

General Hooker stood up and saluted Morrow as he entered the tent. Morrow returned the salute kindly before taking a seat offered by his friend and commander. "I suppose you ought to be called the Duke of Port Royal," said Hooker pleasingly.

Morrow's response was immediate, "Whether I am so called or not depends upon you, General."

Hooker laughed. He seemed to be in a relaxed state considering his army was just pushed back across the river by an outnumbered force. "Well," he said slowly, "if it does you shall be a Brigadier General." He pointed to some paperwork on his small desk. "There are two vacancies in the list of Brigadiers, Henry. I am going to recommend you for one of them, old friend."

The words shocked him. Morrow had done no solicitation. He had done no lobbying as other commanders had. "I am honored, sir. But I must confess that I do not believe I have earned it. There are others whose conduct has been more brilliant, who have had more experience."

"Foolish," replied Hooker. "These commanders you generously speak of are among the reasons this army has turned back in the face of our enemy. If only the rest of the army could have fought like the First Corps, then we would have been successful at that place. We would have driven them from the field, Henry." He angrily turned away from Morrow, hiding the disappointment and frustration on his face. The recent battle had been debated all throughout the army and many officers put the blame on Hooker. "I should just cross the river again and capture the whole Rebel army. Yes, I would push the First Corps in and let the rest of the army see how good soldiers fight. Ah," he sighed, "but this cannot be done. What has happened has happened, and I cannot change it. There are some that blame me, Henry. Do you believe that?"

"I believe the army still has confidence in you, General."

Hooker raised a hand and brushed the comment away. He was

frustrated and upset with the setback. He had touted himself to Washington, the army, and the nation, but he was driven back like all the commanders before him. "It is a great portion of that army that has failed me. No," he suddenly said, changing his argument. "I cannot fault the fighting men of this army. It is not they who have failed me but their commanders." Morrow nodded as Hooker spoke. He was well aware of the strained relations between Hooker and many of his subordinates. "They should be at fault. Had they commanded their units with more precision and given the boys a fair fight, we would have sacked Bobby Lee."

To this Morrow agreed, "Indeed, General."

He watched Hooker lean back casually in the small wooden chair. "Washington may want my head on this, Henry. There has been much politicking by my commanders behind my back. I fear they want me replaced."

"It is not wise to think of such," Morrow replied.

Hooker shook his head. "I will have at them first," he said with a slight smile. "They may call for me to be relieved, and Washington may seek it out. If that happens, then I will resign before these damned political officers strangle my career. I will ensure that I leave the army with my dignity, Henry. I will not let them take that."

The Twenty-Fourth Michigan concluded its participation in the Chancellorsville campaign by quietly shuffling past the rifle-pits and trenches they had stormed so nobly with the Sixth Wisconsin. It was a tragic end to a campaign that had started out with high hopes of ending the war once and for all. As the regiment re-crossed the river, taken so gallantly and earned with blood, there wasn't a soldier in the ranks who didn't think the war would last several more years. They were veterans now, and they realized there would be no easy victories earned in their desperate struggle. They marched with weary hearts, full of pain, sadness, and frustration.

But like good, faithful veterans, they marched on.

THE LAURELS OF WAR

After ten days of marching and fighting, the regiment settled back near Fitzhugh's Crossing and dedicated the welcomed camp in honor of Chaplain Way. Elaborate walkways were designed and built and company streets were laid out over the grounds. The men mingled with comrades and swapped stories around numerous fires. The camp was a lively experience that the men needed after Chancellorsville.

The great George Washington had spent his childhood days around there and not far from the regiment's camp was the land in which a young George took an axe to a cherry tree. Slightly further away was where it was said that the young man threw a stone all the way across the wide Rappahannock, considered quite an impressive feat.

Color Sergeant Peck glanced down to the water and felt the cool spring breeze brush up against his face. He was without the flag and appreciated the rest. But soon he became bored without the many tasks that generally followed him, so he joined a party of Michigan men that wanted to test their strength and one of the legends of George Washington.

Throwing a stone across a river never seemed too trying, but Peck had never come across too many rivers like the mighty Rappahannock. His fixation with George Washington always seemed to return to him during idle times, and he didn't mind the challenge of trying to match the young Washington's feat of getting a stone across the wide river. In order to do so, the men tried to recreate history and stand where they imagined Washington would stand in relation to the property and the house in the background. A few of the men wished to take practice tosses, but all of them soon agreed that this would not be allowed. Although there was no way of telling how many times Washington attempted the throw, they agreed that each of them should throw only once to be fair to the memory of the greatest American.

Peck had been picked to throw first. Stepping back and winding up, he leaped forward and let the small rock fly across the river. He watched the small speck land short of the opposing shoreline, splashing into the shallow water near the edge. "I'm not sure it can be done, boys," he told them as he stepped away. Another soldier stepped forward and heaved a rock toward the other side. His shot too came up short and never hit land. "I'm telling you," Peck added, "I'm not sure that it can be done." A third attempt was made that resulted in the same outcome, and it seemed that Peck's point was being proven.

The fourth thrower told his comrades that his stone would make it to the other shore without a problem. As he let his arm go and released the throw, they were all amazed that the rock had carried that far. There was a soft crack as the rock slammed onto the shoreline, having cleared the wide river with ease. The triumphant soldier hoisted his arms into the air in celebration, for he had matched the impressive feat of the great George Washington.

Seeing that it was indeed possible, other men stepped forward, and their tosses proved just as successful. Peck was called forward again, earning the only second shot at matching the feat. He had watched as the men lined up before making the successful throw, and he tried to copy their motions. Running forward to the edge of the river, he let the stone fly harder than he had ever thrown an object before. To the excitement of his comrades, the rock bounced onto the shoreline, causing the men to explode in cheers. They congratulated Peck by slapping him on the back, while one of the men quickly swam across the river and retrieved the stone, presenting it to Peck upon his return.

Having accomplished the task, the men pulled away from the river under the impression that young George Washington's feat wasn't the least bit remarkable, since several of them had gotten their stones across the Rappahannock. They may have questioned the myth, but they did not question the man as they passed his boyhood home. The buildings and gardens were in bad shape, but Peck imagined what they must have looked like during Washington's stay.

Across the grounds he went, quietly yearning to return to the regiment and reclaim his post and the mighty flag.

Lieutenant Colonel Mark Flanigan slowly policed the camp. The men were scattered about involved in minor chores, gathered around calm fires, or involved in games of all types. Some had retired early to their tents as the usual brigade of prostitutes marched into camp. So, at nearly the same time every evening, Flanigan began his rounds to put an end to gambling and break up the prostitution ring that developed every sunset.

Early in their service, Colonel Morrow had outlawed gambling within the regiment. He did not want the men to carelessly toss aside their money when their families back home could desperately use it. Flanigan thought the same as well and took great strides to ensure that the men obeyed the rules. The games, as Flanigan came upon them, would be presented as a non gambling match. He knew, however, that as soon as he left, the money was placed on the desired spot. In truth, the men wanted to gamble and Flanigan knew that it couldn't be stopped. He didn't like it and tried to stop it as best he could, but the men always found a way to stay cleverly ahead.

As for prostitution, Flanigan took a much harder stance against it. This, he believed, was a moral issue. Besides, several of the Michigan men had come down with illnesses and diseases from regular visits by such women. Not only did Flanigan not believe in the institution, but he saw how if affected the rank and file. A late night with a prostitute could provide a soldier with a terrible disease and miss a coming battle. The regiment, if engaged, would need all the men it could muster, as the number of soldiers in the ranks had steadily decreased since joining the army.

Through his tenure in law enforcement, his eyes were trained to notice the slightest disturbance. As he walked several yards further, he didn't have to look too hard to see activity that needed to be quelled. Ahead of him, gathered around a small tent, was a group of men, maybe ten or twelve of them. As he strolled closer, he could see the men were waving their arms about, money clutched in their hands. There could only be one of two things responsible, either a game or a prostitute. When he came upon them, he forced his way toward the tent by driving his large frame through the crowd. There was no game at all, but he did find a young girl, smile on her face, entertaining the men by dancing and calling out the cost for further, more intimate entertainment.

When the soldiers saw him break through the group, they immediately began to disperse. Flanigan barked at them as they retired, "Back to camp, lads! The fun is over for the evening. Do not return, for she will not be here if you do."

The soldiers grudgingly shuffled away.

He grabbed the girl by the arm and pulled her toward a nearby wagon and sat her on the cart, in between carefully packed goods and wooden barrels. To the driver, a local man bent on selling his merchandise to the soldiers, Flanigan said, "Can you take the poor lass into town?"

The driver nodded. "I'll take her," he replied. "I'll get her back there, but I can't promise you that she won't return. This is the third time this week I've escorted her back. She's from my town, just a ways down that road there. Her name is Ann."

Flanigan returned to the girl. "Ann, is it? Well," he said, his voice calm, his accent smooth, "how old are you, Ann?"

She hid her face under dark brown hair. Her eyes were lowered to the ground, not wanting to look up to the burly man before her. Her lips muttered a quiet response, "Fifteen, sir."

His response was quick, "Poor child." He bent down in hopes of seeing her face. "There are many things a child should be doing, but this isn't one of them, lass. This is no place for a young girl of your age."

"I can't fight," she cried. She pointed toward the camp. "They won't let a woman touch a rifle or nothing! They want us to do *plenty*, except go to war."

"War holds no place for women, lass. And if there is no place in war for women, then there sure is no place for a child." His point had been

277

driven, and it upset the young girl. She folded her arms across her chest with a sigh and then turned away. She was done speaking with him and made it clear. Flanigan looked again to the driver. "Take her back to her mother and inform her all that her child has done. This little one needs to stay away from the army and its soldiers. This is no place for her."

"Well," confessed the driver, "her mother's been touring the army as well. Thing's haven't been the same for those poor ladies since Ann's father was killed out west a year back." The driver wiped his runny nose with a dirty shirt sleeve before continuing on with the conversation. "Life has been hard down here and the county came looking for money. This war costs a lot more than just soldiers, sir. But the mother had trouble with finances and soon took to the streets entertaining soldiers when they came through town. I guess it wasn't long before Ann started working as well. They need money to keep the house."

"It is a shame."

The driver nodded, resting a hand on the cart. He was loaded and ready to travel back home. "Yes, it is." He turned away from Flanigan and climbed into the seat with a grunt. "They've kept their land, though, the same land Ann's father used to farm before the war came calling." The driver whistled and his large horses slowly pulled the loaded cart forward. "I'll take her back," the driver called, "but don't be surprised if you find her here again in the morning."

The Irishman sadly watched as the young girl was carried off on the creaky old cart. Her arms were still tightly folded against her chest in defiance. As the cart creaked away, she finally brushed her hair back from her face and looked to Flanigan with wide eyes. He felt sorry for her and her mother. War had driven them to the unthinkable. There should be countless other activities for the young girl, but the war had forced her to partake in one of the darkest professions. Flanigan could not help but wonder how long Ann had been working, how many men had bedded down with her at night. He shook his head. The thought was horrifying. No young girl should have to live such a life just to get by. He pulled himself away and heard the cart creak and squeak off into the background. He was glad that he had found her and sent her off. If she returned in the morning, then he would try and send her off again. He vowed to repeat the process each and every day, if need be.

Too bad, he thought. Everyone in war must suffer. The soldiers and officers earn medals and acclaim for bravery and gallantry under fire, while those at home are forced to pick up the lives left behind by the soldiers, to care for the businesses, the land, and the families. Women like Ann and her mother are forced into prostitution as a means to survive in a country at war. Oh, how cruel some laurels of war can be, he thought.

Colonel Henry Morrow closed the Bible. He had not read for the last few evenings and promised to devote a greater portion of the night to God in return. Having read for nearly two hours from the divine book, Morrow eventually turned to the paperwork that had accumulated on his small desk. Regimental business called. The nagging bureaucratic work of an army officer waited.

Most of it wasn't hard work. Several of the items were compliments from various commanders, politicians, and important citizens regarding the discipline and skill of the Twenty-Fourth Michigan. It was very rewarding to flip through the pages and read the words, the thanks. There were numerous letters and clippings from Detroit newspapers. He took the time to carefully read each one, marveling the writer's sudden interest in the regiment. And to think the regiment would have never have been organized had it not been for a fortunate string of luck. Wayne County and all of Michigan would never have bathed in the glory of the Twenty-Fourth had it not been for several important players, all deserving a portion of the credit.

He promised to thank them all when the war was over.

Flipping through the loose pages, he stopped when he came across a note, arriving by courier just an hour before, from General Meredith. It told Morrow that the coveted black hats were near arrival, and he had received word from Washington that the shipment was sent out and headed for the army. Morrow slowly set the letter down and leaned back in his chair. His brave soldiers had done it. They had earned the hats. They had earned the confidence and faith of their veteran comrades, but now the entire world would know that they were a part of the Iron Brigade. The thought entertained him and he wondered what his regiment would look like in the tall black hats.

He read the short letter even further and disagreed with Meredith's opinion that the fighting men of the regiment should be thankful for Morrow's diligent service and leadership. Morrow shook his head. He had done only what he could. While it was wonderful and moving to be the recipient of such claim, Morrow wasn't going to take all the glory. He was their leader, their commanding officer, but they were his troops. They were the ones who battled, who forged the regiment in iron. They were the ones that bravely stood among men of iron and learned the art of war, excelled at it.

Promotions and personal gain would come soon enough, he realized. When it came time for him to depart the proud Twenty-Fourth Michigan, he would do so with a heavy heart. The regiment was his family, the only home he knew away from Detroit. He had cared for them, and they had cared for him. They took care of each other.

And even if he should be called upon to leave them for a higher position, he would ensure that his old regiment was taken care of, that they would be left in good hands, be led by a brave and true commander. Morrow felt comfortable that Flanigan could do the task. The Irishman was a good man, a moral man. He had a firm understanding of troop movement and positioning. Besides, the men had grown to love him, to follow him faithfully into battle. There were other officers considered to fill the post if needed as well, Captain Edwards ranking among the best of them.

Morrow took a deep breath and closed his eyes. He was tired, very tired. As he slid the paperwork off to one side, he rubbed his aching forehead. He had not slept well for nearly a week and suffered from terrible headaches. Morrow finally gave up and collapsed upon the cot. His eyes were heavy and he could feel himself drifting off to sleep, thinking of possible promotions and what would become of his regiment if he had to leave them. The thoughts sprinkled about until he finally fell asleep, dreaming of heartache and glory.

The moon was perched high that night, and it gave plenty of light for Morgan to swim across the river and meet with one of the Confederate pickets. Through earlier conversation they had found out that the Rebel soldier was a cousin of Emmy. The two had witnessed friendly exchanges of coffee and tobacco between the lines all day and finally agreed that they should meet at a large rock centered in the river.

He arrived at the rock first and climbed onto it soaking wet, the water dripping down from his elbows and fingertips. Carried with him was the most recent picture of Emmy, protected from the water by being wrapped in a rubber blanket. With attentive eyes he watched the Confederate soldier step down into the cold water and swim toward the large slab of stone that had become a center of friendly trade all day.

After a few short moments, the Rebel took his place opposite Morgan on the large rock. The two soldiers looked at each other in silence, perhaps gauging the strength and soldierly appearance of one another. The night was calm around them and they could see several fires on both sides of the river dotting the landscape. Eventually breaking the awkward silence was the Rebel soldier, who extended a hand in which Morgan warmly received. "You are the man I have been talking to," he said to Morgan. "You are the one who has married my little cousin."

"Yes," replied Morgan. He unfolded a portion of the rubber blanket and handed Emmy's picture over to the soldier. "I assume it has been a long while since you have seen her. This is my Emmy. This is your little cousin."

The southerner took the picture into his hands and angled it for better light. "She has grown," he muttered. "She is very beautiful. I can see she has much of my dear old aunt in her. She looks a little like my mother." The soldier handed the picture back and dug deep into his pockets, pulling out a picture of his own. As he handed it over to Morgan, he said, "This is my girl, Mattie."

Morgan tilted the picture and saw the beautiful, soft face of the woman. "She's lovely," he said politely, honestly. "I'm sure that you miss her as much as I miss Emmy."

"Not a day goes by where I don't."

"I know."

The two shared another awkward moment of silence, each man looking to the picture of his dear wife, the young woman awaiting their return. Soft memories played in their heads.

Sensing that the two should depart, it was the southern soldier who again broke the silence. He looked to Morgan with warm, sad eyes. He was calm, no longer nervous about the meeting. "Are we really that different, you and I?" he asked.

Morgan shook his head. "I don't think so."

"That is good, I suppose, for I have often wondered."

"As have I," Morgan quietly replied.

"Well," said the southerner, again extending a hand, "when this cruel war is over, I hope that you and my cousin will come and visit me in North Carolina. I would be honored to have you as guests."

Morgan accepted the hand warmly once again. "We would like that very much. And when this war is over, we would like to have you in Michigan. Your cousin would like to see you again. I will write her and tell her that you are well and that we have met on peaceful terms."

The southerner nodded, his sad eyes twinkling in the moonlight. He gently placed the picture of his wife back into his pocket and stepped back down into the water. He looked back to Morgan and gave a smile before sliding in and swimming back toward his side of the river.

Morgan wrapped the picture of Emmy in the rubber blanket and tucked it away. He gently slid into the cool water, and without looking back, swam toward the Union side of the river. He moved slowly because he knew that when he returned, he would have to once again consider his wife's cousin an enemy.

The Twenty-Fourth Michigan was again called for service, it being among four regiments of the Iron Brigade under the command of Colonel Morrow for an expedition up the peninsula between the Potomac River and the Rappahannock River. Days prior, the Eighth Illinois Cavalry had gone down there, and the horsemen were feared cut off from the rest of the army. Morrow had once again personally been selected to lead the expedition by order of General Hooker and further approved by General Reynolds.

Colonel Morrow led the twelve-hundred men under his command through the countryside in search of the cavalry and the enemy. His party encountered Rebel pickets and shoved them aside by firing a few rounds at them, but failed to see anymore than a small body of mounted Confederates. One unfortunate Rebel officer stumbled across the river into Morrow's lines and was captured. Near the end of their journey, the expedition came across the advance guard of the Eighth Illinois and Morrow waited for the rest of the separated command to link up before they headed back to camp. The cavalrymen had a large wagon train of captured goods and several contrabands with them, which Morrow thought nothing more than the result of cruel raiding. This, he deemed, was not important enough to have sent out a unit from the main body to search for the supposedly endangered cavalrymen. When the footsore expedition returned to the army, they had marched one hundred and thirty miles in five and a half days.

Upon rejoining the army, the regiment finally received their black hats, long overdue since Fredericksburg.

Captain Edwards sat alone, his hands pinning up one side of the tall black hat's brim. The fire crackled before him, and his company was sprawled out enjoying the peaceful weather. Every now and then he would look up and see them working hard on their new hats. He smiled when he saw several of his men prance around camp with their new hats, showing off the prize to the veteran regiments of the brigade. The men acted like happy children, nearly skipping along.

Once the pin was fastened, Edwards added a feather given to him by a member of the Seventh Wisconsin. He remembered the soldier telling him, "I carried this into my first fight and I came out well. I hope it will provide you with the same fortune." Carefully sliding the worn feather into place, Edwards smiled. He was honored to receive such a treasured gift. The hat completed, he shuffled it around in his hands for several minutes before removing the old kepi from his head and replacing it with the new black hat. He felt immediate pride as it slid onto his head. It had been earned through fierce trial and danger. It felt good to finally wear it. It felt good to have something to show for his service.

Before the hat could settle, he quickly removed it. Taking it once again into his hands, he looked upon it as if it weren't real, it didn't exist. Could something as simple as a hat mean so much? Yes, he thought. He shuffled it around with his fingers once again, remembering the names of those fallen comrades who never had the fair chance to wear it, to feel its pride. Edwards sat so still that only his hands were moving, slowly spinning the hat with his fingers. The names still racing through his thoughts, the faces of those lost appearing through the shadows of his mind.

They were sad memories, he realized. The old soldiers that had fallen from sickness and combat were nothing more than memories. Their bodies had been buried in empty fields, alone and cold. And as he looked upon his newly won hat, he could not help but think of all of them as the reason he was able to don it, to earn it. They had given everything for the cause and got nothing in return. Those soldiers didn't receive their just acclaim. They didn't receive the sincere thanks of their commanders. They didn't receive their black hats. Yet those were the soldiers that had helped forge the Twenty-Fourth. They had walked the path as far as God was willing to let them. He believed they should be entitled to the same fame, the same acclaim and reputation as their surviving comrades. The only way to make that possible was to claim victory. If the Union lost the war, then the names and faces would forever remain sad memories. If victory was earned, however, then all of those fallen before the last shot was fired, before the last Rebel flag was lowered, would be heroes, patriots, martyrs.

The black hat in his hands was more than just a hat. It meant something more than the Twenty-Fourth, the Iron Brigade, or the entire Army of the Potomac. It was a symbol of his country, the United States of America and all that it was, and all that it could become. It was a symbol of all of those fallen, and all of those still fighting for something better than each other, better than their homes and personal gains.

Thinking of all that it was worth, he placed it back onto his head, finally ready to accept it.

Color Sergeant Abel Peck stood with the flag as he watched a company of cavalry drill on the field before him. They saw him standing there and noticed the tall black hat on his head. The cavalrymen rode by him with cheers. They had heard of the old Iron Brigade, the myths and the legends. Peck waved in response. His appearance must have given credit to the rumors and stories, as he stood erect and stiff as iron with the flag waving about above him. As the horsemen came by him once more, they cheered again.

He was called back into position by Colonel Morrow, who was demonstrating how the color guard should behave in battle. They had been over the drills time and time again, but Morrow ordered them to continue. They would master the process until they could complete it in their sleep, until it became second nature. Peck swung around and joined the demonstration, stepping forward at Morrow's order. The color guard surrounded him and Peck couldn't have been happier as to how they rushed in. Morrow called the men back into line, correcting their staggered line. "You will act as one," Peck could hear the colonel holler. "This flag is your priority. You are to protect it and its bearer at all costs. Should it fall in battle, then it is your responsibility to pick it up." Morrow ordered the men to redo the drill. He expected the maneuver to be flawless. Before he ordered the line to commence the drill again, he said, "We have earned those black hats, gentlemen. Let us intend on keeping them."

Peck smiled. He felt like a veteran now, a true member of the Iron Brigade. He only wished that his wife and daughter could see him, see how he transformed into a hardened soldier in the famous black hat.

He leaped forward at Morrow's order. The color guard gathered more closely, rallying around the flag. "Very good," complimented Morrow. "Mr. Peck," the color bearer heard him say, "I believe you to be the bravest soldier in the regiment. The flag is entrusted to the ablest man. Do not disappoint, sir. We have faith in you. Have faith in your color guard. They will stand with you always."

Peck smiled again. Yes, if only his family could see him, the bravest soldier, new black hat and all. What a different man they would find.

Received our black hats, wrote Morgan. *You should see your husband in his. You would come to our camp and no longer be able to recognize a Michigan man from a Wisconsin man or an Indiana man. All the soldiers now look alike, and we are all very pleased. The veterans said we earned our hats in December and that they were slow in coming. Governor Blair called upon us the other day. He said we excelled so much in our practices that he was surprised and inspired.*

He rubbed his forehead in the flickering candlelight. *We saw nearly twenty regiments of the enemy in full dress parade yesterday while out on picket near the old Fredericksburg battlefield. Colonel Morrow believes they are up to something, but what it is we do not know. It is rumored that a regiment or two will be sent out to see. I hope we are not selected, as we have been very busy and need the rest. Soldiering is very tiring and the regiment has worked at it more than most. We don't complain, as Colonel M. says it has made us good soldiers and worthy of our brigade name and our new hats.*

He struggled to write as the light began to fade. The wax candle was nearing the end of its life. In the growing darkness, he concluded his letter. *All is well and we are in fine shape and good spirits. I will write you when I have more time and more light, but for now I must bid you an affectionate farewell, my dear Emmy. Love, Morgan.*

Morgan stuffed the letter into an envelope and slid it into his coat. He would send it off at breakfast in the morning.

He fell to his back in exhaustion and looked up to the canvas roof of the tent. He was lonely and homesick, so he moved out under the stars, hoping they would offer him some comfort. Morgan made a nice spot for himself just outside his tent. When the blanket was down, he rolled upon it and shifted so that his eyes were fixed on the sky above. It was a beautiful night. The stars were twinkling. The moon was high, full, and bright. The glow was soothing to his soul. Fires crackled and popped in the distance. He could almost hear the army breathing, gently drifting off to sleep.

He began to drift off with them, too.

Under the bright moon and the twinkling stars, Morgan clung tightly to his newly received black hat. Before surrendering to sleep, he removed the picture of Emmy and looking at it, wished her goodnight. He missed her so much, perhaps more than he had ever missed her before.

He eventually fell asleep under the clear night sky, his treasured black hat in one hand, and his beloved picture of Emmy in the other.

During this time, the Union First Corps was reduced in numbers by expired enlistments. Before long, the Corps was whittled down from sixteen-thousand to nine-thousand men, making it the smallest in the Army of the Potomac. In light of this, General Hooker reorganized his army as of June 1, 1863. The Iron Brigade became the First Brigade of the First Division of the First Corps.

The Twenty-Fourth Michigan had been in the service for ten months by the time the Army of the Potomac shifted gears and pulled from camp, their heavy marching eventually leading them toward a quiet hamlet, nestled somewhere between the rolling hills of Pennsylvania.

THE GREAT RUSH NORTH

The Twenty-Fourth wearily drove forward. The marches were long, hard, and several of them were forced. The men stopped for only a few short breaks before being ordered back to the roads. It was a tiring affair, but the men knew it was necessary. Rumors brought word of Confederate General Lee's rapid march into northern territory, hoping to strike against Washington or Baltimore, Maryland.

The men were eager for another go at the Rebels but exhausted from the long marches. Stragglers began to clog the roadways, slowing regiment after regiment. The Twenty-Fourth lost several men to exhaustion, while several more straggled far behind, defiantly refusing to give up despite the pain of their blistered feet and weary legs. The line didn't stop, however. It simply couldn't, for too much was at stake.

Colonel Morrow rode slowly past the line and urged his tired men forward. There had been several requests from the soldiers, most of which consisted of them seeking breaks. Morrow denied them all. He had been ordered to push his men until ordered to stop. The army had an objective and was in a race against time to complete it. So he ordered just a few more steps from his men, just another hour or so.

His men had marched hard and for many miles. He knew this but couldn't stop it. At each brief stop he would see the men drop themselves to the ground and quickly remove their shoes. He would ride by and tell the men to hurry and eat and drink what they could, for they would soon be ordered back to the march. As he did so, he would see their bloody and blistered feet. He would hear them moan and see them wince in agony as they forced the shoes back on.

Even as night fell around them, the regiment marched on. The men in line questioned him as they saw him ride by. He could hear them call to him from the dusty and sweaty ranks. "How much longer, Colonel?" they would ask, looking to him for answers. Morrow didn't know how much longer they would have to march. He would ride by them offering encouraging words but no answers. And at a short stop for a quick dinner, he was asked the same question again.

He said to them, "It is necessary for us to go further still tonight. It is now a question of speed between us and our enemy. The army that pulls ahead will take the advantage. I for one am not willing to *surrender* it to them, so I believe it in our best interest to drive forward and give them a fair chance to *take* it from us."

The men would frantically eat their dinner, nearly swallowing it whole. It was hard for him to order them back into the road after only an hour's break. It seemed that the men had just settled and got comfortable when the drums flared up again, calling them back into their lines. Morrow mounted his horse after nibbling on some hardtack and set out to put his regiment in motion. It became a constant routine. The regiment would stop. The drums would roll seemingly minutes later. Morrow would climb his horse and order the men back to their sore feet. The motions became second nature.

He rode hunched over in the saddle, catching himself before he fell asleep. He dared not rest in front of the men. It wasn't fair if he did so. If they were expected to stay awake and march, then he expected the same from himself. He certainly wasn't going to let them suffer alone. He had promised them that he wouldn't. "Keep it up, boys," he would cheer them. "It'll get easier the next ten miles."

"No," said Lieutenant Colonel Flanigan to the curious soldiers, "I don't believe that Lee will see Washington. We will have him in our hands before that, lads. Don't worry about it. We've marched harder and faster than I have ever seen a body of troops march." He turned back to them, saw their hopeful faces. "I think we have got a leg up on him for once. I think we will make something of this."

The soldiers continued the march. "If he did," said one of them, "I don't think he'd take it. Don't you remember how well it was fortified? Didn't you see the big guns bearing down on the fields around the city? I don't care how brave of a general Lee is, if I were him and I saw a place like that, I would think twice."

"Worry not, lads," Flanigan cautioned again. "Lee won't get to Washington. Never mind the rumors you hear. They are foolish. Besides, there are bigger prizes for Lee and his army to bag."

"What can be a bigger prize than Washington?" asked one of others.

"Us," replied Flanigan.

"You mean Lee is after us?"

The Irishman smiled, said, "From what I know of Lee, he is a fighter.

He will not get the fight he desires from a city. Oh, no. He will eventually turn to us. Only after he gets us out of the way will he consider taking the city." He gently tugged on the reins, reminding his horse that he was in control. "It would be far too trying for him to take the city with us somewhere in his rear."

"I never thought of it like that," said another.

"There are some things we shouldn't worry about," reasoned Flanigan. "We shouldn't be concerned with what Lee is doing until we meet him on the field. Then his intentions will be made very clear. But we must remember, lads, that our intentions will then become clear to him as well."

The soldiers fell silent. Flanigan could hear the shuffle of their feet, the dull rhythm of the march. He could also hear the soft beating of the drums, politely reminding the men to keep step. The army was moving forward, its destination unknown. Flanigan again turned and looked at the soldiers behind him. Their eyes appeared heavy, but they scanned the countryside as it slowly passed. Birds could be heard in the near treetops. Deer could be seen leaping through the tall grass. It was lovely country, and the men appreciated it. They were tired and sore from the hard march, yes, but they enjoyed the peace. It had seemed so long since they experienced such a strange calmness.

Flanigan enjoyed it as well. The sky was blue and the heat thick and heavy, but the day was rather enjoyable. Despite their condition, the men were in good spirits and were rather talkative. He could hear several different conversations behind him. There was further talk of Lee's chances on taking Washington. There were complaints over how much the sutlers had charged for notebooks and pencils. He could hear friendly arguments as to who was the better shot with the rifle. A few of the soldiers sang songs and urged their comrades to join. Most of them, however, simply kept to themselves and kept pace with the march. They were content just moving along with the army, waiting for their chance to finally break from the road and catch a little sleep.

It was marvelous to see the men hold up during the grueling march. Flanigan couldn't have been happier with their conduct. It was hard, he knew, but the men were once again proving up to the challenge. If it was a race the Rebels wanted, then he knew the Twenty-Fourth Michigan would give them one.

The long journey eventually took the regiment to the battlefield of Bull Run, the inglorious Union defeat that set the stage for years of continuous warfare. They pushed across the plains and over the fortifications that Confederate General Beauregard had built during that first battle. They saw the sight of the Union collapse, where the line broke way and a flood of chaos followed. Off in the distance, they were told, were the outer defenses of Washington, standing firm over the horizon. The march across the Bull Run battlefield was very humbling to the men, but to others, it meant more.

Captain Albert Edwards pointed toward the location where he had been captured. From there he shifted his arm, and with finger outstretched, showed some of the men the small grove of trees where he had spent his first night in captivity. "There were three hundred of us packed in there," he told them. "I can remember it like it was yesterday. Everything seems so clear, even though it was a long time ago."

Not a man listening envied Edwards.

As they moved along with the line, he stayed behind and gazed across the field. He was still, wanting to take in the moment. He had thought he would never see the field again, never stand on the grass where he first saw action in the bloody war, where the terrible musketry began on a large scale. His eyes shifted about the land as if the battle played out before him. He could imagine a Rebel line here, a Union line there. He could hear the thundering of the cannon. Oh, how the memory played. There, in a shallow ditch, the two lines finally collided, the inexperienced soldiers thrashing about like wild animals. Above him, on the hills surrounding the historic field, he could still feel the eyes of the dignitaries and politicians, gathering for the event as if it were a stage play.

He cynically hoped they enjoyed the show. Thinking of it, he could see them streaming across the land, mixing in with the panicked soldiers, all of them heading for the safety of Washington.

Eventually he pulled himself from the field, no longer wishing to visit the painful memories. He followed the regiment until it settled in the woods near Bull Run. He came upon Company F as the men gathered for dinner and talked of bathing in the cool waters. They had not bathed for several days, and they thought it best not to pass up the opportunity. With wide, begging eyes, they sought permission from Edwards. Before he let them go, he told them to eat their dinner. He moved among them and dug into his knapsack and began to nibble on a piece of dried meat. There, he began to tell his men the importance of their location. "The fight was opened here," he told them. "The Second and Third Michigan stood right where we sit and met the Rebels."

The memories came to life again.

He shook them away as he bit into the meat. The men agreed that the contest must have been confusing, as the troops from both armies had little or no experience. Their training had been hurried. Their skills were not yet honed. The men settled the conversation by agreeing that had their regiment been there, it would have been a different battle. The war would perhaps have been over by sundown. "We have been drilled," reminded Edwards, the veteran of the battle. "We have grown into soldiers. When we marched across this field we thought we were, but we had much to learn."

The men hushed. Edwards felt sorry for ruining the moment. "But," he quickly followed, "should the Twenty-Fourth have been there, knowing then what it does now, I do believe things would have been different." The men lightened up once again, the smiles returning to their faces, the confidence back in their voices.

Finished with dinner, Edwards finally allowed Company F to head to Bull Run for a bath. He told them to take their time and enjoy it because it would probably be the last bath they would have for quite some time.

As he watched his men run toward the cool water, he could not help but remember the sight of three dead bodies laying face down in the stream, blood trickling from them, turning the water red.

He forced himself to turn away.

The Twenty-Fourth Michigan continued its northward advance with the Army of the Potomac. The men learned after leaving the old Bull Run battlefield that the Confederate Army of Northern Virginia had crossed into Maryland and Pennsylvania. The invasion was on. The Union men quickened their pace and vowed to drive the enemy from northern soil.

Under the scorching sun, the troops marched. Over steep hills and dusty roads they moved. They marched endlessly through thunderstorms and heavy rain. There was the sound of distant rumbling as the Union cavalry tangled with the Confederates. General Hooker carefully positioned his army between the enemy and Washington, all the while keeping the marches long and the pace quick. It appeared he would go as far north as Lee wanted.

The regiment marched through peaceful countryside. They passed waving schoolchildren, gathered around their schoolhouses to watch the army pass. Women stood along the roadside, passing out water and fresh bread, thanking the men for their presence and their protection. The young women wished the brave soldiers luck in their journey, expressing interest that they might one day pass again through their village. The men cheered for the women. Colonel Morrow and Lieutenant Colonel Flanigan were the recipients of flowers and other offerings, which they politely waited until the town was well to the rear before disposing the gifts. Every man had been ordered to carry only what was necessary. Along the long march, many of the men even further shortened their load by leaving behind books and other items deemed unimportant enough to lug around through the summer heat and storms.

Stopping for an evening, the regiment camped near a large farmhouse with plenty of green land. Neatly separating the land was a complex series of fences, which the men quickly took apart to build fires for cooking and coffee. There was a disturbance when the farmer realized that the soldiers were tearing down his fences. He stomped about the regiment in search of an officer, hollering at soldiers carrying his wood, condemning them for not seeking his permission first. He pleaded with them that he was an honest Union man, but that he couldn't stand for what was being done. He told the soldiers that he had worked hard on the fences. With them gone, how would his cattle stay in place? When the soldiers heard the word cattle, many of them questioned the farmer as to the location. Wisely, the farmer refused to provide an answer, not wanting his cattle to become government property either.

Color Sergeant Abel Peck saw the old farmer race toward him. As soon as his eyes met the farmer's, and the old man saw him there with the flag, he knew he was in for an earful. The farmer was very polite but angered. It was evident in his voice. He came upon Peck and immediately demanded the color bearer to take him to the nearest officer. Peck attempted to reason with the old man, to cool him down. "What is the problem?" he asked.

The farmer ran his fingers through his silver hair, shaking his head in disbelief of the question. He raised his arms around, showing Peck what was going on. "They are taking my fence! They are burning it! That is the problem," he shouted. "I demand that I see an officer. I have grievances."

"We mean you no harm," Peck pleaded.

"It is not harm I am concerned with, son. If I have no fences left in the yard by morning, then I lose all my cattle. If I have no cattle, I cannot feed my family. Those men there," he said as he furiously pointed, "have been taking down my fences for nearly an hour, and I have yet to see an officer in control."

Peck nodded, said, "It is imperative that we build fires for food and coffee. If we don't eat and drink, then we won't be able to fight when the battle comes. Our strength will fail us, and the enemy will advance to victory. What will come of your field when the enemy arrives? This, I pray, never happens, but I assure you if we leave here hungry and thirsty for another day, it is very likely."

"I suppose it must be so."

"I understand your plight, old man," said Peck. "I know that if you want an officer, I will tell you the way. I will then tell the men to use only what wood they need and be careful not to take down too many fences. I will try this. I do not want your family to go hungry on the account of us."

The old farmer nodded. Peck told him the simple directions, assuring him that he would find an officer down the roadway. In his departure, the old man asked from which state Peck hailed, and the reply was clear, "Michigan." The farmer waved an arm about and said that he appreciated the kindness, and added that he would offer a prayer for the Michigan men. Peck thanked the old man but begged that the prayer be for the Rebels, for they would need it when the Union army fell upon them.

Turning back, Peck watched as countless fires sprung up in the growing darkness. He called for a color guard and asked the soldier to take the flag. Moving down along the visible fence, Peck found several soldiers carrying armloads of wood worth more than they would need. He shouted for them to return the extra wood, demanding that they take only what was necessary. He worked very hard in keeping his part of the bargain, not wanting the farmer's family to go hungry if the cattle snuck out. After all, Peck had a family of his own, so he knew how trying it was to feed them in hard times. He had been there before.

"Now, now," he cried to a young soldier carrying a large stack of rails, "is that really needed, boy? How much of that wood are you planning to use? How long do you think we're staying here?" He pointed to the downed fence. "Go and put half of it back. Put up the fence while you're there. We shouldn't be taking too much from these good and honest people."

Onward the army advanced, determined to keep between the enemy and Washington. By late June, however, another setback nearly brought the army to a grinding halt. General Hooker was relieved from command of the Army of the Potomac, being replaced by General George Meade. The general that had taken a liking to Colonel Morrow and the Twenty-Fourth Michigan, had called it quits.

Colonel Morrow sat in the saddle nervously and looked to General Hooker. The general had stopped by before departing, wishing to see his old friend one last time. "Where will this war take you, General?" asked Morrow.

Hooker shrugged his shoulders and said, "I know not, Henry. My journey has perhaps come to an end for the time being. I shall one day hope to return to a command, but for now I am weary and I am in need of rest." The general cocked his head from side to side, carefully stretching out his neck. He looked completely drained. His skin was pale. He looked like he had not eaten for several days and Morrow was concerned. "I told you I would do it, that I would give it to them," Hooker added. "I am a man of my word, Henry. I want you to know that had I retained command of this army, had I not been pressured by cruel politics, I would have promoted you as I said, as I promised. I had given you my word. I want you to know that I would have kept it. You could have done great things, Henry. This I know."

Morrow smiled. Hooker was always flattering, always offering compliments. He turned away from the general and looked back to his regiment. "I think I am destined to stay here with my men, General. I am comfortable with that for now."

Hooker bowed in the saddle. It was time for him to go. He had done all that he could for the army. Politics had once again damned him, he was sure of it. He glanced over to Morrow's regiment. "Wherever I am, Colonel Morrow," he said proudly, "I shall look forward to reading of all the glory, the success of the Twenty-Fourth Michigan." He lifted the reins and slowly pulled his horse away. Looking back to Morrow, he said, "I have never seen a finer regiment." A smile grew on his saddened face. "I am a man of my word, Henry."

He watched as Hooker rode away. Since their first meeting, he had always kept an eye out for Morrow and the Twenty-Fourth. The commander and regiment seemed to be a favorite of the general, and he wasn't timid about letting the army know it. Hooker had given the Michigan regiment plenty of opportunities to excel and the regiment met every expectation.

The two had been cordial friends. They believed in many of the same ideals. They were excitable, nervous, and brave soldiers. There were differences, of course, but nothing ever seemed to come between them. Hooker had made an impact on him, and he made one on the general. It was a bond that could have been exploited, but Morrow stayed put. He had agreed with Hooker's reasoning that politics had no place in an army. Politics had scuttled the massive force too many times before. Some of the brightest generals and commanders had lost their commands because of politics. Despite Hooker's hatred for such, Morrow knew that it was political mingling that did his friend in. It wasn't Chancellorsville. It wasn't any battle except for the one in Washington, the one that swirled about behind the general's back. He was well aware that Hooker was playing a dangerous game.

Morrow just couldn't understand why his friend gambled away the army.

Such could be the fate of a general, he thought.

With his confidence unbroken, he looked ahead toward the coming battle. He could feel it building, the pressure swelling. Soon it would all come to a head. It was the same feeling he had before Fredericksburg and Chancellorsville. It could not be denied. Hooker was gone. He and the army would have to come to grips with that. Meade was in command now, and the army was still in motion, still setting its sights on the enemy.

The nation had begun to hold its breath once again.

Having reached Adams County, Pennsylvania, the Twenty-Fourth Michigan settled for the day, and the ranks were mustered for pay. As the men stood in the ranks awaiting their dismissal, there was great talk about the change in commanders and how much it would affect the morale of the army. The conversations were steady even after the regiment was dismissed and campfires were built and roaring.

Sitting around the flames peacefully, the regiment received, from the noncommissioned officers, word of General Meade's latest directive to the army. The men were told that the enemy had indeed invaded northern soil and that the entire country looked to the army to vanquish the foe. They were also informed that Meade had given the commanders permission to put to death any soldier who failed to do his duty at that most pressing hour.

It was a bitter pill for these men to swallow, as they were part of the famed Iron Brigade. Despite their short term of service compared to the more veteran regiments, the Twenty-Fourth had seen and done its fair share of hard fighting. The men were outraged that their lives should be threatened in such a manner, that the commanding general would dare issue the order to his troops. The tempers cooled when the fires faded, however, and there was no further talk of the insult.

As July 1, 1863 dawned, the men of the Twenty-Fourth rose early for breakfast. They knew that a battle was fast approaching, but they had no idea that the enemy was just a few short hours away.

Morgan swallowed down his hardtack first, wanting to save the savory pork for last before taking a slow sip of coffee. He conversed with several comrades about the expected battle, and all took guesses as to when it would come. A few of the men figured it would be in no more than two days. Morgan thought it a good chance to rise later in the day, but bet that the regiment wouldn't see combat until the following day. Others kindly disagreed, saying that there was too much business in the army. Things were moving faster with each passing minute. The army was once again coming to life. They believed the fight would in fact happen sometime during the day.

As the drums beat and rolled, Morgan grabbed his belongings and headed for Captain Edwards and Company F. It had been a delightful and pleasant morning, and he was eager to rejoin the march in hopes of catching the enemy. When he got back to his camp, he found Captain Edwards directing everybody over to an open field off to the right. Morgan could see the rest of the regiment gathering and could make out the figure of Chaplain Way standing at the head, towering over the men with the Bible in hand.

He followed the stream of men and took position with his comrades near the back of the group. Most of the regiment had gathered by the time Morgan sat down, but when Way greeted them that morning, he could hear the words clearly. As the chaplain spoke, Morgan took out his small pocket Bible and held it in his hands. It all began by Way welcoming the regiment to another dawn and asking that the Lord protect them in their coming trials. There was a quick prayer offered, but a light gust of summer wind prevented Morgan from hearing the words. As the wind settled and slipped away, the chaplain's voice grew louder and more defined.

As the words rained down upon him, Morgan pressed the small Bible to his heart.

Color Sergeant Abel Peck closed his eyes and thanked God that he was granted another day. As Way's words carried around him, he offered several prayers for the protection of his family. He wanted nothing more than to see them at that instant, to hold them, to tell them that everything was going to turn out well. They were far from his loving reach, however, but he knew that they weren't too far for God, for His care.

His lips opened and compressed as he repeated Way's prayers.

He felt comfortable and balanced. Never before had he felt so. He realized that if he were to die that day, then it had been God's will that he should so fall. He would accept his fate with open arms. Fate could not be questioned, altered. Peck felt relaxed and at peace as the booming voice of Way thundered around him. He was in good company. He knew that his regiment would protect him, but more importantly, they would protect the flag.

As Way continued to speak the wisdom of the Bible, Peck again thought of his wife and daughter. What would come of them without him? Death was prevalent in his mind. He had a firm sensation that it would be his last day alive. If it must be so, he thought, let it come. He slowly shifted his eyes over to his trusted color guard, the men that would rush in with him, swarm him as bees swarm a nest, and protect him and the cherished regimental flag. Peck looked to their faces and saw their confidence. He saw their undying faith in the cause, in each other. He saw them look back at him, every single soldier, and nod a comforting nod, as if telling him that all would be well. Peck would be their beacon in the raging storm, and they would be the protective rocks, thwarting back wave after relentless wave.

Everything seemed right for battle, the air, his comrades, the prayers, and the feeling that he would perish in the fight. It was a sense he couldn't shake, wouldn't shake. He was frightened and unsure of what the day would hold for him, but he looked ahead with anticipation. Let it come, he told himself again.

The thought of carrying the bold flag into the unknown excited him and made him rise above the fear. It was his duty, an honorable one at that, and Peck would not disappoint his regiment. Not on this day.

Captain Edwards shuffled about the men and quietly handed them hardtack as Chaplain Way continued with the service. Food would replenish the hunger and fill the stomachs of brave patriots before they dashed off to battle.

He offered the men no words. There was nothing he could say that would prepare them any more than the words Way offered. He simply roamed around and distributed the pieces of hardtack, gently dropping them into soldiers' laps as they listened.

Several soldiers looked up to him when he gave them their piece, but he just shook his head and nodded toward Way. He wanted the men to listen, to find some comfort. He knew a battle was approaching, and the regiment would be involved. He feared the worst, that the fight would be like no other the regiment, perhaps any regiment, had seen in the war thus far.

There were soldiers he came upon that were whispering personal prayers or handing notes to relatives in case they didn't make it out of the coming fight. Edwards could see the look of uncertainty on their faces, but he was amazed at how strong and fearless the men appeared. They seemed eerily calm, despite the sudden service and the countless prayers offered for their protection. Things were different, he thought. The regiment had never acted the way they were, so calm, so collective. They acted as if they were hardened veterans, having served since the war's outbreak. It didn't look like the green regiment that had only been engaged on a few occasions anymore. This was something different, something more defined. The men had a look of iron about them. There was distinct determination and dedication to the great task before them.

Edwards quietly continued his rounds, feeling confident that whatever the regiment came up against, they would stand together.

Lieutenant Colonel Mark Flanigan helped the young officers disperse ammunition cartridges to the men during Way's service. Time was an important factor that morning, and Morrow ordered that none of it be wasted. There was no reason the regiment couldn't do two or three things at once to prepare for the day.

Flanigan believed it would all culminate with a battle, at the very least the beginning stages of a battle. He had heard many rumors of the proximity of the Rebels. Such had been heard countless times before, but there was something unique with these premonitions and fears. More men were having them. It was as if a large storm had gathered in the skies above, but the rain and thunder had not yet appeared. Each man was capable of looking to the dark clouds and sensing the brewing trouble. It was just a matter of time before the storm was unleashed, before the darkened heavens trembled in anger.

He helped prepare the men by giving them their cartridges. Flanigan handed them to the men and pointed to their cartridge boxes. "Keep them handy," he whispered. He did not want to tell them that they would need them, for he believed that every man had to feel the pressure, had to see the darkening skies of war gathering above.

The Irishman paid little attention to Chaplain Way. There simply wasn't enough time to do everything. Besides, he had spent nearly the entire morning reading from his Bible and praying for the regiment and his family. He had prayed so much that he had to confess to himself that he was out of prayers and that God had perhaps grown tired of listening to all of his. The service wasn't for him, anyway. It was for the men. Way thought it would be a good idea for him to address the men before they marched off to possible battle. The chaplain too had heard the rumors and believed the Rebels not far from their position. If the regiment was headed toward conflict, then he would send them forward the only way he knew how, with God.

Flanigan gave a reassuring smile as a soldier looked up to him as the cartridges were handed out. "It'll be fine, lad," he comforted the soldier. "It's just a precaution." He quickly moved on, his large hands tossing out the paper cartridges. The men caught them and immediately knew what to do with them. He saw them load their cartridge boxes while listening to Way. Flanigan could see the others scattered about, bent over, handing the cartridges off.

He looked behind him and saw Morrow, standing with his arms folded, behind the regiment. To him, he nodded, silently informing the colonel that the job was nearly done, the ammunition nearly distributed. The men were getting ready to battle the threatening storm.

Colonel Morrow thought his regiment, gathered in the open ground before him, resembled a calm blue sea. He watched as Way commanded their attention by raising his arms into the air and reciting the words from the Bible. The men were captivated by the invocation. Their eyes adjusted upward. Their faces were still and attentive. He watched them sit still and wondered what would become of them in the coming days.

He turned his thoughts to his dear wife. Morrow hoped that everything was well with her and the baby. He wondered how she was getting along in Detroit all by herself, how she was getting through the long days without him. He wondered if it was as hard for her as it was for him. He missed her very much, perhaps more than he had ever missed her since his departure.

Way said something about honoring fallen comrades.

Morrow thought of them too. The regiment had suffered. Not just from battles but from all aspects of their hard lives. When the men first arrived, they were so green and raw that the slightest disease would take them down. Immunities had been built over time, however. The men hardened with each passing day, forever entombing the shells that were their former selves. He had guided them. He had watched them grow. Under his care, they sprouted from simple civilians into veteran soldiers. Through them, he grew from his nervous shell and became the leader they knew he could be, the leader they had faith in. Perhaps they would follow him anywhere.

The Twenty-Fourth had grown more than he realized, more than he imagined.

He quietly excused himself from the service and headed back to his tent. When he arrived, he went over to the small desk and chair and slowly flipped through the pages of his personal Bible. He enjoyed reading the words. He always felt refreshed and recharged when he closed the book. Way's words would do the same, he believed, but Morrow needed a more personal setting to get in touch with God. He needed to be alone, even if just for a minute, to establish the connection. From his private sanctuary he would offer prayers and thank God for all that was given to him. He would ask for comfort and protection, for his family, the regiment, and the bloodstained nation. Morrow would ask for forgiveness for drawing his sword against his fellow man. He would also seek guidance if needed. There were times, however, where he would just want to sit alone and read from the divine book. God never needed a reason to be visited.

That was what he wanted to do. He skimmed through the pages in search of a particular passage that jumped out at him. It took him several minutes before he found one that he had marked nearly a week prior but had never gotten around to reading. He placed the book on the desk in between his elbows and bent down to read the text. His lips moved as he read along. Sure enough, the words brought him comfort and soothed his nervous soul.

In the background, piercing through the canvas tent, he could hear Chaplain Way concluding his service with his booming voice. Morrow quickly scanned the last few lines before closing the book. Drum rolls rattled in the distance. There was a soft bugle call carried through the air. He knew that it was time to go. The Twenty-Fourth had once again been called to action. For now they would have to part ways with God, knowing, however, that His watchful eyes would always be upon them, protecting and guiding them.

Soon he could hear the clamor of men in motion as the ranks around the regiment began to form. The company officers, experienced through drill and battle, took it upon themselves to form the lines. They gathered and cluttered the men into neat rows and columns on the Emmitsburg Road. Morrow finally exited the tent, the Bible in his hands, and mounted his horse. The men looked to him as he sat atop the large animal. As he slowly rode by them, they cheered him.

Colonel Morrow was about to bring them to battle yet again.

The Twenty-Fourth Michigan drove up the Emmitsburg Road toward the town of Gettysburg. Since joining the Army of the Potomac, disease and battle had whittled the regiment down to just under half its original strength. As the blue columns marched forward, there were nearly five hundred Michigan men left in the ranks.

To Hold at All Hazards
—The Battle of Gettysburg—

The Twenty-Fourth Michigan was ordered forward with three other regiments of the Iron Brigade, the Second and Seventh Wisconsin, and the Nineteenth Indiana. The Sixth Wisconsin had been detached for service elsewhere in the corps that morning and did not join their comrades in the march to Gettysburg.

The pace was usual and the men's spirits were cheerful. Morgan could hear raspy voices singing songs, joined out of tune by nearly a thousand feet pounding at the ground. It was quite a spectacle, one that his ears enjoyed, and found intriguing. As had been customary with the countless marches of their past, the men passed the time swapping stories and chatting along.

"Some say we'll have a go with the enemy up ahead," a soldier beckoned from the rank and file. "I suppose it will come soon enough. Don't know if it will be today, though. I think the Johnnies have had enough of this for a while. Besides, it's too hot to worry about fighting.

Don't want to fight in this weather, sure don't." He spat toward the ground. Morgan saw beads of sweat drip from the soldier's chin. "What do you think, Morgan? Do you think we'll see them today?"

He shrugged his shoulders, tugging at the leather strap to adjust his rifle. The soldiers still sang all around him. There was this feeling in his stomach, a tightening of his insides that told him there would be more to the day than just marching. "I figure we'll see them when we're meant to see them. If it be up this road, then there is no reason to worry on it. We're all heading this way anyway. Whether it is an empty field for camp or the enemy ahead, we're going that way for sure. I don't suppose old Reynolds is looking to stop us or slow us down." Morgan pointed forward with a stiff arm. The men around him seemed to notice at that instance that his boyishness had faded. His youthful nervousness and fear of the uncertain seemed faded memories of the past. "We're moving fast," he told them. "Whatever waits for us at the end of this road, friends, will sure have to greet us in a hurry."

The march was merry until the men heard the thunder of artillery ahead. Only then did the last of the men, those still not wanting to believe the rumors, feel the dark storm of battle rise. They moved swiftly. A fight had been started, and it soon became clear that they would more than likely have a part in it. That too became evident when the white puffs of cannon fire could be seen in the distance. Immediately all noncombatants and pack mules were ordered back to the rear.

Marching further down the road, the brigade was shifted off the road to the left and continued to march toward the town, the home and property of a family named Codori visible on the horizon ahead.

As the summer of 1863 broke into full swing, Robert E. Lee, commanding the Confederacy's Army of Northern Virginia, pulled camp and drove north for his second invasion. From tactics learned from previous engagements, Lee separated his army, appointing each section with directions. Not until late June did Lee learn that the Union Army of the Potomac, under its new commander George Meade, had crossed the Potomac and were moving north as well. Not wanting his scattered command torn apart piece by piece, Lee began to concentrate his army in the vicinity of Gettysburg and Cashtown. Confederate Lieutenant General Ambrose Powell Hill was the first to convene in the area near Gettysburg. Wanting to investigate Union forces reported there, he ordered Major Generals Henry Heath and William Pender forward to the town.

The Gettysburg area was not far from the mind of Union Major General George Meade, either. While he was not looking for a general engagement, at least not yet, Meade began to turn his army toward the area of concern. Reporting from Gettysburg was a trusted veteran cavalry commander, General John Buford. Buford knew the Confederate army was gathering and approaching. After careful deliberation with his senior commanders, he deemed that the high ground around Gettysburg was too valuable to give to the enemy. Ordering his troopers to dismount and scatter across the open fields, Buford looked to bottle up the enemy columns as they headed down a single road named Cashtown Pike. Union Major General John Reynolds received Buford's reports. Reynolds was in command of the left wing of the Army of the Potomac, the closest to supporting Buford. He ordered his troops on the road early, and the Iron Brigade was first in line with the old First Corps.

As the First Corps swung into action, they were overwhelmed with a heavy sense of duty. These men had earned their veteran scars, however, and knew what was demanded of them. Before them the cavalry pickets, pressed by wave after wave of the enemy, stubbornly fought off attack after attack but were being driven from the field. The roar of musketry and the thunder of cannons greeted the Michigan men as they filed past the Codori House into the fields of Gettysburg. With little time to load their rifles or fix bayonets, the Iron Brigade is tossed forward into the growing fight to relieve Buford's exhausted cavalry.

Colonel Morrow's uncontrollable nervousness came back to him. He could hear the battle thundering around him. He could see the smoke rise from the earth as the two forces collided in epic battle. Of the terrain and strength of the enemy, he did not know. His regiment ran into position with the brigade and drove straight toward a slight rise in the earth, still not yet seeing the battle or meeting an enemy.

The unloaded rifles concerned him, so he cried out for the regiment to halt. The line officers and company commanders struggled to pull the eager soldiers back. They were ready and didn't want to waste any time in confronting the Rebels. The line wavered and then came to a sudden stop. It took time to slow the excited line, and the motion was choppy. Falling behind the rest of the brigade, the Twenty-Fourth eventually settled in line where Morrow was about to order them to load their rifles. Before he could even shout the command, a staff officer from General Wadsworth fell upon him and demanded that he get his regiment into motion again. "General Wadsworth wants the Twenty-Fourth to the front, Colonel, sir," called the aide above the rising din of battle.

Morrow shook his head. There was a desperate fight ahead of them, and he wasn't going to throw his regiment into the violent mix with empty rifles. His hesitation was momentary. With the young officer still present, Morrow called for the regiment to step forward and regain the momentum lost. "Inform the general that the Twenty-Fourth will come up immediately," he said to the officer, sending him away.

His men surged forward, the line struggling to stay together. They streamed toward the slight rise and met up with the advancing brigade just before the men reached the top of the hill. Spurring his horse well ahead of the regiment, he turned back and saw many of his men load their rifles on the run. They knew what was expected of them. They knew a good fight was in store. Urging his horse over the rise, he received the order for the brigade to halt and sent the message back to the oncoming Twenty-Fourth. From this vantage point, he could see the enemy advancing, their rifles blazing away. There was a series of woods near a ravine. He could see even more enemy troops massing below. As his regiment shuffled up, they were shifted to the left of the brigade by order of General Wadsworth. Morrow left the idle rightwing of the brigade and joined his regiment advancing around the rise and headed straight for the woods, swinging around the forest toward the rear of the enemy.

He met up with them just as they passed the slight rise and saw the right wing of the brigade creak forward, spilling over the land. Morrow could hear a roar of musketry turn up against the brigade's right. The left hadn't been fired upon yet and were streaming toward the unsuspecting flank of the enemy troops gathered below. He cheered his men forward, and they cheered in response, their battle-christened legs driving forward in great strides.

Confederate General Archer had maneuvered his Tennessee brigade into the woods in hopes of pressing the flank of the Union horsemen. His position concealed him well from the fire of the Union cavalry, but the location was what eventually did him in. As he looked to the slight rise before him and saw a flood of blue break above the horizon, he tried in vain to shift his troops accordingly. Bracing for the coming tide, he had little idea that the other half of the charging line was pressing upon his endangered flank and rear.

Union General John Reynolds, commander of the First Corps, personally rode with the Iron Brigade and ordered them forward into the woods. He cheered the men on and saw them driving the enemy skirmishers from the field. From his saddle he readied himself to again order the men forward but met his death from a Confederate bullet. Slumping forward in the saddle, he was pulled from his horse by several men and died on the field as soon as they brought him to the ground.

When the rushing Twenty-Fourth finally came into view, several Tennessee regiments further shifted their lines and opened a severe volley in hopes of shattering the new threat on their flank. There was a cry from the southern ranks that it was not a token force they were dealing with. Noticing the tall black hats of the advancing Federals, several cried out, "Here comes those damned *black hats*!"

Lieutenant Colonel Flanigan towered above the men on horseback and waved them forward. The first crash of Confederate musketry was hurried, and the shots buzzed overhead. Again he waved the men forward. "Come on, lads! Give it to them! Take every inch of the field from them."

Whip. The air snapped as a slug careened by him.

He remained fixed in the saddle, determined to carry the regiment toward the enemy no matter what the danger. The men gathered around Flanigan and rushed forward, stepping quickly in line of battle. The Irishman watched as the Confederate line again prepared to meet the charge with a wall of musketry. He could see the men load their rifles and see them toss aside the empty cartridges. Flanigan responded by again waving the men on. It was the only thing they could do. They would have to advance in the face of the severe fire. They would have to wrestle the position away from the determined Confederates.

As the rifles readied across from him, Flanigan closed his eyes and silently said a prayer. He made a worthy target on horseback, and he firmly believed that it would be the last he would see of the world. Still ignoring the aimed Confederate rifles, he asked God to protect his wife and family if he was to die in the charge. Satisfied that his prayers would be answered kindly, the Irishman opened his eyes, and a devilish smile grew on his face. "Forward, Twenty-Fourth!" he hollered, his accent seeping through.

The Confederate line exploded in response.

Flanigan pressed the men forward as the shots slammed into them. Such a volley should have driven the regiment to a standstill, but these men had been forged of iron. They were not about to let their veteran comrades down. There was still something for these Michigan men to prove.

The line drove on and another Confederate volley was readied.

Color Sergeant Abel Peck swooped forward toward the enemy line with the flag guiding the regiment forward, his faithful color guard at his side. As the first Confederate volley tore into the ranks, he saw many men fall. The regiment, however, did not stop, did not waver. He was proud of them. Not wanting to disappoint, he rushed forward with the flag in hand.

As the smoke cleared from the first volley, he saw the Rebel line stand with rifles ready once again. He steadied himself for the second barrage, gripping the flagstaff tightly to keep it afloat in the terrible storm of battle. As the yards separating the lines quickly decreased, Peck grew close enough that he could nearly make out the "CS" on several of the southern soldiers' belt buckles. He could see their dirty and thin faces, and almost see the dirt under their fingernails.

He tilted the flag forward to brace for the coming onslaught as he neared the enemy. With level rifles the Confederates waited to greet them before the engagement erupted into a deadly hand-to-hand bout. There was time for one last coordinated volley. With precision and skill of hardened veterans, the Rebels waited faithfully until they received the order.

Peck could hear the thick accent of the officers shout for the line to fire. He looked to the leveled rifles and saw the wall of flame and smoke splash out from the line. His legs continued to carry him forward for several feet before they went numb. As the smoke swirled around him, he saw the red and white streaks of the flag as it dropped to the ground before his eyes. Peck tried to reach for it but found that he had no strength, had no command over his arms and hands. He tried to move his fingers, but couldn't. The noise around him was muffled, as if he had been submerged underwater. He could hear his heart rate slowing. There was a salty taste in his mouth as a thick fluid rose from his stomach. He bent over at the waist and coughed up blood.

He saw the dark puddle seep into the ground and stared at it in shock. He then felt the last beat of his battered heart before slumping to the ground. His last thoughts were of his wife and little daughter. Peck missed them very much.

And then the world went black.

As the Iron Brigade slammed into the unsuspecting Confederates, the southerners stumbled back in confusion. By the time the Twenty-Fourth arrived to confront them, they were pushing a skirmish line, the rest of the enemy having been driven back by the forceful blow of the rest of the brigade. These skirmishers, however, were more determined to hold back the blue flood than their shocked and battered comrades. Quickly forming thin but sturdy ranks, these men attempted to hold their ground against the rushing northerners, hoping to buy time for their comrades to regain their composure and renew the attack.

Morgan ran forward through the wall of musketry and dashed upon the surprised soldiers. Two desperate volleys had been fired, but yet the Yankees came at them. The land was filled with men storming and crashing around. Rifles and pistols discharged at close range. Morgan fired his rifle quickly, shooting a Rebel in the neck. Blood sprouted like a fountain from the horrible wound, and the enemy soldier struggled to cry out, his voice muffled as the blood rushed through his throat.

The water of the stream splashed under his feet as he thundered toward the staggered Rebel line. Once he reached a large tree, he loaded his rifle and again took aim. The shot took down another southern soldier, the slug hitting the fleeing man in the shoulder. It was only a painful wound, thought Morgan. He contemplated rushing the fallen soldier and putting him out of his misery, but he saw several of the enemy raise their hands in surrender as the regiment surrounded them. He refrained from giving chase to the wounded soldier. Pop. Pop. There was still fight left in the Confederates as they attempted to break out from their Union captives, more dangerous men to strike at. He would give them his full attention.

The rage of war was very much alive in him again as he looked to reenter the bloody contest. After again loading his rifle, he leveled it against a thick branch and aimed for a Confederate who had perched himself in a tree. Apparently the soldier thought the position safe enough to shoot from, and he had taken down several Michigan men from the concealment of the green leaves. Morgan took a breath before he squeezed the trigger. The green leaves ruffled, and there was a thick crack as the man's weight finally broke the branch and the body fell to the solid earth with a thud.

His soul aflame and his heart brave, Morgan stepped forward to personally round up some prisoners. For now the rage settled to replenish its strength. There would be more killing in time.

Captain Edwards could see the door slamming against the pressed Confederates. Both sides of the Iron Brigade had met and a desperate struggle ensued between the lines of blue and gray. There was much smoke. He could see strange patterns and shapes as the smoke danced across the confined space. Looking to his left and right, he saw his men form around him and begin to gather prisoners. Several of them stood in ranks and blazed away, their rifles trained on running shadows and even men who held their arms high in surrender.

He rushed to them and ordered them to stop. Edwards had been in the same position before, just on the opposite end. His life could have been taken in the same manner at Bull Run when he was captured and surrounded. The Rebels let him live that day, however, so he was determined to pay it back.

His men were flushed with the fever of battle. War had a way of making sane men mad. Edwards had seen it too many times in his career. There had been brave and honorable commands torn apart from the inside by the fever, the rage of war. Good and honorable men committed terrible acts of murder. He did not want his men involved in such brutality. War involved killing, he knew, but there were limits. Men such as the Confederates before him, surrounded and demoralized, were ineffective. Their only choice was to either attempt to flee from the field and risk being killed or drop their arms and surrender. Yes, he had been on their end before. He knew that it was a much wiser thing to surrender than to try and carry on a hopeless fight.

Despite the danger, there were those southerners of a braver class. They gathered together and fought against the swarm of Federals. These men were offered fair treatment if they put down their arms, but they refused to cooperate. They considered it a better choice to fight it out. They were met with shots. They were clubbed down motionless with fists and rifle stocks. For these men too, Edwards tried to stop the tide of war. But there was nothing he could do. The men had refused to go peacefully, to admit defeat. They stood together and shot at the Michigan men. Angered, the Michigan men retaliated by bashing them, finally forcing them to stand down.

Edwards moved about Company F and cautioned them to settle down. There would be plenty of work ahead of them, and the men needed to save their strength. He told them to ready their rifles and stand in line. He detailed only a few men to assist with the movement of prisoners. He detached several others for use in the litter corps. There were wounded men all over the place. Edwards could hear their cries for help.

He moved through the line and saw the blood on their faces. There was no attempt to wipe it away. It was their *war paint*. Beyond the line he could hear the angry calls for the prisoners to move faster. There was still a battle to be had, and the guards weren't planning on sitting it out.

The regiment quickly gathered around him, preparing for more bloodletting.

The maneuver had captured a great portion of General Archer's Tennessee brigade, including the general himself. A large number of them escaped and made their way to the unfinished railroad cut somewhat to the north of the bloodied terrain. They didn't find any rest there, either, as they were soon after routed and captured by the Sixth Wisconsin of the Iron Brigade.

The Twenty-Fourth continued its push and drove the enemy for another one hundred yards beyond. As soon as they made it to the crest, having driven the Rebels over the top, they were soon confronted with another enemy line, hastily put together to thwart off the expected counterattack.

Colonel Morrow received the orders to withdraw to the east bank of the stream just taken from the enemy. The brigade had been ordered to change front, turn around, and move into the woods, locally known as McPherson's Woods. Morrow felt a steady uneasiness as he ordered his regiment into position. He fixed his regiment at the desired location as the Confederates made attempts to hamper the movements. Rebel lines of battle formed and harassed the redeployment of the brigade.

Morrow nervously ordered the men to be still and not worry about the danger. "Conserve your ammunition," he said to them. "You will be in great need of the supply soon enough, boys."

Having found a wounded soldier desiring some form of soldierly work, Morrow incorporated the young man into his staff and sent him toward Flanigan. "Tell Mark that I wish him to take our left and make sure we hold with the Nineteenth Indiana over there. Tell him that I will see to the right for now and make sure we are within reach of the Seventh Wisconsin." The young soldier happily took the assignment and dashed off toward the left to find the Irishman.

Calmly settling into the saddle, Morrow spurred his horse toward the regiment's right flank. He wanted there to be no gaps, no holes in the line. As he rode he avoided the quick volleys from the Confederates taking aim at the still regiment. He could feel the warm air separate in front of his face as a round barely missed him. It did him good, however, to move under fire. His nervousness soon fell under his control again, so he shelved it. There was no need for it in battle. There were far too many other things to be concerned about.

Advancing several yards down the line, he saw the mighty flag of the regiment still high above. There were holes in it, openings cut into the bold colors. When he rode forward to inspect the wounded flag, he was surprised that he did not find the reliable Peck at his post. When Morrow asked what had come of the brave soldier, the new color bearer sighed and pointed to a body thirty feet behind the line. They had covered it with a blanket, the soldier told Morrow, so that his comrades would not see the fallen soldier.

It saddened him to think that the faithful and brave Peck was gone. There was no time to grieve, though. A fresh line of Confederate infantry advanced upon them and fired a rushed volley before advancing several more yards and repeating the maneuver.

Morrow hurried his horse toward the right of the regiment.

The wounded soldier, acting as a messenger for Morrow, ducked as the volley carried safely over his head. He heard the cheers of the advancing Confederates and then heard the reply by the Michigan men and the Iron Brigade. His right arm was in pain, having taken a shot that probably broke the bone. Falling back was not an option. He was not willing to leave his comrades. He knew he was still able to help them.

His mission was to find Lieutenant Colonel Flanigan and relay the order that he was to lead the left of the regiment. He found the Irishman on the ground in thick grass, surrounded by several soldiers. The men nervously clamored with the litter and carefully lifted the officer's large frame onto it. The young soldier stepped forward in hopes that Flanigan was still alive, and found him to be so, seriously wounded, however. The soldier saw the blood pouring from the horrible leg wound. He heard the soldiers asking if Flanigan was comfortable, to which an affirmative reply came back.

One of the men turned to the wounded soldier and called for him to join Flanigan in the rear. The soldier shook his head and informed him that he had already declined the service for the present. He had come bearing a message for Flanigan from Morrow and inquired as to what happened. "The lieutenant colonel was ordering us to hold the line when the volley came and dropped many a man. We saw him on his horse and thought he had come out of it, but he clutched at his leg and called for assistance. We believe he will live, but fear that the leg will have to be amputated," was the reply.

The wounded soldier broke away from the group while Flanigan was carted off toward the rear of the growing Union line. Unfortunately for the soldier, he would have to bear the news to Morrow that the regiment's second in command had fallen and had been removed from the field.

The readjustment had cost the Twenty-Fourth dearly. When Morrow returned to the center of the regiment, he learned that both his lieutenant colonel and his adjutant had been removed from service. Furthermore, the regiment had taken many casualties, and its ranks were already thinning. Morrow had lost his first color bearer and several men of the color guard. True to their duty, the brave men of the color guard rallied around Peck before he fell, and secured the flag after.

The position of the regiment was another concern. His right had to angle back to connect with the skirmishers of the Seventh Wisconsin. He could hear that portion of the line slowly engage as the Union and Confederate lines met once again. His left side of the line extended down a rise and was completely cut off from view of the right side. It met there with the brave soldiers of the Nineteenth Indiana, but the ground was covered entirely by the infantry and cannon of the enemy. Realizing this advantage, the enemy withdrew its skirmishers and commenced shelling the woods.

Colonel Morrow reported that during the shelling he received no word of casualties. During the bombardment, he sent his first of several requests to have the brigade moved to a more suitable position, where they could command the ground instead of the enemy. The reply from Wadsworth was sharp and simple: the ground was to be held by the Iron Brigade at all hazards.

By eleven that morning, an eerie calm settled over the field. The Confederates gathered their strength and information, replacing weary and depleted regiments with fresh and lively ones. The shelling of the woods continued but did little more than annoy the hardened men of the Iron Brigade. Company B of the Twenty-Fourth Michigan was sent out by Morrow as skirmishers in anticipation for the restart of the desperate contest. The lull in action proved unnerving to all of those in the ranks of the Iron Brigade. They preferred to be in constant action, so that their thoughts would not catch hold of them, so that they wouldn't have to reflect. But war had never been kind to these western men.

Morgan poured a little water from his canteen onto his hands. They were dirty and bloody. He tried to scrub at them, hoping to cleanse himself of the red stains that were evidence of his actions. He worked a small knife under his fingernails, prying away loose fragments of dried dirt and blood.

There were wet spots on his uniform. To remedy this, he tossed a handful of dirt against the dark red stains. When the dirt cemented, he attempted to scrape it off with his knife and then his fingernails. This act too proved to be in vain. The blood had stained and wasn't coming off. He could not part with the convicting evidence.

His regiment had been tattered. The ranks were thin. He could see that when he looked around. What had become of the many men who made the march? Morgan glanced back toward the rising hill in the background. He could see bodies spread across the landscape. Birds flew down upon them and pulled from the already decaying carcasses. It was a gruesome sight. There were dozens of wounded soldiers stumbling toward the rear. He could make out both blue and gray uniforms, torn and bloodied by the quick battle of the morning.

Morgan called for old friends and comrades who didn't answer in reply. Ignoring the shells crashing through the trees around him, he walked a few yards behind the line and saw the body of a childhood friend. The soldier's mouth was open, and his eyes were wide and dark. His rifle had fallen at his side, one arm outstretched as if to reach it, the other resting sill on his motionless chest. Morgan could not see the wound that had claimed the soldier's life from where he stood, but he dared not get any closer. A large tree toppled some distance away as a solid shot tore through the thick trunk. He heard the call from Edwards for the company to line up. The captain was seeking a roll call to see how many men Company F could muster for the coming fight. It couldn't be much, Morgan thought as he strolled back to them.

In the distance he could hear the cannon silence. The shells no longer endangered the thinning command, no longer slammed into the protective woods. Morgan fell back in line and knew what was coming. There would be another push. The Iron Brigade had gained ground, and the Confederates were determined to get it back. They would come in much stronger now, probably with reinforcements. As he stood in line, he eagerly looked out ahead to hear if Company B had met with the advancing enemy, for he knew that it was just a matter of time. There was nothing, though, just an eerie stillness.

It was gladly broken by the voice of Colonel Morrow, who had dismounted from his horse and sent the animal to the rear. He made his way through the thinning lines and offered words of encouragement. "You have done well, boys. You have made your colonel very proud." Morgan smiled. He settled down and felt at ease, finally ignoring his bloodstained hands.

As the whirlwind of battle hushed to a standstill around the woods sheltering the Iron Brigade, arriving elements of the Union Army of the Potomac steadied into a staggered line, hoping to defend the town and the high ground that was deemed so valuable. It was at this time, this break in the action, where word first trickled to the Twenty-Fourth that Reynolds had been killed while placing the brigade into line. Word spread that the brave general was near the forefront of the fight, a most gallant and brave soldier he had been. There was little time for sorrow, however, as the scent of battle grew stauncher, thicker. The day was hot and the sun blistered their bare heads and narrowed their eyes as they looked to the land before them, eagerly awaiting the revitalized thrust of the enemy.

To the right of the Iron Brigade's position, arriving a little after noon were the leading elements of the Eleventh Corps, "those damned Dutchmen," as they had been labeled. Panting and out of breath the men clamored toward Gettysburg having been pushed at the double-quick for miles. Reaching the field just as the Confederate line began to realize the shortened position of their Union hosts, the Dutchmen on the scene were determined to rid themselves of that unfair name that had haunted them since Chancellorsville.

Back in the woods, Colonel Morrow couldn't get over the dangerous position the brigade sat upon. Again he sent an aide to the rear asking Wadsworth to allow the brigade to shift back to better ground. Again the aide returned with the same answer: hold the ground. Wadsworth knew that his commander, General Doubleday was determined to make the stand on the ground the fallen Reynolds had chosen for the brigade, even though it hindered the effectiveness of one of the army's most hardened and celebrated units.

The Confederates would not wait long to reopen the battle. Although General Lee had made it very clear to all of his subordinates that he desired no general engagement, his commanders present on the field smelled blood. Their noses had been bloodied but they realized their numerical strength over the Union forces planted before them. Intelligence identified the enemy elements they were engaged with, the First Corps, and the arrival of the Eleventh Corps, two of the smallest corps in the Army of the Potomac. Despite this, there was some hesitation until the sounds of battle erupted again. Whether by design or by mistake, the Confederate drums rumbled again, and this time they were intent on driving the two isolated Union corps from the field.

Two thick lines of battle were formed and thrown toward the tiny band of Union soldiers holding McPherson's Woods. Their line completely outstretched the left flank of the battered Iron Brigade. As soon as the lines became visible, Colonel Morrow ordered the regiment to hold their fire until the enemy had come within good striking distance. He would have to make up for the terrible ground, which would shield most fire at long ranges. Again, the Confederates held the advantage. They could fire as soon as they came into contact with the Federals. The withering Union line would have to wait for their enemies to advance before opening up.

At some point, General Meredith, commander of the Iron Brigade, was wounded and forced to retire from the field. Command of the brigade then passed to Colonel Robinson of the Seventh Wisconsin.

As news spread of the change of command, Confederate Generals Pettigrew and Brockenbrough drove their brigades headlong into the Twenty-Fourth Michigan and Nineteenth Indiana. Another body of troops fell upon the Seventh Wisconsin, hoping to drive them from the field at the same time. Colonel Morrow again directed his men to hold their fire until the enemy advanced and decreased their advantage by marching onto better ground for the defenders. Having let the enemy march within some eighty paces of his first line of battle, Morrow gave the order for the regiment to fire.

The battle between the Twenty-Fourth Michigan and the Twenty-Sixth North Carolina began. The Carolinians, having been under the impression they were marching against local militia, exclaimed, "Here are those damned *black hat* fellows again! This is no militia!" It was the second of such realizations that day.

Colonel Morrow coughed in the smoke as the two lines slugged it out. He had allowed the enemy to advance upon him and had suffered heavily for it. My God, they march so beautifully, he thought. He silently counted the massed bodies marching toward him and wondered how many more the enemy could throw against him. They came at him in great hordes, while he defended with small bands. But the advantage the enemy held folded as soon as they stepped into his firing range and Morrow let the regiment open up for the first time since witnessing the second Confederate attack.

He raced among his line and told the men to keep up a hot fire. As he had complained to General Wadsworth, the ground the brigade was placed on was terrible. Even within effective range of the regiment's rifles, he could see the enemy had suffered little. Onward the enemy advanced, rapidly approaching the first line of battle. His attention then focused to the left of his line, where he saw the Confederates pressing the flank of the noble Nineteenth Indiana. Sensing the coming threat, he immediately ordered his leftmost companies to shift slightly to confront not only the attack at their front, but the one that would soon arrive on their left as well.

His worst fears were realized when the ranks of the brave Indiana regiment broke for the rear. Having fought valiantly, the veterans were forced to fall back by the pressure of superior numbers. The enemy had the clear advantage and the Nineteenth suffered great loss as they attempted to shift their line back against the growing tide.

Vacancies in the regiment's officer ranks were appalling. Junior officers had to fill the spots left by the wounded and dead. Because of this, Morrow turned to Major Wight, who was acting as lieutenant colonel since Flanigan fell and ordered Captain Speed, who in turn was acting major in place of Wight, to the left of the line to command the companies there. "Order them to turn and confront the coming assault. We must not let them cave us in. I will work on a way for us to get out of this," he said. Wight obliged the order and demanded that Speed bravely go to lead the left, in which Speed sprinted off to do. As he got about thirty yards from Morrow, the colonel saw the young captain instantly fall to his death.

Morrow kept his word and just as the regiment was withered to pieces by a terrible crossfire, he ordered the regiment to fall back to a new line. To his second color bearer, a man by the name of Charles Bellore, he shouted, "Charles, take the flag several paces to the rear and try and link up with the Nineteenth. I will bring the regiment there!" As he sent the color bearer off, there was another volley that tore into the ranks, slicing through the flag and bearer alike. Without hesitation, a brave soldier from Company K, Augustus Ernst, took the flag and positioned it where Morrow intended to rally his staggering line.

Captain Edwards ordered Company F to fall back in the face of the enemy fire, telling two other companies to fall back before them. "We will cover you," he cried out. "My men are stubborn enough to stay here for as long as they can."

Edwards resorted to firing with his revolver since the Rebels were within range. Pop. Pop. Crack. Whip. Pop. Crack. Thud. The battle grew more intense as the Confederates pressed their larger numbers against the depleted Twenty-Fourth. Bullets filled the air but Edwards and his company stayed put to hold off the enemy for as long as it took for the other companies to pull away. To his surprise, the two companies refused to vacate the field unless it was together, so they hinged on Company F and fired as they reluctantly gave up the bloodied ground.

Eventually he had no choice but to order his company to the new line with the rest of the regiment. The Confederate pressure was too great, and his ranks were thinning so much that he dared not keep them in between the two forces anymore. He urged the men to stream toward the new line as fast as they could and to not worry about firing back at the enemy. It was important that they reach the new line and make another stand with their comrades. "Move!" he shouted to them, as the bullets riddled the ground around him.

Morgan reached the line and quickly bent down to a dead soldier and stripped him of his ammunition. He was careful not to look at the soldier, not wanting to know who had fallen and who he was stealing from. No sooner had he stood back up from gathering the vital supplies, when the Confederate line unleashed another volley. He saw the white smoke and flames belch from the rifles and felt the slug slam into his arm. Falling to the ground, he fought to pull himself back up. He used both his arms, forgetting that he had been hit, but fell abruptly when the wounded arm's bone broke in two. He screamed in pain as he rolled over, bullets whirling above his head.

His comrades fell about him. One of them fell on his legs, pinning him to the ground. Morgan gently kicked the wounded soldier off of him but was again trapped as one fell onto his body. He lifted his good arm and reaching up to the man's chest went to push off. His hand slipped into the moist, warm tissue, nearly up to his forearm. Morgan quickly pulled his bloody hand from the dead soldier's body. Sitting up, he looked and saw that his hand had entered the wound created by several slugs piercing the soldier's stomach. Frantically he tried to wipe the blood away.

A comrade helped the wounded Morgan to his feet and instructed that it would be best if Morgan headed for the rear. Pausing, ignorant of the epic storm crashing around him, Morgan took a breath and looked toward the thinning regiment. He did not want to leave them, but his wound needed care. The soldier again beckoned to Morgan, telling him to head for the rear. Morgan shook his head, "I'm not going."

The soldier pointed to the horrible wound. "You need to go," he pleaded.

"No," replied Morgan.

Quickly the soldier tore a shirt from a dead comrade and dressed the wound. His fingers felt the broken bone protruding slightly from the skin. He felt the rise in the skin once more with his fingers. "Can you move it?" he asked Morgan.

"I cannot."

"Then you are of no use here, not anymore. Go to the rear and seek help." He finished dressing the wound and told Morgan that he did not think the arm would need to be amputated. "It is broken, but I do not think it very bad."

Reluctantly, Morgan began his slow trek toward the Union rear.

He had been forced to abandon his comrades.

The second line of battle for the Twenty-Fourth further heated the contest between the two primary enemy regiments, men from Michigan and North Carolina. The thinning Michigan line began to waver yet again and was forced to fall back to a third line of battle before the charging Confederates.

Once readied, the Michigan men sent a volley that staggered the North

Carolinians and brought their assault to an abrupt standstill. On this line, the brave soldier Ernst was killed, and the flag retrieved by Andrew Wagner, of Company F, one of the last color guards surviving. He took the flag where Morrow directed it and there helped rally the weary troops before being wounded in the chest and removing himself from the field. Not wanting his third line to cave in, Morrow leaped for the fallen flag.

Colonel Morrow took the flag and raised it into the air. The men gathered around him and blazed away at the driving Rebels. Their ranks had been thinned and torn apart, but they continued to band together despite the great odds confronting them. Sharp volleys were tossed between the opposing lines, both growing weary, both suffering heavily from the knock-down-drag-out fight.

Their colonel called them to their duty, and they responded quickly. Morrow fluttered the tattered flag about and heard the fabric rip and tear as more bullets riddled the bold colors. He stepped out before the line until he heard one of his soldiers call for the flag. From the ranks of Company E came William Kelly. He reached for the flag with outstretched fingers. "The colonel of the Twenty-Fourth shall never carry the flag while I am alive," he said bravely.

Morrow passed the flag into the hands of the brave soldier. He lifted his sword and called for the regiment to rally, to hold its position. Pop. Pop. Pop. Pop. Pop. The musketry roared across the field. To his right, he could hear the Federal guns of Battery B blasting away in desperation. To his front he saw the endless lines of Rebel soldiers. They were everywhere, slithering toward him, letting loose a raspy cry as they came.

He turned to Kelly just as the private fell to his death, the flag in his hands for only a brief moment. Morrow seized the banner in time as the last of the surviving color guard rushed to grab it. The soldier brought news that Major Wight had been wounded and removed from the field. He further reported that Lieutenants Safford, Shattuck, and Wallace had been killed. Morrow shook his head. How many more before this will end? How many more brave patriots must fall before the fire?

To his feet he went, and Morrow ordered the regiment to fall back to yet another line of battle. He asked for several volunteers to stay with him and protect the rest of men as they shifted back. There was no problem in requiring an ample amount of men, as they did not wish to leave their colonel to such a deadly task. They reasoned with him to fall back with the rest of the regiment. He agreed to do so, only if the men made quick of their work. Morrow wasn't about to leave them alone in the field. "God bless you, gentlemen," he told them.

To a fourth line of battle the Twenty-Fourth went. It seemed that each regiment in the Iron Brigade was acting under their own orders, selfishly not wanting to give ground to the enemy. Colonel Morrow took the flag once again, hoping to further rally his depleted regiment, but another brave private offered to carry it instead. For over two hours the battle raged, cutting through the regiments on both sides of the field. For over two hours the flag floated, fell, and then was defiantly raised again.

Captain Edwards had never seen such a terrible firefight. To his left he saw the Nineteenth Indiana bow once again under the relentless pressure. To his right he saw the sturdy Wisconsin regiments holding their ground against growing numbers. He simply found no sanctuary from the great battle. Company F had been torn to shreds, and he had sent the men into other companies to fill gaps as necessary.

The dead and wounded littered the ground in front of him. He could see where the regiment had formed earlier lines of battles because several of the dead were lying in a neat and orderly line. They had answered the call to rally, but they had paid for it. The Confederates drove over the bodies rapidly, their rifles blazing. He could hear their shrieks and yells as they advanced. Again the dwindling Twenty-Fourth attempted to hold its ground. There wasn't but a company of men left in the regiment.

What had become of the gallant men? Where did they all go?

To their graves many of them did march. He could see the still bodies through the breaks in the smoke. His ears perked when he heard the cries of Colonel Morrow, commanding the regiment to shift once again. To his amazement, Edwards saw the ground the regiment repositioned itself on as open with no cover. Morrow ordered what men were left to stand the ground and offer a rear guard action for the rest of the brigade, slowly caving in before them. He hoped it would buy enough time for those building another line on the ridgeline behind him, knowing that nothing then was more important than time. The irony almost made him smile amid the chaos and bloodshed. Morrow had always been a man who valued time. Never had its worth been so high, however.

The Michigan men loaded their rifles and looked through the smoke toward the deafening noise of battle. They had been whittled down to nearly nothing, but they stood strong and leveled their rifles. There was still plenty of fight left in them. Up they went to makeshift barricades built around the seminary buildings.

Colonel Morrow took the flag in his hands yet again and rallied his shattered command. The men swarmed around him, determined to make the final stand with him. He waved the flag about, inspiring his troops and attempting to rally several retiring remnants of the other regiments. They stopped and looked to him and couldn't help but return to their ranks. Morrow rose above his men and raised the riddled flag above his head, clearing away the smoke blanketing him.

He saw before him the Iron Brigade regiments stumble backward, no longer able to ward off the gray tide. He called for his men to ready themselves. Their comrades needed protection. It would be up to the small band of Michiganders to provide them with it. "They have done much for you," he commented. "It is time that we repay them."

His hands no longer trembled. The doubts no longer surfaced in his head. He knew what he had to do, what his men had to do. An aide from General Wadsworth found him and asked him to depart with his battered regiment. Morrow refused. "We are of the Iron Brigade," he told the frightened soldier. "We shall stand as such."

Several soldiers pleaded with Morrow to give up the flag, but Morrow declined their requests. He felt it his personal duty to rally the men, to inspire them. And with the tattered flag in hand, he looked forward toward the advancing Confederate line. He saw his dead and wounded spread across the field. He saw the Rebel dead too. The fallen southerners were numerous. The grass was sprinkled with gray and blue. Stepping over them, he saw the last of the Iron Brigade regiments fall back, the Confederates giving them quick chase. He braced himself when a new Confederate line approached to the left and center of his line. He watched, helplessly, as their rifles were lowered, and they let loose a volley that cut through the already thinned Michigan ranks.

He ordered the men to hold the line. He saw some of them drop to a knee and take careful aim. Many of them stood at his side, responding to the threats from all angles. They blasted away, this small band of brothers, determined not to give another inch until the battered brigade had reunited. They fought like demons, yelling and screaming. Another exchange of volleys came between the two lines, and Morrow felt a sharp pain as a projectile hit him in the head. Everything went black for a second. When he stood up, his hearing was gone, and he was dazed and confused. His eyes scanned the line in search of the rest of his command, but they were not there. They were spread out all across the field before him. Soon the blood seeped down into his eyes. His hands shot up to wipe it away.

When he came to his senses, he looked for the fallen flag. He couldn't find it. He knew that he had carried it, but it was gone. Disappointed, he shuffled across the narrow line and found Captain Edwards rallying the men into position, preparing for the next Confederate volley. With each step Morrow lost strength, nearly collapsed to the ground.

Morrow looked to him and said nothing. Edwards saw the blood stream down from his colonel's head. "You must head to the rear," ordered the junior officer. Morrow still said nothing. He just looked to Edwards with a blank stare. "Colonel Morrow, sir, I beg of you, please retire to the rear."

Edwards finally got Morrow to speak. "Captain Edwards," he heard the wounded colonel say, "I leave you in command of the regiment." The words were shocking. "You are the highest ranking officer left in the field of this regiment," Morrow concluded. Edwards nodded, and watched as the colonel vacated the line, stumbling.

He turned to the command that was now his. He saw a soldier standing out in front of the regiment, the shredded flag in his hands. Edwards pointed to the few that remained. "Go there, boys! Go to that soldier and stand with the colors." He moved down and joined the command just as the Nineteenth Indiana linked up with them. When the veteran regiment came upon the Twenty-Fourth, many of them removed their black hats in respect. There was a quiet sense of compassion between the two bloody lines, a vast difference from the raging storm of war capturing the landscape.

The regiment fired away, taking ammunition and rifles from the dead and wounded. Edwards moved before them and shouted out the commands. He inched his way toward the lone soldier with the flag and saw that it was Morgan. The wounded soldier had returned from the rear, not wanting to leave his regiment. Edwards met the soldier there and told him to move the flag back and guide the regiment away from the enemy. The men had done all they could. A courier raced from General Wadsworth and instructed the Twenty-Fourth Michigan to finally retire. Edwards received the note with a sigh of relief. He ordered the wounded Morgan to carry the flag to the front of the regiment and lead them up the hill.

As Morgan pushed along, the Confederate line advanced yet again and fired upon the few Michiganders left. Leaping toward the front of the regiment, Edwards found Morgan lying still on the ground, having been hit once again in the shoulder. A small pool of blood gathered underneath the soldier. Edwards pried the flag from Morgan's still hands and waved it in the air. The men rallied once again behind the bold colors, and men from Michigan, Wisconsin, and Indiana all banded together under the ripped folds of the American Flag. But soon, the last line too proved unable to hold back the rush of the sweeping Confederates. Outnumbered and outgunned, Edwards ordered the regiment to retire to the rear.

He had no choice but to leave Morgan where he fell, just as the others had been left in the field behind them. Slowly the shattered remains of the mighty Twenty-Fourth made its way toward town with the decimated Iron Brigade.

The weight of the Confederates finally punched through the line held by two determined corps of the Union Army of the Potomac. The First and Eleventh Corps had slugged it out and stubbornly held the ground all day. Eventually their lines were flanked and driven from the field, as the Confederate Army of Northern Virginia crashed upon them. Through the town these weary and bloody Union soldiers were driven, desperately hoping to escape the clutches of the victorious enemy, closely chasing them through the streets. Cries of halt and demands of surrender were heard, followed by quick rifle shots, an indication that the orders were being ignored by the fleeing Union men. In a few instances, men stood against the rushing Confederates, waving a fist at them, damning them, and vowing that they would meet again. Others scampered for hiding places, hoping to sneak away from the enemy during the night.

What had been the staunch Union defense and the bold Confederate attacks, had now become pandemonium and confusion. The ranks melted away. Confusion made no difference between victory and defeat, as both armies suffered from exhaustion and shock. What had once, perhaps a half hour before, been an organized pursuit of the routed Union enemy, became a mass of men sprinting down streets and alleyways, staggering across the bloody fields, and stopping to drink in the bloody stream. The Union men, having worked together for survival during the day, broke apart as their units dashed to the rear, toward the growing Union presence on a ridge outside of town.

As the flood of men spilled from the fields, commanders of all grades dashed out to regroup them, to reorganize the masses. Captain Edwards was among those trying against all odds to collect his scattered regiment. He was able to mass a few of them, but there was no resemblance to the mighty body of men that had stood with him in the morning. Listening to random cracks of rifles and hearing the muffled shouts of cheering Confederates, Edwards wondered how many of the proud Twenty-Fourth would rally under the banner one last time before the night claimed the field from both sides. He did not believe there would be a great many, but he prayed that he would be wrong.

The Twenty-Fourth Michigan made its way through the streets of Gettysburg and up toward the cemetery. They moved stubbornly behind the flag. Each step they took they furthered themselves from the enemy, whom they were surprised did not give a relentless chase. The men banded together despite the great loss they had suffered. Colonel Morrow had been wounded and was missing. Lieutenant Colonel Flanigan was wounded and taken to the rear. Most of their officers had been either killed or wounded and every member of the cherished color guard had been brought down during the desperate fight.

Ahead of the small band was Captain Edwards, proudly carrying the flag that had been riddled, by the young officer's count, with twenty three bullet holes. It had been tattered and torn. There were several bloodstains visible on the cloth. The staff was splintered worthless, with countless bloody fingerprints dotting the wood, attesting to the number of men that held the flag aloft in the battle. Carefully following behind Edwards, making their way toward the cemetery, were only twenty-six members of the regiment.

FINALE

Captain Edwards moved the flag over to a battery later that evening and planted it in the ground. The soldiers watched him. He felt their eyes upon him. "We should let the boys retire under the bold colors," he said to them. Moving over to a grave, he sat down and waited for the remnants of the regiment to join them on the hill.

His soldiers continued to look to him. He wanted to say something, but the time wasn't right. He could not find the words. They had all survived a terrible conflict that withered away the best and bravest among them. The soldiers gathered on the hilltop were fortunate to have come through the ordeal. Edwards didn't know how to describe it to them, how to comfort them. Out in the field before them, among the enemy's lines and mingled with their dead, were friends and families. There had been too much bloodshed. There was too much pain. Edwards wasn't ready to justify it all, not yet. He sat on the gravestone and waited, hoping that more of his soldiers would turn up to join him.

The men were tired, hungry, and thirsty, but there were no complaints. They simply gathered with their captain and impatiently awaited the return of their comrades, many of whom they knew would never again meet up with them. Breaking the silence, one of them confidently summed up the results of the day. "They have the field," he said aloud, "but we have the high ground."

Colonel Morrow fell into Confederate hands that day. At one point in the evening, a Confederate soldier approached him. He got close enough to Morrow so that only he could hear the words. "Well, there, Colonel, how do you do?" asked the weary Rebel. Morrow raised a finger, pleading with the man to keep quiet. "Well," sighed the soldier, "you probably don't know me, but I know you." Morrow struggled to recognize him. "Your regiment captured me sometime ago, damn you!"

Morrow happily replied, "Glad of it. Did they not treat you well?"

"Bully!"

"Then treat me the same," Morrow added.

The soldier nodded, rubbed his forehead, and then smiled. "We will, Colonel." He leaned forward and nudged at Morrow with a closed fist. "Where are your straps?"

Morrow glanced down to his shoulders. "I have lost them for the time being."

The southerner smiled again. He turned his head away from Morrow and nodded in approval as columns of Confederate infantry burrowed through the streets. Morrow watched the proud soldiers file by. He wondered what had become of his regiment, if there was anything left. They had given their all, deserving a better fate than the one they received.

Later on in the evening, he was rounded up and sent with a large number of prisoners to the center diamond of Gettysburg, where Confederate General Ewell had set himself up. Here, with the thunder of battle behind them, Yankees and Confederates mingled and conversed rather freely. There it was discovered that Morrow had commanded one of the regiments of the Iron Brigade and Ewell thought it his position to lecture the Union officer. "Although you fought like demons," said Ewell, "you should not have stayed as long as you did when your cause was hopeless," the Confederate commander preached in front of the crowd.

Morrow stepped forward, his nervousness long faded, and proudly declared, "General Ewell, the Twenty-Fourth Michigan came here to fight, not surrender."

Captain Albert Edwards looked into the darkening sky and took a breath. He tried not to think of what he had just been through, but it was hard. The staggering losses of the regiment reminded him with each glance across the field. A longtime friend was missing and presumed dead. For another it was a father, son, brother or cousin. Each Michigander felt the pain as they looked across the field that night toward the glowing fires of the gathering Confederate Army of Northern Virginia.

The Union army was materializing around him, but it was much too late for the Twenty-Fourth Michigan and the fabled Iron Brigade. They had been shattered. Despite the devastation in the ranks, they were still able to hold the ground General John Reynolds had believed so important to the battle. In time, it would become the brigade's legacy for doing so.

Listening to the moans of the wounded and the silence of the dead, he knew there was nothing he could do for them. The wounded would soon fall into enemy hands. Colonel Morrow was out there as well, feared captured or dead. Edwards was now responsible for piecing the regiment back together after the storm. It had been a terrible fight and none of them would forget it. The men had suffered more than most, but still rallied with the old flag on the hill. Throughout the evening, men funneled into the camp and returned to the regiment, all realizing that it would never be the same.

There were less than one hundred of them when he rose to address them. Perhaps learning what to do from a manual or from training, he thought it best to speak to them. He had formulated the talk all evening, while sitting alone on the gravestone. "All the field officers of this regiment have been wounded, and the senior captains killed or wounded, I hereby assume command." Edwards looked to each sad face as he spoke. "I congratulate you, brave soldiers, upon your splendid achievements." He stopped quickly, fighting back the haunting images of the day's fight. "The enemy's dead in front of your lines attest to your valor and skill. Again you have merited a nation's gratitude. Again you have shown yourselves worthy of the noble state you represent and the glorious cause for which you are fighting." He turned away from them. "Our joy in the glory of our arms is mingled with sadness for the heroic dead on the field of honor." He returned to them with another deep breath and sad eyes. "Let the memory of our lamented comrades inspire your hearts with new life and zeal to emulate their heroic virtues and avenge their untimely fall," he concluded.

There was a great deal of commotion through the darkness. Soldiers scampered this way and that. The town had been taken by the Rebels, so daring parties of wounded Union men attempting to reach their commands were spread out over the ridgeline in the distance, scurrying through the darkness.

Two soldiers streamed toward the fires of the Union camps, bearing a wounded man on a litter. They had found him out in the field and had talked a Rebel guard into letting them take him back to the Union hospital. They moved quickly and carefully up the line, wanting to pull away from the Rebels but not disturb the wounded soldier they carried. At several points the men looked back to him because of his silence, believing the soldier had died before they could get him help. Each time they did, however, they found him looking calmly at them. One of his arms had been wrapped from an earlier wound and the men could see the bloodstains on his coat from a shoulder wound. Having inspected him on the field, they saw the bullet passed clean through, but believed because of the loss of blood, the soldier might not make it through the night. But he had surprised them on their long journey back to Union lines.

When they came to the makeshift hospital of the First Corps, a surgeon met them and introduced himself by the name of Beech, proudly announcing he served with the Twenty-Fourth Michigan. The angelic soldiers pointed back to their cargo, and when Beech brought the soft candle down to view the wounded soldier's face, he was pleased to recognize the soldier.

Beech looked him over and tended to the wounds, the worst of which was the broken arm. He had him carried inside. There he told the soldier that everything would be well and that he would feel much better in the morning. Beech offered him some water and some bread, but made sure not to overdo it. Relaxed and as comfortable as he could possibly get in his condition, the soldier politely requested a pencil and a piece of paper.

My dear Emmy, he began to write.

Darkness soon wrestled the battlefield away from the weary armies. They had battled out for as far as both sides were willing to go. Both armies had suffered tremendous casualties, especially in the area around McPherson's Woods. The field was haunting. Strange shadows bounced across the rolling countryside. The wounded tried to pull themselves to their respective lines. The dead forever slept where they had fallen. Cartridges and rifles littered the land. There were moans and whispered prayers echoing across the field. The dead of the Twenty-Fourth Michigan and the Twenty-Sixth North Carolina confronted each other in death as they had done in life. Among the fallen Carolinians was Emmy's cousin, whom Morgan had swam across the cold river to meet.

The Twenty-Fourth Michigan had entered the battle with four hundred and ninety-six men in its ranks. There were ninety-nine men remaining at the end of the night.

The Twenty-Sixth North Carolina had entered the battle with nearly eight hundred men in its ranks. Following the storm, there were only ninety-two men remaining in their ranks when the moon reclaimed the sky.

The Michiganders left with Captain Edwards could attest to the fury of the battle. They had withstood the punishment of several times their number and stubbornly refused to yield ground just as they had done at Fredericksburg when confronted by the enemy artillery. The two lines on the plain fields of Gettysburg had gnawed at each other, pounded away like two weary boxers entering the final round. For every inch of ground the Michigan regiment gave, they made the southerners pay. For every inch of ground they refused to give up, the southerners made them pay as

349

well. The two lines slammed away at each other, both of them with dreams of ending the war once and for all, both of them refusing to break before the other.

It was a standoff between beliefs more than anything. The Confederacy came to the fields of Gettysburg on July 1 hoping to brush aside the expected Pennsylvania militia, hoping to inch closer to drawing in European intervention, if it would ever materialize, and hoping to force the Union to the peace table. The Union came to Gettysburg that day determined to vanquish the foe from their territory once again, moving swiftly to stay between the enemy army and Washington. With them, they brought hopes of restoring the Union and abolishing slavery. Both sides sought an end to the already long and bloody war, and they would continue to seek it in Pennsylvania for two more bloody days. Soon, places like Culp's Hill and Little Round Top would become famous. But this mattered little to the Michigan men left on the hill that night.

They were concerned only with the names and faces of the soldiers that had perished in the fighting during the day. They struggled to express themselves, often relying on silent prayers. Many of their friends and family members were out alone in the field, waiting to be buried far from their beloved homes, far from the peaceful and pleasant valleys and hills of Michigan.

Lieutenant Colonel Mark Flanigan spent the lonely night in the hospital surrounded by surgeons and under the watchful eyes of the attendants. His leg had to be amputated and he spent the night in a drug induced slumber, replaying the chaos and destruction of the battle in his memory alongside with the horrible images of the wounded soldier in the hospital in Washington. He never could forget him. When he awoke, as he did occasionally throughout the night, he would softly mutter a haunting line that sent shivers down the spines of the weary doctors and surgeons, "Oh, it is a shame that we should grow so accustomed…"

He would survive the wound.

Colonel Morrow slowly walked the field and looked upon the dead and fallen soldiers of his command. He bent down in hopes of finding a few of them still alive, but each man he rolled over was dead. He found the eyes black and the bodies bloated from the heat, which prevailed even into the night. The stench was terrible, but he put up with it. These were his men, Michigan men. They had stood where he ordered, had fought like brave and honorable patriots, and had fallen in death where he placed them.

A few Rebel officers asked him to leave the field, but Morrow refused, telling them that he was among some of his men, that he knew them, and wanted to spend just a little longer with them. Left alone, he thanked the countless men strewn across the field, down into the bloody ravine, and sprinkled about the woods. "I have stood among men of iron," he whispered, as tears flowed down his dirty cheeks.

He stood among them in silence as he had for so many months before. They had given their all for him. The least he could do was pay his respects, honor their faithful service.

God bless the Twenty-Fourth, he thought.

He would return to his regiment following General Lee's retreat from the bloodstained fields of Gettysburg.

As he felt the men huddle around him, Captain Edwards looked up to the moon. Along the building battle line, several regimental bands sparked up a humbling tune. He stood with the men as they looked down the ridge and listened as the soft summer breeze carried the delicate music across the field. Each man looked to the other as they immediately recognized the tune. It was *Amazing Grace*.

It was the same tune that was played at Fredericksburg, where it was received very coldly by the Twenty-Fourth. They had been a green and untested regiment prior to that battle, and they didn't understand the song's peaceful and soothing intentions. On the night of July 1, however, they looked to each other not in disgust, but in pride, in memory of those that had sacrificed themselves for the national cause, for each other.

The small band realized what Gibbon had told Morrow about the veterans of the Iron Brigade. There was something there that bonded them together, that made them stand where few dared to stand. They had an undying faith in each other that allowed them to do all the things the hardened brigade was known for.

The Twenty-Fourth had given their all on the fields of Gettysburg. They fought the enemy with the ferocity and determination that even the veterans of the brigade had to admire, had to confess was impressive for the junior regiment. They were different men who stood together for common beliefs and a common goal. They came from all walks of civilian life but stood together as brave soldiers in the woods and beyond. Six different battle lines the regiment did draw and six different times did they turn and confront the enemy with shot and yell. They did so because they had faith in their glorious cause, but more importantly because they had faith in each other.

And that is what made them men of iron.

The tune continued down the line and several of the men could be heard whispering the hymn. No, they had not understood its meaning at Fredericksburg.

But it was understood as they gazed across the bloody fields of Gettysburg.

How sweet the sound indeed.

"The last thing the boys think of is what those at home think of them. They feel proud of themselves, and they want you to feel proud too. Write them cheering letters. Encourage your soldiers. Bid them God speed. Tell them they are fighting in a just and holy cause, as they certainly are."

—from a letter of Colonel Henry A. Morrow